T-Mac cleared his throat. "Since you don't need me, I'll go."

Kinsley's eyes flew open. "Do you have to?"

He shrugged. "No. My buddies are covering for me with my commander."

She held out her hand. "I think they gave me a sedative. Could you stay until I go to sleep?" Her lips twisted. "You don't have to if you don't want to."

He chuckled. "Playing second fiddle to a dog isn't quite a compliment, but I'll take it."

T-Mac pulled the chair close and gathered her hand in his, reveling at how small it was in his, yet how strong and supple her fingers were.

Agar leaned his long snout over Kinsley's body, sniffed T-Mac's hand once and then laid his head back on Kinsley's other side, seemingly satisfied T-Mac wouldn't harm the dog handler.

For a long moment, she said nothing.

T-Mac assumed she was sleeping.

"Don't tell anyone," Kinsley whispered, her eyes closed, her breathing slow and steady.

T-Mac stroked the back of her hand. "Tell anyone what?"

"That the tough-as-nails a a navy SEAL's hand."

VALIANT TRACKER

NEW YORK TIMES BESTSELLING AUTHOR

ELLE JAMES
& ELIZABETH HEITER

Previously published as *Six Minutes to Midnight* and *K-9 Defense*

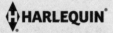

ISBN-13: 978-1-335-45482-9

Valiant Tracker

Copyright © 2020 by Harlequin Books S.A.

Six Minutes to Midnight
First published in 2018. This edition published in 2020.
Copyright © 2018 by Mary Jernigan

K-9 Defense
First published in 2019. This edition published in 2020.
Copyright © 2019 by Elizabeth Heiter

Recycling programs
for this product may
not exist in your area.

This edition published by arrangement with Harlequin Books S.A.

For questions and comments about the quality of this book,
please contact us at CustomerService@Harlequin.com.

Harlequin Enterprises ULC
22 Adelaide St. West, 40th Floor
Toronto, Ontario M5H 4E3, Canada
www.Harlequin.com

Printed in U.S.A.

CONTENTS

Elle James, a *New York Times* bestselling author, started writing when her sister challenged her to write a romance novel. She has managed a full-time job and raised three wonderful children, and she and her husband even tried ranching exotic birds (ostriches, emus and rheas). Ask her, and she'll tell you what it's like to go toe-to-toe with an angry 350-pound bird! Elle loves to hear from fans at ellejames@earthlink.net or ellejames.com.

Books by Elle James

Harlequin Intrigue

Declan's Defenders

Marine Force Recon
Show of Force
Full Force
Driving Force
Tactical Force
Disruptive Force

Mission: Six

One Intrepid SEAL
Two Dauntless Hearts
Three Courageous Words
Four Relentless Days
Five Ways to Surrender
Six Minutes to Midnight

Visit the Author Profile page
at Harlequin.com for more titles.

SIX MINUTES
TO MIDNIGHT

Elle James

I'd like to dedicate this book to the military working dogs, who are such an important addition to our fighting forces. They are loyal, smart and dedicated to doing what they do best. Friends of mine adopted a retired military working dog, which gave me the idea to include him in this book. Agar, thank you for your service!

Chapter 1

"Four days and a wakeup," Trace McGuire, T-Mac to his friends, said as he sat across the table in the chow hall on Camp Lemonnier. They'd returned from their last mission in Niger with news they were scheduled to redeploy back to the States.

He glanced around the table at his friends. When they were deployed, they spent practically every waking hour together. In the past, being stateside was about the same. They'd go to work, train, get briefed, work out and then go back to their apartments. Most of the time, they'd end up at one of the team members' places to watch football, cook out or just lounge around and shoot the crap with each other. They were like family and never seemed to get tired of each other's company.

T-Mac suspected all that was about to change. All

of his closest SEAL buddies had women in their lives now. All except him. Suddenly, going back to Virginia wasn't quite as appealing as it had been in the past. T-Mac sighed and drank his lukewarm coffee.

"I can't wait to see Reese." Diesel tapped a finger against the rim of his coffee cup. "I promised to take her on a real date when I get back to civilization."

"What? You're not going to take her swinging through the jungle, communing with the gorillas?" Buck teased.

Petty Officer Dalton Samuel Landon, otherwise known as Diesel, shook his head. "Nope. Been there, done that. I think I'll take her to a restaurant where we don't have to forage for food. Then maybe we'll go out to a nightclub." He tipped his head to the side. "I wonder if she likes to dance."

"You mean you don't know?" Big Jake Schuler, the tallest man on the team, rolled his eyes. "I would have thought that in the time you two spent traipsing along the Congo River, you would know everything there was to know about each other."

Diesel frowned. "I know what's important. She's not fragile, she can climb a tree when she needs to, she doesn't fall apart when someone's shooting at her and she can kiss like nobody's business." Diesel shrugged. "In fact, I'm looking forward to learning more. She's amazing. How many female bodyguards do you know?"

Big Jake held up his hands in surrender. "You got me there. None."

"I can't wait to see Angela." Corpsman Graham "Buck" Buckner, the team medic, smiled. "She's interviewing for positions around Little Creek."

"With her doctor credentials, and the work she did with Doctors Without Borders, she's sure to get on pretty quickly," Big Jake said. "If not one of the military hospitals, there are lots of civilian hospitals and clinics in the area."

Buck nodded. "I can't believe after all these years, she'd want to be close to me." He smiled. "I'm one lucky guy."

"Yeah, and maybe she'll talk you into going back to school to finish your medical degree." Built solid like a tank, Percy Taylor had the tenacity of a pit bull, thus his nickname, Pitbull. He gave Buck a chin lift. "You'd make a good doc."

"What?" Buck spread his arms wide. "And give up all this?"

T-Mac chuckled. "I know. It's hard to believe anyone would want to stop being on call at all hours of the day and night, deploying to some of the worst hellholes on the planet and not getting back to see your family for months on end. Who would want to give up all that?"

"Hey, are we getting cynical in our old age?" Harmon Payne clapped a hand on T-Mac's back. "We're the ones who are going to suffer. We all have women to come home to now."

"All except T-Mac," Buck pointed out. "Maybe we should fix him up with someone? You think one of our women knows someone who could put up with his being a computer nerd and all?"

T-Mac shook his head. "I don't need help getting a date, thank you very much."

"I'll bet Reese has met some pretty hot chicks in the DC area through her work as a bodyguard," Diesel said. "Or maybe she still has some connections in the mixed-martial-arts community. One of those women are bound to be able to stand toe-to-toe with our guy."

"Seriously." T-Mac pushed to his feet. "I don't need a woman in my life. You all know how hard our lives are without relationships. I'm surprised all you self-confirmed bachelors broke the cardinal rule."

Pitbull stabbed the mystery meat on his tray with his fork and held it in the air, inspecting it with a frown. "What cardinal rule?"

T-Mac pounded his fist on the table. "Don't get into a permanent relationship as long as you're a full-time SEAL."

"Nope." Harm's eyes narrowed and his lips twisted. "I don't remember that line in the BUD/S training manual."

"Before we came to Africa," T-Mac reminded them, "we were drinking beer and talking about how we didn't have wives and kids—"

"Ha!" Pitbull held up a finger. "We were drinking beer. That's where we got off track."

Swallowing his irritation, T-Mac continued. "We all agreed that relationships were doomed to failure as long as we were doing the jobs we do. No woman will be satisfied being on a part-time status, what with us shipping out as often as we do to fight some battle nobody else wants."

"Then I found Marly," Pitbull said. "She can stand on her own two feet. And we get along pretty well." He smiled, his rugged face softening. "She's even getting me to like flying in crop dusters. And she's found a charter company in Virginia that wants her to pilot for them. She won't be waiting around for me to come home. Hell, we'll be lucky to be home at the same time."

"Exactly," T-Mac said. "And how's that going to work for you? You won't see each other."

Pitbull frowned. "We'll find time." His frown turned upside down. "And when we do…yup." He nodded. "We'll find time. I'm not ready to give up on her, and I don't think she'll give up on me."

"The point you're missing, T-Mac, is that we found women who can stand on their own," Harm said. "They don't need us any more than we need them. We *want* to be together. And that makes all the difference."

"Uh-huh." T-Mac knew they wouldn't listen. His five friends were so besotted by their women, they couldn't see past the rose-colored glasses to reality. He might as well save his breath.

"Guys." Buck stared around the table at everyone but T-Mac and lowered his voice to a conspiratorial whisper. "We've got to get T-Mac laid. He's strung way too tight. He's likely to blow a gasket soon."

"What's the use?" T-Mac pushed to his feet. "We're headed home in four days. Let's not screw anything up between now and then."

"What could possibly go wrong?" Buck asked with a grin and then ducked as everyone else threw their napkins and food at him.

Pitbull snorted. "Thanks for jinxing us, dirtbag."

"You guys can hang around talking about your women you'll rarely see. I'm going for a run." T-Mac walked out of the chow hall to the laughter of his friends.

"Gotta get him a girl," Buck said.

As T-Mac rounded the corner of one of the stacks of shipping containers that had been outfitted to become sleeping quarters, a hard object landed at his feet.

He jumped back, his heart racing, his first thought *Grenade!* Then a hair missile barreled toward him, all four legs moving like a blur.

T-Mac braced himself for impact.

The black-faced, sable German shepherd skidded to a stop, pushing up a cloud of dust in the process. He grabbed the object in his teeth and raced back the way he'd come.

"Agar, heel!" a female voice commanded.

The animal stopped immediately at the female soldier's side, dropped the hard rubber object on the ground and stared up at the woman as if eagerly awaiting the next command.

"Good dog." She patted him on the head and then glanced up. "Sorry. I didn't know you were there until after I'd thrown his KONG." Her hand continued to stroke the dog's head.

T-Mac stared at the woman, who was wearing camouflage pants, boots and a desert-tan T-shirt. Her hair was pulled back in a bun that had long since lost its shape. Coppery red strands danced in the breeze. She returned his stare with a direct green-eyed gaze. "If you're afraid of Agar, I'll hold him while you pass." She cocked an auburn eyebrow.

"What?" T-Mac shook his head. "I'm not afraid of the dog. Just startled."

"Then don't let us keep you." She snapped the lead on the dog's collar and straightened.

Curiosity made T-Mac ask, "You're new at Camp Lemonnier?"

She shrugged. "I've been here a week, if you consider that new."

He laughed. "I do. And I just got back to camp, or I'm sure I'd have seen you." There weren't too many good-looking redheaded females in the world, much less in Djibouti. "Hi, I'm Petty Officer Trace McGuire. My friends call me T-Mac." He took a step forward, slowly so as not to alert the dog, and held out his hand.

She clasped it in a firm grip. "Specialist Kinsley Anderson." She glanced down at the dog. "And this is Sergeant Agar."

T-Mac dropped to one knee in front of the German shepherd and held out his hand.

Agar placed a paw in his palm.

With a chuckle, T-Mac shook the dog's paw and then stood. "He's very well trained. What's his mission?"

"Bomb sniffing."

"Bomb sniffing?" T-Mac glanced again at the woman. He hadn't really thought about females on the front line. But with the army graduating females from Ranger School, it was a natural progression.

"Well, I hope you don't have to put that skill to use anytime soon."

Her eyes narrowed and she lifted her chin. "We came here to do a job. I'm not afraid."

Having seen his share of action and lost members of his team to gunfire and explosions, T-Mac didn't wish any of it on anyone. But a person had to live through the horrors of war to truly understand how terrible it was. He couldn't begin to explain it to the shiny new specialist who'd probably never been shot at or stood next to a man who'd been blown away by an IED.

And he had no business chatting up a female soldier when fraternization was strictly forbidden on deployment. Especially since it could lead to nothing and he and his team would be shipping out in four sleeps and a wakeup. "Well, it was nice to meet you."

"Same," she said, then grabbed the KONG and took off with Agar in the opposite direction.

As T-Mac continued on toward his quarters, he couldn't help sighing. He'd never considered dating a redhead, but something about Specialist Anderson made him reconsider. Perhaps it was the way her coppery hair seemed out of control, or the light dusting of freckles across her nose and cheeks. Or maybe it was the way she absently, or automatically, stroked the dog's head, showing it affection without having to think about it. Either way, she was off-limits and he was leaving. Once again he reminded himself, *Don't get involved.*

Kinsley hurried past the navy guy. She'd spent the past two hours working with Agar, keeping his skills fresh and helping him burn off energy. Now it was her turn.

Though she'd been in the country for a week, she and Agar had been tasked only with inspecting vehicles entering Camp Lemonnier. Thankfully, they hadn't found any carrying explosives. Training sessions were a must, or Agar might forget what he was looking for and Kinsley might not pick up on the behavior Agar displayed when he sensed he'd found something.

Meanwhile, her male counterpart had gone out on

missions with the Special Operations Forces into more hostile environments, working ahead of the teams to clear their routes of IEDs.

Kinsley had signed on as a dog handler because she loved dogs and because she wanted to make a difference for her country and her brothers in arms.

Her heart contracted as she thought about one in particular. Cody, her best friend from high school, had been killed in Iraq when he'd stepped on a mine.

Kinsley wanted to keep other young military men and women from the same fate.

On her first deployment, she'd hoped to land in Afghanistan or Iraq. Instead she'd landed in Djibouti, a fairly stable environment but also a jumping-off point to other more volatile areas. She hoped that her being female wouldn't keep them from mobilizing her to support missions outside the safety of the camp's borders.

Kinsley reached her quarters, filled a bowl full of water for Agar and stripped out of her uniform pants and boots. While Agar greedily slurped the entire contents of the bowl, Kinsley slipped on her army-issue PT shorts and running shoes and switched her desert-tan T-shirt for her army PT shirt. After strapping her flourescent belt around her waist and pulling her hair back into a ponytail, she planted a black army ball cap on her head and stepped out the door, leash in hand.

She moved smartly, walking past the rows of shipping-container quarters and other buildings, working her way through the complex toward the open field designated for PT.

She passed the motor pool and offices set aside for

contractors who were providing additional support and building projects for the camp.

A silver-haired man stood at the corner of one of the buildings, smoking a cigarette. He wore khaki slacks and a polo shirt, incongruous with the multitude of uniforms from all branches of the military.

As she approached, he smiled. "Good afternoon," he said.

Not wanting to be rude, Kinsley slowed, though she'd rather speed by without engaging. "Hello."

He stepped in front of her. "You're new to the camp?"

"Yes, sir." She frowned, her gaze running over his civilian clothing. "I'm sorry, I don't think we've met." She held out her hand. "Specialist Anderson."

"William Toland." He reached out and shook her hand. "No, we haven't met. I'd remember a woman and her dog."

Kinsley's hand automatically dropped to Agar's head. "Sergeant Agar is a Military Working Dog."

"I assumed he was." The man reached out as if to pet the dog.

Agar's lips pulled back in a snarl and he growled low in his chest.

Toland snatched back his hand. "Not very friendly?"

Kinsley stepped between Agar and Toland. "He wasn't trained to be friendly. He's trained to sniff out explosives, not to be petted by strangers."

"Handy skill to have in a war." Toland stepped back. "And message received."

Kinsley nodded toward the construction crane at the far end of the camp. "Are you working with the contractors to build the new water towers?"

"I am," Toland responded. "But please, don't let me keep you from your exercise. I'm sure Sergeant Agar needs a good run to keep him in shape, too." He waved his hand as if granting her passage.

All in all, Kinsley was irritated by the man's arrogance in stepping in front of her in the first place. And even more convinced Agar was right to growl at the man. She'd learned to trust her dog's judgment of character.

Toland hadn't said or done anything too far out of the ordinary. Even so, Kinsley couldn't put her finger on it, but she wasn't sure she trusted the man. After all, why did a man stop a lone female soldier just to talk? Didn't the contractors get the same briefing as the military personnel?

Don't fraternize. Period.

As soon as she cleared the buildings, she shook off the prickly feeling at the back of her neck and quickened her pace into a slow, steady jog, with Agar easily keeping up at her side.

Running had never been a joy, but she did it to stay in shape for the semiannual fitness test and to be able to keep up with the physical demands of the job. She had to be in shape to walk long miles carrying a heavy rucksack. She might also be required to run into and out of bad situations. She expected Agar to be fit; she required nothing less of herself.

She ran along the track circling the containerized living units, staring at the stark desert beyond. She could glimpse a bit of the blue waters of the Gulf of Aden. No matter how hot, she preferred running outdoors than in the air-conditioned fitness center on the treadmills set up for residents of the camp. If Agar had to run in the heat, then she would do no less. The peace of the desert, with the wind off the water and the salty tang in the air, lulled her into a trance, nearly clearing her thoughts of the man Agar had come close to slamming into earlier.

Kinsley had to admit McGuire had appeal, unlike William Toland, who was perhaps old enough to be her father. Knowing McGuire was a SEAL made her all the more curious about the man. Anyone who had gone through BUD/S training had to be not only physically fit, but also mentally equipped to handle the most extreme environments and situations.

Based on the man's broad shoulders pulling tautly at his uniform, he was fit. But she wasn't sure about his mental fitness. For a long moment, he'd stared at her before actually opening his mouth. Perhaps he'd been hit once too often in the head and had suffered a brain injury.

At least that's what Kinsley told herself. She preferred to come up with reasons she should stay away from the man rather than reasons to fall under his spell. She hadn't joined the army to get married. And fraternization at Camp Lemonnier was strictly forbidden.

Footsteps sounded behind her, disturbing her not-so-peaceful escape.

She tightened her hold on Agar's lead and moved to the outside of the dirt path, making room for the other runner.

Instead of passing her, the runner slowed to match her pace.

She frowned over at him, ready to tell him to move on, when she noticed it was him… Petty Officer Mc-

Guire, the navy SEAL who had been occupying entirely too many of her thoughts since she'd run into him minutes before.

"Mind if I join you?" he asked with a grin.

She shrugged and kept moving. "Can't stop you."

"All you have to say is *shove off*, and I'll leave you alone," he said. "Sometimes it's nice to have a running buddy to fill the time."

"I actually have one," she said, and tipped her head toward Agar.

As if he could understand, Agar glanced up at her, his tongue lolling to the side.

"I see." With a twist of his lips, McGuire gave a curt nod. "Then I'll leave you two to your workout." And he picked up his pace, leaving Kinsley behind.

For a moment, Agar strained at the leash, wanting to keep up with the jogger ahead.

Kinsley gave him a sharp command. "Heel."

The German shepherd immediately fell in step with her, looking up at Kinsley and back to McGuire as if to tell her he could easily catch the man.

"I suppose I was rude," Kinsley admitted to Agar.

Agar looked up at her words, his mouth open, tongue hanging out the side. He appeared to be smiling, when in fact he was only trying to keep cool in the incredible heat.

"It's just as well. He has red hair. I make it a point not to get involved with men while I'm deployed. But even if we weren't deployed, I couldn't date the man. He has red hair. Our babies would all be doomed to red hair." She shuddered. "I wouldn't wish all of my children to that lot in life. Not if I have a choice."

Her gaze followed the SEAL as he ran to one corner of the huge field, turned and kept running, his powerful thighs pushing him forward with ease.

Kinsley's heart beat faster and her breathing became more labored as she watched the man's tight buttocks and well-defined legs. If she were into gingers, he'd be the one to catch. Thank goodness she wasn't.

Nevertheless, she slowed to a fast walk, letting McGuire widen the gap between them. She didn't want to risk running into him again at the end of her run. The man had *complication* written all over him.

When she arrived back at her quarters, she found a note stuck to the door.

Meeting at command center ASAP.

Kinsley had never received a message like that. Her pulse kicked up a notch, but she focused on staying calm. For all she knew, someone might have lodged a complaint about her exercising Agar too close to the living quarters. Or they were switching her to night shift.

She refused to get excited and dare to think she might be sent on an actual mission.

Chapter 2

T-Mac had just stepped out of the shower facility when Big Jake found him.

"Meeting in the command center, now," Big Jake said.

"Give me two minutes to get dressed." T-Mac hurried in his flip-flops toward his quarters, threw on his uniform, hat and boots and ran out the door, buttoning his jacket as he went. He jogged all the way to the command center and stepped inside the air-conditioned containerized office unit.

Inside, his team sat around a long, narrow table. Navy Commander Trevor Ward stood at the head of the table, his gaze on T-Mac as he entered. "Now that we're all here, let's get this party started."

T-Mac remained standing near the door, his curiosity piqued, his adrenaline pumping. He preferred missions to boredom any day.

"We're all ready to mobilize back to the States—" the commander held up his hand "—and as far as everyone is concerned, we will still be leaving in four days. However, we just received intel on a trade deal going down tonight on the border of Somalia."

The team waited quietly for Commander Ward to continue.

"You might ask what we have to do with trade in this area. But here's the deal. Someone from around here has been funneling shipments of weapons from around Camp Lemonnier to the Al-Shabaab terrorists in Somalia. Intel intercepted a text communication from a burner cell phone nearby. Apparently, there will be handoff of a shipment conducted tonight in one of the abandoned, shelled-out villages on the other side of the border between Djibouti and Somalia." He nodded to his assistant, who clicked the keys on a laptop.

A map of the Horn of Africa blinked up on the whiteboard behind the commander.

Commander Ward turned to point at the location marked with a red dot. "The mission is simple. We go in, capture the traitors involved and return them to camp."

"All in a night's work," Harm said. "What's the catch?"

"Previous attempts by army rangers to recon this village were met with explosives."

"As in mortars and rocket-propelled grenades?" Buck asked.

The commander's lips pressed into a thin line. "Not

so easy. IEDs and land mines. That's why we'll have two additional members on our team."

As if on cue, the door behind T-Mac opened and a German shepherd entered, followed by Specialist Kinsley Anderson, still dressed in her PT uniform of shorts, a T-shirt and running shoes.

The woman glanced around the room full of men and lifted her chin. "I'm sorry I'm late. I got here as soon as I received word of the meeting."

"No worries," the commander said. He waved his hand toward her. "Team, meet Specialist Anderson and Sergeant Agar. They will be with us on this mission tonight."

All eyes turned to the only female in the room.

T-Mac's pulse quickened. He'd never been on a mission with a female. Would having a woman in the mix change the dynamics of his team? Not that he was superstitious, but would the others be worried that a woman would jinx their mission?

He glanced around the room at the others' gazes. For the most part, they appeared more curious than apprehensive.

"Anyone have any issues?" the commander asked.

Specialist Anderson's chin rose another notch, her gaze sweeping the room full of men, challenging them with just that one look.

Big Jake shrugged. "I'd be glad to have a dog ahead of us. I've seen what one can do. They're pretty amazing."

"Same," Buck said. "Rather sniff out the bombs than step on one."

The rest of the men voiced agreement.

"Then get ready, you leave in—" Commander Ward glanced down at his watch "—one hour."

T-Mac followed Anderson out of the building. "Do you need help getting ready?" he asked.

"I think I can figure it out," she said, stepping out smartly and moving toward the containerized living quarters.

Falling in step beside her, T-Mac hustled to keep up. "Is this your first mission outside the wire?" he asked.

She tensed and frowned. "I know my job, and I know what to carry and wear into combat. You don't have to coddle me because I'm female."

He held up his hands. "Oh, believe me, I wouldn't dare do that." Then he ruined it with a chuckle. "I'd help out the new guy, male or female. I like to come back with all the people we left with intact."

Her shoulders relaxed. "Sorry. I shouldn't be so defensive."

"I'm sure you have a right to be."

She lifted her shoulders and let them drop. "I get tired of people underestimating my abilities just because I'm a woman."

"I've seen you two in action. I have complete confidence in you and Agar."

The dog lifted his head at the sound of his name and then looked forward again, trotting alongside his handler.

"Well, you don't have to worry about us. We can handle our job. We'll keep you and your team safe from explosives."

"And we'll do our best to keep you and Agar safe from loose bullets."

She shot him a hint of a smile. "Thanks." By then, they were standing in front of her quarters. Specialist Anderson frowned. "I didn't ask where we should meet."

T-Mac's lips twisted. "We'll be loading up in helicopters. If you like, I can swing by and we can walk over together."

Her frown cleared. "Thanks. I'd appreciate that."

"My pleasure," he said, and left her at her door to hurry toward his own quarters, where he'd gear up for the mission ahead.

In the back of his mind, he couldn't help but worry about the addition to their team. The SEALs trained together. They hadn't trained with a dog handler working out in front of them. Specialist Anderson and Agar might know what they were doing when it came to sniffing out bombs, but they had no experience in hostile environments.

When T-Mac entered the containerized quarters he shared with Harm, his roommate glanced up from assembling his M4A1 rifle with the SOPMOD upgrade. "Hey, T-Mac."

"Harm." T-Mac pulled a hard plastic case out from under his bunk, extracted his rifle and pulled it apart piece by piece. He'd cleaned it after his last mission and had assembled and disassembled it a number of times since. Handling his weapon was second nature.

"Saw you walked the dog handler back to her quarters," Harm said.

"Yeah." T-Mac stiffened. "So?"

Without looking up from what he was doing, Harm

continued. "You know we were just kidding about fixing you up with a female, right?"

T-Mac snorted. "No. I fully expect you guys to bombard me with women."

Harm gave a twisted grin. "You're right. But we'd wait until we got back to the States. What with how touchy folks are about not fraternizing while deployed."

With a frown, T-Mac shook his head. "If this is about Specialist Anderson, forget it. I only offered to help her get ready for the mission. She hasn't actually been on one before."

Harm's head shot up. "Never?"

His chest tightening, T-Mac pressed his lips together. "Everyone has to have a first time."

His roommate frowned. "I'd rather it wasn't with us."

"Would you rather she went out with some teenaged infantry soldiers who are barely out of boot camp?"

Harm sighed. "I suppose not. But I don't like the idea of babysitting when we have a mission to accomplish."

T-Mac pulled the bolt from his weapon, inspected it and shot it back home, reassembling the weapon in record time. "I'd almost rather take my chances with the mines and IEDs than risk losing her and the dog."

"Not me," Harm said. "Remember what happened to Roadrunner when he got too far ahead of the rest of us on that extraction mission in Afghanistan?"

T-Mac's stomach clenched at the memory.

Roadrunner had been point man when he'd stepped on a land mine. Thankfully for Roadrunner, he'd died instantly. The team had been left to pick up the pieces, physically and mentally.

"Hopefully Anderson and Agar know their stuff," T-Mac muttered.

"Yeah. But they're all about sniffing out explosives. We have to worry about the snipers. A lot of money goes into training dogs and handlers."

"And SEALs," T-Mac reminded him.

Harm nodded. "That's a given. I'd like to make it back to the States in four days. Talia will be waiting at my apartment. I let her use it for a place to stay while she's house hunting."

T-Mac shot a glance toward his teammate. "I thought you two were a thing?"

"We are. But I want her to be sure. Moving from Africa back to the States is a big deal. And dating a SEAL won't make it much easier." Harm lifted a shoulder and let it fall. "I don't want to pressure her. She needs time to make up her own mind and be comfortable with herself."

"Before she commits to you?"

"Yeah." Harm grinned. "You know our lives aren't easy even for us. I want her to know how it is and what she can expect before we tie the knot."

"What happened to being confirmed bachelors? I thought we were a team. And now you all have women." T-Mac shook his head. "I don't get it."

Harm chuckled, pulled his steel-plated vest out of his go bag and laid it out on his bunk. "You'll get it when you find the woman who makes you reconsider everything you ever thought to be true."

"Now you're starting to sound sappy. I'm not sure I want to find a woman who makes me go soft." T-Mac strapped a scabbard around his calf and stuck his Ka-

Bar knife into it. "Next thing you know, you'll be sec-ond-guessing yourself on the battlefield."

"Never." Harm shrugged into his vest and secured several empty magazines into the straps. "Let's quit flapping our gums and go meet up with your cute dog handler."

"She's not *my* dog handler."

"No?" Harm gave him a side-eye glance and raised one eyebrow. "Sure looked like it to the rest of us."

"She's not my dog handler," T-Mac insisted, his tone hard, his lips tight.

"Whatever you say." Harm grabbed his helmet and stepped out of the box. "But between the two of you red-heads, you'd make some really cute redheaded babies."

"She's not my redhead," T-Mac said through clenched teeth as he snagged his helmet and followed Harm. "And we're not having babies."

"Who's having babies?" Buck fell in step behind Harm and T-Mac. "If T-Mac is planning on marrying the dog handler, they can start their own ginger bas-ketball team. Or hockey team. Or whatever team they want. They'd all be gingers."

"We're not getting married. She's not my dog han-dler, and I'd appreciate it if you wouldn't say anything around her about babies and basketball teams." T-Mac picked up the pace, hoping that by walking faster, his teammates wouldn't have the time nor desire to poke fun at him.

Pitbull and Big Jake stepped out of the quarters they shared.

"What's this about babies and basketball teams?" Pitbull asked. "Is T-Mac marrying his dog handler?"

T-Mac threw his hand in the air. "She's not my dog handler."

Big Jake chuckled. "I think he protests too much. I swear I saw something between the two of them."

"You can't see something that wasn't there." T-Mac sighed. "I get it. This is all part of razzing me because I choose to stay a bachelor and have my pick of women out there while you losers commit to being with one woman for the rest of your lives. I think I have the better deal."

"What deal?" Diesel jogged to catch up to the team. "What did I miss?"

"T-Mac's met his match," Buck said.

T-Mac gritted his teeth. "I didn't."

"His dog handler?" Diesel guessed.

"She's not my dog handler." T-Mac might as well have been talking to a wall.

"Oh, he's going to fall hard," Diesel said. "She's got attitude and a dog. A killer combination. What's not to love about that?"

"I'm not in love. She's not my handler, and I don't even think the dog likes me." He glanced toward the container where Specialist Anderson was staying and debated walking past and letting her find her own way to where the helicopters were parked. But he'd promised to walk with her. He slowed, hoping the rest of the team would walk on without questioning why he was stopping.

But he knew them better than that. They weren't stupid and they would figure it out pretty quickly.

"Look, guys, could you be serious for once?" He turned and raised his hand to knock on the door.

All five of his friends came to a complete stop.

T-Mac groaned as the door opened.

Agar came out first and immediately sniffed T-Mac's crotch.

A rumble of chuckles sounded behind T-Mac.

"I guess the dog likes you after all," Buck muttered.

More chuckles sounded.

Heat rose up T-Mac's neck into his cheeks as he glanced up at Specialist Anderson. "Don't listen to anything these yahoos say. They're all full of... Well, they're full of it, anyway."

Kinsley tore her gaze away from the SEAL standing in front of her looking all hot and incredibly sexy in his combat gear. Beyond Petty Officer McGuire stood five of the other men who'd been in the command center minutes before. She stepped out of the doorway, looped the strap of her rifle over her shoulder and double-wrapped the dog's lead around her hand. "What am I not supposed to listen to them about?"

"Tell her, T-Mac," one of them encouraged.

"We don't have time for games," McGuire said. "We have a mission to accomplish before we head home."

"You're heading home?" Kinsley asked.

"Four days and a wakeup," the tallest of the group answered.

"Where's home?" Kinsley fell in step with them as they wove their way through the temporary buildings to the landing strip where planes and helicopters parked.

"Little Creek, Virginia," McGuire answered.

"What about you?" one of the guys asked. "Where is your home base?"

"San Antonio, Texas, was my last PCS assignment," Kinsley said.

"That's where they train Military Working Dogs, isn't it?" McGuire asked. "They have a facility at Lackland Air Force Base. Is that where you and Agar received your training?"

She nodded. "I spent the past year in training."

"T-Mac says this is your first assignment since training."

Again, Kinsley nodded. "That's true. Agar was the best in his class. He could find trace amounts of explosives that none of our own detection equipment could pick up." She patted the dog's head. "He's good at what he does. If there are IEDs or land mines, he'll prove himself tonight."

As they reached the helicopters, more SEALs gathered. Ammunition was dispensed. Then it came time for them to load into the helicopters.

Kinsley started for one of the choppers away from McGuire and his group.

The navy commander who'd briefed them caught up to her. "You're riding in the other bird. Stick with T-Mac. He'll make sure you're safe."

"I can take care of myself," Kinsley insisted.

"I understand," the commander said. "But the team isn't used to working with a dog and its handler. It's for their safety as well as yours."

Kinsley couldn't argue with that. Apparently, she was to have a handler. "Yes, sir."

The commander escorted her back to the other helicopter where McGuire, or T-Mac, as his team nicknamed him, stood, waiting his turn to climb aboard.

"T-Mac," the commander called out.

The SEAL turned when he saw who was with his superior.

"I have an assignment for you," Commander Ward said.

"Yes, sir," T-Mac replied.

"You're to keep up with Specialist Anderson and Sergeant Agar. Bring them back safely."

T-Mac's eyes narrowed. "Sir?"

Kinsley stiffened.

The SEAL didn't look too excited.

"You heard me," the commander said. "Take care of them out there. You don't know what you'll be up against."

"Yes, sir." T-Mac nodded.

When the others in the helicopter chuckled, T-Mac shot a glare their way.

With the odd feeling she wasn't in on the joke, Kinsley stepped up to the chopper.

"Has Agar been in a helicopter?" T-Mac asked.

Kinsley nodded. "Not only has he been up, he's been hoisted in and out on a cable multiple times. He's calm throughout."

"Good." T-Mac offered her a hand up.

Ignoring the hand, Kinsley motioned for Agar to go first. Then she stepped up into the chopper and found a seat between the tallest guy and one who was stout with a barrel chest. She settled between them and buckled her safety harness, keeping Agar close at her feet.

"I'm Jake," said the tall man. "They call me Big Jake."

Kinsley shook hands with the man. "Nice to meet you, Big Jake."

"I'm Pitbull." The barrel-chested guy stuck out his hand. "Here, you'll need these." He handed her a head-set.

She removed her helmet and settled the headset over her ears. Immediately, she could hear static and the pilot and copilot performing a communications check with the passengers.

She watched and listened as each of the SEALs answered, and she committed their names to memory.

"Diesel."

"Pitbull."

"Buck."

"Big Jake."

"Harm."

"T-Mac."

Her heart skipped several beats when T-Mac spoke. He sat in the seat opposite, his gaze on her. When no one else spoke, he winked and touched his finger to his own microphone.

Kinsley realized she'd forgotten to say her name. With heat rising up in her cheeks, she spoke into the mic. "Anderson and Agar."

T-Mac grinned.

A moment later, the helicopter lifted off the ground, swung out over the Gulf of Aden and then turned south, back over the Horn of Africa.

The sun had sunk low on the horizon, bathing the land in a bright orange glow.

If they hadn't been headed into a potentially hostile environment, Kinsley would have enjoyed the view, the sunset and the warm wind blowing in her face. But this was her first real combat assignment. She wasn't scared, but she was anxious to do well.

She sat back in her seat, forcing herself to be calm. Agar needed her full focus. He sensed her every mood and emotion. He needed to know she was in full control of herself as well as him. They'd trained to save lives by finding dangers lurking beneath the surface or behind walls.

For the duration of the flight, she concentrated on reducing her heart rate, breathing deeply and going over everything she'd learned in the intensive training she'd been through with Agar. Dogs weren't deployed unless they were ready. And dog handlers didn't last long in training if they weren't capable, consistent and calm. She'd excelled along with Agar.

All of her training had been for more than inspecting vehicles entering through the post gates.

Agar nudged her foot with his nose and looked up at her.

Kinsley rubbed the dog's snout and scratched him behind his ears.

He laid his head on her lap, as if sensing her unrest.

When Kinsley glanced up again, it was to stare across the darkening fuselage at the SEAL seated across from her. Though she resented feeling like she had to be babysat, she was glad she had someone with more combat experience watching her back.

All too soon, the helicopter touched down. The second one landed beside it.

Kinsley removed the helicopter headset, slipped her helmet on and latched the buckle beneath her chin. She exited the aircraft and stood to the side with Agar while all twelve SEALs alighted, checked their gear and waited for the signal to move out.

T-Mac approached her and handed her a small electronic device. "You'll need these earpieces to hear the team as we move through the village. You'll have to keep them up-to-date while they're looking for our traitor."

Kinsley fitted the device in her ear and spoke. "Testing."

Big Jake took charge, giving directions, performing one last communication check on their radio headsets.

After everyone checked in, Big Jake gathered them in a circle. "The village should be another four clicks to the east. We need to get in, clear the rubble of any enemy combatants and wait for the handoff. Any questions?"

Big Jake nodded toward Kinsley. "Take it, dog soldier."

Kinsley's heartbeat quickened. This was it. She and Agar had a job to do, lives to save and explosives to find.

She tugged on Agar's lead, sending him in the direction Big Jake indicated. She allowed the dog to run out at the extent of the retractable lead and walked behind him. She carried her rifle in her right hand, the lead in her left.

T-Mac fell in step beside her, his specialized M4A1 at the ready position.

Darkness had settled over the landscape with a blanket of stars lighting their way.

Agar zigzagged back and forth in front of her, his nose to the ground, tail wagging, moving swiftly enough that Kinsley had to hustle to keep up.

One kilometer passed without incident. Then two. As they neared their target, Kinsley slowed Agar, encouraging him to take his time. The team had chosen to approach the abandoned village from the west, establish a defensive position and wait for the party to start. The handoff was supposed to take place at midnight. That gave them a few hours to get in place and hunker down.

From what some of her more experienced counterparts had reported, sometimes it took hours to navigate a quarter-mile stretch. If their adversary considered the location to be worth the effort to defend or sabotage, they could have rigged it with land mines or trip wires hooked to detonators.

Glad for T-Mac's protection, she led the SEALs toward the crumbled buildings at the edge of the little village.

As they neared the closest of what was left of a mud-and-stick hut, Agar stopped, sniffed and lay down on the ground.

Kinsley's pulse quickened. "He found something."

She marked the spot with a flag and bent to scratch Agar behind the ears, then gave him the command to continue his search. Within a few feet he lay down again.

Marking the new spot, Kinsley worked with Agar, moving a few feet at time, ever closer to the village, at what felt like an excruciatingly slow pace.

"I don't like it," T-Mac said. "If they have a sniper waiting in one of those buildings, they can easily pick us off."

"Unless they figure the explosives will alert them to

anyone coming in from this direction," Big Jake said into Kinsley's ear.

She ignored the chatter and continued until she and Agar had identified a clear path to the village through what appeared to be a short field of submerged mines.

Once inside the crumbled walls of the village, Agar moved from structure to structure, sniffing without lying down.

Kinsley didn't let her guard down for a moment. After encountering the mines, she wouldn't put it past whoever set them to have more hidden treasures to keep unwanted visitors out.

She had Agar enter huts along the way, clear them and move on, aiming toward the center of the village and the road that led through the middle.

All the while, T-Mac remained at her side, his weapon ready, hand on the trigger.

As Agar neared the building on the edge of the road, he slowed. His hackles rose on the back of his neck and he uttered a low and dangerous growl.

Kinsley dropped to a squat in the shadow of the nearest building.

T-Mac followed her movement and knelt on one knee at her side. "What's the growl mean?"

"Someone's nearby," Kinsley whispered.

T-Mac held up a hand where the others could see his command to stop.

Kinsley didn't dare look back. All her focus was on Agar and what was in front of the dog.

"We'll take it from here." T-Mac rose and started forward.

Kinsley caught his arm before he could move past her. "But what if there are more explosives?"

"You're not going any farther." T-Mac glanced down at her. "Bring Agar back."

Kinsley didn't like being relegated to the rear. She'd come this far; she wanted to complete her work.

Before she could bring Agar back, the dog turned and entered a building, his growls increasing in volume and intensity.

Kinsley hurried after him.

"Wait," T-Mac called after her.

She had to know Agar was all right. As she ran forward, she pulled her flashlight from her pocket. When she turned into the doorway of the building, she flipped on the switch and shone the light, filtered with a red lens, into the room.

Agar stood with his feet planted and his lips pulled back in a wicked snarl.

As she panned the light around to see what Agar was growling at, a man's face appeared in the glow... a face she knew.

Kinsley gasped but didn't have time to react when the man lifted his rifle and fired point-blank into her chest.

The bullet hit with enough force to knock her backward through the door. She landed flat on her back and lay stunned.

Before she could catch her breath, the world erupted in gunfire around her.

Agar flew out of the building and landed on his side.

"No!" Kinsley screamed silently, though nothing would come from her lungs. She rolled to her side and tried to rise.

Agar yelped, the kind of sound only emitted when an animal was hurt.

Pushing past her own breathlessness and the pain in her chest, Kinsley crawled toward the dog, her heart in her throat, her need to reach Agar foremost in her mind.

Then an explosion went off in the building in front of her, shooting mud, rock and shrapnel in all directions.

Kinsley felt the force of the blast against her eardrums. Her body was peppered with rock and shrapnel like so many pellets from a shotgun shell. Dust billowed outward, choking the air, blinding Kinsley before she could reach Agar.

A sharp pain ripped through her side; still she staggered to her feet, crying out, "Agar!"

A high-pitched whistling sound screamed through the air.

"Incoming!" T-Mac yelled. Then he hit her from behind, sending her flying through the air to land hard on the packed dirt.

T-Mac landed on top of her, knocking the air from her lungs yet again. At the same time, another explosion rocked the ground she lay against.

Her ears rang, and for a moment she couldn't breathe or move. Dust and debris rained down on them. A darkness so deep closed in on her, threatening to pull her under.

"Agar." She reached out her hand, patting the ground, unable to move or crawl forward. Then her fingers touched fur. A sob rose in her throat as her vision faded and the ringing in her ears became a roar. She couldn't pass out. Agar needed her.

The next thing she knew, she was being lifted into the air. She struggled to get free. "No."

"Be still, Kinsley." T-Mac's voice sounded in her ear. "I'll get you out of here."

"No," she croaked, choking on dust. "Can't leave—"

Gunfire sounded all around.

"I have to get you out of here," T-Mac insisted. "You've been hit."

"Can't leave." She fought him, pounding her fists against his chest.

Big Jake appeared beside her. "Get her out of here."

T-Mac fought to retain his hold on her. "She refuses to go."

"Agar." Kinsley pushed against T-Mac's chest.

"He was hit," T-Mac said.

She swung her legs out of T-Mac's grasp and dropped to the ground. "Not leaving without him." Her knees buckled and she would have crumpled into a heap if T-Mac hadn't been holding on to her.

Again he scooped her up into his arms. "You can't stay here."

"I'll get the dog." Big Jake ran into the swirling dust and reappeared a moment later, carrying Agar.

"Oh, God," Kinsley sobbed. "Agar." Tears streamed from her eyes. "Let me help him."

"Not until we're out of here." T-Mac ran through the village, back the way they'd come. He passed his team as they moved in the opposite direction.

Over T-Mac's shoulder, Kinsley watched for Big Jake. The big man appeared out of the cloud of dust, still holding Agar.

Then, as they cleared the edge of the village, Big

Jake staggered and fell to his knees, his arms hitting the ground first, cushioning Agar's landing.

"Stop!" Kinsley screamed. "Big Jake's down."

"I can't stop," T-Mac said. "I can only carry one person at a time."

Behind Big Jake, another one of the SEALs appeared, looped Big Jake's arm over his shoulder and half carried the big man down the path between the flags Kinsley had planted to identify the buried land mines.

Agar remained on the ground...left behind.

"Let me down," Kinsley begged. "Please." She didn't dare struggle, afraid that if she did, she'd make T-Mac stumble and veer into one of the mines. Her strength waned, and a warm wet stickiness spread across her right arm and leg.

"Please, you can't leave Agar. He's my partner. He trusted me." Her voice faded to a whisper as tears trickled down her face and darkness threatened to block out the stars shining above.

The crackle of gunfire and the boom of explosions seemed to be coming from farther and farther away.

Kinsley must have passed out. When she came to, T-Mac was laying her on the floor of a helicopter. When she tried to sit up, her body refused to cooperate. All she could lift was her head, and only for a moment before it dropped to the hard metal floor. "Agar," she said on a sigh.

"Buck, do what you can," T-Mac said. "She's bleeding in several places."

"Don't worry about me," she said. "Please, go find Agar."

No one seemed to be listening as they pulled off her

helmet, unbuckled her protective vest and applied pressure to her wounds.

"Shh, you're going to be all right." T-Mac leaned over her, brushing her hair from her face, while someone else ripped her uniform jacket away from her leg.

The rumble of rotor blades sounded and the helicopter lifted from the ground.

As they rose into the air, Kinsley reached out a hand. "Agar."

T-Mac took her hand. "We'll take care of you."

"But who will take care of Agar?" she whispered.

And then the sounds of the rotor blades faded, and the world went black.

Chapter 3

T-Mac stayed with Specialist Anderson from the moment he carried her out of the village until they wheeled her into the medical facility at Camp Lemonnier. At that point, the medical team on standby grabbed him and made him take a gurney as well.

"You're bleeding," one of the medics said.

"I don't care. I promised to take care of Anderson." He pushed to his feet and slipped in something wet on the floor.

The medic grabbed his arm and steadied him. "She's in good hands. And you can't go back with her."

"But it was my responsibility to take care of her." And he'd failed. Miserably.

The physician on call appeared in front of T-Mac, a frown furrowing his brow. "You might not care about your own injuries, but you're putting everyone else in this facility in danger with the amount of blood you're getting on the floor. Take a seat, SEAL."

At the command in the doctor's voice, T-Mac sat on the gurney.

The medics stripped him of his body armor and uniform jacket and cut away the leg of his trousers.

In minutes the doctor had fished out the shrapnel, stitched the wound and applied a bandage.

The medics cleaned up the blood from the floor and set his gear on a chair beside the examination table.

T-Mac pushed to a sitting position and reached for his boots. Once he had his feet in them, he slid off the table to stand on the floor. He swayed slightly.

The medic was there, helping him stay upright. "Hey, you're going to rip a stitch if you're not careful."

"I want to see Specialist Anderson."

"They're taking care of her now." The young medic, who couldn't be more than nineteen years old, released his arm. "I'll go check on her and let you know how it's going." He helped him out of the room and nodded toward the front of the building. "In the meantime, you can take a seat in the lobby. I'll bring your gear."

Gritting his teeth, T-Mac turned away as another gurney entered the building with Big Jake on it.

His face was pale, but his eyes were open. He grabbed T-Mac's arm as he passed. "How's the dog soldier?"

"They're working on her now." T-Mac scanned his friend. "Where were you hit?"

"Took a bullet in the buttocks." Big Jake laughed and grimaced. "Only hurts when I laugh, or move, or hell, anything. I'll be glad when they get it out."

T-Mac stood back, his gaze going to the medics pushing the gurney. "Take care of my friend."

"We've got this. You might want to take a seat while you're waiting," the medic who'd helped him said. "You lost a little bit of blood yourself."

T-Mac made his way to the lobby. The window looking out was still dark.

As promised, the medic delivered his gear, setting it on the floor beside a chair.

Wearing his torn pants, the air-conditioned air cool on his exposed leg, T-Mac paced the short distance between chairs. He prayed the female dog handler and Big Jake would be all right. Part of him wanted to be back in the bombed-out village, wreaking havoc on those who'd hurt his team.

Seeing Anderson blown back out of the building by the power of a point-blank attack made his gut clench. He'd tried to grab her arm before she went in, but she'd been too fast, worried about her dog. He should have known she'd do something like that and thought ahead. She was his responsibility. Even if the commander hadn't tagged him with the job, he would have taken it anyway.

As he stared at his body armor and helmet, he wondered if the rest of his team was still fighting or if they'd brought the little village under control.

The whole mission had felt as if it had been a fiasco from the very beginning…as if they had been led into the chute like lambs to slaughter.

Unfortunately, Specialist Anderson had been first up. She'd taken a bullet to her armor-plated chest. Thankfully, she'd worn her protective gear, or she'd be dead.

As it was, the mortar having landed near them had taken its toll. If she didn't die of a punctured or collapsed lung from the blunt force of being fired on at close range, she might die from the multiple shrapnel wounds across her arms and legs. Or suffer from traumatic brain injury.

He didn't feel the stitches pinching since the doctor had given him a local anesthetic, but he felt ridiculous in his one-legged pants.

All the while he sat in the lobby, his teammates could be facing the fight of their lives, and he wasn't there to help.

An hour passed, and the medic came out. "Your friend, Petty Officer Schuler, is going to be okay. He should be out shortly."

Minutes later, Big Jake limped out into the lobby, wearing what T-Mac assumed were borrowed gym shorts and his T-shirt.

A medic carried his body armor and helmet, as well as his shirt and the remainder of his pants. "I can help you get back to your quarters when the shift changes in an hour," he promised. He glanced over his shoulder. "I have to get back in there."

"Wait." T-Mac took a step forward. "What's the status of Specialist Anderson?"

The medic shook his head. "They removed all the shrapnel, but she's still unconscious. They were waiting to see if she'd come out of it on her own, but she got kind of combative, so they sedated her. The doctor thinks she might have a concussion. We've called for transport to get her to the next level of care. They'll either take her to Ramstein in Germany or back to the States."

T-Mac's chest tightened. "How soon?"

"As soon as we can scramble a crew and medical staff to fly out on a C-130." The medic turned. "Now, if you'll excuse me, I need to get back." He disappeared before T-Mac could ask any more questions.

Big Jake laid a hand on T-Mac's shoulder. "I'm sorry about your dog handler."

For every time T-Mac had corrected his teammates, he knew he'd been lying to himself. He didn't know Kinsley Anderson well, nor did he have any ties to her, other than having been assigned to protect her. Still, he had felt she was his dog handler and that he was responsible for seeing to her safety.

The door to the medical facility burst open behind T-Mac and Big Jake. Buck, Harm, Diesel and Pitbull pushed through, covered in dust and smelling of gunpowder.

"Thank God you're both okay." Buck clapped a hand to T-Mac's back.

"We didn't know what had happened to you when you took off," Pitbull said.

Diesel nodded toward their pant legs and grinned. "New fashion statement in uniform trousers?" Then his smile faded. "You're okay?"

Big Jake snorted. "Other than a stitch here and there, we'll survive."

"What about T-Mac's dog handler?" Harm asked.

T-Mac's jaw tightened. "They're going to ship her out to the next level of medical support." He turned to Harm. "What about Agar? What happened to the dog?" T-Mac knew the first thing Kinsley would want to know was if her dog made it out alive.

Harm shook his head. "We got him onto the helicopter and carried him to the camp veterinarian. I can't tell you whether he'll make it. He was nonresponsive when we delivered him, but I think he still had a heartbeat."

When Kinsley recovered enough to ask, she'd receive yet another blow if the dog didn't make it. T-Mac wanted to know more about Agar's condition, but he wasn't leaving the medical facility until the army specialist did.

"You might as well get some rest," Big Jake said. "You can't do anything for her now."

"I know. But I'm staying," he said.

Big Jake nodded. "You know it wasn't your fault she was hurt."

T-Mac's fists knotted, but he didn't say anything.

Big Jake touched his arm. "You couldn't have known the dog would dart into that building, or that someone was there waiting to shoot her."

"That's right," Buck stated. "She's lucky she had on her body armor, or she wouldn't be alive—"

Pitbull elbowed Buck in the ribs. "She's going to be okay. The docs will take good care of her. And when they get her to a real hospital, they'll make sure she gets even better care."

T-Mac knew all that, but he wouldn't feel better about any of it until he saw the dog handler standing in front of him, giving him attitude.

"If you two are up to it, the CO wants a debrief," Harm said. "He's out for blood. The way we see it, we were set up, plain and simple."

"Did you find the guy who shot Specialist Anderson?" T-Mac asked.

Harm's lips thinned. "We thought we'd find pieces

of him after the explosion, but he got away. There was a back door to that hut."

Anger seared through T-Mac's veins. "He got away?"

"Yeah," Buck said. "And the only guy they left behind was in no condition to give us any answers."

"He was dead," Pitbull said.

"Shot in the back," Diesel finished.

"Not only were they waiting for us," Harm said, "but they had their escape plan in place before we got there."

Buck's eyes narrowed. "Someone tipped them off about what time we left. We got there well before the arranged trade deadline."

"Any others hurt besides the three of us and Agar?" T-Mac asked.

"No," Pitbull said. "When the dust settled, they were gone in a couple of pickup trucks. We would have gone after them, but we figured the dog needed medical attention."

"What exactly happened to the dog handler?" Harm wanted to know.

"She was shot in the chest by whomever was in that hut."

"That'll give her nightmares." Diesel shook his head. "Seeing the face of the man who shot you would leave an indelible image in your mind."

T-Mac snorted. "She was more concerned about Agar being hurt than the fact she'd nearly been killed."

"I hope they make it." Big Jake gently rubbed a hand over his backside. "The whole mission was a disaster."

T-Mac ran a hand through his hair. "Absolutely. Tell the commander what I told you. I'll be here, if he wants to hear it from me in person."

"Will do." Big Jake limped out of the facility with the others on their way to the debrief.

T-Mac paced the lobby again, his frustration growing with each step. He hoped he could be around when Kinsley came to. He wanted to let her know how sorry he was for not keeping her and Agar safe.

Just when T-Mac was ready to ignore the rules and march back to Kinsley's bed, the medic returned.

"She's still out of it," he said. "But you can come back and sit with her."

Kinsley hovered between the dark and the light. Every time she felt as if she were surfacing from a deep, black well, she stretched out her hand only to slip back into it. No matter how hard she climbed and scraped her hands on the hard stone walls, she couldn't seem to get to the top. Her fingers grew chilled from the coldness of the stones.

And then warmth wrapped around her hand.

She quit fighting to climb and lay back, basking in the warmth radiating from her hand up her arm and throughout her body.

A deep voice came to her through the black abyss.

"Kinsley, wake up and tell me I'm wrong."

That voice made her want to wake, but that well she'd been clawing her way out of wouldn't let her go.

"Kinsley, you're going to be okay. You just need to wake up and give me all kinds of grief for not taking care of you."

Who was talking to her? And what was he talking about? She tried to open her eyes but she didn't have the strength. So, she lay listening to the warm, deep tones, letting them wash over her, fill her, hold her up when she couldn't stay afloat in the bottomless well. The voice permeated her insides while a strong hand cupped hers, providing heat when she felt so very cold.

Images and sensations swirled in an endless cyclone, refusing to coalesce into anything she could recognize. Faces, dust, fur, sounds, blinding flashes, all spinning inside, making her dizzy, forcing her back into that well, away from the light.

"Kinsley, sweetheart, you're going to be all right. Open your eyes. You'll see. I should have been the one entering that building. You and Agar wouldn't have been hurt if I'd gone first. You have to be okay. Agar is going to need you."

Agar? The word was odd, yet familiar. Still, she couldn't remember why. Nothing made sense. The only anchor keeping her from drowning in the whirlpool threatening to take her under was the voice in the darkness urging her toward the light.

As the black abyss pulled her under, she tightened her hold on the big hand.

Minutes, hours or days later—Kinsley couldn't tell—she blinked her eyes open and stared at the top of an auburn head lying on the sheet beside her. She wasn't in her apartment back in San Antonio. Then she remembered—she'd deployed. Her brow furrowed. To where? She thought hard, the truth just out of her grasp.

She was in the army. They'd sent her on a long flight to…

Nothing.

Frustration made her want to hit something. But

when she tried to clench her fist, she couldn't. Someone was holding her hand.

Again, she stared at the head on the sheet beside her.
Perhaps the man who owned the head was also the one
holding her hand.

But why?

The astringent scent of disinfectant assailed her nostrils. Her gaze moved from the stranger's head to the
walls around her. Once again, she realized she wasn't in
an apartment, and based on the unusual bed, the bright
overhead lights and the monitor tracking her heartbeat,
she had to be in some kind of hospital.

Had she been hurt? Kinsley took inventory of her
body. Twinges of pain answered for her. Stinging on
the surface of her arms and legs let her know she had
cuts and abrasions. Her chest felt bruised, and breathing deeply made it slightly worse.

But who was the man with his head on her bed?
And what was she forgetting that was so important?
Something tugged at her mind, something she should
remember, but couldn't.

"Psst," she said.

The man remained facedown on the sheet.

"Hey." When she spoke, her voice sounded like a
frog's croak.

The head stirred and lifted. Blue eyes opened, and
ginger brows knitted together. "Kinsley?" the man said.

"Yes, that's me." She frowned. "But who are you?"

He sat up straight in the chair beside her bed and
pushed a hand through his hair. "I'm T-Mac. Don't you
remember me?"

Her frown deepened, making her head hurt. "If I remembered, would I be asking?"

He chuckled. "You still have your bite. We met yesterday, near your quarters."

"Quarters?" She looked around. "These aren't my quarters."

His brows pinched together again. "No. You're in the Djibouti medical facility."

"Why am I here?" she asked.

"You were injured in a skirmish in Somalia."

"Skirmish?" she asked, feeling like she was missing a chunk of her memory. And it was scaring her. "What day is it?"

He told her the date. "You were shot and involved in an explosion."

She gasped, her heartbeat fluttering uncontrollably. "What was I doing in Somalia?" The green line on the monitor jumped erratically.

The auburn-haired man pushed to his feet. "Let me get the doctor."

"I'm okay," she said. "I'm okay," she repeated, as if to remind herself. "I just can't remember any of that."

He didn't listen, leaving the room in a hurry.

Kinsley lifted her head. A sharp pain slashed through her forehead. She lay back, closed her eyes and let it abate before she opened her eyes again.

By then T-Mac had returned with a man in a white coat. He introduced himself as her doctor. She couldn't commit his name to her memory with the pain throbbing in her head.

He shone a light into her eyes. "Do you remember what happened to you?"

She tried to shake her head, remembering too late that it caused pain. Kinsley winced. "No." Her heart beat fast and her hands shook as she pressed her fingertips to her temple. "I can't remember what day it is."

"Do you know who the president of the United States is?" the doctor asked.

She thought, but couldn't come up with a name. "No."

"What about where you were born?" he persisted.

The more she tried to remember, the worse her head hurt. "I can't remember." A tear slipped from the corner of her eye to run down her cheek.

The doctor patted her hand. "Don't be too alarmed. You had a concussion. Temporary memory loss can be a side effect."

"Will it come back?" Kinsley asked. "Will I remember where I'm from and who the president is?"

He smiled down at her. "You should. Give yourself time to recover. We're trying to get a transport to send you back to a higher-level medical-care facility, but we can't seem to find a C-130 we can tap into for the next couple days. You might be stuck with us."

"I'm fine," she said, and pushed up on her elbows. "I need to get back to work." She shook her head. "If only I could remember what work I do."

The doctor touched her shoulder. "Don't strain your brain. The memories will return, given time."

She lay back on the bed, her gaze following the doctor as he left her room. Kinsley wanted to call him back, to make him give her some pill or potion to force her memories to return. Not knowing things was confusing and frightening.

Her gaze shifted to T-Mac. "Why are you here?"

He smiled. "I wanted to make sure you were going to be okay."

"I'm okay. You don't have to be here. I'm sure you have more important things to do."

"Do you mind if I stay? I'm not on duty or anything. After being here all night, I feel invested in your well-being."

She shrugged. "Suit yourself. I'm probably going to go back to sleep. Maybe when I wake up again, I'll remember what I've forgotten." She laughed, the sound catching on a sob. "I don't even know what I've forgotten."

He lifted her hand and gave it a light squeeze. "I'd fill you in, but I barely know you."

"Then you're no help." She closed her eyes but didn't try to pull her hand free. Holding on to T-Mac was the lifeline she needed at that moment. If that made her weak…so be it. Until she got her memories back, she felt as though she'd been set adrift on an ocean, far from shore.

"What exactly happened?" she asked.

His eyes narrowed as if he were assessing her.

She waved her free hand. "I'm a soldier. Don't pull your punches. Give it to me." Then her eyes widened and a smile lifted her lips. "I'm a soldier."

T-Mac smiled. "See? Your memory's already coming back." He nodded. "We entered a village with the intention of getting there ahead of people coming to make a weapons handoff. We ran into resistance. You were shot in the chest. The team was overwhelmed by incoming grenades and mortars, and we backed out to regroup. Fortunately, you were wearing body armor, or the outcome could have been very different."

"That's it?" She studied T-Mac. He wasn't telling her everything. "What else?"

"Agar was injured."

That name. She should know that name. She didn't want to say it, but she couldn't remember who Agar was.

T-Mac's gaze pinned hers, his lips pressing together for a moment. "Your dog."

As if a floodgate had been unleashed, images and memories poured over Kinsley, all revolving around Agar, his training, her training as a dog handler and the heat of summer in San Antonio, Texas. She tried to breathe, but her lungs were constricted, the air refusing to enter or leave. "Agar," she mouthed. Her hand squeezed his tightly.

"He's with the veterinarian. I haven't been there yet to check his status."

Kinsley pushed to a sitting position. Her head spun and pain knifed through her temple. "Have to see him."

T-Mac pressed a hand to her shoulder. "You're not going anywhere until the doc clears you to move."

"I'm going." She shoved his hand away and swung her legs over the side of the bed. That's when she noticed she was only wearing a hospital gown and not much else. "Where are my clothes?"

"They cut away the trousers and shirt to get to your shrapnel wounds."

"Great. I don't suppose I can walk across the camp in this gown?" She glanced down at the flimsy hospital dress and back up at T-Mac.

"I'll bring a change of clothes for you."

"Thanks." Her brows rose.

"Oh, you mean now?" He grinned. "I should say, I'll get your clothing when the doctor releases you to go back to your quarters."

"I'm leaving." She scooted her bottom to the edge of the mattress. "With or without clothes."

"Specialist Anderson, you haven't been released from my care." The doctor chose that moment to return to her room. "Until that time, you're under my command. You leave, and I'll have to report you as AWOL."

Kinsley frowned. "I need to see my dog."

"You can see your dog when I release you. I want to keep you one more night. If everything looks good in the morning, I'll sign your release orders." The doctor shone his penlight into her eyes, listened to her heartbeat and then left her alone again with T-Mac.

"I'll check on Agar and let you know how he's doing," T-Mac said.

Kinsley wanted to see for herself, but she couldn't risk her career by disobeying orders. "Okay. But could you go now?"

T-Mac chuckled, the rich tone warming her in the air-conditioned room. "Going." He performed an about-face and marched to the door, where he turned back. "Don't go anywhere. I'll be back in a few minutes."

"You might want to shower before you return." She wrinkled her nose. "You smell."

He leaned close and inhaled. "You're no bed of roses either, Specialist." He moved out of range of her swinging arm and winked.

She watched him leave in his torn pants and dirty

uniform jacket. Even with dried blood smeared across his leg, he was handsome.

Kinsley crossed her arms over her chest, every nerve in her body urging her to jump out of bed and race after him, to go to the vet's office. Agar had to be okay. He was more than just a working dog to her. He was her only friend.

The image of T-Mac's head lying on the bed beside her returned. He'd been by her side throughout the night when he didn't have to be. Why had he stayed for a relative stranger?

Now that T-Mac was gone, Kinsley felt alone and overwhelmed. At least she had part of her memory back.

Agar. She could remember every detail of her dog and the training they'd gone through to make him the best explosives-sniffing dog he could be.

But no amount of training made either one of them bulletproof.

Kinsley prayed Agar would be okay. And she hoped T-Mac would hurry back. Not only for news on her dog, but because she already missed holding his hand.

Chapter 4

T-Mac hurried to his quarters and grabbed a clean uniform and his shaving kit. After a quick trip to the shower unit, he felt almost human. His leg stung where his stitches were, but he'd get over it soon enough. The injury wouldn't keep him from a mission, and it sure as hell wouldn't keep him from checking on Kinsley.

On his way back to the medical facility, he swung through the chow hall and snagged a couple of sandwiches and pieces of lemon pound cake. He had them wrapped in cellophane and tucked them in the large pockets of his jacket.

Next stop was the camp veterinarian. When he entered, he found Harm talking to the vet with Agar sitting at his feet.

"It's the darnedest thing," the vet was saying. "One

minute he was unconscious, the next he was up and moving around as if nothing had happened. I watched him through the night, but he seems to have suffered no lasting damage from the explosion." The vet handed over the lead to Harm. "He's been fed and has had plenty of water for now. You might test his abilities before he returns to duty. And he could use some exercise. He's been cooped up in a crate until now."

"Will do," Harm said, and handed the lead to T-Mac. "I'm sure your dog handler would like to see her dog."

T-Mac grinned. "I'm sure she would." He reached down to scratch Agar behind the ears. "I'll take him out for a run first." He nodded toward the vet. "Thanks."

"My pleasure. He's a well-behaved animal."

He had to be. Military Working Dogs were selected based on physical ability, temperament and intelligence. Agar had all that going for him, plus a rigorous training program of which Specialist Anderson had been a major part.

T-Mac and Agar followed Harm out of the veterinarian's building.

Harm stopped and faced T-Mac. "How's your dog handler?"

T-Mac smiled. "She's awake and talking." His smile faded.

Harm's brow creased. "But?"

"She's suffering some temporary amnesia."

"Not good."

"No kidding. The doctor thinks she'll get most of her memory back."

"Do you think she saw the man who shot her?"

He shrugged. "It was dark. Even if she did see him, there's no guarantee she'll remember."

"That's too bad."

"It's too bad he got away." T-Mac clenched his fists. That man had fired with all intentions of killing Kinsley. She would be dead had her body armor not protected her.

"The CO wants to see you when you get a chance." Harm held up his hand. "He was satisfied with what we told him, so he said no hurry."

"Good." He wanted to get back to Kinsley as soon as he exercised Agar. "I'll stop by later, after she goes to sleep."

"I'll let him know."

"Did he say anything about the mission?"

"He was hot." Harm bent to smooth his hand over Agar's head and then glanced up at T-Mac. "Someone around here tipped off our quarry. They were ready for us."

"The only people who knew where we were going were our team and the helicopter pilots."

"The commander has the intel folks interviewing the crews and maintenance people," Harm said. "I'll let you know if they learn anything."

"Thanks." T-Mac glanced toward the containerized living units. "Big Jake doing okay?"

"He's sore, but he'll live. The commander wanted him to sit out the next mission, but Big Jake laughed and told him he might as well go. Sitting wasn't an option."

T-Mac chuckled.

"What about you?" Harm pointed to his leg.

"Just a flesh wound. I'm in if they go after the people who did this to us."

"We're all in. You think your dog handler will join us?"

"God, I hope not." He hated to think of Kinsley back in the line of fire. She might not be so lucky next time. "The doc said they're trying to get a transport to carry her to the next level of care. But now that she's awake and coherent, they might change their minds."

"Awake and coherent is a good sign," Harm said. "I can see you're anxious to get back to her. Don't let me hold you up."

"Thanks for checking on Agar." T-Mac left Harm and half walked, half jogged around the camp, giving Agar the exercise he needed. From what he could tell, the dog had completely recovered. At one point, while they were passing the motor pool, Agar growled low in his chest.

With a quick glance around, T-Mac couldn't identify what set off the dog. He'd seen Agar's behavior when he found explosives. He hadn't growled, just lain down beside the find. The only other time he'd seen the dog growl had been before he'd gone into the building with the rebel who'd shot Kinsley.

After he'd walked Agar for fifteen minutes, he headed for the medical facility and strolled through the door as if he owned the place. Bravado might get him past the guy manning the front desk.

"Excuse me," a voice called out behind T-Mac.

He slowed, pulling Agar up on a short leash. "Yes?"

"I'm pretty sure animals aren't allowed in the facility." The young man stood.

"This isn't just an animal. This is Sergeant Agar. He outranks you. You might show him a little more respect."

"You're kidding, right?" The young man's brow twisted.

"Sergeant Agar is on his way to see his handler, Specialist Anderson."

"Oh." The young man sat back in his seat, a worried frown still pulling at his brow. "I guess that's okay, then."

"Right." T-Mac marched past him to the room where he'd left Kinsley. When he entered, he did a double take. The bed was empty. He walked back out and went to the next room only to turn around and come back.

Agar tugged at his lead.

T-Mac released him and he ran for the door to the adjoining bathroom and sniffed at the gap beneath.

The door opened and Kinsley stepped out, holding the back of her gown together behind her. When she saw Agar, she let go and dropped to her knees to hug the German shepherd.

He nuzzled her, licked her face and wagged his tail.

"Thank God you're okay," she whispered, tears running down her face. She ran her hands over his body and legs. "Did you get hurt?" She checked him over thoroughly, blinking back her tears. When she was done, she looked up at T-Mac. "Thank you for bringing him."

T-Mac smiled. "I think he missed you."

"Even if he didn't, I missed him." She hugged the dog's neck.

A twinge of envy rippled through T-Mac. He found himself wishing he was the dog, being lavished with all the attention and hugs. But the smile on Kinsley's face made T-Mac's day brighter. "Now that you have Agar, I suppose you don't need me anymore."

Her eyes widened and she straightened. "You can stay, if you like. Though it's horribly boring being stuck in bed all day. I don't know why the doctor doesn't let me go. I feel fine. And Agar needs to be exercised. I have to know, the next time we're out, that he'll be able to sniff out explosives."

"I walked him before we came into the facility. And tomorrow should be soon enough to test his skills," T-Mac assured her. "In the meantime, do you want me to take him back to my quarters?"

Her eyes widened and her hold on Agar tightened. "He sleeps in my room, with me."

He leaned close and dropped his voice to a whisper. "I bet if Agar's really quiet no one will notice if he stays."

Kinsley pushed to her feet and walked to the bed.

Agar followed, his body pressed against her legs.

Kinsley slipped beneath the sheets and lay back.

Agar paced around the bed, lifting his nose to sniff at Kinsley. Then he leaped up onto the foot of the bed.

Kinsley laughed and moved over.

Agar stretched out beside her and rested his snout on her arm.

The image of the two of them lying against the white sheets made T-Mac's heart swell. For a fleeting moment, he wished he was Agar, and that he'd put that happy smile on Kinsley's face.

She closed her eyes and sighed. "I guess I can stay another night as long as Agar's with me."

T-Mac cleared his throat. "Since you don't need me, I'll go."

Kinsley's eyes flew open. "Do you have to?"

He shrugged. "No. My buddies are covering for me with my commander."

She held out her hand. "I think they gave me a sedative. Could you stay until I go to sleep?" Her lips twisted. "You don't have to if you don't want to."

He chuckled. "Playing second fiddle to a dog isn't quite a compliment, but I'll take it."

T-Mac pulled the chair close and gathered her hand in his, reveling at how small it was in his, yet how strong and supple her fingers were.

Agar leaned his long snout over Kinsley's body, sniffed T-Mac's hand once and then laid his head back on Kinsley's other side, seemingly satisfied T-Mac wouldn't harm the dog handler.

For a long moment, she said nothing. T-Mac assumed she was sleeping.

"Don't tell anyone," Kinsley whispered, her eyes closed, her breathing slow and steady.

T-Mac stroked the back of her hand. "Tell anyone what?"

"That the tough-as-nails army soldier needed to hold a navy SEAL's hand."

"I could find another poor soul to hold your hand, if you like." His fingers tightened around hers. "Maybe even an army puke," he offered, but he really didn't want to relinquish his hold.

"No need to disturb anyone else." She lay for a while with her eyes closed.

T-Mac studied her face. Freshly washed, free of any makeup, she had that girl-next-door appeal, with a sprinkling of freckles across her nose and cheeks.

T-Mac had the sudden urge to kiss those freckles.

"Why did you want to be a SEAL?" Kinsley's voice yanked T-Mac back to reality.

He barely knew this woman. They were deployed. Fraternization could get them both kicked out of the military, or hit with an Article 15, which would put a black mark on their records and keep them from getting promoted.

"I joined the navy because I didn't want to be a farmer," he said. "My father owns a farm in Nebraska. I grew up running tractors and combines through the summer. He inherited the farm from his father, who inherited it from his father."

"Was your father disappointed when you didn't want to take over the farm?"

T-Mac shrugged. "Not really. I think when he was a teenager, he had dreams of traveling the world and doing something else with his life. But his father had a heart attack and he stayed to take care of the crops and his mother. And he never left."

"Any siblings?" she asked.

"A younger sister." He grinned. "And she's all about the farming. She's in college now, studying agriculture and researching all kinds of things that will help improve crops and yield. My father is so proud of her."

"And he's not proud of you?" Kinsley asked.

T-Mac nodded. "He is. I'm doing what he would have wanted to do. Whenever I can, I send pictures of some of the places I've been. I think he lives vicariously through me. One of these days, I hope to take him and my mother to Europe on vacation. I want them to see Italy, Greece, Spain and France. My father is a big history buff. He'd love it."

Kinsley smiled, her eyes open, the green color seeming deeper. "Sounds like you had a good childhood. You must love your folks a lot."

He nodded. "I miss them, but I also love what I'm doing." T-Mac tilted his head. "What about you? What made you join the army?"

Her lips twisted. "I didn't feel like I had a lot of choices. My mother didn't have the money to send me to college. I joined the army to build a better life for myself. When I get out, I plan on going to college."

"What do you want to study?"

"I don't know yet. I might go into nursing. But for now, I love working with the dogs. Agar in particular."

As if he knew she was talking about him, Agar rested his head over her belly.

Kinsley stroked the dog's neck. "Working with Agar has taught me more about life and living than all twenty-something years of my life."

"How so?"

"I grew up with a single mother. She worked two jobs to keep a roof over my head and food on the table. I didn't see her enough."

"Sounds like you were pretty much on your own."

"I was, from about ten on. I didn't have many close friends in school because I didn't join any extracurricular activities. I couldn't. I had to ride the bus home. Walking wasn't an option. Between home and high school were some pretty sketchy neighborhoods. So I went home on the bus and locked the doors. I guess you could say I was pretty introverted. Handling Agar taught me patience with others and helped bring me out of my shell."

"How did you get in with the dogs?" T-Mac asked.

"I was working on a detail near the canine unit at Fort Hood, Texas. I asked how I could get into the program. My first sergeant helped me apply, and here I am." She laughed. "My first real mission and I blew it."

"You didn't blow it." T-Mac squeezed her hand. "Someone tried to blow you away."

She touched a hand to her chest. "Feels like it."

"Bruised?"

"Just sore." Her eyebrows dipped. "But not too sore I can't go back to work."

"I'm sure you let the doctor know."

"Damn right I did." Her chin tilted upward. "Agar and I have work to do…lives to save."

"Yes, you do." Though he didn't like the idea of Kinsley and Agar going out on point again. "About last night… Did you see the face of the man who shot you?"

Kinsley closed her eyes and scrunched her face. After a minute, she shook her head. "I can't remember even going out with the team. How did we get where we were going?"

T-Mac shook his head. "By helicopter."

Her eyes narrowed. "That's right. You walked me to the helicopter pad."

"Just me?" he prompted.

Kinsley sighed. "That's all I remember. Everything else is a blank." She looked up at him with her pretty green eyes. "Why can't I remember? I feel like I'm forgetting something important."

"Like someone shooting you point-blank in the chest?" T-Mac snorted. "That's something you might want to forget. Or maybe it's your mind's way of protecting you." He brought her hand up to his mouth and pressed a kiss to the back of her knuckles. "Don't let it worry you. When you're ready, you'll remember." He kissed her hand again before he even realized what he was doing.

Her gaze went from her hand to his face. "Why did you do that?"

Heat rose up his neck into his cheeks. "I don't know. I'm sorry. I shouldn't have." He laid her hand on the sheet. "Maybe I should go."

"No." She reached out and snagged his fingers with hers. "Please, don't go. Unless you have to." Her cheeks flushed. "I didn't say I didn't like it."

"Yeah, well, I shouldn't have done it anyway. I don't know why, but it just felt right." He held out his hand. "I'm sorry. It won't happen again."

An awkward silence ensued. One in which T-Mac couldn't look Kinsley in the eyes.

Finally, she squeezed his hand and let go. "I've kept you here long enough. I plan on sleeping until tomorrow and then initiating my escape plan."

T-Mac chuckled. "I'm sure Agar will be a big help in your endeavors." He stepped away from the bed and looked around. "If Agar is staying with you tonight, we need to see to his comfort as well as yours. I'll be right back."

He turned away, kicking himself for kissing the woman's hand. What if a nurse or doctor had walked in? He was taking advantage of the woman when she was at her most vulnerable. And worse, his actions could have been construed as fraternization, which could not only get him in trouble, but Kinsley as well.

T-Mac searched through the cabinet in the room.

He found a bedpan and some kind of sterile bowl. He pulled the bowl off a shelf, filled it with water from the sink in the adjoining bathroom and set it on the floor.

Agar leaped down from the bed, trotted over to the bowl of water and licked it dry.

T-Mac chuckled. "Hey, boy, you must have been really thirsty."

"I swear that dog is part camel." Kinsley laughed. "I keep expecting him to grow a hump from all the water he consumes."

Squatting next to the dog, T-Mac rubbed the animal behind the ears. "You're lucky to have Agar."

"I know," Kinsley said, her voice low. "I'm sick that I almost lost him."

T-Mac glanced up to catch Kinsley staring at him. Not the dog. His pulse pushed blood through his veins at an alarming speed. He didn't know what was wrong with him, but if he didn't leave soon, he'd do more than just kiss the woman's hand. And he couldn't let that happen. "I'm sorry, but I have to go."

She nodded. "I know. You can't babysit the dog handler forever."

He turned to leave.

"T-Mac." Kinsley's voice stopped him from making good his escape.

He made the mistake of turning back.

Kinsley lay against the sheets looking small and vulnerable.

"Yes?" T-Mac kept his distance, while clenching his fists to keep from reaching out to take her into his arms.

"You're an amazing man. Thank you for rescuing me."

"Don't mention it," he said, and left the room.

Chapter 5

The nurses and the doctor who visited Kinsley through-out the rest of the day and into the night didn't seem at all put out by Agar's presence. Kinsley suspected T-Mac had something to do with their casual acceptance. And for that she was grateful.

Having Agar with her helped her make it through the nightmares that woke her several times in a single hour.

At one point, she woke up calling out T-Mac's name. When she realized what she'd done, she looked around quickly, hoping no one else had heard. Once she as-certained she was well and truly alone, she was able to relax. At the same time, she missed having the navy SEAL there in her room, holding her hand. And, if she were honest with herself, she wanted him to kiss her again. But not on her hand.

The sun and Agar's soft whining woke Kinsley the next morning. She rolled out of the narrow bed and landed on her bare feet. The cool tile flooring against her toes and the draft through the back of her gown made her shiver.

Agar danced beside her, ready to go outside for his morning run.

"Sorry, boy, we have to get permission from the doctor."

"Speak of the devil…" The doctor entered the room. "And here I am." He chuckled at his own joke and then got serious. "Headache?" The doctor pulled a penlight from his breast pocket.

"No, sir."

He shone the light into her eyes. "Dizziness?"

"No, sir."

"How are those ribs?" He patted his hand on the bed. "Hop up and let me look you over."

"The ribs are mildly sore, but livable." She scooted her bottom onto the edge of the bed and swung her legs up.

"Lie down on the bed," the doctor ordered.

After a nurse joined them in the room, the doc lifted her gown to inspect the bruising on her ribs, pushing here and there until he was satisfied nothing was broken.

Kinsley bit down hard on her tongue to keep from crying out a couple of times. It hurt, but she refused to be put on profile until the bruising went away. She wanted to get back out and make sure no one triggered an unexpected explosion and lost lives or limbs. She and Agar had a job to do, and by God, they were going to do it.

"As much as I'd like to keep you and have someone for my staff to work on, I can't find enough wrong with you."

Kinsley sat up, grinning. "Really?"

"The nurse will give you discharge instructions."

"So, I can return to duty?"

The doctor held up a single finger. "Light duty for a day, to make sure you don't have any residual effects of the explosion or gunshot."

"Thank you." Kinsley was so relieved she wanted to cry.

Agar's tail pounded the floor beside the bed.

"I'm really releasing you to get this hairy beast out of my facility." The doctor brushed a dog hair from his white coat. "Now, get out of here before I change my mind."

"I will." Kinsley hopped off the bed, grabbed Agar's lead and made for the door.

"Eh-hem." The doctor cleared his throat. "Aren't you forgetting something?"

The cool tile beneath her feet and the draft on her backside made a rush of heat climb up her cheeks. Her heart sank. "I don't suppose I can borrow some scrubs or something?"

"As a matter of fact, I have what you need." The nurse reentered the room carrying a stack of clothing. "A handsome navy SEAL delivered these this morning for you. He apologized about the size but said he didn't have access to your room to get your own things." She grinned.

Kinsley took the shorts, T-shirt and socks from the woman. "These will do."

"Let me know if you need any help," she offered.

"Thank you."

Once the doctor and nurse left the room, Kinsley stripped out of the gown and pulled the T-shirt over her head. The hem fell down around her knees. Undaunted, she slipped into the shorts and dragged them up over her hips. They were too big, but she was able to tighten the string at the waist to keep them from falling off.

The heels of the socks came halfway up her ankles, but they were fine to get her to her quarters. She found her boots in the corner and pulled them on. Feeling like an orphan in hand-me-downs, she grabbed Agar's leash and headed out of the medical facility and across the compound to the containerized living units.

Agar trotted alongside her, his steps light, tail wagging. Thankfully, he seemed to have no ill effects from his own brush with death.

As she walked past the motor pool, a man in an army uniform smiled and waved in her direction.

Kinsley nodded and waved back.

Another man stood on the front bumper of one of the big trucks, leaning over the open engine. He raised his head for moment but didn't acknowledge her. Instead, his gaze followed her.

Agar growled.

"I agree. He wasn't very friendly," Kinsley whispered, and walked faster until she moved out of sight of the motor pool.

As she passed by the command center, the navy commander who'd called for the mission that had almost gotten her killed stepped out of the building. "Ah, Specialist Anderson. I'm glad to see you up and about." His gaze swept over her outfit.

Kinsley lifted her chin. "I was just released from the medical facility. I'm on my way to my quarters to change into a uniform."

The commander's brow dipped. "Should you return to work so soon?"

"I'm on light duty for a day, then I'm back to regular duty." She motioned for Agar to sit. "I wanted to let you know I'm ready and able to perform my mission, should you need me."

"Good to know. I might have something coming up soon. I'll keep you in mind."

"Thank you, sir," she said.

"Can I interest you in some fabulous food from our neighborhood chow hall?" He waved his hand toward the dining facility. "I'm headed there now."

"No, thank you, sir," Kinsley said. "I need to change and exercise Agar."

"Don't overdo it," the commander said.

"Yes, sir." Kinsley hurried along, determined to reach her quarters before she encountered anyone else. She didn't like being out of uniform in the oversize shirt and shorts, looking goofy in a pair of combat boots. She'd seen worse while she'd been there, but she held herself to a higher standard. And she was grateful for the clothing to get across the compound. She couldn't imagine traipsing across Camp Lemonnier in nothing but boots and a hospital gown.

Thankfully, she didn't encounter anyone else on her way to her quarters. Her skin crawled with a strange feeling someone was watching her. She flung open the door.

Agar stepped inside.

Then Kinsley slipped into the shipping container, closed the door behind her and stood for a moment, listening for footsteps outside.

The crunch of gravel sent a shiver along her spine.

Agar pressed his nose to the door crack and sniffed. Then he sniffed again, his hackles rising.

Kinsley knew she should look outside and see who was there, but she couldn't bring herself to do it.

Then, as quickly as Agar's hackles rose, they fell back in place and he trotted over to her bed and lay down.

"What was all that about?" Kinsley asked.

When the dog looked up at her from his lounging position on the floor, he cocked his head to one side.

"You're hopeless." Kinsley yanked off the T-shirt that smelled amazingly like T-Mac. She pressed it to her nose, inhaled his scent and tossed the shirt on the bed.

The shorts were next.

Wanting to prove she was up to working again, Kinsley changed into a clean uniform, brushed her hair and pulled it back into a tight bun at the nape of her neck. Sore around the stitches on her leg and achy around the ribs, she didn't slow down, but called for Agar. She snatched up his lead, his KONG and the training aid she used with the trace scent of explosives inside.

Agar leaped to his feet as soon as he saw the dog toy. He loved chewing on the KONG and would do almost anything she asked just to get to play with it for a few seconds.

Feeling a little more like normal, if somewhat beaten up, Kinsley left her quarters and walked out to the camp trash containers. With the sun rising high in the sky, barely a breeze to stir the air and the sun's heating the earth and the trash, the smell was barely tolerable and perfect to help disguise the training aid.

Kinsley tied Agar to a post and then ducked between trash bins to hide the toy.

When she returned, Agar's ears perked. She gave him the signal to find the explosives and let him out to the end of his lead.

Within minutes, he found the aid. Kinsley's heart swelled and she praised the dog for his find. She rewarded him by throwing his KONG and letting him run to fetch it. Repeating the exercise several more times, she was satisfied Agar hadn't lost his touch. She took him for a long walk around the perimeter of the camp, hoping to stretch the kinks out of her body and work thoughts of a certain navy SEAL out of her mind.

She'd have to return his clothes soon, and the thought warmed her all the way to her core. Which scared the crap out of her. She did *not* need to get involved with a navy guy. Nothing could come of it. They were both committed to their military careers.

Besides, nothing could happen while they were deployed together. And when they returned stateside, he'd end up in some navy base on the East or West Coast and she'd be at an army post, probably in the middle of the country, like Texas or Oklahoma. They might as well be on different continents.

The sooner she got the man out of her head, the better. But the more she walked, the more she thought about Petty Officer Trace McGuire. The man with the strong hands and big heart, who'd rescued her when she'd been knocked down and stayed by her side in recovery.

* * *

After a terrible sleepless night, T-Mac left his bed early and went for a run around Camp Lemonnier. Then he hit the weight room for forty brutal minutes pumping iron. And he still couldn't get Kinsley out of his head.

He'd purposely resisted going straight to the medical facility and checking on her. But the longer he stayed away, the more he wanted to go. He showered, put on a fresh uniform and stepped out of his quarters. Despite his effort to stay away, his feet carried him to the medical facility. The closer he got, the faster he walked until he burst through the door.

He didn't stop to say anything to the guy at the desk, but kept walking straight to Specialist Anderson's room. About to barge in, he stopped himself short and forced calm into his fist as he knocked.

When no one answered, he knocked again. Was she asleep?

When no one answered the second time, he pushed open the door and marched in.

The bed was freshly made and completely empty.

Damn! Where had she gone?

"Specialist Anderson was discharged first thing this morning," a voice said behind him.

He turned to face the nurse who'd checked on Kinsley the day before.

"Is she well enough?"

The woman smiled. "She was. The doctor signed her release papers. She practically ran out the door with her dog. Oh, by the way, thank you for bringing the clothes. I think she would have walked out of here in her boots and the hospital gown if she hadn't had them to change into."

A smile tugged at the corners of T-Mac's mouth. "I'm sure she was happy to be free."

The nurse's lips twisted. "It's not like we're a prison in here."

He chuckled. "No. And thank you for taking such good care of us."

She nodded. "Not many guys have the patience or desire to sit in a hospital room for hours on end. She's lucky to have you."

T-Mac didn't try to correct the woman. Kinsley didn't have him. He'd just done the right thing to take care of a fallen comrade. Nothing more.

"Thanks again," he said, and turned to leave.

"Do you want us to check your stitches?" the nurse asked. "We don't often get shrapnel wounds here. Most people come in with colds, allergies or the occasional broken bone from playing volleyball or football."

"No, thank you. You all did a good job. It's healing nicely," he said as he turned to leave. He didn't want to stand around and chitchat. He wanted to find Kinsley and see for himself that she was well enough to be back on her feet.

His first stop was her quarters. Once again, he knocked. No one answered.

When he raised his hand to knock again, someone spoke behind him.

"T-Mac, there you are. I've been looking all over for you."

T-Mac turned to find Harm standing behind him.

The SEAL wore his desert-camouflage uniform and a floppy boonie hat instead of his Kevlar helmet.

"What's up?" T-Mac asked.

"The CO wants us in the command center for a briefing in fifteen minutes. I'm headed there now."

His fists tightening, T-Mac sighed. So much for finding Kinsley. He'd have to wait until after the briefing.

T-Mac fell in step beside Harm.

"How's your dog handler this morning?" Harm kicked a pebble in front of them.

"The doc released her." He didn't tell him that he wanted to see her and had yet to find her. Harm didn't need to know how the dog handler had him tied in knots. He'd get a big kick out of it and razz him even more than he already did.

"Glad to hear it," Harm said. "When will she be able to return to duty?"

"Tomorrow." Too soon, by T-Mac's standards.

"What about the dog?"

"Agar spent the night with her at the medical facility. He seemed to be no worse for the wear."

"Good to hear. We might need them on the next mission."

"We've done just fine on most missions without a bomb-sniffing dog."

"What? You don't want Anderson and Agar in the heat of things with us?"

"Not really."

Harm grinned. "You really like her, don't you?"

"I didn't say that," he grumbled. "I just think she's a distraction we can ill afford."

"There's probably a little truth in that statement."

Harm glanced toward the command center. "You were quick to load her up and get her out of there without looking back."

"My point exactly." T-Mac stopped in front of the building. "Don't you dare tell her I said that. She'd skin me alive if she knew I didn't want her on a mission."

"Too late," a female voice said behind him. "So, you don't want me on a mission?"

T-Mac balled his fists, dragged in a deep breath and turned to do damage control with Kinsley.

"Look, Kin—Specialist Anderson, I didn't say you weren't good at your job. I'm just saying that we're used to working as a combat team. The night before last was the first time we've integrated a dog team in a mission. And, well, you know what happened. It wasn't a raging success."

"And that was my fault?" she asked.

"If you hadn't been there…" T-Mac started.

Harm cleared his throat. "You might reconsider going there, buddy."

Kinsley held up a hand. "No, let him go. I want to know how deep he'll dig his own grave."

Anger rose up inside T-Mac, and he plowed right into waters he knew would be over his head in the next few words out of his mouth. "If you hadn't been there, one of us would have breached that building in a way we've been taught that doesn't involve walking through the door as if we expect a big hug and a hallelujah."

Her eyes narrowed. "And you think that's what I was doing?"

Harm crossed his arms over his chest and shook his head. "Told you to think before you opened your mouth." He held up his hands. "Now you're on your own. I'll see you two inside." Harm bailed on T-Mac and entered the command center.

"So, you think I don't know what I'm doing?" Kinsley asked.

"I think you're more concerned about your dog than your own life."

"Maybe you're right. I care about Agar." Her chin lifted even higher. "At least I care about someone."

"I'm sure you and Agar are good at sniffing out IEDs and land mines, but clearing buildings might not be the right fit for you."

Kinsley's face grew redder and redder. "It's a good thing you're not my boss, or anywhere in my chain of command. Now, if you'll excuse me, I've been summoned for a job. A job you don't think I can do." She spun on her heel and marched into the command center without looking back.

Once again, T-Mac could kick himself for opening his big mouth. The woman had a right to be spitting mad at him. He just couldn't see going through what he'd been through two nights ago again.

When Kinsley had been blown out of that hut and lay on the ground like she had, T-Mac's heart had stopped and then turned flips trying to restart and propel him forward to pick up the pieces. What had him all wound up was the possibility that next time, Kinsley might not be as lucky. She might actually be in pieces. And he didn't want to be the one to pick them up.

Chapter 6

Kinsley stood in the command-center war room, too mad to sit. How dare T-Mac tell his teammate he didn't want her on another mission?

Hadn't she and Agar gotten them through a mine-field upon entering the abandoned village?

The CO paced at the front of the room, waiting for everyone to enter and take a seat. He raised his brow at Kinsley, who still stood. "Please, take a seat."

"Sir, if you don't mind, I'd prefer to stand," Kinsley said. The only empty seat happened to be beside T-Mac. And she sure as hell wasn't going to sit next to him. Not when he'd impugned her honor and spread doubt about her abilities as a dog handler and soldier.

"Suit yourself," the commander said. He addressed

Kinsley and the room full of SEALs. "The mission two nights ago didn't go the way we expected."

Several snorts were emitted by various members of the SEAL team.

Kinsley held her tongue.

"We were lucky to come out with as few casualties as we did," the commander continued. "As it is, having Specialist Anderson join the effort was a welcome addition to the team. Without her, our SEALs might have stepped on and triggered half a dozen or more mines on their way into the village where the arms trading was to take place." He held up a hand. "I know I'm repeating old news, but I want to be clear... We cannot have a repeat of what happened that night."

"Sir, does that mean we're going out again?" Big Jake asked.

"I'm not sure you are," the CO said. "But the rest of the team is going."

Big Jake placed both hands flat on the table. "Sir, I might have taken a hit in the rear, but the rest of me works just fine. I won't be sitting on a mission. And where my guys go, I go."

The CO stared hard at Big Jake. "If you think you're up to it."

"I am, sir," Big Jake said without hesitation.

"Good." He stared around the room again. "What happened two nights ago was an ambush. They knew you were coming and they were waiting for you to enter the village before they attacked."

Kinsley gasped. Having been in the hospital since the incident, and being the only army personnel in a sea of navy SEALs, she hadn't been included in the scuttle-butt. "You think we were set up?"

The commander nodded. "Someone leaked information about the mission. We still don't know who did it, but we suspect it's someone here on Camp Lemonnier."

Kinsley glanced around the table of men, all loyal, career military men who'd risked their lives on many occasions for their country. "You don't think it was anyone in this room, do you?"

"No, not anyone in this room," the commander said.

"I should think not," Kinsley said.

T-Mac's lips twitched, as did others in the room.

"We have a traitor amongst us on Camp Lemonnier. And that traitor is quite possibly connected to the illegal arms trading going on."

"What's being done about it?" Harm asked.

"We've interviewed everyone involved with the helicopters. We don't know for certain, but we don't believe any of them were the culprit." The commander sighed. "And if one of them is, we haven't found the connection yet."

He paused for a moment before continuing.

"But we can't sit back and wait until we find him. We have new intel, and we need to move on it before it becomes useless."

The SEALs all leaned forward in their chairs.

"We have infrared satellite images from two nights ago. When our guys bugged out of that village that night, two trucks left in the opposite direction." The CO stared around the room. "Bottom line is, we know where they went."

"Where?" Kinsley asked.

The commander shook his head. "I can't say. Until we launch a mission, I'm not revealing any specifics about any part of that mission until the choppers are off the ground."

"Radio signals can be intercepted," T-Mac said.

"I didn't say I was going to use radio signals."

Pitbull frowned. "Then how will we know where we're going?"

The commander stared around the room. "I'm going with you. I will have the mission-specific information necessary to carry out the assignment."

"Sir, you haven't trained with the team," Buck pointed out.

"Won't that make the mission higher profile?" Big Jake asked. "If someone is leaking information and learns you're going along for the ride, won't that make the rest of us collateral damage when they're targeting you?"

"First of all," the commander said, "this information is not to go outside this room. No one other than the people here are to know we have intel on a potential location of the attackers from the village the other night. No one outside this room should know what we know. Not the helicopter pilots, the mechanics, anyone in the mess hall or anywhere else."

The commander continued. "Every one of you should be ready to go at a moment's notice. When we take off, you will have only a few minutes to prepare. Can you be ready?"

"Sir, yes, sir!" Kinsley shouted along with the SEAL team.

"Then for now, not a word to anyone." The commander's eyes narrowed. "Not even to each other. We can't risk being overheard. Understood?"

Kinsley stood at attention and shouted, "Sir, yes, sir!" along with the others in the room.

The commander nodded, apparently satisfied. "Then you're all dismissed until further notice."

One by one, the SEALs filed out of the room but without the usual banter.

Kinsley stood in the corner, waiting until the others were gone. Then she and Agar approached the commander. "Sir, do you still plan on using me and Agar in the next mission?"

"Specialist Anderson, I would not have allowed you in the room with the others if I didn't plan on taking you along." He stared hard into her eyes. "Are you up to another mission so soon?"

She nodded. "Yes, sir."

"That's all I need to know. You proved invaluable on the last one. I see no reason to leave you out of the next one."

"Thank you, sir."

"You realize that some of the men might consider you a distraction to the mission."

Her blood pressure rocketed and her jaw tightened. "Did T-Mac say that?"

"Not actually." The commander smiled. "His report to me was that you were fearless." His smile turned into a frown. "Why? Are you and T-Mac at odds? Do you want me to assign a different SEAL to look out for you?"

Fearless? He thought she was fearless? And yet, he didn't want her on a mission.

"I could get Harm or Buck to look out for you," the commander offered.

"No," Kinsley said, her pulse racing. "T-Mac was there for me. I trust him." And she did. She'd bet her life on him. But was she betting his life on her being a part of the mission? Was it right for her to want to go even though she was a distraction to them?

She stiffened her spine and pulled back her shoulders. Based on what had happened on the last mission, and finding all those land mines buried along the path the SEALs were destined to follow, she had to go. Whoever would set those up the way they had could do it again.

Not only did she want to go, she *had* to go. Otherwise, she would be sitting back at Camp Lemonnier, safe and sound, while the SEAL team could be walking into a minefield. They needed her and Agar. She had to be with them. If something happened to them that she and Agar could have helped them avoid, she could never live with herself.

She looked the commander square in the eye. "Sir, I'm ready whenever you are. Just say the word."

He nodded. "That's what I wanted to hear."

"Walk with me," Harm said as they left the command center.

T-Mac would rather have waited for Kinsley, but he didn't want to admit it, so he fell in step beside Harm.

Instead of turning toward their quarters, he headed toward the flight line where the helicopters were parked.

"You know you can't always protect her, don't you?" Harm said.

T-Mac knew it would serve no purpose to pretend he

didn't know who Harm was talking about. "Who said I always want to protect her?"

Harm stopped short of the helicopters and stood staring at them. "She's special. I didn't expect her to be so brave about sniffing out land mines."

His lips twitching, T-Mac rolled his eyes. "She doesn't sniff out the mines. Agar does."

"You know what I mean."

"Yeah, I do. You should have seen her go after Agar when he ran into that hut." The image was etched indelibly into T-Mac's mind. "And then watch as she was blown back out by the force of the bullet that hit her vest."

Harm laid a hand on T-Mac's shoulder. "That shook you, didn't it?"

"I've never been more shaken," T-Mac admitted.

"I know what you mean. We anticipate our own deaths and meet that possibility head-on. But when it comes to someone else, we have a more difficult time accepting or even processing it."

T-Mac nodded. "You hit the nail on the head. All I could think about was how to get her out of that place as quickly as possible. I would have felt the same had it been one of my teammates."

Harm snorted. "I know you would rush in to help if one of us was hit, but I think it was more than that with the dog handler."

A frown pulled T-Mac's brow downward. "Don't read more into my actions than what's there."

Harm held up his hands. "Just saying. You don't have to bite my head off."

"You and the others think that just because you have

women, I need one, too. I don't need a woman in my life. And Specialist Anderson isn't that woman anyway."

"You don't think so?"

"I wouldn't know," T-Mac said. "We haven't known each other for very long."

"Speaking from my experience," Harm said, "it doesn't take long to fall in love. Sometimes you just know she's the one."

"Like you and Talia?" T-Mac asked.

"Yeah. Like me and Talia." Harm smiled as he stared at the helicopter. He was probably seeing Talia, the petite beauty with the black hair and blue eyes, not the smooth gray hulks of Black Hawk helicopters.

T-Mac shook his head. "How do you know?"

"At first, I didn't recognize it, but the more I was around her, the more I wanted to be around her. And then when we were apart, all I could do was think about her."

That's not me. T-Mac refused to believe that was what he was feeling about Kinsley. Yeah, he'd seen her around camp. And he'd fantasized about getting to know her better, even how it would be to kiss her. But love?

Oh, hell no.

But, like Harm, he couldn't stop thinking about her and counted the minutes until he could see her again.

What was wrong with him? He did not need a woman in his life, despite what his buddies thought.

He turned away from the choppers. "We should go prepare."

Harm touched T-Mac's arm. "Falling for a woman is not a bad thing."

"I wouldn't know," T-Mac insisted.

"It doesn't make you weaker," Harm continued. "In

fact, it makes me stronger, more determined to do the right thing and be a better person. The kind of person Talia would want to be with."

"Well, that certainly isn't me. Not with Kinsley. I told her I didn't want her to be on the next mission."

Harm's eyebrows shot up. "Kinsley?"

"Specialist Anderson," T-Mac corrected.

"That's why she looked mad enough to spit nails." Harm chuckled.

"Yeah." T-Mac started walking again. "She sure as hell doesn't want to be with me now."

"An apology goes a long way to smoothing a woman's feathers," Harm advised.

T-Mac shot a horrified glance his buddy's way. "Apologize? I'm not sorry I told her that. She's one hundred percent a distraction on a mission."

"Maybe for you, since you're into her."

"I'm not into her." He couldn't be. It made no sense.

"No? Then why did you spend the night at her bedside, holding her hand?" Harm raised an eyebrow. "And don't say you'd have done the same for one of us."

T-Mac opened his mouth to tell Harm that holding Kinsley's hand didn't mean anything, but he knew it would be a big fat lie. So he closed his mouth, sealed his lips in a thin, tight line and stepped out smartly for his quarters.

Harm jogged to catch up. "You can run, buddy, but you can't hide from the truth."

T-Mac came to an abrupt halt.

Harm ran into him.

"Let's get this straight." T-Mac turned and poked a finger into Harm's chest. "I'm not into Kinsley. We're not together. She's just an army puke with a dog. Nothing more. Period. The end."

Harm stared into T-Mac's eyes and then burst into laughter. "Damn, dude, you've got it really bad for the woman."

T-Mac balled his fists and cocked his arms.

The smile left Harm's face and he held up his hands. "Hey, remember me? I'm on *your* side."

Still ready to hit someone, T-Mac kept his fists up.

"All right. I'll stop razzing you." Harm dropped his hands and tipped his head toward the living quarters. "We'd better get ready. Who knows when we'll get the call?" He stepped out.

For a long moment, T-Mac stood with his hands up, jaw clenched and anger simmering. Finally, he let go of the breath he'd been holding and turned to follow his friend.

They were almost to the living units when T-Mac spoke again, as if they hadn't ended the conversation. "It doesn't matter anyway."

"What?" Harm asked.

"Nothing could ever come of something between us."

"Between who?" Harm grinned and jerked his thumb between T-Mac and himself. "You and me? You're right. I'm taken."

"Shut up. You know who I'm talking about."

Harm nodded. "Yeah, but I also know things have a way of working out."

"Like Talia's resort burning down so she's forced to move back to the States to be with you? Or Marly's airplane blowing up so she can move back to the States and be with Pitbull?"

With a frown, Harm kicked at a rock. "When you put it like that, it sounds bad. But maybe there's something to fate."

"I don't wish anything ill on Kinsley or Agar. They've worked hard for what they do. If I was interested in Kinsley—which I'm not—I couldn't ask her to give up her career to follow me around. Nor would I want to give up my career to follow her. So it doesn't matter. Nothing could ever come of a relationship between me and Kinsley."

With a shrug, Harm opened the door to the quarters they shared and held it for T-Mac to enter. "All I know is, you never know."

T-Mac snorted. "Sounds like double-talk to me."

"Maybe. Maybe not. Just wait and see. If she's worth it, you'll find a way."

T-Mac went to work preparing for the next mission, not knowing what it would be, where they would go or how he'd make it through the tough times and keep Kinsley out of the line of fire. One thing he did know, but wouldn't admit to Harm or anyone else, was that Kinsley was definitely worth the trouble. She was brave, loyal and beautiful.

He cleaned his M4A1 rifle and his nine-millimeter handgun. Then he spent time sharpening his Ka-Bar knife and checking his communications equipment. When he was finished, he stood, stretched and asked, "Ready to hit the chow hall?"

Harm nodded. "Give me a minute to lay out my gear."

While Harm set out his body armor, helmet and night-vision goggles, T-Mac did the same.

By the time they finished, T-Mac's belly rumbled.

They left their quarters and walked toward the dining facility.

As T-Mac passed Kinsley's unit, he noticed a package sitting on the ground directly in front of her door. Wrapped in brown paper, it looked like something the postmaster might have delivered. Except the camp postmaster didn't make deliveries.

At that moment, Kinsley opened the door.

Agar started to step out on the ground and stopped. He sniffed the package once and lay down, blocking Kinsley's exit, his tongue hanging out, his gaze seeking her.

Kinsley nearly tripped over the dog, expecting him to exit. When he didn't, she looked past him to the package, her brow furrowing. She hesitated and stepped back into the unit. "Good boy, Agar. Good boy."

T-Mac stared from the dog to the package and back again. "Did you place that package there?" he asked.

Kinsley's gaze locked with T-Mac's, her eyes going wide. "I was going to ask you the same question."

"Don't bother." T-Mac turned to his friend. "Harm, get back to the command center and report a potential bomb located inside the perimeter."

Harm nodded. "On it." He turned and ran back in the direction from which they'd come.

"Is Agar ever wrong?" T-Mac asked.

Kinsley shook her head. "He tests out at one hundred percent, even with trace amounts of explosives in the decoy."

"Can you step around it?" T-Mac asked.

"Probably?"

T-Mac moved closer to the package and held out his

arms. "You can lean on my shoulders and I can help you out."

"No," she said.

With a frown, T-Mac dropped his arms. "No, you can't? Or no, you won't?"

"No, I won't leave Agar." Her lips pressed into a straight line.

"Step back—I'm coming to you."

Her eyes widened. "No! You can't. What if it explodes?"

"Then we'll go together." He winked. "Won't that be romantic or something?"

"Are you insane?" She held up her hands. "I'm going inside the unit and closing the door. Let me know when the unexploded-ordnance guys are done." She backed up a step, held the door wide and called to Agar to follow.

Agar rose and entered the unit, trotting past Kinsley.

When Kinsley stepped back and started to close the door, T-Mac made his move. He took a giant step over the package and fell through the door frame.

"What the—" Kinsley said as he caught her around the waist and took her to the ground with him.

With his foot, T-Mac kicked the door shut behind him and covered Kinsley's body with his own.

He waited for several long minutes, trying to shield Kinsley from the shrapnel sure to pepper their bodies should the package explode.

After three minutes passed, Kinsley stirred beneath him. "T-Mac," she said, her voice barely a whisper.

"Yes?"

"What are you doing?" Kinsley breathed.

"Saving your life."

"Is that what this is?" Her breathing came in short, shallow gasps.

"Of course."

"Sweetheart, you're killing me," she wheezed.

Sweetheart? Had she really called him *sweetheart*? His chest swelled and warmth spread throughout his body from every point of contact with hers. Which was practically everywhere. All that warmth pooled low in his groin. And his body reacted to the heat and he grew hard.

"T-Mac?" Kinsley said.

"Mmm," he murmured.

"I can't breathe," she whispered.

Immediately, he rose up on his elbows, giving her chest the space she needed to take a deep breath and fill her lungs. "Sorry."

"It's okay. I didn't die." She chuckled. "And the package didn't explode."

"No. But we don't know if it will. What if whoever put it there can trigger it to explode at any time?"

"I would think he would have triggered it when I opened the door."

"Maybe, or maybe he's waiting for a bigger crowd. In which case you won't be safe until the ordnance-disposal guys arrive."

"We can't lie here for that long," she said, her voice all practical but still a little breathless.

T-Mac refused to move. He couldn't risk leaving her exposed. "What does it hurt to stay put for a little longer?"

"I don't want you to shield my body with yours. The navy put a lot of training into you."

"And the army put a lot of training into you and Agar. Speaking of which…can you get him to lie down in case the explosives go off? I'd hate for either one of you to be injured."

"Agar, lie down," she commanded.

The dog dropped to his belly beside Kinsley.

She stared up into T-Mac's eyes. "So, does this mean you care?"

T-Mac frowned. "Only because my commander put me in charge of making sure you're okay."

"Really?" She tilted her head. "That's the only reason?"

"Of course."

Her pretty, peach-pink lips twisted. "Your commander tasked you with that responsibility during our last mission," Kinsley pointed out. "We're not on that mission now."

"I take my responsibilities seriously," T-Mac argued, refusing to admit that he probably would have protected her even if his commander hadn't tasked him with the job. Something about Kinsley drew him, and like a moth to the flame, he couldn't resist. And like that moth, he figured he'd eventually be burned in some way or another. Navy SEALs, by the nature of their work, were doomed in the relationship department.

But at that moment, when they faced the possibility of being blown to bits, he stared down into her face, his gaze zeroing in on her pouty lips.

And he couldn't resist.

He leaned down, his mouth hovering over hers. "I take my responsibilities very seriously," he repeated.

"T-Mac?" Kinsley's breath warmed his mouth. "Are you going to kiss me?"

He nodded. "Yup. Do you have a problem with that?"

"Yes," she said, her voice a hot puff of air against his lips. "You're taking too long."

He claimed her mouth in a long, hard kiss that shook him to his very core. She wrapped her arms around his neck, her fingers threading into the hair at the back of his neck and pulling him closer.

When he ran his tongue across the seam of her lips, she opened to him.

He dove in, deepening the kiss, sliding his tongue along hers in a warm, wet caress, one he never wanted to end.

Kinsley wrapped her calf around his and pushed her hips up, making him even harder.

By the time he raised his head, his body was on fire and he couldn't get enough of her.

He rested his forehead against hers and dragged in air. "What the hell just happened?"

Kinsley chuckled and her breath hitched. "You tell me."

T-Mac brushed his lips across hers in a feather-light kiss. He couldn't get over how soft they were, or that she tasted of mint.

Agar crawled forward and laid his head on Kinsley's shoulder.

Laughter bubbled up in T-Mac's chest. Despite the fact there was a bomb outside the container unit, he'd never felt so light. All because he'd kissed Kinsley.

"T-Mac?" Harm's voice called to him from outside the container. "Are you two in there?"

"If we're really quiet, do you think they'll go away?" Kinsley asked.

T-Mac liked that she could joke when the circumstances could go south quickly. "I doubt it."

"Well, damn." She cupped his cheeks between her palms, leaned her head up and pressed a hard kiss to his mouth. "Then you'd better answer."

He drew in a deep breath, every movement reminding him he was lying on top of a female with curves in all the right places. "We're in here," T-Mac called out.

"Hang tight," Harm said. "The EOD guys are going to remove the package. Stay down."

"Will do," T-Mac said, his gaze never moving from Kinsley's.

"I don't like that you're not wearing body armor," she said.

"I'm liking that I'm not. A little too much." His shaft pressed into her pelvis. He shifted his body to ease the pressure.

Kinsley's eyes flared and her hips rose as if seeking to reestablish the connection. Then she dropped her bottom back to the floor. "You should probably move." Her voice sounded as if she'd been running, her chest rising and falling in shallow breaths.

"Sorry, sweetheart," T-Mac said. "I'm not moving until the danger's over."

"I'm not sure where it's most dangerous...outside my door, or in here." She held his gaze.

"Specialist Anderson, are you afraid of me?" he asked, his tone deep, his body humming with a rush of heat.

"No, Petty Officer McGuire." Her gaze shifted from his eyes to his lips. "I'm afraid of me."

Chapter 7

Lying sandwiched between the hard metal floor of the container unit and the muscular planes of T-Mac's chest, torso, hips and thighs, Kinsley could barely breathe. And it had nothing to do with T-Mac crushing her chest. He'd removed his weight, balancing over her on his arms.

The man stole her breath away by his sheer alpha maleness.

He could have run away from the package of explosives on her doorstep and left her and Agar to whatever happened.

But he hadn't. He'd sacrificed his own safety to protect her.

Kinsley's estimation of the man increased tenfold. Hell, he'd already proven he could rescue her from tight situations.

But when he'd kissed her…

Sweet, sweet heaven. He'd changed everything in just that one meeting of their lips.

Now she couldn't stop thinking about him and really wished he'd kiss her again.

He lowered his head, his gaze shifting from her eyes to her lips. "This could get us in trouble."

"Big trouble," she whispered, her lips tingling in anticipation of his.

"Hang in there, T-Mac. They're moving the package now." Harm's muffled shout reached her through the walls of her quarters.

They had only seconds to live if the explosives detonated. Or seconds to kiss if they didn't.

Kinsley didn't want to die without just one more…

She reached up, her hand circling the back of T-Mac's head, and pulled him down to her mouth.

She'd never felt so empowered and yet vulnerable as she did in that one desperate kiss.

"They're gone!" Harm shouted.

The rattle of the doorknob alerted Kinsley to impending danger. She planted her hands on T-Mac's chest and shoved him over.

He went willingly, springing to his feet just as the door swung open.

"EOD saved the day," Harm said.

T-Mac reached out a hand. Kinsley placed hers in his and let him bring her to her feet to face T-Mac's friend.

"Are you all right?" Harm asked, his gaze slipping over her face and narrowing in on her lips.

She nodded, her cheeks heating. Could he tell she'd just been kissed? Kinsley fought the urge to press her palms to her cheeks and further incriminate herself. No one had seen what had happened between her and T-Mac. No one had to know. She didn't need an Article 15 on her record. She could lose her position as a dog handler.

Command Order number one when deployed was No Fraternization.

And she'd just fraternized.

She shot a glace toward T-Mac. His gaze was on her, making her entire body burn with desire. What was it about this man that made her feel completely out of control?

"What was in the package?" T-Mac asked.

"We won't know until the EOD guys can either dismantle it or blow it up. I suspect they'll blow it up. Either way, they'll let us know."

T-Mac's lips pressed into a thin line and his jaw firmed. "What the hell? We're inside the wire here in Djibouti."

Harm nodded. "Which means we have a traitor among us."

"Someone who doesn't like me," Kinsley added.

"Why?" Harm asked.

"My guess is whoever left the package could be the one who shot Kinsley point-blank." T-Mac's chest tightened. "He's afraid she'll recognize him and blow his cover."

"But I can't remember anything about that incident," Kinsley said.

"He probably knows that," Harm said. "Word gets around camp quickly."

"He probably also knows that your memory could

return at any time. He just wants to make sure it doesn't happen before he can get rid of you." T-Mac faced Kinsley. "Until we determine who it is, you're not safe here."

A shiver rippled from the base of Kinsley's neck down her spine. "In that case, we might as well go on another mission. Agar and I will be as safe, if not safer, with your SEAL team."

"True," Harm said.

T-Mac's jaw tightened.

Kinsley almost laughed. The man was torn. He didn't want her on any mission with them, but she could tell he didn't like the idea of her staying behind and being the target of a traitor.

Finally, he sighed. "You're right. In the meantime, I'm hanging out with Specialist Anderson until further notice."

"You know you can't stay in her quarters," Harm reminded him.

"I know, but I sure as hell can camp out on her doorstep."

"I don't need a babysitter," Kinsley insisted.

"No, but you need a bodyguard." T-Mac held up a hand to keep her from saying more. "Just go with this. If this were happening to one of us, we'd do the same."

Harm nodded. "That's true. You always need someone watching your back."

T-Mac winked. "I've got your six. Think about it. If Agar hadn't warned you, what would have happened?"

A chill swept across her skin. She could have been blown to bits.

"Come on." Harm jerked his head toward the command center. "We need to report to the CO. He has to know what just happened."

Agar nudged her hand.

Kinsley rubbed her fingers over the top of his head. "It's okay, boy." Then she snapped on his lead. He couldn't know all of what was happening, but he was unsettled by the number of people in her quarters and Kinsley's physical distress, no matter how she tried to hide it.

T-Mac and Harm marched her to the command center. The other four members of T-Mac's immediate team joined them, asking questions and expressing concern.

Once they reported what had happened to the commander, his face appeared as if set in stone. "We knew we had a possible leak among us, but this takes it to a different level." He nodded toward T-Mac. "You know what you have to do?"

T-Mac nodded. "I'll cover for Specialist Anderson."

"We'll all look out for her and Agar," Harm promised.

"Good." The commander glanced around at the rest of the team. "We all need to be ready and keep our eyes peeled for anything that might lead us to our traitor."

All six SEALs and Kinsley snapped to attention. "Yes, sir!"

The commander touched Kinsley's arm. "Are you good with all this? If not, we can ship you out on the next transport."

"No way," she said, and added, "Sir. I'm in this for the long haul. Whoever is betraying us and our country needs to be brought down. I want to be a part of the takedown. That bastard needs to pay."

The commander grinned. "That's what I like to hear." He clapped his hands together. "Be alert. Be ready."

As they left the command center, Harm asked, "Anyone up for chow?"

"I'm not particularly hungry," Kinsley said.

"Yeah, but you need to fuel up," T-Mac said. "We never know when we'll be called up."

She nodded, knowing he was right. Her stomach was still knotted from the scare of the explosives package and the kiss from the man at her side. She wasn't sure any food would help her stomach relax, but she had to maintain her strength in order to keep up with the SEAL team. Kinsley refused to slow them down in any way.

In the dining facility, she choked down half a sandwich and a few chips and waited while the others finished their meals. By the time they were done, day was turning into evening.

They exited the dining facility and headed toward the living quarters.

Harm, Buck, Diesel, Big Jake and Pitbull peeled off at their quarters, but T-Mac continued beside Kinsley.

"Agar and I are going for a run. You don't have to go with us. We'll be out in the open and safe."

"I need to go for a run, too." He patted his flat abs. "Can't keep up my girlish figure by eating bonbons and sitting around."

"Seriously, I don't want to monopolize your time. Surely whoever left the package won't try anything out in broad—" she caught herself and continued "—out in the open."

"We don't know what he'll try. And if it's all right by you, I'm not taking any chances."

Kinsley sighed. "I don't like taking up all of your time."

"What else do we have to do?" He waved his hand at their surroundings. "It's the typical military deal—hurry up and wait."

"In that case, meet me outside in five minutes."

He planted his feet in the dirt and crossed his arms over his chest. "I'll wait here."

"No, really." Kinsley touched his arm and immediately retracted her hand when sparks seemed to fly off her fingers and up into her chest. "What could happen in five minutes?"

"A lot."

"You can't go with me everywhere, and I can't go with you. Five minutes will be fine." She pointed toward his unit. "Go change into your PT uniform."

"I'm wearing it," he insisted, though he was in his full uniform, boots and all.

Kinsley planted her fists on her hips. "I'm not going anywhere until you change into your shorts. And I'd have to wait for you outside your unit if I followed you. Just do it, and get back. I promise not to get blown up in the meantime."

He stood for a moment longer, staring into her eyes, and then sighed. "Okay, but I want to check your room before you go in."

Kinsley glanced down at her dog. "Agar does a pretty good job of it for me," she reminded him.

"Humor me, will ya?"

She raised her hands. "Okay." Unlocking the door, she pushed it open and released Agar's lead. "But let Agar go first."

T-Mac's lips twisted. "Deal."

She gave Agar the command to search, pointing into the building.

Agar entered, nose to the ground. As small as the unit was, it took only seconds for him to trot back to her side. He displayed no behavioral signs that anything might contain explosives.

She nodded toward T-Mac. "Your turn."

The navy SEAL entered the small box of a room and searched high and low. What he was looking for, Kinsley had no clue.

When he returned to the door, she raised an eyebrow. "Find anything?" she asked, knowing the answer.

His eyes narrowed. "Don't get smart with me, Specialist."

Her eyes widened as she feigned innocence. "Me? Never."

T-Mac's lips curled on the corners and he lowered his voice until only she could hear him. "Don't tempt me to kiss you again."

Her heart fluttered. "Never," she whispered. Although, at that moment, she'd give anything to feel his lips on hers again. But they weren't locked behind a door, away from prying eyes, with the chance of a deadly explosion threatening to take their lives.

"Five minutes," she whispered.

"Close the door behind me," he said, and stepped out of the doorway.

Kinsley entered and closed the door behind her. Then she leaned against it and dragged in a deep breath. The man made her forget to breathe.

Agar nudged her hand, bringing her back to reality and the need to change quickly.

She rushed around the small space, tossing off her jacket and desert-tan T-shirt. She pulled on her army PT shirt, untied her boots and kicked them off. In short order, she switched her uniform trousers for shorts and her boots for running shoes.

A knock sounded as she pulled her hair back into a ponytail.

She grabbed Agar's lead and flung open the door.

T-Mac stood there in a pair of shorts and running shoes, nothing else.

All those muscles on his broad, tanned chest sucked the air right out of her lungs.

"Ready?" he asked.

She nodded mutely, exited her quarters with Agar and locked the door behind her.

They took off at a jog, past the rows of containerized living units and out to the open field.

Though she was in good shape and could run several miles without stopping, Kinsley didn't have the long stride of the much-taller SEAL. But she held her own, aware that T-Mac slowed his pace to match hers.

Agar trotted alongside them, happy to be outdoors.

They didn't talk, but ran in companionable silence for a few laps around the open field. When they approached the living quarters again, Kinsley slowed to a walk, breathing hard. "Any clue as to who might have planted that package?"

T-Mac walked beside her, barely having broken a sweat. "None."

"I wish I could remember anything from that night I was shot."

"Don't worry about it," he said. "The guy will surface. And when he does, we'll get him."

"Hopefully before anyone else is hurt." As they reached her unit, she turned. "I'm going to grab my things and hit the shower facility. You can't follow me inside, so don't argue."

"I'll wait outside. But take Agar with you. I'm sure he could use a shower as well."

Kinsley laughed. "I will. He loves the shower."

T-Mac muttered something low, almost indiscernible, but it sounded like *lucky dog*.

Kinsley chose not to read into the comment she might not have even heard correctly. Leaving her door wide open, she entered her unit, grabbed her toiletries kit, towel and clothes, kicked off her running shoes and slipped on her flip-flops. She was outside again in record time.

T-Mac escorted her to the shower facility and waited outside while she and Agar went in. They had the shower to themselves.

Kinsley shampooed Agar first and rinsed him beneath the spray. Then she washed her hair and body, all the while aware of the man right outside the thin walls of the building. As she stood naked under the cool spray, she thought about what it would feel like to share a shower with the SEAL. The man was all muscular and glorious. Would he be disappointed with her pale, freckled body and soft curves? Or would he touch her all over and light her entire body on fire?

Sweet heaven.

Her core heated. The lukewarm water did nothing to tamp down the flames of desire coursing through her veins. Kinsley had to quit thinking about the man and his soft, firm lips, broad shoulders and narrow hips, or she'd melt into a puddle of goo.

Agar stepped out from beneath the spray and shook. Kinsley rinsed one last time and shut off the shower.

Running the towel over her skin, she dried off briskly, trying not to take too much time. When she was finished, she dressed, brushed her hair back from her forehead and smoothed the tangles free. Agar would dry quickly in the Djibouti heat.

T-Mac was still there when Kinsley stepped out of the shower facility.

He walked her back to her unit and waited for her to enter. "Harm is going to stand guard until I can get showered and changed. But I'll be back for the night."

Kinsley frowned. "You can't sleep in my quarters with me. That would be construed as fraternization."

T-Mac shook his head. "I'm sleeping outside."

"No way. You shouldn't have to sacrifice the comfort of your bed for me."

"I don't consider it a sacrifice. You're doing me a favor. I love to sleep under the stars, and an army cot is what I sleep best on."

"No. This is too much. I can go sleep in the office with whoever is pulling charge of quarters duty. You don't have to babysit me through the night."

He touched her arm. "Anyone ever tell you that you argue too much?"

"Only when I'm right," she replied sharply.

"Well, this time, you aren't going to win the argument. Harm will be here until I return. I'm staying the night outside your unit. The end."

She pressed her lips together. The stubborn set of his jaw brooked no further argument. She'd be talking to a brick wall.

Harm trotted up to stand beside T-Mac. "I'm here." He clapped a hand on T-Mac's shoulder and wrinkled his nose. "Whew, buddy, you smell. Go get your shower."

T-Mac grimaced. "Thanks, Harm."

"I heard from the EOD guys. They said the bomb in the package had a pressure detonator. If she'd stepped on that box, it would have exploded."

T-Mac's gaze went to Kinsley, warming her with the concern in his eyes.

"It's a good thing I have Agar," Kinsley said. "He found it before I would have."

"Maybe I should skip the shower." T-Mac's brow lowered.

"Trust me, dude, you need the shower," Harm said.

T-Mac tipped his head toward Kinsley. "Keep an eye on her."

Harm grinned. "Will do."

"I guess I don't have a say in this?" Kinsley asked, though secretly, she was glad to have such great bodyguards.

Harm glanced at T-Mac.

T-Mac gave a quick head dip. "Nope."

Kinsley rolled her eyes. "Fine. Then keep the noise down. Agar's a light sleeper." She stepped into her unit and gave Agar the command to follow. Once they were both inside, she closed the door.

Three days ago, she had thought the assignment in Djibouti was going to be boring. Now, with the current threat to her life and the other threat to her heart… Djibouti was anything but boring.

T-Mac hated being even a minute away from Kinsley. He couldn't be certain whoever had planted the package bomb wouldn't try again, or when.

He made it to his quarters and back to the shower facility in record time. He scrubbed clean and shaved, wishing he had time to get a haircut. But he'd already been gone more than eight minutes.

Back at his quarters, he grabbed a folding cot and returned to Kinsley's building.

Harm leaned against the corner of the unit. When he spotted T-Mac, he straightened. "What took you so long?" Then he chuckled. "Just kidding. Did you even wash behind your ears? That was faster than a shower at BUD/S training."

T-Mac clapped a hand onto Harm's shoulder. "Didn't want you to suffer for too long."

"Suffer? Or you didn't want me to tell your dog handler all your faults?"

"Both," T-Mac said.

Harm moved closer. "Big Jake hobbled by while you were AWOL from your post."

"And?" T-Mac prompted.

His friend glanced around and lowered his voice. "He was at the command center."

T-Mac drew in a breath and let it out slowly. "Are we a go?"

"Soon." He looked over his shoulder at the door to Kinsley's unit. "Are you ready?"

"I am."

Harm tipped his head toward the door. "Are you ready for her?"

"For Specialist Anderson to come along?" T-Mac sighed. "I don't have much choice, do I?" He shrugged. "I guess I am. Any idea when?"

With a shake of his head, Harm squared his shoulders. "Nope. Just be ready."

Which meant no sleep.

Harm left T-Mac alone.

He set up his cot in front of Kinsley's unit. A few people walked by, giving him strange looks, but he ignored them and stretched out with his hands locked behind his head. If he slept, it would be just a catnap, with one eye open. Darkness had settled in on Camp Lemonnier and the stars popped out, a few at a time, soon making enough light that he didn't need a flashlight to see.

The beauty of the night sky, filled with an array of diamond-like stars, made up for the daylight drabness of the desert surroundings.

A soft click sounded behind him.

He turned as the door to Kinsley's unit opened.

Agar trotted out.

Kinsley stood in the crack and gave Agar the command to lie down.

Agar dropped to his belly on the ground beside T-Mac's cot.

Before he could tell Kinsley that he didn't need Agar's protection, she closed the door.

Agar lifted his head beside the cot. T-Mac reached over and smoothed his hand over the dog's back. "She has a mind of her own, doesn't she?"

When T-Mac's hand stopped moving, Agar nuzzled his fingers.

"Needy guy, aren't you?" T-Mac scratched behind Agar's ears and rubbed his back again. He'd rather be running his hands over Kinsley's naked body than over her dog's back, but this was safer.

He must have drifted off, because the next moment, he awakened to the low rumble of Agar's growl.

T-Mac popped to a sitting position, his fist clenched, ready to defend.

A dark figure disengaged from the shadow of one of the container units.

"T-Mac," Harm's voice called to him in a half whisper.

"Yeah."

"It's time."

Chapter 8

A finger pressed to her lips and a voice sounded in the darkness. "Kinsley, wake up."

Immediately, Kinsley knocked the hand away, and she shot to a sitting position. "What the hell?"

"I knocked lightly, but you didn't answer. I couldn't knock louder without waking others."

She pushed the hair out of her face and stared up at T-Mac. "It's okay. You just startled me."

"You left your door unlocked."

Agar nudged her fingers with his cool, damp nose.

Kinsley smoothed a hand over his head and neck. "I know. With you out there, I wasn't worried someone would break in."

"What if someone slit my throat?"

She yawned and stretched. "Agar wouldn't let that

happen." The room seemed smaller with T-Mac in it. "Why did you wake me?" Her eyes widened. "Oh. Is it time?"

He nodded. "Get your gear. Harm's outside. I'll be back in less than five minutes to get you."

She nodded.

He turned toward the door. "Oh, and did you know you snore?"

"No, I do not." She frowned. "Do I?"

He grinned. "You do. And it's cute as hell. Don't let anyone tell you otherwise." He left her sitting on her bunk with her mouth open.

As soon as he shut the door, she was off the bed and dressing in her uniform, body armor loaded with ammunition and a first-aid kit. She pulled on her helmet, grabbed her rifle and snapped Agar's retractable lead onto his collar. By the time she was ready, a soft knock sounded on the door. She opened it to find T-Mac standing on the other side.

Without a word, she stepped out with Agar, closed the door softly behind her and locked it.

They hurried toward the helicopters on the flight line where the rest of the SEAL team had assembled. Already the rotor blades were turning. If someone didn't know they were about to go on a mission before, they knew now.

The SEAL team loaded into the helicopters. Agar jumped in, and T-Mac gave Kinsley a hand up. Even before she had her safety harness buckled, the chopper left the ground and rose into the air.

Kinsley settled back in her seat and willed her pulse to slow. Agar sat between her legs, his chin on her lap.

She stroked his fur, calming him as well as herself. The mission seemed to be happening so fast. The silence made it seem all the more dangerous.

She could imagine what it would be like to be one of them on a mission without her and the dog. They probably moved like a well-oiled machine. Each had a position or a part to play, and they did it well. Perhaps T-Mac had been right in concluding she was a distraction. She didn't belong in this group of highly trained fighters.

Sure, she was a good shot and knew basic fighting tactics, but she wasn't like them. They were finely honed weapons in and of themselves.

Then again, the SEALs weren't like Agar. The dog would help to protect them when they couldn't sniff out danger lurking beneath their feet.

She tried not to be so completely aware of T-Mac's thigh pressed against hers. She couldn't move away from him, since they were packed tightly together and Agar gave her no room to shift her legs.

The heat from T-Mac's thigh scorched her own, sending electrical currents through her leg and straight to her core, making her burn with sexy images of him in his PT shorts and bare chest. Her fingers tingled, itching to touch him, to run her hands over his taut muscles and down to… Sweet heaven, how could she even think naughty thoughts of the man when they could be descending into yet another hotbed of enemy activity?

Her mind should be on the task ahead, not the man beside her. She should be planning her and Agar's next moves. But T-Mac was right there beside her, tempting her like no other man ever had.

After half an hour in the air, she'd settled back in

her seat and tried to relax, determined to conserve her energy for whatever lay in store for her next. But she was too wound up, thinking about the last time she'd gone out on a mission. Her heart pounded in her chest and her ribs were still sore from the impact of the bullet on her armored vest. At her current pulse rate, she'd be worn out before they landed. She let her hand fall to her side between her and T-Mac.

A moment later, T-Mac's fingers curled around hers, hidden between them from anyone else's view.

His touch at once calmed her and excited her for an entirely different reason. She didn't question it, just drew on his strength.

By the time they landed, she had pulled herself together, ready to face whatever fate had in store for her and Agar.

As soon as the helicopters landed, the SEALs leaped to the ground. Agar was quick to exit, and Kinsley jumped down beside him.

T-Mac was there with a hand on her elbow to steady her until she had her balance.

As soon as they were all on the ground, the helicopters lifted into the air and headed back the way they'd come. The crew would wait within radio distance for the call to extract the team.

Kinsley couldn't help but feel a little stranded as she watched the choppers disappear into the night. She hefted her rifle in one hand and gripped Agar's lead in the other.

"Comm check," Big Jake said.

Kinsley worried that his slight limp would slow him down. But the big guy seemed as determined as the rest to find the people responsible for the attack on them in the last operation that had gone south.

One by one, all six of the SEALs checked in with only their call signs.

Once all of the SEALs had called out their names, T-Mac nudged Kinsley.

"Dog handler and Agar," Kinsley added to the tail end of the comm check. She could hear her voice in the radio and was reassured by the sound. If nothing else, she was connected by radio. If she got separated from the others, she could still connect this way.

"Let's do this," Big Jake said.

T-Mac touched Kinsley's shoulder and nodded in the direction they were heading.

"I'm right next to you," he said into his mic. "We have a lot of ground to cover between us and our target."

Kinsley warmed at his voice coming through the radio in her ear. With T-Mac at her side, she didn't have to worry if she was going the right way. While she concentrated on Agar, T-Mac would make sure they were on track.

Giving Agar the command to search, she followed the dog, moving out quickly. If they wanted to get there in a hurry, Agar had to work his magic without interruption.

As before, the dog sailed past the first mile without stopping.

The second mile, they traversed over rougher terrain, heading into hills with lots of scrub trees and bushes blocking their view ahead.

Agar kept his nose to the ground, working his way back and forth across the path.

Kinsley never let her guard down, constantly watching for any sign from the animal that things weren't all they should be.

"We're getting close to the target coordinates," T-Mac warned. "Slow the dog."

Kinsley pulled back on Agar's lead, checking his progress. The dog immediately returned to her side and looked up at her, his tongue lolling.

She would like to have given him some of the water she carried in her CamelBak thermos, but they didn't have time to stop. Keeping Agar on a shorter lead this time, she sent him forward to sniff for explosives.

"Half a click," T-Mac whispered. "Be on the lookout for guards on the perimeter."

"Roger," Big Jake answered. "You, too."

Ten steps later, Agar lay down.

Kinsley stuck a flag in the ground where he lay and moved on. Five flags later, Agar was moving faster again.

She gave him more of a lead, allowing him to swing wider from center. When he didn't come up with anything, he raced back in the opposite direction, clearing a wider path.

Kinsley understood the need to move slowly, but she also knew the element of surprise could require striking swiftly. The SEALs liked to get in and get the job done.

But she focused on her work with Agar, determined to deliver the team safely to the coordinates. That was her and Agar's primary responsibility. If they didn't accomplish that, what was the purpose of including them on the mission?

T-Mac grabbed her arm and pulled her to the ground.

"Tango at two o'clock." He held up his fist for the guys behind him, indicating they should stop in place.

Agar was as far out as his retractable lead would go, still sniffing out bombs and land mines.

Kinsley couldn't call him back without alerting the man pulling guard duty on the perimeter. She tugged the lead.

Instead of coming, as he usually did, he braced his paws in the dirt and strained against his lead.

Kinsley tugged again. Resisting a touch command was not like Agar. The dog always came when he was called or tugged.

"Why is he just standing there?" T-Mac asked.

"Something or someone is out there, not too far from where Agar is standing." Her heart pounding, Kinsley remained in position with one knee on the ground. She aimed her rifle in front of her, ready to take down anyone who tried to attack the team or Agar.

"I'm going forward," T-Mac said.

Kinsley wanted to hold him back, but knew she couldn't. Agar had cleared the path between them, but not beyond. All she could hope was that there were no more land mines or other explosives between Agar and the Tango crouched out of sight beyond.

When T-Mac moved past Agar, Kinsley tugged hard on his lead, calling the dog back to her side.

This time Agar complied, as if he knew he'd done his job and T-Mac would take it from there.

Kinsley held her breath, praying no explosives lay in T-Mac's path. She squatted low to the ground, her hand on Agar's back, her heart pounding an erratic tattoo against her ribs.

T-Mac moved from bush to tree, clinging to the shadows cast by the starlight. Before long, even Kinsley couldn't make him out against the gloom of darkness. The man was like a cat moving through the night after his prey.

A movement beside her made Agar growl low in his chest.

Harm dropped to his knee at her side. "Do you see him?" he asked quietly into her headset.

"No," she responded. "I lost him."

"He's almost to the guy." Harm pointed into the darkness. "Let's hope the guard is asleep."

Kinsley nodded, never taking her gaze from the last place she'd seen T-Mac.

"One down," T-Mac whispered into her headset.

Then a shadow leaped up from a different location and ran away from the team.

"Got a live one on the loose," Harm called out softly.

"Hold your fire. We can't alert the rest of the camp until we can no longer avoid it," Big Jake warned.

"But he's going to alert the others," T-Mac said.

"Not if I can help it." Kinsley unclipped the lead from Agar's collar and gave him the command to take down.

Agar leaped forward and chased after the running man. Within seconds, he hit the man in the back, knocking him to his knees.

The SEAL team closed in.

Kinsley ran to catch up to Agar.

But before she could reach him, a shot rang out.

Shouts sounded ahead and lights flared out of the darkness. Half a dozen pairs of headlights came to life, chasing away the darkness and ruining any night vision they could have hoped for.

"Get down," Big Jake spoke sharply into the headset.

Kinsley didn't have to be told twice. She dropped to her knees, then down to a prone position, her rifle in her hand, aimed at the headlights, waiting for movement.

"Things are about to go sideways," Big Jake said. "Take out who you need to—save a live one to bring back."

Shouts sounded from the camp and gunfire echoed in the sky.

The men moved forward, slipping into the shadows now cast by the many vehicle headlights glowing.

Kinsley eased her way toward Agar and the man whose arm he held between his razor-sharp teeth.

Harm had been there a moment before, dispatching the man with a clean swipe across the neck with his wicked Ka-Bar knife.

Kinsley shuddered and gave Agar the command to release. Agar shook the dead man once more and then let go of his arm and returned to Kinsley's side.

Harm moved on, leaving Kinsley and Agar alone with the dead man.

As Kinsley moved past the man on the ground, he reached out and grabbed her ankle.

Kinsley screamed and dropped to the ground, kicking at the hand.

Agar leaped to her defense, sinking his teeth into the man's arm.

Kicking wouldn't release the man's grip. She reached down and peeled back the fingers on the hand, finally freeing her ankle.

"Kinsley, are you all right?" T-Mac's voice sounded in her ears.

"I'm okay," she said.

"Where are you?" he demanded.

"I don't know," she admitted. "Not far from where you left me, I think."

All the SEALs had converged on the camp.

"Stay put—I'll find you."

Moments later, T-Mac appeared in front of her.

Kinsley leaped to her feet and fell into his arms.

More headlights flashed from another direction, heading toward the position where Kinsley, Agar and T-Mac stood.

"Come on. We have to get out of here." T-Mac took her hand.

Together they ran around the perimeter, away from the vehicles heading into the camp.

At one point, T-Mac pulled her down to a crouch.

He glanced back in the direction from which they'd come. For a moment, he remained silent. Then he spoke into his headset. "Gang, you need to get out of there. Four trucks loaded with at least ten men each, all armed, are on their way in. You're about to be grossly outnumbered."

"Calling for extraction." Big Jake's voice came over the radio. "Meet at the alternate pickup point, ASAP."

"Where's the alternate pickup point?" Kinsley asked.

"Two kilometers north of our original drop zone."

"Aren't we—"

"South of the camp and our pickup location?" T-Mac grunted. "Yes."

"And aren't those trucks filled with all those reinforcements standing between us and our ride back to Camp Lemonnier?"

"Give the girl a prize." He touched her shoulder. "We'll be okay."

"We have a man down," Harm called out. "We've got him, but we're moving slowly toward the pickup point. Someone cover our backs."

"Gotcha covered," Diesel said. "Go!"

"Getting hot in here," Buck reported. "Heading out. Don't shoot me."

"Those trucks are less than a kilometer away," T-Mac reminded him. "If you're getting out, now would be a good time."

"What about you?" Big Jake asked. "Give me a si-trep, T-Mac."

"We're between a rock and a hard place. Get the injured back to the Lemon. The dog handler and I will stay low until you can send reinforcements back to collect us."

"We're not leaving without you," Big Jake said.

"You can't delay getting that man some medical attention. We'll be all right."

The chatter stilled.

Kinsley held her breath, her heart pounding. "Are we staying?" she asked.

"Looks like it," T-Mac answered. "We can't delay the choppers from getting the men back to Camp Lemonnier."

"Okay." She was with T-Mac. He'd promised to keep her safe. She trusted he would keep that promise. Kinsley sucked in a deep breath and let it out. "What now?"

T-Mac didn't like that he and Kinsley were trapped more or less behind enemy lines. He had to get her safely away from the terrorist camp and hunker down somewhere safe and out of sight until the helicopters could return to pick them up.

His night-vision goggles were useless with all the headlights lighting up the sky. But as long as they weren't pointed directly at them, they could move without being obvious. If their night vision was compromised, so too would the terrorists'.

He checked his compass using a red-lensed flashlight and nodded in the direction they should travel to get away from the commotion. "Let's go."

"Wait." Kinsley touched his arm. "Let Agar go ahead of us."

"We don't have time."

"And we don't have time to be blown up. You saw the mines were set out between one and two kilometers outside the camp. If they set them out on all sides, let Agar find them for us."

"Okay, but we have to move fast. Right now they're probably concerned about the larger group of SEALs. When they're gone, they'll have time to look for others. That would be us. We can't let them see us, or our ducks are cooked."

Kinsley laughed. "Ducks are cooked?"

T-Mac liked the sound of her laughter, even if it was only nerves. "You know what I mean."

"I do, but ducks?" She laughed again but fell in step, moving hunched over.

They crouched as low as possible to the ground to keep from being seen or captured in the light from a moving vehicle.

Agar searched ahead, his nose to the ground, a silent shadow moving back and forth at the end of his lead.

So far, he hadn't found anything, but that didn't mean he wouldn't.

A loud explosion sounded from the other side of the camp. T-Mac's heart plummeted.

"Oh, no," Kinsley said softly.

"One of our guys stepped on a land mine," Buck reported over the radio headset. "He's in a bad way. Really bad."

T-Mac stopped and cursed. He hovered between getting farther away and heading back to help his team. But he had an obligation to protect Kinsley. If he took her with him to help his teammates, she'd be in danger and might either be shot or captured.

"We have to go back," Kinsley said.

Her words brought him back to reality. Even if he could get past the four truckloads of men entering camp, he couldn't drag Kinsley into the middle of the mayhem.

"We can't go back." His jaw hardened. "My team will return to collect us after they get the injured to safety."

"But Agar could have gotten them out without unnecessary injuries."

"SEAL teams don't usually have the benefit of a Military Working Dog looking out for us. However, we wouldn't have made it as far as we have tonight without you and Agar."

"I wish we could have kept that SEAL from stepping on the explosives."

"We can't second-guess our decisions. Right now we have to lie low and hope we aren't discovered." He kept moving, farther and farther away from the terrorist compound until they could barely see the individual headlights. All they could discern were lights shining out from the camp center.

"How does your team know where to pick you up if you get separated?"

"I'm carrying a GPS tracking device. And when they get close enough, we'll reestablish radio communication with our headsets."

"In the meantime, shouldn't we conserve the battery on these?" She pointed to the device in her ear.

"Yes." He pulled his radio headset off and stuffed it into one of the pockets on his uniform.

Kinsley did the same. "Are we stopping for a few minutes?" she asked.

"We can." T-Mac pulled his night-vision goggles down and glanced around the area, careful not to look directly at the terrorist camp with its bright headlights still burning. He didn't see the green heat signatures of people moving about in the area, and they were far enough away that they couldn't see them. He raised the NVGs and nodded. "Rest for a few minutes."

"Good. Agar needs water." She looped her weapon strap over her shoulder, cupped her hand and squirted water into her palm from the CamelBak water-storage device she wore like a backpack over her body armor.

Agar eagerly lapped up the water and waited while she repeated the process several times until he was satisfied. Then he lay on the ground beside her, seemingly content to rest as long as she was still.

"How long do you think it will take them to come back for us?" she whispered.

"I'm not sure. But it would be good for us to get as far away from the compound as we can before they attempt to bring the helicopter back. Now that the terrorists know we know where they are, they will be moving. And we don't know which direction they will go."

"They could be heading this way?" Kinsley rubbed her hands up and down her arms. "We are south of them, right?"

"Right."

"Wouldn't it be better if someone knew where they were headed?" she asked.

T-Mac didn't like the question, or the direction of her thoughts. "What do you have in mind?"

"If you have a GPS device on you, couldn't you attach it to one of their vehicles? That way we wouldn't have to rely on satellite images to find them again."

"But then our guys would have no way of finding us. And believe me, it's a long way back to Camp Lemonnier on foot."

Kinsley stared at the ground beside Agar and ran her hand over his head. "It's a shame. These terrorists will probably be gone by morning."

"Military intelligence could pull more satellite photos. They'll find them again."

"You heard the commander. The intel guys said it was lucky they actually found them the first time." She shook her head. "Those bastards could get away again. They'll only go on to hurt more of our military personnel, not to mention the innocent people they terrorize on a daily basis."

"It's too bad we don't have one of the vehicles we saw tonight," Kinsley mused. "We could plant the GPS device and make our way back to Camp Lemonnier on our own."

"To do that, we'd have to steal one of their vehicles," T-Mac said. "It would be insane to try." Then why the hell was he considering trying to steal one of the trucks he'd seen that evening?

But the more he thought about it, the more he liked the idea. He could do it. But would he put Kinsley at too much risk by even attempting such an idiotic feat?

He glanced down at where Kinsley sat beside Agar. "I know you're good at finding land mines and IEDs, but how are you with setting detonators in plastic explosives?"

Chapter 9

After a quick refresher on detonators and C-4 explosives, Kinsley worked with T-Mac to divvy up what he'd come with into three separate setups.

The camp would still be in a state of disarray, with everyone loading up whatever they deemed valuable in preparation for bugging out. They wouldn't want to stay in one place knowing their location was compromised. After the Navy SEAL attack, they would be expecting even more grief in the way of rockets launched by either UAVs or other military aircraft. If they didn't get out that night, they would be easy targets.

"Since we haven't seen guards out searching for anyone left behind, we can assume they think all of the personnel who participated in the attack are gone for now," T-Mac said. "We have surprise on our side. They will not be expecting anyone else to launch an offensive anytime soon."

Kinsley squared her shoulders, excitement building in her chest. "That's where we come in."

Even in the limited lighting from the stars overhead, she could see the way T-Mac's brow dipped. "Not *we*," he said. "*I* will set the charges in strategic locations."

"Right," she agreed. "While Agar and I hide nearby."

"Exactly." T-Mac continued. "Then, while the Al-Shabaab terrorists are confused by the explosions, I'll see what I can appropriate in the way of a vehicle. You'll need to be ready once I roll out of the camp."

She nodded, wishing she could play a bigger role in the attack. "Agar and I will be ready."

T-Mac pressed a button on the side of his watch. "They should be scrambling out of the camp soon. If we're going, we should leave now and get as close as possible without being seen." He nodded toward Agar. "Will you be able to keep him quiet while I'm setting the charges?"

"Absolutely," she replied, confident in Agar's ability to take command.

"Then let's go." Together, they loaded the detonators into pouches and secured them on his vest. Then they loaded the C-4 into another pouch and secured the pouch to his vest. In order to move quickly, he would leave his rifle with Kinsley and carry only his handgun, Ka-Bar knife and a couple of hand grenades.

Now that they were actually going back to the camp, Kinsley was positive her idea was insane. But no matter how much she wanted to change T-Mac's mind, he was set on his course.

Once he had everything where he could reach it

quickly, he stared down at Kinsley. "You can stay here, if you like. I could make it back to you in whatever vehicle I can commandeer, or if that's not possible, I can return on foot and we'll get the hell out of here."

"I'm coming as close as I can get. If you run into difficulties, I can cover for you while you get out."

He shook his head. "I don't know. The more I think about it, the more I'm convinced you'd be better off staying here."

"I'm not staying. You can't go it completely alone. You might get in okay, but getting back out will be more difficult. They'll be looking for whoever set off the explosions." She touched his arm, ready to do what it took to convince him she was an asset, not a liability. "I'm a pretty decent shot. I qualify expert every time I've been to the range. The least I can do is provide cover for you."

"Being that close to camp puts you at risk."

"I signed up for this gig when I asked to train with the dogs. I knew we'd be on the front line at some point. I'd say this is pretty damn close to the front line." She lifted her chin. "I'm not afraid."

"You might not be afraid for yourself." He cupped her cheek in his palm. "But I'm scared for you." He tipped his head toward the dog. "And Agar."

Her heart warmed at the concern in his voice. She leaned her cheek into his palm. "Don't worry about us. I'll stay low and still. They won't even know I'm there. You just do your thing and create the biggest, loudest distraction you can. I'll be waiting near the road they drove in on. It should be clear of all land mines or they wouldn't have driven in from that direction."

"And you'll have Agar if you get into trouble." He stared down into her face.

T-Mac's eyes were inky pools in the starlight, and Kinsley couldn't read into them. By the way he leaned toward her, she could sense he wanted to say or do more. When he hesitated, she made up his mind for him and leaned up on her toes, pressing her lips to his. "Be careful, will ya? I kind of like kissing you."

He laughed. "You know we could be court-martialed for fraternizing."

She shrugged. "And we might not live to see the dawn of a new day. I'll take my chances." And she kissed him again.

T-Mac gripped her shoulders and pulled her into his embrace, their body armor making it difficult to get closer. "This doesn't end here," he promised.

"I'm banking on that, frogman." She squared her shoulders. "Let's do this."

Though she was scared, adrenaline kicked in and sent her forward. She gave Agar the command to search ahead of them. While he sniffed for explosives in the ground, Kinsley looked at the activity going on in the terrorist camp. They appeared to be loading trucks. Men moved in front of headlights, carrying boxes and other items.

If T-Mac didn't hurry, he might miss the opportunity to tag one of the vehicles and claim one of them for their own.

Kinsley couldn't make Agar move faster. He was doing his job, but apparently between them and the camp there were no land mines. The terrorists must have thought the threats wouldn't come from the south, deeper into Somalia.

Within minutes, they were back in shooting range of the camp.

Kinsley's heart beat faster and her level of fear intensified. She didn't like the idea of T-Mac slipping back into camp to set explosive charges. She couldn't even imagine if he got caught. She prayed it wouldn't happen, that he'd make it in and back out unscathed.

Just outside the camp, close to the road T-Mac was due to escape on, they hunkered low in the brush.

Kinsley sought out T-Mac's hand, having massive second thoughts. "Don't worry about swiping a vehicle. Just get in, plant the GPS and get back out. We'll find our way back to Camp Lemonnier on foot. In fact, let's not do this at all. I'd rather not lose you at this point."

He squeezed her hand and brought it to his lips. "I'll be fine. But thanks for caring." He kissed the backs of her knuckles. "Remember, I'll be driving with the lights out. I'll give three beams of my flashlight in quick succession."

Kinsley smiled. "And I'll return it with a beam from my red-lensed flashlight."

"We might have to repeat the cue a couple of times if I'm off on distance."

"I'll be watching." She sighed and stared up into his eyes. "Hurry back. I'm kinda getting used to having you around, big guy." Kinsley cupped his cheek. "And don't do anything stupid."

"Stupid isn't in the repertoire of a SEAL," he said. "Hang tight. This shouldn't take too long." He kissed her hard on the lips and took off.

Agar strained at the lead, eager to follow, but Kinsley held firm. For the first few minutes, she could follow T-Mac's silhouette moving through the brush and past trees, working his way toward the vehicles and people milling around the camp. Once he reached one of the tents still standing, he disappeared.

Kinsley's heart lodged in her throat and her pulse pounded so hard, she could barely hear herself think.

Minutes ticked by like hours.

If he didn't come out, she and Agar were on their own to make it back to Camp Lemonnier. But that didn't scare her as badly as the fact that if he didn't make it out, it meant he was either dead or captured and would be tortured by the terrorists.

Kinsley didn't know which would be worse. But she knew one thing... She was falling for the navy SEAL, and she didn't want what she felt for him to end like this.

Making it into the camp hadn't been that difficult. The terrorists were in a frenetic hurry to break camp, pack the trucks and get the hell out before their attackers returned with mortars or missiles.

T-Mac hid in the shadow of a tent, studying the layout of the camp, determining where would be the best place to set his charges. To make the biggest bang for his effort, he'd have to take out a couple of the trucks. The pile of empty crates at the north end of the camp would be a good target, drawing attention to the north while T-Mac attempted to take a vehicle and head south, as if one of the terrorists had gotten a jump start on leaving the compound.

Once his decision was made, he went into action, stealing from shadow to shadow. Men in black robes and turbans raced past him, their weapons slung over their shoulders, each carrying something to load into the backs of trucks.

T-Mac slipped up behind one at the back of a lone truck at the north end of the compound, grabbed him from behind and snapped his neck, killing him instantly. He dragged him under the truck, stripped off his turban and robe and dressed in them. He'd have a better chance of mixing in with the bad guys dressed like them.

Then he planted the plastic explosives near the engine of the vehicle and pressed a detonator into the clay-like material. Lifting a small crate, he ran through the camp like the others until he arrived at another vehicle on the northwest side and stood behind another man loading a box into the back. He handed his crate up to the man in the back of the truck and turned to leave.

The man in the truck shouted something to him.

T-Mac didn't catch what he said, so he couldn't translate. He pretended he didn't hear and hurried toward the front of the truck, where he pressed another glob of plastic explosives into the metal and jammed a detonator into it.

Once he had the two trucks tagged with explosives, he hurried toward several barrels that he assumed contained fuel of some sort. As he walked with his hands under the robe, he pressed another detonator into the C-4. Once he reached the barrels, he mashed the explosive compound into the side of one of the barrels that felt full.

A shout from behind made him turn.

Fortunately, the man wasn't shouting at him, but at another man who'd dropped a container full of boxes of ammunition, spilling its contents over the ground. Bullets spilled out and rolled across the sand.

A couple of the men ganged up on the one who'd dropped the box.

While all attention was on them, T-Mac slipped to the south side of the camp, eyeing two vehicles already pointed toward Somalia. Men were loading boxes and weapons into the backs of the trucks. On the one closest to him, a driver sat in the cab, his weapon resting across his lap.

T-Mac hoped the fireworks would distract all of them long enough for him to get the truck and get the hell out of camp before anyone knew any better.

He found a position behind the hulk of a vehicle that had flat tires and had been stripped of anything that could be removed, cannibalized or destroyed. Once he was safely in place, he covered his ears, hunkered down and pressed the button to detonate the first charge.

The explosion shook the ground beneath him.

Screams and shouts rose up around him.

From the corner of his hiding place, he watched as half of the men who'd been loading his target truck and the one beside it ran toward the explosion.

Five seconds later, he set off round two.

Again, the explosion made the earth tremble beneath his feet and debris rain down from the sky.

Daring to peek out, T-Mac checked the truck he hoped to steal. The driver had stepped down from the cab, his weapon raised, his gaze darting around, apparently searching for the person setting off the charges. Yet he didn't move away from the vehicle.

T-Mac would have to take the guy down.

He gauged how far he'd have to run out in the open to get to the driver, knowing he could easily do it, especially since he was disguised as one of them.

Gunfire sounded as the terrorists ran to the north end of the compound.

Knowing it was his last chance to create a huge distraction, T-Mac waited a few seconds before detonating the last charge.

Boom! The charge went off. A second later, another, louder bang ripped through the night, sending a tower of flames into the air as the fuel in the barrel ignited.

The truck driver hit the ground and covered his head.

T-Mac made his move. He sprinted across the open space, bent to the man on the ground and slit his throat. With the driver out of the way and the others all concentrating on the north end of camp and the raging fire sending flames a hundred feet into the sky, T-Mac had the chance he'd been hoping for.

He dragged the man beneath the truck, ran to the other vehicle and stashed the GPS tracker in a ripped hole in the driver's seat. Once he had the reason for his visit to the camp in place, he ran back around the front of the truck he hoped to take, leaned into the cab, set it in Neutral and started pushing it toward the perimeter of the camp.

At first, the truck barely moved. But once he got the momentum going, it rolled faster and faster. When he reached the edge of the camp, he jumped into the cab, twisted the key in the ignition and cranked the engine.

A shout sounded beside the driver's door. A man in the black garb of the Al-Shabaab ran alongside the truck, shaking his fist at T-Mac.

T-Mac slowed enough to position the vehicle just right, then shoved the door open fast and hard, hitting the man in the head.

The guy fell to the ground and lay still.

T-Mac didn't wait around to see if he revived. He didn't have time. As soon as the excitement of the explosions waned, the men in the camp would notice one of their vehicles had disappeared and some of their men were down. Someone else might have seen the truck leaving camp and the direction it had gone. T-Mac had to find Kinsley fast and get as far away from the terrorists as they could.

Once outside the camp, he pressed the accelerator to the floor, sending the truck leaping forward. He couldn't go far at that speed or he'd be forced to use the brakes without knowing if the brake lights would light up.

When he got to within range of where he'd left Kinsley, he pulled out his flashlight and hit the on-off switch three times. He scanned the darkness, praying for a red light blinking back at him.

For the longest moments of his life, he waited. When he didn't see anything, he repeated the three bursts of light.

Damn, had he gone out in the wrong direction? Had she been discovered and captured? Where was she? If he didn't find her soon, he wasn't sure they'd make it out of there undiscovered. He searched the darkness, desperately looking for the silhouette of a woman and a dog, praying they were all right.

Just when he considered turning back, a red dot appeared in the darkness.

Chapter 10

Kinsley hated waiting, not knowing what was happening. The first twenty minutes were hell, with every possible bad scenario rolling through her mind.

With all the terrorists running around the camp, how could T-Mac get in and do the job without being seen? The operation wasn't like one where they sneaked in while everyone was sleeping. He was going into a stirred-up hornets' nest to stir it up even more.

The more she sat waiting, the more she convinced herself this mission was a very bad idea.

When the first explosion went off, she jumped. She felt an immediate mixture of relief and even more tension.

T-Mac had managed to get in and set at least one charge.

Agar whined softly beside her, but stayed in his prone position, head down, resting. He could be up and running at her command.

The second explosion went off. The corners of Kinsley's lips quirked upward. Two down, one to go.

"Come on, T-Mac," she whispered softly.

At the third explosion, she wanted to cheer, but the ensuing fireball rising into the air made her heart drop into her belly.

Had something gone wrong? Had T-Mac been caught up in whatever caused the fireball?

Her heart pounded so hard, her pulse beat against her eardrums, making it hard for her to hear.

Men ran around the camp, shouting, their bodies black silhouettes against the bright orange blaze of what Kinsley suspected was burning fuel.

She didn't care how T-Mac got out of the camp as long as he got out alive. If he didn't find a way to commandeer a vehicle, they'd figure out a way to get back to Camp Lemonnier on foot.

He just needed to hurry.

The giant flame held Kinsley's attention, destroying her night vision. She didn't see the truck racing toward her until it was close enough she could hear the engine.

She prayed T-Mac was driving. What had he said? He'd give her three flashes from his flashlight?

Kinsley held her breath, waiting as the dark hulk of the truck grew closer.

Then a bright white light shone out from the cab.

Her pulse sped and she laughed out loud. "It's him, Agar!" she cried.

Agar jumped up, jerking the lead right out of her hand.

Afraid the dog would run out in front of the truck, Kinsley gave him the command to sit.

Agar sat.

Kinsley patted the ground, searching for the lead. When she found it, she looked up again.

The truck was much closer, moving slowly but almost to where she lay waiting in the brush. Another three flashes of light blinked into the night.

Oh, no.

Kinsley fumbled to unclip her flashlight from her web gear. She was supposed to flash her red-lensed flashlight back to indicate where she was. If she didn't hurry, he'd pass her. Then she'd be left behind. T-Mac couldn't shine his bright beam back toward the camp without alerting the terrorists to their location.

Her hand trembled as she pressed the switch. Nothing happened. Damn. Now wasn't the time for an equipment malfunction.

She slapped the device against her palm and the red light came on. Quickly, she held it up, aiming the red orb at the oncoming truck.

She heard the engine throttle down as if being placed into low gear. It slowed, rolling past her so slowly, she jumped up and ran after it, Agar trotting alongside her.

The screech of an emergency brake sounded, and the truck stopped with a jerk.

T-Mac dropped down from the cab, ran back to her and wrapped her in his arms. "I thought I'd come out of the camp on the wrong road."

"I thought you'd never get here." She laughed and stood on her toes to press a kiss to his lips. "Let's get out of here."

"Good idea." He held the driver's-side door.

Agar leaped up into the cab.

Kinsley climbed in and scooted over.

T-Mac hopped in, shifted into gear and took off as fast as he could without headlights to guide them. Thankfully, the stars shone bright enough to light their way.

With Agar in the passenger seat, Kinsley sat in the middle, her thigh pressed against T-Mac's, the reassuring strength of him warming her all the way through. She could breathe again.

"GPS?" she quizzed as she removed her helmet.

"Planted," he shot back.

"Thank God." Kinsley settled back in her seat, hesitant to pull off her armored vest so soon. "How far south are we going?"

"Not very." He glanced sideways at her. "We need to find a place to hide and wait for Al-Shabaab to move past, however long that takes."

"Aren't you worried we'll run into more of them coming up from the south to see what the fire is all about?"

"A little. The sooner we find a place to hide, the better."

Kinsley stared out into the darkness, focusing on anything large enough to hide a truck behind. For the first few miles, the land was flat and dry. Only a few bushes and scrubby trees stood out against the desert landscape.

As they traveled farther south, the road turned west. No headlights shone behind them and no one pulled out in front of them to block their escape. Soon, they passed the rubble of a small deserted village.

T-Mac drove past quickly.

Kinsley turned in her seat, looking out behind them. "Why didn't we stop there?"

"That was the first place we could hide. If the terrorists figure out we took one of their vehicles and headed south by the only road in this area, that would be the first place they'd look."

She nodded. "True."

"We should be getting into more hills the farther west we go."

"Can't we pass into Ethiopia? Would it be safer for us to travel back to Camp Lemonnier that way?"

"Al-Shabaab doesn't care about borders, but that's the plan for now. After what I did to them, they'll be hoppin' mad and out for blood."

"Other than the three explosions, which were bad enough, should I ask what you did that was so bad?"

He shook his head. "No. But they are three men fewer."

Kinsley shrugged out of her heavy body-armor vest and laid it on the floorboard. "Here, let me get your helmet."

He lifted his chin, keeping his eyes on the road.

Kinsley unbuckled the chin strap and slid the helmet off his head, without blocking his view of the road in front of him.

She would have offered to help him with his vest, but that would require more effort and he'd need to stop to pull it off. He'd have to wear the heavy plates until they came to a full stop long enough to remove it.

The road grew steeper as they climbed into the hills in northwest Somalia. Soon, they found a turnoff to the north, taking them deeper into rugged terrain, the road turning into more of a path than one used for four-wheeled vehicles.

T-Mac pulled the truck in behind a giant boulder that had fallen from an overhanging cliff. He checked the gas gauge before turning off the engine. "We have three quarters of a tank left. Whatever we do tomorrow, we might have to find more fuel, or find a way to contact my unit for a pickup. But for tonight, we camp here."

Sitting so close to T-Mac for the past two hours, Kinsley had felt a shiver of awareness and anticipation ripple across her skin. Alone in a vehicle with T-Mac was one thing. Alone lying under the stars with the navy SEAL was entirely different.

She gulped back her sudden nerves and blurted, "Let's see what we have in the back." Kinsley started to reach over Agar to open the passenger door.

T-Mac opened his door first. "Come out this way."

Since getting out the other side would be more difficult with Agar in the way, Kinsley followed T-Mac out the driver's side. Before she could step down from the truck, T-Mac grabbed her around the waist and lifted her out to stand on two feet. Agar jumped down behind her and wandered off to sniff at the rocks and brambles.

T-Mac didn't release her immediately, his hands resting on her hips. "You don't know how crazy it made me when I didn't see your red light."

She laughed. "Trust me. Had you been the one waiting the entire time things were blowing up in that camp, you would have gone off the deep end." Kinsley cupped his cheek and stared at him in the starlight. "You don't know how glad I was when I saw those three blinks of your flashlight."

"What took you so long to respond?" He brushed a strand of her hair out of her face.

"Agar and I got excited when he heard the rumble of the truck's engine. He jerked his lead, and I dropped the handle. I had to grab it before he took off after the on-coming truck. At that point, I didn't know if you were the driver, or someone else." She smiled up at him.

"Well, I was pretty happy to see your red lens shin-ing back at me." He touched her cheek with his fingers and kissed her forehead. "I almost turned around and headed back into that mess."

She pressed her hand over his on her face. "Are you crazy? They would have killed you."

"I thought I'd missed you, or gone out of the camp in the wrong direction."

She laughed, the sound shaky in the night. "Need help getting out of your body armor?"

"I can do it myself," he said.

She laughed. "And where would the fun be in that?" She reached for the fasteners, unbuckling them one at a time. When she had them free, she shoved the vest over his shoulders.

He caught it and laid it on the floorboard of the ve-hicle and then turned to face her, captured her hands in his and lifted them to his lips. "You amaze me."

She shook her head. "I don't know why. You're the one doing all the heavy lifting on this gig."

"You hold your own, no matter the situation. Most females I know would fall apart."

"Then you don't know the right females." She lifted her chin. "I joined the army, not a sorority."

He laughed and took one of her hands in his. "Come on—let's see what they were loading in the back of the truck."

Kinsley liked the sound of his laughter and the way his hand felt wrapped around hers. No, she wasn't a scared little girl needing the protection of a big burly man, but she liked having T-Mac around. And he had a way of making her feel more feminine than she'd felt in a long time. Kinsley knew she was a strong and courageous soldier. Somewhere along the line, she'd had to bury the woman inside in order to fit in in a man's world. T-Mac brought out the desire and longing she thought she'd never feel again.

And he was a navy SEAL and she was an army soldier. In no scenario could they be together for the long haul. Being with him on a dangerous mission in middle-of-nowhere Africa brought it home to her that they might not be in it for the long run. They might not make it to morning. Every minute they were together now was a gift that should not be squandered.

So she reveled in the touch of his hand. They couldn't hold hands on Camp Lemonnier. Someone would see and report them for fraternization. But out in the hills of Somalia, where every day could be their last, no one was watching. No one would know.

Feeling only a little guilty, Kinsley was also titillated and anxious to see what would happen next. Especially since they would be alone all night.

Chapter 11

At the back of the vehicle, T-Mac hit the switch on his flashlight and shone it up into the back of the large utility truck. He reluctantly released Kinsley's hand and passed the flashlight to her to hold while he lowered the tailgate.

The back of the truck contained crates and boxes.

T-Mac climbed up into the truck bed and picked through, opening boxes, moving some and setting others to the side.

"These cardboard boxes are full of food and rations marked WHO."

"World Health Organization," Kinsley said. "They must be stealing food and medical supplies destined for refugee camps."

"The wooden crates aren't marked WHO and they

weren't destined for refugee camps." His gut knotted as he lifted out a brand new M4A1 rifle and held it up for her to see. "We definitely found the opposite end of the snake, selling illegal arms to the enemy."

Kinsley shone the flashlight away from the boxes for a moment and then back into the bed of the truck. "Holy crap, T-Mac. You need to see this." She pointed to the rear bumper of the truck.

T-Mac dropped down out of the vehicle and stood beside Kinsley as she pointed the flashlight at a smear of black spray paint half covering numbers and letters stenciled onto the desert-tan paint.

"You've got to be kidding." T-Mac rubbed at the paint covering the numbers. "That's one of ours from the motor pool."

Kinsley nodded. "And those M4 rifles?"

"The armory isn't missing any, that we've heard of, but they're the same style and military grade as what is issued to our soldiers. Plus, they have the bullets to go with them. I saw someone drop a case in the middle of the camp."

"Great. Someone is arming Al-Shabaab with our own weapons." Kinsley rubbed her arms, as if trying to chase away the chilly night air. "I get that people would be able to sell weapons directly to our enemies, but how would Al-Shabaab get their hands on one of our vehicles without us hearing about it?"

"All the more reason for us to get back to Camp Lemonnier…with the evidence."

"Right." Kinsley tilted her head toward the back of the truck. "I don't suppose you found any blankets or immediately edible food in that truck, did you?"

T-Mac shook his head. "Sorry. Only guns, rice and medical supplies on this truck."

Kinsley dug into the pockets on her uniform pants and in her jacket. "Fortunately, I brought some protein bars and some snacks for Agar."

He took one of the protein bars and held it up to the flashlight. "Are you always this prepared?"

"I've learned to be." She reached into another pocket for a ziplock bag of food for Agar. "I know myself and Agar. We work better when we're not hungry."

"Good to know," T-Mac said. "We should get a little sleep before dawn. We might be out here for a day if the terrorists take their time moving from their previous location."

Kinsley glanced around at the rock outcroppings nearby. "I can stay awake and stand guard for the first shift."

"There's not much of the night left."

"You've been driving and did all of the work setting off those charges. I'm sure you're exhausted. You need to recharge."

"I'm fine," T-Mac assured her. "I've gotten by on a lot less sleep. You sleep first."

She frowned. "Only if you wake me in a couple hours so that I can pull guard duty while you get a little rest." She crossed her arms over her chest and raised her brows, waiting.

He sighed. "Okay. But for now you need to find a place to sleep."

"How about in the cab of the truck?" she suggested. "The bench seat is the softest thing around, and if we need to make a quick escape, we don't have to make a dash for it."

"Good thinking." He held the passenger door for her.

"I'll sleep behind the wheel," Kinsley insisted. "That way you can stretch out beside me without any obstructions."

"You mean, if we have to beat a hasty retreat, you'll do the driving?" He grinned and let her get in first.

"If I have to, I will." Kinsley slid across the seat to the driver's side. When he didn't get in, she stared out at him. "What's wrong?"

"Nothing. I just figured Agar needed a warm place to sleep. He needs some rest, too." He patted the dog's head and then leaned the seat forward, opening up the back seat for a passenger. "He worked hard tonight."

Kinsley smiled at how easily Agar got along with T-Mac. She gave the dog the command to climb up into the vehicle.

Agar leaped up and settled on the floorboard between the driver's and passenger's side.

Kinsley reached back to pat the animal's head.

When T-Mac still hesitated with his hand on the door, Kinsley frowned. "Aren't you getting in?"

"I think I'd be better off standing guard in the open where I can see someone coming."

Kinsley's frown deepened. "Would it make any difference if I said I need you with me?"

His lips turned upward on the corners. "It might."

She shook her head. "Then please, stay."

"For the record, I don't think it's a good idea."

She smiled. "For the record, I agree. But we're out here alone. The only people who will know or care will be us." Kinsley patted the seat beside her. "You need rest, even if you don't sleep."

"I've been sitting for the past couple of hours while driving."

She raised her brow. "Fine. Suit yourself. I'm going to get some sleep so I can take the next shift." She leaned back against the seat and closed her eyes.

T-Mac stood in the open door of the truck, staring at Kinsley, knowing that if he got into the truck, he might not be able to keep his hands to himself.

The woman was sexy without trying. She tipped back her head, exposing the long line of her very pretty, and kissable, neck.

His lips tingled, and he longed to press them to the pulse beating at the base of her throat.

Her lips tipped upward at the corners and she chuckled. "You might as well get in and close the door. It gets cold at night in the desert." The husky tone of her voice made his groin tighten.

Getting into the truck beside Kinsley was a very bad idea when all T-Mac wanted to do was touch her, taste her and kiss her until they both begged for air.

Despite what his head was telling him, T-Mac followed his gut. Or was it his heart? Whatever. He climbed into the truck and sat beside Kinsley.

She tilted her head toward him and opened one eye. "That wasn't so hard, was it?"

"Sweetheart, you have no idea," he murmured.

She closed her eyes and sighed. "Wake me in two hours."

T-Mac forced himself to stare straight ahead. But

every time Kinsley shifted, he couldn't help glancing her way.

Her head fell back against the headrest, tipped at an uncomfortable-looking angle.

Before he could think better of it, he found himself saying, "It might be more comfortable lying across the seat."

She gave a weak smile. "Thanks. I've never been very good at sleeping sitting up." Kinsley tipped over and tried to fit herself between the driver's door and T-Mac's thigh.

"Seriously." He snorted. "You can lay your head on my thigh. I promise not to bite."

Kinsley sat up, frowning. "Are you sure? I don't want to make you uncomfortable."

"Oh, babe, I'm way past uncomfortable." He shook his head. "Just use my leg as a pillow."

"But I don't want to make you uncom—" she started again.

"Woman, are you always so argumentative?" He gripped her shoulders and pulled her across his lap. "You can't help but make me crazy, and you don't even have to touch me to accomplish that." He kissed her lips hard and then lifted his head. "I've wanted to do that since we stopped. And I want to do so much more. But this is neither the time nor the place." He sighed and leaned his forehead against hers. "You're an amazing woman, and I want so much more than just a kiss."

Kinsley's eyes widened. "Oh." Then she snuggled into him. "What's stopping you? Because it sure as hell isn't me." She cupped his face between her palms and kissed him. She pulled back until her mouth was only a breath away from his, and then whispered, "It could be a very long night, or far too short. Depends on how you spend it."

T-Mac didn't need more of an invitation than that. "You realize we'll be breaking all the rules?"

"Damn the rules." She kissed him again, this time pushing her tongue past his teeth to slide along the length of his.

T-Mac held her close, his heart pounding against his ribs. After all that had happened and that short amount of time he'd thought he'd lost her...he couldn't hold back. He had to hold her, touch her, bury himself in her.

Her fingers flew across the buttons on his jacket, popping them free of the buttonholes one at a time. When she had his jacket open, she ran her fingers across his chest, the warmth of her hands burning through the fabric of his T-shirt.

He slipped his hand beneath her uniform jacket and smoothed it up her back and down to the base of her spine. "Once we start down this path, I can't guarantee I can stop."

"I don't want you to stop. I want you, Trace McGuire. We might not have tomorrow, but we can make good use of tonight."

"What about not getting involved with a navy guy?"

"Tonight, we're neither army nor navy. We're just two people, alone in the hills."

He chuckled and brushed a kiss across the tip of her nose. "And what happens in the hills stays in the hills?"

Kinsley nodded. "Something like that." She raised her hands to her own uniform jacket and pushed the top button free. "Now, are you going to talk, or are we going to make out?"

He laughed out loud and pulled her into his arms. "I feel like a teen on his first date. All we need is a cheesy song to play and a cop to shine his light into the window."

She smiled. "I can do without the cop with the flashlight, but we can make our own music."

"I like the way you think, Army."

"I like the way you feel, Navy."

He helped her with the rest of her buttons and pushed the jacket over her shoulders.

They became a tangle of hands and clothing in an effort to remove the T-shirts.

All the wiggling on his lap made him even harder and more desperate to be with her.

When she reached behind her back to unclip her bra, he pushed her hands aside and flicked the hooks loose and then slid the bra from her shoulders and down her arms.

Her small, perky breasts spilled into his hands.

Kinsley inhaled deeply, pressing more firmly into T-Mac's palms. She cupped the backs of his hands and held him there. "You don't know how good that feels."

He chuckled. "Oh, I think I do."

Kinsley shifted her legs until she straddled his hips and slid her center over his growing erection.

"Darlin', it doesn't work that way."

"What?" she asked, her voice breathy, as if she couldn't get enough air past her vocal cords.

"We have too much between us."

Kinsley sighed. "I know. Can we hurry the foreplay along? I'm not a very patient person."

T-Mac set her away from him. In a flurry of awkward movements, bumping into the windows, doors and each other, they got naked and spread their clothing out on the seat.

By then, T-Mac was breathing hard, his body on fire from touching hers so many times in the process of undressing.

"Uh, this could be a bad time to ask," Kinsley started, "but I don't suppose you brought protection?" She laughed nervously. "I mean, it's not like you think about things like that when you're gearing up. I wouldn't expect you to have anything like that. I know I didn't think to pack it."

T-Mac sealed her mouth with a kiss. "Knowing you were on this mission, I packed extra first-aid supplies and even tossed in some protection. Don't ask me why. My gut instinct has never steered me wrong."

"Hear, hear for your gut." She kissed him hard and once again straddled his hips, skimming her already wet entrance over his rock-hard staff. "So, where is it?"

"You were serious about skipping the foreplay," he said.

"Damn right. Life's short—you have go for what you want… Be in the moment. You never know when fate will hand you a treasure or stab you in the heart."

"Speaking from experience?" he asked softly.

She nodded. The starlight shining in through the window glinted off moisture in her eyes.

He gripped her arms. "Did you lose someone you cared about?"

Again, she nodded without speaking.

His heart wrenched and he asked the question he wasn't certain he wanted the answer to. "Someone you loved?"

* * *

Kinsley had spent the past two years trying to heal her broken heart and pushing past her fear of losing someone she cared about enough to let herself fall in love again. She thought she was well on her way to doing just that, until she'd hunkered down outside an Al-Shabaab camp, waiting for T-Mac to appear. All that old fear and anxiety had surfaced and practically consumed her.

Now that T-Mac was safe and in her arms, she couldn't let another moment go by without really being with him. She'd spoken her truth about seizing the moment. They might not have tomorrow together. If Al-Shabaab caught up with them, or the rules of Camp Lemonnier kept them apart, they would have only this one moment in time to pack into their memories. Kinsley was determined to make the most of it.

Their military careers would keep them apart tomorrow, but they had the night.

Kinsley held out her hand. "If you'll hand me the protection, we can get this show on the road."

T-Mac shook his head. "Not so fast. You might not think foreplay is necessary, but I want you to be every bit as turned on as I am before I come into you."

A shiver of anticipation rippled across her skin. "What exactly did you have in mind?"

"This." In one fluid motion, he turned her over and pinned her to the seat and cushion of clothing.

She giggled. "Are you always so eager with your women?"

T-Mac kissed her forehead and the tip of her nose, and nibbled her left earlobe before replying. "Just so you know, I don't have women. I'm not celibate, but there's no woman in my life except the one lying beneath me at this moment."

Her body heated at his warm, resonant tone. "I'd understand if you had a female in every port."

"That's nice. But I don't." He trailed kisses down the side of her throat and lingered at the base, where her pulse beat hard and fast.

Kinsley squirmed beneath him, wanting more than just his lips, more than kisses.

Then he moved down her body, trailing his mouth, his tongue and his hands. He slowed to suck one of her nipples between his teeth and rolled it around.

She arched her back off the seat, pressing her body closer, a moan rising up her throat.

He flicked the hardened bud of her nipple with his tongue again and again. Then he moved to take the other nipple into his mouth and gave it the same delicious treatment.

Kinsley's core tightened, coiled and heated. She threaded her hands in his hair, urging him to take more.

He did, pulling hard on her breast, alternating between flicking and nipping at the tip.

Then he abandoned her breasts and moved lower, skimming across her ribs, tonguing a warm trail, stopping to dip into her belly button. When he reached her mound of curls, he parted her folds and dragged his finger across that strip of flesh tightly packed with nerves.

A moan rose up Kinsley's throat, and she dug her fingernails into his scalp. "Oh…dear…sweet…"

He touched her there with the tip of his tongue.

Kinsley moaned again, her hips rising to meet that tongue, willing him to do that again.

T-Mac swept a warm, wet path through her folds and dipped a finger into her slick channel.

Her entire body quivering, Kinsley ached for what came next. She wanted him. Inside her. Now.

But he wasn't finished with her. Apparently, he wanted to torture her into submission, one incredibly delicious lick or stroke at a time.

His tongue worked magic on her nubbin while his fingers teased her entrance and dipped in, first one, then another until three stretched her opening, preparing her for him.

Tension built inside, centering at her core. Her muscles tightened and she dug her feet into the seat cushion, pressing upward. "Please," she begged.

"Please what?"

"I want you."

He chuckled, his warm breath playing across her wetness. "Sweetheart, you have me."

"No. Now. Inside me," she said, her voice breathy. She couldn't breathe, she was so caught up in the sensations he evoked. "I need you."

"But you're not there yet." He blew a stream of warm air across her nubbin and then flicked it with his tongue.

A shock of electricity ripped through her from the point where T-Mac touched her all the way out to the tips of her fingers, tingling all the way.

He flicked again and again, refusing to let up and give her a chance to fill her lungs, think or pull herself together. She came apart at the seams, rocketing to the stratosphere, any modesty left in the dust of the African desert gone. She soared into the heavens, crying out his name as she launched.

For a long moment, she remained suspended, somewhere between earth and heaven, every nerve on fire, her blood moving like molten lava through her veins.

When she finally came back to earth, she tugged on T-Mac's hair. "Now. I need you now," she said, her voice hoarse with emotion.

He crawled up her body, leaned up on his knees and grabbed the foil package he'd set on the dash earlier. He tore open one end and shook out the protection into his palm.

Impatient, and past caring how pushy she looked, Kinsley snatched the item from his palm and rolled it over his distended erection.

When he was fully sheathed, she positioned him between her legs.

T-Mac took over, pressing against her entrance, his gaze meeting hers. "Tell me to stop, and I will." He gave her a crooked grin. "It'll be hard, but I can walk away if you change your mind."

Before he finished talking, she was already shaking her head. "You're not walking away now." She gripped his buttocks in both hands and pulled him closer. He penetrated her, easing in, careful not to hurt her, giving her channel time to adjust to his girth.

The deliberateness was excruciating. More painful than anything, and she could do nothing to stop it. She almost pounded her forehead in frustration. Why did he insist on going so slowly? Gripping his bottom, she guided him in and out, setting a rhythm both comforting and exciting.

T-Mac drove deep, filling her to completely full,

stretching her inside and creating a friction so wonderful, it set her body on fire.

She urged him to go faster and faster, until he pounded into her like a piston.

Kinsley rose up to greet each thrust with one of her own. The slapping sound of skin on skin echoed inside the truck cab.

T-Mac's body stiffened. He thrust one last time, going as deep as he could get and froze, his shaft pulsing with his release. His breathing came in ragged breaths, his chest heaving, a sheen of perspiration making his body glisten in the starlight penetrating through the windshield.

When at last he relaxed, he lay down on her, covering her body with his. He gathered her in his arms and kissed her long, hard and thoroughly, stealing her breath away and caressing her tongue.

When at last he eased off to let her fill her lungs again, she let go of a shaky laugh. "Wow."

He chuckled. "That's all? Just *wow*?"

"You so rocked my world, my brain is mush and my vocabulary reduced to one-syllable words. Thus…*wow*."

He lifted her off the seat, removed the condom and settled his body on the cushion, draping her over his chest. "This way I don't crush you."

"I'd die a happy death." She laid her head against his heart and listened to the fast, steady rhythm. "Think Al-Shabaab will find us tonight?"

"I doubt it," he said.

"Good." Her fingers curled softly into his chest. "Then you can stay with me."

He rested his hand over hers. "Someone needs to stay awake in case they find us."

"I'm willing to risk it if you are."

He inhaled deeply, the movement raising her up and then lowering her downward. "Much as I'd like to lay here with you and feel your body against mine all night, I'd better get out there and keep both eyes open."

She sighed. "Wake me in an hour and a half. I'll take the next watch."

He didn't answer, just shifted into a sitting position, levering her across his lap. He cupped her breasts in his palms. "You know, you're beautiful beneath all that camouflage."

She wiggled against his stiff erection. "You're not so bad yourself." Kinsley leaned into his palms. "Care to go for round two?"

"I'd love to, but I only had the one condom."

"It's too bad we're not close to a drugstore." She cupped his cheeks and bussed his lips with a hard kiss. "Thank you."

He smiled. "For what?"

"For not being selfish, and making it just as good for me as it was for you." Kinsley frowned. "It was good for you, wasn't it?"

"Darlin', if it had been any better, I would be passed out or dead from a heart attack." He lifted her off his lap and set her on the seat beside him. He dragged on his trousers and boots and then slipped out the passenger door to stand on the ground.

Kinsley dressed in her bra, T-shirt and panties, her gaze on T-Mac as he covered his glorious body one item of clothing at a time. What a shame that he had to cover all that taut skin and those bulging muscles.

She dragged her trousers up her legs and buttoned them, then pulled on her boots with a sigh. They were back in uniform, back to reality. Soon, they would be back at Camp Lemonnier, where they wouldn't even be able to hold hands or kiss without the threat of an Article 15.

"Sleep. You don't know what tomorrow might bring," T-Mac said. "You'll need your strength." He left her alone in the truck and disappeared around the giant boulder to take up a position where he could watch the road.

With a yawn, Kinsley leaned over the back of the seat to check on Agar.

He lifted his nose and touched her hand.

"At least I will have you after the SEALs redeploy back to the States."

Agar nudged her hand and licked her fingers.

There had been a time when she thought loving Agar was enough. His loyalty was unquestioned, his love unconditional. But he wasn't a man. Kinsley hadn't realized just how much she needed the warmth and physical contact only a man could give her.

Until T-Mac entered her life.

She hadn't known what she was missing.

Now she did. And he would ship out, leaving a giant hole in her heart and soul.

She lay on the seat, her head resting on her bent arm. A single tear slipped from the corner of her eye and splashed onto the seat.

Crying accomplished nothing. So she limited it to the one tear. When T-Mac was gone, she might have to shed a few more. Until then, she wouldn't think that far ahead.

Chapter 12

T-Mac didn't wake Kinsley after an hour and a half. Nor did he wake her at two hours. Not a single vehicle had gone by on the road. He couldn't be certain one hadn't passed while he was making love to Kinsley, but he doubted it.

Which meant the Al-Shabaab faction hadn't made it out of the camp at a decent hour, unless they'd slipped by him while he'd been otherwise occupied.

He cursed himself for losing his concentration and focus. Their lives depended on him staying aware and on top of the situation. Sex in a truck wasn't going to keep them alive.

But oh, it had felt amazing. Having Kinsley in his arms hadn't gotten her out of his system. If anything, holding her made him want her even more.

The woman was tough as nails on the outside and all soft and vulnerable on the inside. And she'd fit perfectly against him, their bodies seemingly made for each other.

He found himself trying to figure out how a navy SEAL and an army dog handler could make a long-distance relationship work. Throughout the night, he worked it over in his mind and came to one conclusion. As long as they were both on active duty, a relationship between them was doomed before it started.

Who was he kidding? They would never be on the same base, and probably not in the same state or even the same continent. Why go through the heartache of separation, as often as he was on call and deployed?

Why was he even thinking that way? He was a navy SEAL. He didn't have any right to expect a woman to give up all she knew and loved to follow him around the country or world, only to be stuck somewhere, waiting for him to come home.

He'd been an idiot to make love to her. Satisfying his base needs could only hurt her in the long run. And make it harder to let go when he left.

A couple times during the night, he'd almost nodded off. Each time, he'd imagine Kinsley wearing a dress, standing in the doorway of a cute little cottage with a white picket fence, sending him off or welcoming him home.

But that image clashed with the reality of what and who she was. She'd trained to be a dog handler. Surely, she would never be content to stay behind and keep the home fires burning.

He admired his teammates' ability to find love and

the ways they'd worked out the difficulties of maintaining a relationship even when they were separated. If they could do it, why not him?

Because Kinsley belonged to the army. She had a commitment to serve. She couldn't move around from navy base to navy base and still do what she did. The army didn't care if she was married to a navy guy. They'd send her wherever they needed her.

T-Mac wished Big Jake or Harm were there. He could sure use some advice, or just a sounding board. He had a lot on his mind and he couldn't seem to push any of it aside.

The first gray light of dawn pushed over the tops of the hills, creating long shadows and warming the air.

They needed to get on the road to Djibouti. The sooner the better. He'd made up his mind that they would take the route through Ethiopia, hopefully avoiding Al-Shabaab all together.

As much as he hated doing it, he got up, brushed off the dust and walked back to the truck to wake Kinsley.

When he looked inside, the truck was empty. His heart leaped into his throat and he shot a glance around the truck, the cliff and the giant boulder. Kinsley was nowhere to be seen.

With his heart pounding and a sweat breaking out on his forehead, T-Mac spun in a circle.

"I'm over here," Kinsley called out, emerging from around another, smaller boulder. "I had to relieve myself."

T-Mac didn't answer, taking a moment to drag air back into his lungs and calm his racing pulse. "You scared me."

She smiled. "I'm sorry. I didn't think about letting you know."

"It's imperative that you let me know where you are at all times. Al-Shabaab isn't above kidnapping women, drugging them and abusing them. They will give you even less slack because you are dressed as a soldier."

Kinsley squared her shoulders. "Bring it on."

T-Mac frowned. "You can't take on all of the Al-Shabaab faction. They have weapons, and they aren't afraid to use them. They don't follow any government. They aren't governed by the Geneva convention and they don't have a code of honor like ours."

Kinsley crossed her arms over her chest. "I can take care of myself, navy guy."

He cupped her chin. "You might think you can. But if these men gang up on you, you have to be ready for the worst."

She pushed her shoulders back and lifted her chin. "Yes, sir." Then she leaned her face into his open palm. "I'll play it safe."

"Good." He bent to kiss her, unable to resist her lips, swollen from his kisses. "What am I going to do with you?"

"I asked myself the same question all night long," she admitted.

He stared down into her eyes.

Kinsley met his gaze, unblinking. "How do two people from two totally separate military branches even dare to get together? You have to be all kinds of stupid to allow it to happen."

He chuckled. "Call me stupid."

"And me." She turned her face and pressed a kiss

into his palm. "But we can't get hung up on what's going on here."

"You're right," he agreed. "We have to get back to Camp Lemonnier and report what we found in that Al-Shabaab camp."

"Right." She cupped the back of his hand. "And what happened here, last night, will stay here." Her lips twisted into a tight frown. "It can't go any further."

T-Mac wanted to disagree. He opened his mouth to do just that, but closed it nearly as fast. Kinsley was right. They couldn't go there. Anything between them was doomed. "You're right. We have a job to do. We need to focus on getting it done."

Though he knew it would only prolong the pain, he pulled her into his arms and kissed her hard.

At first she stood stiffly. Then her hands slid up the back of his neck and cupped his head, pulling him closer. She opened to him, allowing him to sweep in and caress her tongue with his. He accepted her offering, greedily tasting her, holding her and giving back all she gave him.

Agar brought them back to their senses. He pressed a warm, wet nose between them.

Kinsley leaned back and laughed shakily. "Hey, boy. Are you not getting the attention you deserve?" She lowered her hand to his head and scratched him behind the ears.

T-Mac dropped his hands lower, cupping the small of her back. He leaned forward and kissed her forehead, then swept his mouth lightly across her lips. Then he stepped away. "We have to get going. The sooner we get back, or find a phone to call for a lift, the better."

Kinsley pressed a hand to her lips and nodded. "I'm ready."

Agar jumped up into the cab of the truck and sat in the middle between Kinsley and T-Mac.

T-Mac would have preferred Kinsley sitting beside him, but having the dog between them was perhaps the only way he'd keep his hands off the woman.

He needed to concentrate on the road ahead, not on the woman. The men from the Al-Shabaab site would be out for revenge and wouldn't stop short of killing the people responsible for setting off the explosions in their camp and offing three of their men.

T-Mac turned the key in the ignition. The engine didn't make a sound. He did it again with the same result. Damn.

Kinsley held up a hand. "Pop the hood."

"I'll look," he insisted.

"No, you need to turn the key. I had some training in the motor pool. Let me try the usual quick fixes." She hopped out of the truck and ran around to the front.

T-Mac released the hood. Kinsley pushed it up and climbed on the bumper to lean over the engine.

T-Mac tried to see what she was doing, but the hood blocked his vision.

"Try it now," she called out.

He turned the key, and the engine started right away.

Kinsley closed the hood and climbed up into the passenger seat with a grin.

"What was wrong?" he asked as he shifted into Drive and pulled around the big boulder.

"Corrosion on the battery terminals. All I did was wiggle them and break loose some of the crud. If we stop again soon, we need to do a more thorough job of cleaning the posts and connectors."

T-Mac admired the female for her ingenuity. He knew too many who wouldn't have had a clue about engines. "You are an amazing woman, Kinsley."

She shook her head. "Not at all. I just use the brain I have."

T-Mac's chest tightened. The more he knew about her, the more he loved. When the time came to part, he'd have a tough time saying goodbye.

Kinsley sat in the passenger seat with her hand on Agar's back. The dog usually had a way of calming her when she was upset. All she had to do was rest her hand on his fur and the world would right itself.

Not this time. Since losing Jason to an IED explosion, she hadn't thought she'd fall for another military guy. Too much could go wrong and her heart couldn't take another loss like that.

She'd dated Jason for two years and thought she was in love with him, but what she felt for T-Mac seemed much stronger and harder to push aside.

Who would have thought she'd find a man who could rival Jason? Or that she would fall so fast and so hard? She was insane to even consider another relationship with a guy so entrenched in his military career.

No. Just no.

She stared at the road ahead as they angled west toward the border between Somalia and Ethiopia without actually seeing any of the terrain. Her thoughts remained pinned to the man in the driver's seat. In her peripheral vision, she could see him over Agar's head.

T-Mac's lips pressed tightly together, and his hands gripped the steering wheel as he kept the truck on the dirt road, his gaze sweeping the road ahead, the hills to each side and the rearview mirror.

He had a strong jaw and high cheekbones to go with his auburn hair and the dark auburn shadow of his beard.

If they somehow managed to get together, they'd have beautiful redheaded children. She could imagine a little girl with bright hair and T-Mac's startling blue eyes. And a little boy with auburn hair and her green eyes.

Kinsley looked straight ahead. Why was she daydreaming the impossible?

As soon as the SEAL team left, T-Mac would forget she ever existed.

She wouldn't forget him. Not for a long time. But she'd get on with her life, complete her commitment to the army and decide what she wanted to do next. She loved training dogs. Maybe she'd start her own training and boarding facility. And when Agar was retired from duty, she'd apply to adopt him. He deserved a happy forever home. A place with a big yard and lots of room to run and explore.

The truck leaped forward, jerking Kinsley out of her reverie.

"What's wrong?" she asked.

T-Mac's lips thinned and he glanced in the side mirror. "We've got trouble behind us."

Kinsley turned in her seat and stared through the back window, over the boxes and crates. Emerging from the dust cloud behind them were a truck and two motorcycles. The men riding the motorcycles wore the black garb of the Al-Shabaab fighters.

Her pulse banging against her veins, Kinsley fumbled on the floorboard for her rifle.

The truck bounced on the rough dirt road.

T-Mac pushed the accelerator all the way to the floor, but the truck and the motorcycles behind them were catching up.

"Stay down!" he shouted over the roar of the road noise. "They have guns."

No sooner had the word *guns* left his mouth than a bullet hit the back window and exited through the front, leaving a perfect round hole in each.

"Get down!" T-Mac ordered.

"The hell I will." Kinsley crawled over the back seat.

"What are you doing? You're going to get killed."

"No, but I'm going to put the hurt on them." She hit the bullet hole in the window with the butt of her weapon. The glass shattered, but didn't fall. She hit it again. This time shards spilled outside and onto the seat beside her.

Bashing the jagged shards again and again, she cleared the rear window, pointed the rifle through the open space and aimed at the vehicles following them.

One of the motorcycles raced up to the back of the truck.

Though she was being jostled by the bumps in the road, Kinsley steadied her arm as much as possible and stared down the sights at the man on the motorcycle, who was getting close enough that he could eventually hop into the truck.

She took a breath, held it and caressed the trigger.

Her aim was true. The man on the motorcycle jerked sideways, lying over the bike, skidding along the dirt road for a long way before coming to a stop.

"One down!" T-Mac called. "Good shot."

Kinsley didn't respond, her attention on the other motorcycle and truck.

The motorcycle had slowed to run alongside the truck, both of which were speeding toward them.

Kinsley aimed for the driver's window.

Just as she pulled the trigger, their truck hit a rut, throwing her aim off. The bullet went wide.

Undisturbed, she aimed again and pulled the trigger before they hit another bump.

The bullet must have hit close to the driver. He swerved, sending the truck off the side of the road for a moment before straightening and pulling back into the middle.

The motorcycle stayed on the road, gained ground and headed for the driver's side of T-Mac's truck.

Kinsley took aim, sighted down the barrel and pulled the trigger.

The weapon jammed.

"Damn!"

"What?" T-Mac asked.

"Jam." She slapped the magazine from the bottom and pulled the trigger again. Still jammed.

The motorcycle rider pulled alongside the truck. "Watch out!" she called. "Motorcycle coming up on your side." Kinsley pulled back the bolt and found a bullet lodged at a bad angle. She dug in her pocket for the knife she kept handy. She dug out the bullet, slammed the bolt home and rolled down the window in the back seat as the motorcycle rider pulled up beside the truck, holding a handgun.

Kinsley aimed through the window and pulled the trigger.

The weapon jammed again.

Her heart hammering, Kinsley turned the weapon around, leaned out the window and, holding the barrel, used the rifle like a baseball bat and swung as hard as she could, knocking the handgun from the rider's hands and the rider from his seat. He crashed to the ground, the motorcycle slipping sideways under the truck's wheels.

The resulting bump nearly threw Kinsley out of the truck. She was so concerned about keeping hold of her rifle, she forgot to hold on to something to keep from being thrown from the truck. Thankfully, she had her heel hooked beneath the back seat and was able to pull herself and her rifle back inside.

Just in time for the truck behind them to ram into the rear of their vehicle.

Kinsley slammed into the back of T-Mac's seat.

"Are you okay?" he asked.

She pulled herself off the floorboard and up onto the seat, shaken but not injured. "I'm okay."

Then she cleared her weapon, braced it on the rim of the back window, aimed at the driver's windshield and prayed her rifle wouldn't jam.

The trailing vehicle raced forward, full speed.

Kinsley focused down the sights and pulled the trigger.

The bullet flew through the window and into the truck, directly into the driver's-side windshield.

For a moment, the vehicle stayed its course, heading straight for the back of T-Mac's truck.

Kinsley braced for impact, closed her eyes and held on.

A moment passed. Then two. Nothing happened. The truck behind them didn't hit theirs.

Frowning, Kinsley opened her eyes.

The Al-Shabaab vehicle was going so fast that when it spun sideways, it rolled over and over, coming to a halt on its side. Steam rose from the engine, but no one crawled out.

Drawing in a deep breath, Kinsley stared out the back window until the toppled truck became a speck in the distance. She crawled over the seat and settled in the front, her weapon across her lap.

Agar nudged her hand.

She laughed and patted his head, glad she was still alive to do it.

"You weren't kidding when you said you were a good shot," T-Mac said.

"I'm just lucky you were able to keep your cool and drive on."

"We make a good team," T-Mac said.

"Yes," Kinsley agreed. Too bad the military wouldn't keep them together to see how far they'd go on synergy.

Hell, too bad they wouldn't be together for the long haul. But Kinsley couldn't be too sad. Not after what had just happened. At least they were still alive.

Without a tail following them, they drove into Ethiopia, hoping to find a town of sufficient size and infrastructure where they might find a working telephone.

After two hours on the dirt road, they finally entered

such a town. And none too soon. The gas gauge had dipped low. Fortunately, there was a place to purchase fuel, and that station had a telephone.

After going through several operators, he got one who understood how to connect him to an operator at Camp Lemonnier, and he was able to talk with his commander.

Kinsley waited nearby, feeling more hopeful than she had since they got separated from the rest of the SEAL team.

When T-Mac completed the call, he smiled in her direction, making her day brighter. "They're sending a helicopter to collect us. They should be here in two hours."

"What about the motor-pool truck?" she asked.

"I mentioned it to Commander Ward. He didn't give a damn about the truck." T-Mac grinned. "He was just glad to hear from us. They sent a couple of Black Hawks out to the site this morning. Everyone was gone."

"We expected that. They were packing up when you hit them with the explosions."

T-Mac nodded. "The commander figured we might have had something to do with the abandoned vehicles and scorched fuel barrels."

"You did a number on them." Kinsley glanced around the little town. "I don't suppose we could find some food here?" she suggested.

"I'm hungry too, but I'd just as soon wait until we get back to Camp Lemonnier. At least I'll know what I'm eating."

"Agreed." Her belly rumbled loudly. "Where will they land the choppers?"

"On the road headed northeast out of town," T-Mac

said. He paid the man for the fuel, thanked him for the use of the phone and held the passenger door while Kinsley climbed up into the cab.

In silence, T-Mac closed the door and climbed into the driver's seat. He sat for a moment with his hand on the key. He opened his mouth as if to say something, but closed it without uttering a word.

Kinsley wondered what he'd been about to say, but didn't ask. Her emotions were still on overload from making love to the man the previous night, followed by the adrenaline rush of being attacked.

If he said anything about forgetting what happened, or pretending it never did, she wasn't sure how she'd react. The only thing she was certain of was that her heart was 100 percent involved.

Dang. She didn't need that kind of complication.

Chapter 13

T-Mac drove a few miles out of the small town and parked the truck in a clear area with only one tree for hundreds of yards. The helicopter would be able to land easily, and T-Mac would be able to watch both directions. If Al-Shabaab decided to send more mercenaries their way, T-Mac needed to see them enough in advance to know whether they should stand fast and defend or run.

For the time being, the road was clear and the sun shone down, burning into the roof of the vehicle, making it unbearably hot inside.

"I'll park in the shade." He positioned the truck beneath the low-hanging branches. Then he climbed down, rounded the hood to the other side and opened the door for Kinsley.

He held out his hand. "We'll be back before you know it."

Kinsley laid her fingers across his palm, but didn't get out of the truck immediately. "About last night..." Her voice was low, husky and sexy as hell.

T-Mac's groin tightened at the mere mention of the previous night. "What about it?"

"We're headed back to camp," she blurted out.

He gave her a tight little smile. "Don't worry, I won't tell anyone. My career is just as much on the line as yours."

She laughed, the sound more nervous than humorous. "No. I mean... I just..." Kinsley flung her hands in the air. "What I'm trying to say is—" She threw herself into his arms and kissed him long and hard.

T-Mac gathered her into his arms and held her in the air, holding her tightly against him, his tongue thrusting between her teeth to sweep across hers.

When he at last lowered her to the ground, he lifted his head and sighed. "We won't get the chance to do that back at the base."

She laughed and leaned her forehead against his chest for a moment. "No, we won't."

He tipped her chin upward. "What are we going to do about us?"

Kinsley shook her head. "I don't think there can be an *us*. Not when we're both on active duty, and we'll be going our separate ways as soon as we leave Djibouti."

"It's hard to believe we've only known each other a few days. I feel like I've known you for a lifetime."

"And I you." She smiled. "And yet, I don't know anything about you. Like what's your favorite color? Do you have any siblings? Are your parents still alive? Where did you grow up?" She cupped his cheek. "None of that matters because I know you here." Her hand moved from his face to his chest. "You're loyal. You care about your team. You take your duty seriously and you love animals. Those are the big things. The rest is just data."

He pressed a kiss to her forehead. "Blue." And kissed the tip of her nose. "You already know I have one sister." He swept his lips across hers. "Yes, my folks are still alive, and before you lost your memory, I told you how I grew up on my father's farm in Nebraska." He held her face between his palms and kissed her lightly. "And I know very little about you, but I know you can fire a rifle, you aren't afraid of going into enemy territory, you can hold your own as a soldier in the army, you care about Agar. You care about your country and you care enough about me to take out a truck driver and two men on motorcycles."

"To be fair, you lit their world on fire with a little C-4." She wrapped her arms around his waist and squeezed gently. "I'll be sad when you leave with your team to redeploy back to the States."

"And I'll be sad when I go." He shook his head. "Maybe we'll see each other back home," he said hopefully.

"The most likely scenario is that you'll be in Virginia, I'll go back to San Antonio or somewhere else equally distant, and we'll get on with our lives and never see each other again."

"Wow, a little negative much?" He brushed a strand of her hair from her face. "I prefer my version."

"I do, too. But reality is, we're both committed to our

careers. We've trained hard to get where we are today. Jetting back and forth across the country or around the world isn't realistic."

"I'll tell you what." He rested his hand on her hips. "If we're both still single—and since I'm a SEAL, I'm pretty sure that'll be the case for me—can we at least meet on the anniversary of our night in Somalia?"

She smiled. "Sure. Why not? But only if we're both single."

"Good. Then I'll have a date." He captured her face in his hands. "But for now I'd like to take advantage of the little bit of time we have alone together to hold you and kiss you."

"I'm in." She snuggled close to him, despite the heat of the desert sun cooking the landscape around them.

Kinsley gave Agar some water from her CamelBak thermos. Then the three of them settled on the ground in the shade of the tree and waited for the helicopter to arrive.

Agar slept while T-Mac kissed Kinsley, held her hand and talked.

While they waited for their transport, T-Mac learned Kinsley's favorite color was red, she had no siblings and her father had passed. She liked watching NFL football but sadly wasn't a Dallas Cowboys fan, preferring the Denver Broncos. She grew up in Colorado Springs, Colorado, and joined the army to earn money for college. She stayed because she enjoyed working with the dogs.

"I like camping and fishing but prefer to shoot animals with a camera, not a gun." She leaned her head against his shoulder. "I don't like to dance, because I'm not very good at it, but I do enjoy slow dancing…with the right person."

"And have you met the right person?"

"I won't lie. I fell in love once. I told you about him. He was a dog handler, too. We thought we might one day have a future together." She sighed. "He and his dog had just identified an IED when the ISIS rebel set it off remotely."

"I'm sorry."

She shrugged. "That's part of the reason why I try not to get involved with military guys. What's the use? They might die or be transferred. I don't know if I can go through that heartache again."

"Will you go through that heartache over me?" T-Mac asked, his arm tightening around her shoulder.

"I'm trying really hard not to fall for you." She tipped her head upward to stare into his eyes. "You're making it really hard on me. Can we stick to the facts that don't mean much?"

"Sorry." He raised his hands in surrender. "Continue."

"Where was I?"

"You like slow dancing."

"Right." She took a breath. "There's not much more. I favor daisies over roses, and I enjoy a cold beer on a hot day, like today, and I really like walking in the rain."

"As hot as it is today, I'd enjoy a cold beer and a little rain as well."

"What about you? Ever been in love?" Kinsley asked.

"No," he said. *Until now,* he didn't add. He feared he was falling hopelessly in love with the army dog handler. But telling her would only make it harder for him and for her when they parted. He'd avoided relationships, knowing how hard they were to maintain for a guy in his career field. He'd never been in love. Kinsey tempted him to break all his self-imposed rules. Was what he was feeling for Kinsey love? His heart skipped several beats and then jerked like a jackhammer.

"Do you want a family?"

"Someday, maybe," he replied. "When I'm not shooting bad guys for a living." He could imagine Kinsley's round belly. She'd be beautiful pregnant with their child. The baby girl would have bright strawberry blond hair like her mother and a smile that would melt every male heart.

Kinsley stiffened. "There's a vehicle coming."

T-Mac leaped to his feet and jerked Kinsley up beside him. They both grabbed their rifles and took up defensive positions, using the truck for cover.

A dilapidated truck loaded with bags of grain, people and livestock trundled by. The folks on the back of the truck waved as they passed.

Kinsley and T-Mac lowered their weapons out of sight and waved back, not letting their guard down completely.

When the truck disappeared and the dust settled, T-Mac and Kinsley sat beneath the tree again.

The afternoon passed entirely too quickly. By the time the helicopter arrived, they were both hungry and ready to be back at Camp Lemonnier, yet T-Mac was sad to leave their little patch of shade where they'd had the time to get to know each other better.

When the chopper came close enough and T-Mac

identified it as one belonging to the US, he stepped out of the shade and waved.

The chopper landed and five men jumped out.

"You old son of a gun." Harm was first to greet him, dragging him into a giant bear hug. "We got a little worried about you when we couldn't find you at the Al-Shabaab camp."

"That's right." Diesel gripped his forearm and pulled him into a hug. "Wasn't as much fun going back to camp without our T-Mac."

"How's the guy who stepped on the mine?"

"It was Stucky. They flew him to Ramstein, Germany," Buck said. "He had multiple lacerations and embedded shrapnel, one piece lodged close to one of his eyes. They're trying to get him to a specialist to save the eye."

"Damn. I hope he'll be okay."

"We all hope for the best." Big Jake limped up to T-Mac. "We saw the damage to the camp. Glad you were able to escape. We were confused when your GPS tracker headed deeper into Somalia."

"I didn't want to lose them, so I sacrificed my tracker. Once I planted it on one of their trucks, I stole one of the vehicles they had in their camp and got the heck out."

"This the truck?" Pitbull called out from where he stood by the vehicle.

"It is."

Pitbull shot a glance toward T-Mac. "Who put the bullet holes in it?"

"Three of the Al-Shabaab fighters caught up to us early this morning."

Pitbull shook his head. "I hope they look worse than this truck."

"They're dead." T-Mac grinned. "Our little dog handler is a crack shot."

Kinsley's cheeks flushed.

Diesel held out his hand to Kinsley. "I'm impressed. You can have my back anytime."

She gripped it and shook. "Thanks."

T-Mac busted through Diesel's grip on Kinsley's hand. "Hey, she's my sidekick."

"Yeah, I get that." Diesel shook his hand. "I've got my own sidekick waiting for me back home."

Harm snapped pictures of the truck and the bumper with the writing.

T-Mac walked to the back of the truck and climbed in. He opened one of the crates and held up an M4A1 rifle. "We can't leave these weapons in the back of that truck. They might fall into the wrong hands."

"Load them into the helicopter," Big Jake said. "We'll take them back to camp for disposal. We need to get back. The commander wants a debrief."

The men loaded the crate of weapons onto the chopper. T-Mac helped Kinsley and Agar up into the fuselage and climbed in to sit beside her. He adjusted her safety harness around her shoulders and lap before buckling his.

"Here." Big Jake handed Kinsley a plastic-wrapped package. "Figured you might be hungry."

"Thank you." Kinsley smiled and opened the package to reveal a sandwich loaded with salami, ham and turkey slices. She moaned.

The sound reminded T-Mac of how she'd moaned

when he'd made love to her the night before. His groin tightened and he looked away from her biting into the sandwich.

"We didn't forget you." Big Jake slapped another sandwich into T-Mac's hands. "Eat up. It's a long flight back and the commander won't let you hit the chow hall or the sack until you debrief him on what happened after we left you."

Pitbull faced T-Mac in the seat across from him. He leaned forward and yelled as the rotor blades spun up to speed. "The boss wasn't too happy with us when we came back without the dog handler."

"You didn't have a choice. You had to get Stucky back before he bled out," T-Mac said.

The men settled back against their seats, the roar of the engine and blades making it too difficult to carry on a conversation.

The chopper lifted off the ground and circled back the way it had come.

T-Mac made short work of the sandwich, feeding bits of bread and meat to Agar.

Kinsley ate a third of her sandwich and fed the rest to Agar. Once she finished the food, she stuffed the plastic wrap into her pocket and leaned her head back, closing her eyes. She let her hand fall between them on the seat where T-Mac's rested.

T-Mac captured her hand in his and held on. If someone noticed, too damned bad. That little bit of contact with Kinsley might be the last he would get before they made it back to all the rules and consequences. He'd be damned if he wasted the opportunity to touch her this one last time.

* * *

Kinsley curled her fingers around T-Mac's. Though the past thirty-six hours had been difficult, she hadn't exactly felt scared. Unless she counted the minutes she'd lain in wait for T-Mac to emerge from the rebel camp. Then, she hadn't been afraid for herself, but for T-Mac. He'd walked right into that camp as bold as day and set off those explosions. Anyone could have caught him. Anyone could have shot him on sight.

Kinsley had been more scared than she'd been in her entire life. She felt as if her heart hadn't started beating again until she'd seen T-Mac behind the wheel of that truck.

Her fingers tightened around his. Now she wanted to hold on to his hand and never let go. She was afraid she'd lose him. Which was silly. Their time together was coming to an end. His team was scheduled to ship out in a day or two. They'd leave and she'd be left behind to continue her mission of supporting operations out of Djibouti. Her deployment was for a full year. She'd been there only a few weeks.

When she'd arrived, she'd been excited to actually put her and Agar's skills to use.

Now that she and Agar had been under fire, she wasn't nearly as excited. More cautious, yes. A little frightened? She'd be a liar if she said she wasn't. Her next engagement with the enemy might be without the SEAL team as backup. She might not be as lucky without them.

She had to face it. T-Mac wouldn't be there every time she went outside the wire, and that made her sad.

Her chest tightened and her eyes burned. A single tear slipped from the corner of her eye, down her cheek.

She raised her free hand to brush away the moisture. Her drill sergeant in Basic Combat Training had assured her vehemently that soldiers didn't cry. Now wasn't a good time to start. Surrounded by SEALs who'd been through a whole lot more, she couldn't show any weakness.

Yet another damned tear slipped down the other cheek, closest to T-Mac.

He raised his hand as if to brush it away, but caught himself before he touched her. Instead, he pushed his hand through his hair and let it drop to his lap.

Kinsley had wanted him to touch her cheek. But she knew any public displays of affection were frowned upon and, in front of his buddies, would be purely awkward. So she sat still, hiding her disappointment, wishing she and T-Mac were alone again where they could hold each other, kiss and touch to their hearts' content.

Kinsley must have fallen asleep on the ride back. The change in the speed of the aircraft and the gentle squeeze on her hand brought her back to consciousness.

The chopper came down on the tarmac and the SEALs piled out.

Still a little groggy from her short nap, Kinsley took her time climbing down.

T-Mac stood on the ground, holding out his hand.

She stumbled and fell into his arms.

He caught her and held her briefly, perhaps hugging her harder than he would a stranger. Then he set her up straight and gathered Agar's lead from the ground where she'd dropped it. "Steady there," he whispered.

She nodded, her cheeks burning. "Thanks."

"We're all due to report to Commander Ward in the command center," Big Jake reminded them.

Kinsley nodded, all her grogginess wiped clean. They were back. Rules and regulations couldn't be ignored. She couldn't hold T-Mac's hand or steal a kiss whenever she liked. Tired, grungy and ready for a shower and a real bed, she squared her shoulders and marched alongside the SEALs, her hand wrapped around Agar's lead. The vacation was over.

Ha! Some vacation. They'd been shot at, nearly blown up and on the run for the past thirty-six hours. And somewhere in there had been the most magical point of her life. Making love with T-Mac had changed everything. Inside, her heart bubbled with the need to shout out how good he'd made her feel. How he'd lit a fire inside the woman in her. Couldn't everyone see that? T-Mac had made her feel so very different.

And she could do nothing about it.

Kinsley pushed her hair behind her ears and tried to tuck it into the back of her shirt. She'd long since lost the elastic band that held it off her face. Yet she would stand in front of the mission commander, in her dirty uniform, and tell him everything that had happened.

Except what she considered the most significant… what had happened between her and T-Mac.

If the truth got out, neither one of their careers would survive. Time to suck it up and be a professional. In order to do that, she'd have to cut all ties and forget what had happened between her and T-Mac.

Like that would ever happen.

Even if she'd never forget her night with the SEAL, she would have to pretend it never took place.

Somehow, she made it through the debrief. When she left the command center, T-Mac cornered her in the shadow of one of the buildings.

"Kinsley, I can't pretend what we have together means nothing. I don't want this to be the end."

Her heart pinching in her chest, Kinsley held up her hand and shook her head. "Don't."

He gripped her arms. "What do you mean?"

"We're on two divergent paths, heading in completely different directions. We are destined to be apart. The sooner we accept that, the better off we'll both be."

He held her arms for a moment longer. When footsteps sounded on the gravel, he dropped his hands. "Is that the way you want it?"

She nodded, her eyes stinging with unshed tears. "It is."

"Very well." He took a step back. "I'll let you have time to think about it. But I can tell you now… I don't give up that easily. I wouldn't have come as far as I have… I wouldn't have made it through SEAL training if I gave up on what I wanted." He leaned closer so only she could hear his next words. "And I want you, Kinsley Anderson. I. Want. You."

Chapter 14

T-Mac walked away from Kinsley, his chest tight, his fists clenched. He wanted to turn and run right back to her and kiss her until she changed her mind. He knew, deep inside, that she wanted him as much as he wanted her. She couldn't have faked her response to him when he'd held her in his arms and made sweet love to her. And she couldn't have faked how much she enjoyed kissing him when they were waiting for the helicopter.

She was a rule follower, and the rules were firmly in place at Camp Lemonnier. Breaking them would get them in trouble, and T-Mac didn't want to jeopardize Kinsley's career. He'd pushed the limits, bent a few rules and done things that could have harmed his own career, but he couldn't sabotage Kinsley's. She loved working with Agar. He knew a dog handler might not always get to work with the same dog. Kinsley knew it, too. If she were reassigned or got off active duty, Agar would still belong to the army. Until he was retired, he'd have to go back to work. With another handler.

If Kinsley got in sufficient trouble, she could be kicked out of the military or reassigned to a different skill set and no longer be allowed to train with the dogs.

T-Mac's strides ate the distance as he passed the motor pool. The acrid scent of something burning irritated his nose. A yell made him slow to a stop and glance around.

"Someone help!" a voice cried out. "Man down!"

T-Mac altered his direction and headed toward the sound—and a growing cloud of black smoke.

As he rounded the corner of the motor-pool building, he could see a young marine dragging another man in uniform across the pavement.

T-Mac ran toward them, grabbed one of the inert man's arms and helped the marine drag him out of the smoke.

Harm, Diesel, Pitbull, Big Jake and Buck appeared beside him.

Buck dove in. "Let me check for a pulse."

T-Mac moved aside while Buck put his medical training to good use. He pressed his fingers to the base of the man's throat and stared at his chest. "No pulse and he's not breathing." Immediately, Buck began compressions against the man's chest. "Breathe for him while I work on his pulse." He pointed at the young marine standing by. "You! Get help."

The marine sprinted toward the next building.

Soon they were surrounded by people. A fire truck

arrived and an ambulance pulled up. The trained medics took over from Buck.

The firefighters went to work on the fire burning inside the building. The medics loaded the injured man into the back of the ambulance and whisked him away to the medical facility, leaving the rest to pick up, clean up and get on with their own work.

T-Mac found the marine who'd originally pulled the man out of the motor-pool building. "What happened?"

The young man shrugged. "I don't know. One minute, Jones was fine. I went to the base exchange to get us a candy bar, and when I got back, smoke was billowing out of the building. I ran in to find Jones on the floor. If you hadn't come along…" He shook his head, his cheeks smudged with soot. "Do you think he'll make it?"

Buck stood beside T-Mac. "We did all we could. It's up to the medics and the doctors now."

"I don't get it. What would have started that fire?" He stared at the building where the firefighters were winding up the hoses.

"You should head to the medical facility and have them check you out for smoke inhalation."

The marine squared his shoulders. "I'm fine. But I'll go check on Jones."

"Seriously, man." Buck touched the man's shoulder. "Smoke inhalation might not hit you immediately. Better safe than sorry."

"Okay. I'll check in with the doc." The marine left.

The SEALs stood staring at the wreckage of the motor-pool building.

"What are the chances," T-Mac mused, "that we find a vehicle from this motor pool in the hands of Al-

Shabaab, and the next thing we know, the motor pool building and all its records are burned to the ground?"

Big Jake shook his head. "Too much of a coincidence."

T-Mac's jaw tightened. "I don't believe in coincidence."

"We still don't know who was after your little dog handler," Harm reminded him.

T-Mac turned away from the building. "You're right."

"Her dog should keep her safe," Diesel assured him.

"Yeah, but he can only do so much." T-Mac left his team and walked toward the containerized living units. His walk became a jog, and then he was sprinting toward the one assigned to Kinsley. When he arrived, he pounded on the door.

When he got no answer, he glanced around wildly. She wasn't anywhere to be seen. He pounded again. "Specialist Anderson!"

A female poked her head out of the unit beside Kinsley's and frowned. "Hey, you might want to keep it down. Some of us work nights."

"Do you know where Specialist Anderson is?" he asked.

"No, but she might be in the shower unit." When T-Mac turned in that direction, the woman added, "I wouldn't go barging in on her. They frown on that kind of thing, you know." She chuckled and closed the door.

"Looking for me?" a voice said behind T-Mac.

He turned to find Kinsley wearing her PT gear and shower shoes. She carried a shower caddie of toiletries and her hair was wound up, turban-style, in a towel. Agar stood at her side, his coat slick and damp.

T-Mac caught himself before he did something stupid, like grab her and pull her into his arms.

She frowned. "Is everything all right?"

He shook his head. "I'm not sure you're safe."

"Why? What happened?"

"There was an accident at the motor pool. A fire and a man knocked unconscious."

Her eyes rounded. "That's awful. Is he going to be okay?"

"I don't know." He explained his concern about the fire coming on the heels of finding the motor-pool truck in the Al-Shabaab camp.

"You think the fire and attack in the motor pool had something to do with the stolen truck?" She pulled the towel from her head, looped it over her shoulder and finger combed her hair.

"What do you think?" he asked, wishing he could run his hands through her wet hair.

"Sounds too coincidental to me." She glanced down at the ground. "Do you think someone is trying to destroy the record of who checked it out?"

"That's what I'm thinking."

"Are all records stored online now?" she asked.

"I'm pretty sure they are," T-Mac said. "But the fire could have destroyed the computer." He lifted his head. "And the data might be stored on a database at a remote server." T-Mac smiled. "I'll check on that."

"In the meantime," Kinsley nodded toward her quarters, "I have a date with a blow dryer."

"Okay then." He stepped aside.

As she passed, he touched her arm. "I'm still not giving up on us."

She sighed and stared at the fingers on her arm. "Do you know how hard it is not to throw myself into your arms?" she whispered. Her gaze rose to meet his. "Just leave me alone. I can't be this close to you and not touch you. It's killing me."

As it was killing him. He nodded. "Don't let your guard down for a minute. Whoever attacked the guy in the motor pool might still consider you a threat."

"I don't know why. It's not like I remember anything from the attack in that village." She pressed her lips together. "But I'll be careful. And Agar will be with me at all times."

"Good." He nodded toward her door. "Let Agar go in first."

She gave him a gentle smile. "I always do." Kinsley turned toward her unit and stopped. "For the unofficial record, I miss being out in the desert, just you and me."

"Then why won't you consider seeing me again?"

Kinsley smiled sadly. "Because it will make the parting even harder. We're both married to our careers."

He smiled. "Then I want a divorce."

"You can't. You and I both have a number of years to complete our obligations." She lifted her head and stared directly into his eyes. "We can't tell the army and navy to go take a hike just because we might want to be together."

"Why not?"

"Because of all the attributes we've identified we like about each other, including loyalty and patriotism."

"But I don't want to give up on you…on us," he said, and reached out for her hand.

She stepped back and glanced right and left. "We

can't be together, and it would be foolish to think otherwise. Long-distance relationships rarely work."

"I'm willing to give it a try."

"I'm not willing to hold you to it."

T-Mac pounded his fist into his palm. "Damn it, Kinsley, why do you have to be so obstinate and…and…" He sighed. "Most likely right."

She smiled, her eyes glistening with what he suspected were unshed tears. "Give it time. You'll forget Djibouti ever happened."

"Nope. Not a possibility. I don't want to forget it, and I suspect you don't either."

"For now, respect my decision," she said, and looked up at him, a tear slipping from the corner of her eye. "Leave me alone."

He inhaled a long, deep breath to calm his hammering heart. Then he let it out. "Okay. For now. But this isn't over. I won't let it be."

"I'm sorry," she said. "It has to be." Then she ducked past him and entered her unit with Agar, shutting the door behind them.

Once the door was closed behind Agar, Kinsley let the tears fall unchecked. She threw herself onto her bunk and hugged her pillow to her face to muffle the sobs. She wanted to be with T-Mac more than she wanted to breathe. But they couldn't abandon their careers. They each had a commitment to uphold. She had three more years on her current enlistment. In three years, they could each find someone else. Someone who wasn't so far away.

Yet Kinsley was certain she wouldn't find anyone

she cared about as much as she'd learned to care about T-Mac in the few short days she'd known him. But he had an important job to do. He needed all his focus to be on staying alive and accomplishing his assigned dangerous missions. Trying to work out the logistics of a long-distance relationship would only make him lose focus. And that could be deadly.

After a good cry, she dried her tears, pulled back her hair, dressed in her uniform and went to the chow hall for dinner. She hoped she wouldn't run into anyone from T-Mac's SEAL team. Agar trotted along at her side.

In the dining facility, she collected a tray of food, not really hungry but knowing she had to keep up her strength should she and Agar be assigned to another mission. At the very least, she might be put back on gate-guard rotation. At that moment, she'd almost prefer the monotony of guarding the entrance of the camp. At least then she wouldn't run the risk of bumping into T-Mac.

Her gaze drifted to the door more often than she cared to admit. Part of her wanted T-Mac to walk through. Another part prayed he wouldn't.

"Mind if I sit with you?" a voice said, drawing her attention away from the entrance.

She looked up to find Mr. Toland hovering over her, holding a tray of food. Kinsley shrugged. "Not at all," she said, though she'd rather be alone with her thoughts. But she didn't want to be rude to the contractor.

"I hear you and one of the navy SEALs have been on quite the adventure."

Using her fork, she stabbed the meat on her platter and cut it with a knife. "If you want to call it that," she replied.

"We all thought you and the SEAL were casualties when you didn't make it back with the others."

"We weren't," she said, stating the obvious.

"I was surprised they sent you out again after your last mission resulted in a concussion."

Tired of the man's conversation, Kinsley turned to him and gave him a direct stare. "I'm sorry, sir, but information about missions is classified. I'm not allowed to discuss the details."

He held up his hands. "Of course. I wouldn't want you to get into trouble."

Good. Then maybe you can go away. She wanted to say the words, but she refused to take out her bad temper on the contractor.

"I was just worried about you. You remind me of my daughter." He smiled. "How are you feeling after the concussion?"

Feeling a little guilty for jumping down the man's throat, Kinsley answered, "Perfectly fine, except for a little memory loss."

"Really?" Mr. Toland nodded. "Sometimes situationally induced concussions can result in memory loss. You don't remember anything before the blow that knocked you unconscious?"

She frowned hard, trying to force the memories out. Finally, she shook her head. "Nothing." *But I feel like I'm forgetting something really important.* She stared into the man's eyes. "You know, like it's right there on the edge of my memory, just waiting to come back." She laughed. "Maybe I just need another knock in the head for it to shake loose." Kinsley shrugged. "At least I didn't forget how to work with Agar or how to hold my fork." She lifted her utensil as proof.

"Strange thing, the brain," Mr. Toland said. "I've heard of people never recalling tragic events. Then I've heard of people suddenly remembering all of it."

"You never know with amnesia." Kinsley wished she could forget how much she cared for T-Mac. Then again, she didn't want to forget, because he was such an important part of her life. He'd shown her how real her emotions could be and how much she wanted that in her life.

She stared down at her tray, giving up on refueling her body. "If you'll excuse me, I think I'll go for a run." She stowed her tray, gathered Agar's lead in her hand and left the dining facility.

The only way she could clear her mind was to run until she was too tired to think. Even then, she doubted she'd forget T-Mac. Most likely, he'd haunt her dreams for years to come.

Outside, she hurried back to her quarters and slipped out of her uniform and into her PT clothes. Agar danced around her, knowing he would be included on her run. The dog needed to blow off steam as much as Kinsley. A run around the perimeter would be just what they both needed.

When she stepped out of her quarters and started for the field beyond, she spotted T-Mac jogging ahead of her.

She almost turned around and went back into her container to hide.

Agar tugged on his lead, eager to get out and run.

Kinsley couldn't disappoint the animal. He needed the exercise, and she had to get used to seeing T-Mac in passing until they left to return to the States. Hadn't his commander said something about them redeploying in four days? That had been a few days before. If they were still on track to return to Virginia, they'd be leaving soon.

Good. At least then she could start down the road to recovery. In the meantime, she jogged behind T-Mac, admiring the way his muscles bunched and how graceful he was when he ran.

Her imagination took her back to when they were lying naked on the front seat of the truck. His buttocks were hard and tight beneath her fingertips.

Her heart beat faster and her breathing became more labored than her slow, steady pace warranted.

When he turned at the far end of the field and circled back toward the living quarters, he spied her. For a moment, he slowed, his brows dipping into a fierce frown.

Kinsley focused on putting one foot in front of the other, if a little slower. She prayed he wouldn't stop and wait, or run back to her. She wasn't sure she could keep up her adamant refusal to see him again, when all she really wanted was to be with him always.

How did this happen? How did she fall for a military guy after losing her first love? She knew the dangers of death and separation.

Thankfully, T-Mac kept running toward their quarters without slowing significantly. As he neared the living area, five of his teammates met him. They put their heads together and spoke in low tones. Whatever they were saying didn't carry on the wind.

Having been a part of their mission task force, Kinsley was interested in what was going on. She might have input into the next operation, and she sure as hell wanted to know if they'd followed the GPS tracking device to where the Al-Shabaab rebels had moved.

Kinsley picked up the pace, racing to the group of men, Agar running easily alongside.

"Hey, Specialist Anderson." Big Jake held out a hand.

Kinsley came to an abrupt stop and took Big Jake's hand in a firm shake. "What's going on?"

"Got word back from the doc at the medical center," Buck said, his lips forming a thin line. "The guy from the motor pool didn't make it."

"Smoke inhalation?" Kinsley guessed.

Buck shook his head. "Blunt force trauma to the back of his skull. We couldn't have saved him."

Kinsley's chest tightened. "Why?"

"Either he knew something or he got in the way of someone burning the building is my guess," Big Jake said.

"The weapons, the truck, they're all part of whatever is going on here at Camp Lemonnier." Kinsley frowned, pushing hard to remember. "I get the feeling I should know something or that I saw something that night I was shot in the chest." She smacked her forehead, angry at her inability to pull those few minutes of her life, seemingly lost. "If only I could remember."

"Don't worry about it," Harm said. "It's probably your mind's way of protecting you. It had to be pretty horrific to see a gun pointed at your chest and not be able to do anything to stop the shooter from pulling the trigger."

"Still…" She sighed. "If only I were a computer with a reboot button."

"On the bright side," Big Jake interjected, "the commander had the UAV team track the GPS you two planted on the Al-Shabaab truck." He paused dramatically.

"And?" T-Mac questioned impatiently.

"The truck led them to their new camp." Big Jake's eyes narrowed. "Once they determined there were no civilians in the way, the UAV team dropped missiles in their midst. They won't be using our weapons and vehicles against us anytime soon."

Kinsley crossed her arms over her chest and her eyes narrowed. "Good riddance. But what happened to capturing one of them to determine who their supplier is?"

"That decision wasn't ours to make," Big Jake said. "The commander decided it wasn't worth risking the lives of our SEALs and dog handler again."

"And we're still due to redeploy back to home base tomorrow," T-Mac said. His gaze captured hers. "Our transport leaves at seven in the morning."

Kinsley's heart plummeted to the pit of her belly, and her knees wobbled. She'd known they would leave soon, but she'd selfishly hoped they would be delayed a few more days. "What about the supplier connection? Isn't Commander Ward concerned about finding the link?"

"He is, but he's bringing in an investigator and working with the intel guys looking into the motor-pool database. He thinks they'll be able to trace back to the man responsible. And since we were able to bring the weapons back, they might be able to pull a serial number and find out who shipped them in the first place."

"So you're done here?" She smiled, though her heart hurt so badly she could barely breathe. "I know you'll be glad to get back home."

"Some of us will be happier than others," Harm said, his eyes sliding sideways, aiming toward T-Mac. "We'd better go pack our gear." He gave a chin lift to the others. "And leave T-Mac to fill in Specialist Anderson on anything we might have left out."

"What did we leave out?" Pitbull asked.

Harm glared at the man and jerked his head toward T-Mac and Kinsley. "I'm sure we've left off something. T-Mac will fill her in." He gave Pitbull a shove. "Sometimes you can be so thickheaded."

"Oh." Pitbull grinned. "You want to let T-Mac have some time alone with his dog handler. Why didn't you say so in the first place?"

Harm raised his face to the heavens. "I'm surrounded by morons."

"Watch it, dude." Pitbull shoved Harm. "I have feelings."

The five SEALs left T-Mac alone with Kinsley.

"I hope you have a good flight back to the States." Kinsley refused to look into T-Mac's eyes. Hers were burning with unshed tears, and if she didn't get away soon, she'd lose it in front of him. "Safe travels," she said, her voice catching. Then she turned and would have run but for the hand that grabbed her elbow and held on.

"I want to see you again."

"No," she whispered, staring down at the hand on her arm. "It's better to end it now than to drag it out."

"Will you be there in the morning when we take off?"

"No." She shook her head. "I have to be on duty at the gate," she lied. Since she'd been tasked to aid the SEAL missions, she hadn't been added back to the gate-inspection schedule. But she couldn't let T-Mac see her standing by, watching them leave. She'd be all red faced and tear streaked. And if she didn't get away from him quickly, she'd be that way all too soon. "I have to go." She ducked past him and ran.

Kinsley had marched right into enemy territory, stood face to face with a killer who had shot her in the chest and fought terrorists from a moving vehicle, but she ran from T-Mac because she was afraid.

She was afraid of losing someone she loved. Again. Maybe her reasoning for running didn't make sense, but she had to get away. He was leaving. She was staying. By the time she returned to the States, he'd be off on his next mission or—worse yet—on to his next girlfriend.

Not that Kinsley was ever his girlfriend. Knowing each other for such a short time shouldn't have made her feel this strongly about T-Mac. But there she was, crying like a baby, her vision blurring so much she ran into someone.

Hands reached out to steady her. "Specialist Anderson, are you all right?"

"I'm fine," she said, and then sniffed loudly and blinked enough to clear her eyes and look up at Mr. Toland. "I'm sorry. I'm just…just… They're leaving in the morning," she cried, and the tears fell faster.

"The navy SEALs?" he asked.

"Yes."

"Things always have a way of working out," he said.

She rubbed her hand over her face, knowing her situation with T-Mac would never work and talking it over with a stranger wouldn't make her feel any better. "I'm sorry. I need to go."

With Agar at her side, Kinsley ran all the way back to her quarters, pushed through the door and collapsed on her small cot. She cried herself to sleep, wishing there was another way.

She'd be up early to watch their plane take off, despite telling him she wouldn't.

Chapter 15

Pounding on the door to the unit T-Mac and Harm shared startled T-Mac awake. He glanced at the clock. Two in the morning. "What the heck?"

"Seriously." Harm swung his legs out of his bunk.

"Wake up, T-Mac!" Big Jake called out from the other side of the door. "We've got orders to move out."

T-Mac pushed the door open. "Thought we weren't leaving until seven."

"Plans changed," Big Jake said. "We have one more operation before we bug out. Gear up. We leave in fifteen."

All sleepiness disappeared in seconds. T-Mac grabbed his go bag and upended it onto his bunk. He jammed his legs into dark pants and boots, pulled a dark T-shirt over his head and slipped a black jacket over his shoulders. He knew the drill, knew exactly what he needed, and in under five minutes he was fully dressed, wearing his body armor vest and carrying enough weapons and ammunition to start his own damned war. He settled his helmet, complete with his night-vision goggles, on his head and slung his M4A1 rifle strap over his shoulder.

Harm finished preparing at the same time.

Together they left the unit and headed for the landing strip, where the helicopters sat with rotor blades turning.

Big Jake, Diesel, Pitbull and Buck were climbing aboard when T-Mac and Harm arrived.

T-Mac hopped on board only to find one more person already there with her dog.

He grinned, happier to see her than he could say out loud. He settled his headset over his ears and waited for the others to do the same.

All the while, he couldn't stop staring at Kinsley where she sat beside him. He reached out and scratched Agar behind the ears.

"Comm check," Big Jake said into his mic.

They went around the interior of the helicopter calling out their names.

"You all might be wondering why we were called out without any warning," Jake started as the rotor blades spun faster and louder.

Everyone nodded.

"Commander Ward received a message from intel that our attack yesterday did not take out the leader of the Al-Shabaab rebels. They were able to locate his position. We have the new coordinates and are tasked with taking him out. If this mission goes well, we'll be back in time to ship out. Maybe not at seven in the morning, but at least by noon."

"Good. Marly's supposed to get back from her chartered flight tomorrow," Pitbull said. "She promised not to fly any more gigs until we've had time to really see each other." He patted his flat belly. "And I have a steak with my name on it back at the steakhouse in Little Creek."

"I can't wait to see Reese," Diesel said. "We're finally going out on an honest-to-goodness date. I'm not sure how to act."

"Talia has been busy redecorating my apartment. I can't wait to test out the new king-size bed," Harm said.

"Angela's been too busy at the hospital to care about the furniture in my apartment," Buck said. "I imagine we'll find a house pretty quickly."

"I can't wait to see Alex." Big Jake smiled. "She should be settled into her new teaching job."

Everyone had someone to go home to back in the States. Everyone but T-Mac. He had everything he wanted in the helicopter at that moment. If he could, he'd extend his stay in Djibouti just to be with Kinsley. This extra mission meant he got to see her one more time. He might even get to hold her hand as they flew to their location.

The Black Hawk lifted off the tarmac and rose into the star-studded night sky.

Moments later they were high above the ground. They headed out over the Gulf of Aden and started to turn south.

A loud bang sounded over the noise-reducing headsets. The helicopter shook violently, and shrapnel pierced the shell.

Kinsley yelped and doubled over, grabbing for T-Mac's hand.

The motor shut down and the helicopter fell from the sky.

Over the headset, the pilot's tense voice sounded. "Brace for landing."

As the chopper lost altitude, T-Mac reached his free hand for the buckles on the harness holding him in his seat. They would have only seconds after hitting the water to get out. If the helicopter rolled upside down, the confusion of which way was up and which was down in the dark would be deadly.

He and his teammates had gone through special training on how to get out of a helicopter that had gone down in the water. They knew how to get out. He'd bet Kinsley had not had similar training.

Based on the way she squeezed his hand, she was scared. Her fear was about to multiply.

Right before the chopper hit the water, it tilted, slowed and then slammed into it. As soon as they hit, buckles popped free and SEALs pushed away from their seats.

T-Mac ripped open his seat-harness buckles and floated free.

The helicopter rolled and filled with water so fast, T-Mac barely had time to pull his arms free of the harness. He let go of Kinsley's hand only for a moment, but that moment was too long. He held his breath, his lungs burning, hands reaching in the darkness, searching for Kinsley.

The arms and legs of his teammates floated against him as they struggled to find their way out through the open doors.

Just when T-Mac's lungs felt as if they would burst, a small hand wrapped around his wrist.

T-Mac grabbed Kinsley's arm and pulled her out of the helicopter and swam for the surface, his own buoyancy leading him in the right direction. A moment later, his head breached and he gulped in air.

Kinsley's head popped up beside him. She coughed and sputtered, dragging in huge breaths. As soon as she stopped coughing, she yelled, "Agar!"

Splashing sounded beside them and Agar dog-paddled over to Kinsley, whining pitifully. T-Mac swam toward them.

"Head count and status!" Big Jake's voice boomed across the water. "Buck."

"Alive and bleeding," Buck called out.

"Pitbull," Big Jake yelled.

"Here," Pitbull answered. "Nothing but a goose egg on my forehead from where Diesel kicked me."

"Harm." Big Jake sputtered and coughed.

"Took some shrapnel to my thigh," Harm said. "But I'm alive. Hurts like hell."

"T-Mac and Specialist Anderson?" Big Jake queried.

"We made it. And Agar's here." T-Mac continued to hold on to Kinsley's hand. If anyone wanted him to let go, they'd have to pry his cold dead fingers loose. He wasn't letting go of her ever again. She treaded water with her free hand but clung to him like a lifeline.

"Commander Ward?" Big Jake called out.

A moment went by.

"Commander?" Big Jake repeated.

"I'm here," he said, his voice weak. "I think my arm is broken."

"Gotcha, sir." Buck swam over to the older man and helped him stay above water.

"What about the pilot and copilot?" Big Jake called out.

"Pilot here. We both made it out, but the Black Hawk is toast."

"What happened?" Big Jake swam up to T-Mac and treaded water.

"Didn't you feel it?" the pilot said. "Someone shot us down."

T-Mac's grip tightened on Kinsley's hand. "That's what it felt like."

"Who the hell would shoot us down from Djibouti?" Harm asked.

"Al-Shabaab?"

"Or whoever is supplying them." T-Mac's jaw tightened as he struggled to tread water with one hand.

"Oh, hell." Kinsley rubbed her forehead with her free hand while kicking her feet to keep her face above the surface.

"What's wrong? Besides being in deep water with no life raft?" T-Mac held on to her, helping to keep her afloat.

"My knee hurts like hell, for one," she said. "And I hit my head coming out of the chopper."

"Are you feeling dizzy? Confused?" Buck swam over to where she bobbed in the water.

T-Mac wished he could get her out of the water and to the nearest medical facility. But they'd have to wait until folks at Camp Lemonnier realized what had happened. "It won't be long. They had to have seen the explosion. We'll get you the help you need."

"No. You don't understand." She pressed her palm to the top of her head. "I… I…remember!" She glanced up and stared across at T-Mac.

"Everything?" T-Mac asked, his heart swelling.

She nodded and struggled to tread water. "Everything."

When the chopper had gone down, Kinsley had braced for the landing. She knew the dangers of landing in the water and had her hands on her seat belt before they crashed into the Gulf of Aden. She'd released her harness a fraction of a second too soon. When they hit, she flew out of the harness and slammed her head against the top of the fuselage, and twisted her leg so hard she'd felt something snap in her knee, accompanied by a sharp stab of pain. She'd seen stars and feared she'd pass out. But all she could think about were T-Mac and Agar. She had to get out to save them.

The knock on her head made her disoriented. When the chopper rolled in the waves, Kinsley went under. Like a movie playing at high speed, her memories flashed through her mind, all the way up to, and including, the current crash. She'd seen her first meeting with T-Mac, the time he had thrown himself into her quarters to protect her from an unexploded package. He'd been so darned sexy.

Memories of her first night out chasing down enemies hung in the background. She remembered leading the SEAL team with Agar. They'd found numerous land mines through the rubble of the little village, Agar doing his thing, following his nose.

Kinsley remembered her jolt of fear when Agar entered that hut. She'd turned the corner and charged into the building before she thought through the consequences.

And then she'd shone her light into the face of someone she recognized. "The man who shot me. I remember who it was!" she said, and dipped below the surface, choking on a mouthful of salt water.

T-Mac jerked her back to the surface. "Breathe," he said. "We'll worry about who it was when we're out of the water."

"But I know who it was. It was that contractor working on the improvements to the camp."

"Which contractor?" the commander asked.

"Toland. William Toland." A gate opened in Kinsley's mind and all the memories flooded in. She pushed through the pain in her knee, relying on one leg and her arms to keep her head above water.

The roar of rotor blades sounded, coming from the direction of Camp Lemonnier.

Joyful relief filled Kinsley. Not only would they survive a crash, she remembered who'd shot her.

"Toland has to be the one responsible for the gun trading and the information leaks," T-Mac said. "Wasn't he involved in renovating the command center?"

"He was," Commander Ward said. "He could have bugged the room with electronic devices."

"Look, when we're taken back to the camp, let everyone believe Specialist Anderson didn't make it. We'll have her delivered directly to the medical facility, but have the doctors announce that she's dead."

"Why?"

"We want Toland to think he's in the clear," Harm said. "The only eyewitness to him being in that Al-Shabaab camp will be dead. He might get careless. At the very least, we'll be able to catch him before he tries to make a run for it."

"Are you game to play dead?" T-Mac asked Kinsley.

"I'd rather be in on the action. That man tried to kill me." She treaded water for a few seconds before adding, "But I have to be realistic. Something's wrong with my knee. I'll play dead, but you have to promise me you'll get him."

"Are you sure it was him?" Harm asked.

"Absolutely," Kinsley said, her arm getting weaker as her strength waned. "I remember seeing his shock of gray hair before he pulled the trigger." Her eyes narrowed. Yeah, she'd like to be there at his takedown. He'd tried to kill her.

"We'll take care of him," T-Mac said, his face dark and hardened into stone.

When the Black Hawk arrived, Kinsley and Agar went up first on the hoist as the chopper hovered over the water. One by one, the rest of the men were reeled in. Buck stabilized her leg by applying a temporary splint. The pain was so bad, Kinsley passed out several times en route back to land.

By the time they returned to camp, it was late. Nevertheless, Kinsley was loaded onto a stretcher and into an ambulance to be delivered to the medical facility. She was sequestered in a room at the back of the building, along with Agar. No one was allowed to enter but the doctor and Commander Ward. The doctor suspected she'd torn her ACL or her meniscus. They'd have to send her back to the States to have an MRI. Fortunately, a C-130 airplane was scheduled to leave the next day. She would be on it. They discussed the plan to declare her dead. The doctor set her up with an IV and pain meds before leaving her and Agar alone.

The commander called in the veterinarian to perform a house call and check Agar over. The dog had been limping so badly, he'd been brought into the medical facility on a stretcher as well. He lay on a bed that had been pushed up to the side of Kinsley's.

When the veterinarian came, he gave Agar pain meds and recommended he be airlifted out along with Kinsley and taken to a veterinarian surgical clinic, where they would have the equipment to better treat the animal.

Kinsley couldn't tell how much time had passed. She floated in and out of a cloud of pain, the morphine the doctor had given her barely taking the edge off.

Kinsley lay on the hospital bed and waited for someone to come tell her that Toland had been captured and locked in the brig. At the very least, she wanted to shower the salt water off her skin. A nurse had helped her out of her uniform and into a hospital gown under strict instructions to keep quiet about Kinsley being alive.

Alone in the hospital bed with Agar in drug-induced sleep, whining every time he moved, Kinsley could only imagine what was happening. Every scenario she came up with ended badly. When she heard footsteps in the hallway, she held her breath and prayed it was T-Mac coming to tell her they'd caught Toland.

The pain medication finally took its toll and claimed Kinsley in sleep.

The gray light of morning edged its way around the shades over the window when Kinsley opened her eyes.

She stared up at the ceiling for a moment, trying to remember where she was and what had happened. Her skin felt sticky, and that's when she recalled all that had happened the night before and all that she'd forgotten from when she'd been shot. She turned her head to see dark red hair lying on the sheet beside her, a big hand holding hers in its grip.

"T-Mac," she whispered, and reached over to smooth her hand through his auburn hair. It wouldn't be so bad to have red-haired children. As long as they looked like the navy SEAL who'd stolen her heart.

He raised his head and stared into her eyes. "Hey, beautiful."

She snorted softly. "Hardly. I'm sure I look like I've been dunked in the ocean and put up wet."

"Which is beautiful to me."

"Did they get Toland?"

"They did. And he confessed to trading the weapons. He was also working with a guy in the motor pool to transport the goods."

"The guy who died?" Kinsley asked.

T-Mac nodded. "Toland killed him to shut him up."

"He admitted to the murder?"

His brows dipping lower, T-Mac pressed his lips together in a tight line. "Toland was more afraid of us than of going to jail. He spilled his guts."

Kinsley sighed. "Good. He'll get what he deserves. The man is a traitor."

"Yes, he is." He leaned across her and pressed his lips to hers. "But all that is done. How are you feeling?"

"Better, now that you're here." She wrapped her arms around his neck and pulled him down to return that kiss with all of her heart.

When they broke away for air, she smiled up at him. "Aren't you afraid we'll get in trouble?"

"I don't really care."

She chuckled. "Me either."

"They should be in soon to load you up into the plane and take you back to the States."

She touched his cheek. "I don't want this to end."

He cupped her hand and pressed a kiss to her palm. "Me either."

"It might not have to." She glanced down at her leg. "I might be medically boarded out."

"The doc thinks you tore your ACL or meniscus."

She nodded.

"And if they medically retire you?" T-Mac looked at her. "What then?"

Her hand slid across the sheet to smooth over Agar's head. The dog whined and tried to lick her fingers.

"I'll probably go on and get that college degree I joined the military for." She met his gaze with a direct one of her own. "If Agar is retired as well, I want to give him a forever home with a yard to run in."

"There are some great colleges in Virginia," T-Mac offered.

"Yeah?" Kinsley smiled, tears welling in her eyes. "Will you want to date a gimpy girl?"

"I'll want you no matter what, my sweet, brave dog handler." He slid onto the bed beside her and carefully gathered her into his arms. "You're amazing, and I want to spend a lot more time getting to know you. Like the rest of my life. Baby, you're the one."

She shook her head. "How do you know I'm the one? We haven't known each other very long."

"A wise old friend of mine told me you don't have to know a person very long to know she's the one for you." He pushed a strand of her hair out of her face. "I didn't believe him, until I met the one person who convinced me."

"And who was that?" Kinsley whispered.

"I think you know."

"Hmm. Maybe I do. You better kiss me before my chariot arrives to take me away. This kiss will have to last me until I see you again." She brushed her lips across his. "Because when you know he's the right one, you just know."

Epilogue

Three months later...

"Need help bringing out that platter of marinated steaks?" T-Mac called out.

"No, I can manage." Kinsley limped out to the patio of the house they'd purchased together in the Little Creek area.

T-Mac smiled at her, his heart so full he couldn't believe how lucky he was to have found the love of his life.

"The gang will be here any minute. Should I put the steaks on right now, or wait to make sure they arrive on time?"

"Wait. The guys like them practically raw." She set the tray of steaks next to the grill.

T-Mac captured her around the waist and pulled her

into his arms, kissing her soundly. "I'm the luckiest man alive."

"Oh, yeah, how's that?" She leaned back against his arms around her middle and smiled up at him.

"I have you, don't I?"

"That makes me the luckiest woman alive."

"Even though you had to give up the army?" He kissed the tip of her nose. "Do you miss it?"

She shrugged. "I do miss helping keep our guys safe. But since Agar and I were both injured and retired, it worked out for the best. I can be around to see to Agar's needs, and you and I get to be together."

A damp nose pushed between T-Mac and Kinsley's legs.

"That's right, Agar. You're loved, too." Kinsley reached down and patted the dog's head.

He would walk with a limp for the rest of his life, but he was retired from active duty and would lead the good life with a big backyard to run in and a soft bed to sleep on.

"Hello! Anyone home?" a voice called out. "The gang's all here." Big Jake stepped through the patio doors with Alexandria Parker at his side.

Behind them were Buck and the love of his life, Dr. Angela Vega.

Diesel came out on the patio with Reese Brantley, the former army bodyguard with the fiery auburn hair and mad fighting skills that served her well in her chosen profession.

Pitbull held hands with Marly Simpson, the bush pilot he'd fallen in love with during a vacation in Africa. She'd relocated to the States and was flying for a charter company.

Harm followed Talia Ryan, the former owner of an African resort.

Talia carried a bottle of wine. "I hope you like red. I thought it would go well with the steak."

Kinsley smiled and took the offering. "I'll save it for later."

T-Mac circled her waist with his arms and grinned at Harm. "Nine months later."

"What?" Harm's jaw dropped. "Nine months? Are you saying what I think you're saying?"

"No kidding?" Buck grinned. "Kinsley's got a bun in the oven?"

Angela frowned. "Do people really say that anymore?" She hugged Kinsley. "I'm so happy for you two."

"When's the wedding?" Big Jake asked. "You have to make an honest woman of her now."

"Next weekend. If you all can make it," T-Mac announced.

"Oh, wow!" Marly exclaimed. "That's great. I'm pretty sure I don't have anything on my schedule that can't be pushed off."

"Where's it going to be?" Talia asked.

Kinsley laughed. "We're having a JP perform the ceremony on Virginia Beach. Someplace Agar can be a part of the ceremony."

"Do you need help with the preparations?" Alexandria asked. "I'm really good with decorations and flower arrangements."

"I'd love some help."

"Have you bought your wedding gown?" Talia asked.

Kinsley's cheeks flushed pink. "No, I haven't."

"Oh, sweetie, we have to get on that," Talia said. "I can help you there. How many bridesmaids and grooms-men?"

"None," T-Mac said. "It's just going to be Kinsley, me, Agar and all of our friends."

"Oh, and your parents and sister are coming," Kinsley added.

"What?" T-Mac frowned. "I haven't even told them I'm getting married."

"They know," she said, her face smug. "And they're so delighted you wanted them here to celebrate."

He laughed and pulled her into his arms. "You are the right one for me. Are they happy about their new grandson?"

"I'll let you share that news with them after the wedding." Kinsley lifted her chin. "But I'm sure they'll be ecstatic about their granddaughter."

Reese laughed. "Too early to know whether you're having a girl or boy?"

T-Mac nodded. "Yeah, and we won't until the ba-by's born."

"Oh, that's not fair. We want to know what it is," Buck complained.

"And you will." T-Mac said. "When the baby comes."

Harm shook his head. "I can't believe you're getting married before the rest of us." He pulled Talia into the circle of his arms. "I just got Talia to agree to marry me."

"Seriously?" T-Mac shook his friend's hand and then hugged his fiancée. "I'm really happy for you two." He turned to Talia. "You're getting a great guy."

"I know." She smiled up into Harm's eyes. "He's been patient with me through my move back to the States. I wasn't sure I wanted to get married again. I loved my first husband so much. But I've learned I can love again, and Harm's the man who showed me how."

The others all gathered around to congratulate Harm and Talia, T-Mac and Kinsley.

"Anyone else holding out on us?" T-Mac asked. "Speak now before I put the steaks on the grill."

"Alex got a job teaching at the elementary school around the corner from our apartment," Jake said. "The kids all love her. And so do I." He hugged Alex and gave her a big kiss.

"I have an announcement," Buck said.

"That you're getting off active duty and going back to medical school?" Diesel guessed.

Buck frowned. "Hey, I was supposed to say that. How did you know? But yes, I was accepted into medical school. I start next spring."

Diesel opened the cooler he'd brought with him and tossed Buck a can of beer. "It's about damned time. You're going to make a great doctor. You and Angela can open your own practice when you're done."

"Anyone else?" T-Mac asked.

"I'm giving up my gig as a bodyguard," Reese announced.

Diesel frowned. "That's news to me. I thought you liked it."

"I did, but it's not really conducive to pregnant women." A smile spread across Reese's face.

"Pregnant?" Diesel's face went from shocked to joyous. "Are you kidding?" He lifted her off the ground and spun her around. "Really?" He lowered her to her feet and stared down into her eyes. "Sweetheart, I love you so much." He dropped to his knee and held her hand in his. "Will you marry me?"

Reese laughed. "You don't have to ask me if you don't want to marry me. I like things the way they are now. Why ruin it by getting married?"

Diesel straightened and gathered Reese in his arms. "Because I love you and would be honored if you'd be my partner, my lover and my friend in marriage."

"To love, honor and swing from tree to tree?" Pitbull joked.

"I'd do it, if she said *yes*," Diesel said, his gaze never leaving Reese's. "Will you marry me, Reese Brantley?"

She smiled up at him and nodded. "I will."

"Next week? Can we make it a double wedding on the beach?"

Reese gave T-Mac and Kinsley a nervous smile. "They might want to have a wedding all to themselves. I don't want to butt in."

"The more the merrier," T-Mac said.

"It's a great idea," Kinsley agreed. "And our babies will grow up together. How wonderful."

"Well, damn," Pitbull said. "We're not keeping up with the rest of them." He started to bend down on one knee, but Marly beat him to it.

Marly held up her hand. "Before you start, let me say something."

Pitbull frowned.

"Will you marry me?" she asked, and grinned. "Beat you to it."

"Damn woman. Is this how it's going to be?" He

pulled her into his arms and kissed her on the lips. "Because if it is, I'm in. Yes. I will."

More congratulations were offered.

T-Mac finally got the steaks on the grill, and he stood back with an arm around Kinsley, Agar lying at their feet and surrounded by the men and women who were so much a part of his life, they were like family.

"I'm truly the luckiest man alive," he said.

Kinsley leaned into him and smiled. "I love you, Trace McGuire. I'm glad you didn't give up on me."

* * * * *

Elizabeth Heiter likes her suspense to feature strong heroines, chilling villains, psychological twists and a little romance. Her research has taken her into the minds of serial killers, through murder investigations and onto the FBI Academy's shooting range. Elizabeth graduated from the University of Michigan with a degree in English literature. She's a member of International Thriller Writers and Romance Writers of America. Visit Elizabeth at www.elizabethheiter.com.

Books by Elizabeth Heiter

Harlequin Intrigue

K-9 Defense
Secret Investigation

The Lawmen: Bullets and Brawn

Bodyguard with a Badge
Police Protector
Secret Agent Surrender

The Lawmen

Disarming Detective
Seduced by the Sniper
SWAT Secret Admirer

Visit the Author Profile page
at Harlequin.com for more titles.

K-9 DEFENSE

Elizabeth Heiter

Over the years, I've been lucky enough to have many loyal companions like Rebel. This book is for all my furry, feathered and scaled family members.

Acknowledgments

Thank you to Denise Zaza for suggesting I write a book with a hunky hero and a K-9 partner—I had so much fun creating Colter and Rebel! To everyone involved behind the scenes with *K-9 Defense*— I appreciate everything you do. Finally, thank you to my family and friends, who are always willing to lend their support on my crazy writing journey. Special thanks to Kevan Lyon, Andrew Gulli, Chris Heiter, Robbie Terman, Kathryn Merhar, Caroline Heiter, Ann Forsaith, Charles Shipps, Sasha Orr, Nora Smith and Mark Nalbach.

Chapter 1

"I'm still alive."

Three simple words in a note. A note signed by the sister Kensie Morgan hadn't seen in fourteen years had sent her in a frantic rush across 3,500 miles. Kensie had left a brief message on her boss's voice mail, telling him she needed some time off, then called her family. They'd been less supportive.

But this time, Kensie had to believe, the lead could be real.

The hope had buoyed her from one layover to the next, warmed her as she stepped off the plane in Alaska. For early October, the temperature was way colder than she'd expected, and it had only gotten worse as she'd paid for her rental pickup truck and headed north.

Desparre, Alaska, was the kind of place you came

to to drop off the map. The sort of place no one would think to look—and even if they did, they might never make it out.

After her GPS had given up and she'd made a half dozen wrong turns, she'd finally been able to get directions from a local into town. Now Kensie shivered as she stepped out of her truck for the first time in four hours. Her heavy down jacket was no match for the windchill, so she tugged up the collar as strong gusts whipped her long hair around her face. There was no avoiding the snow covering the walkways, so Kensie trudged through it. Her next stop after the police station was going to be for a new pair of boots.

Her fingers tingled from the cold and she clenched them into tight fists in her pockets, hoping the motion would also ease her nerves. She'd planned to make the store where her sister's note had been found her first stop, but when she couldn't find it, she'd given up and headed into the main part of town.

Kensie glanced around, taking in the assortment of buildings—post office, clothing store, bar, drug store, grocery store, church. She felt like she'd stepped back in time to the eighteen hundreds. The only thing missing was horse-drawn carriages. But it was probably too cold for horses. Even the monstrous all-weather truck parked up the street seemed ill prepared for Desparre once winter descended.

Chicago got cold, but after not even one day in Desparre she was longing for the ridiculously cold-but-not-*this*-cold windchill off the lake.

With the exception of a guy playing with his dog down the road, she was the only fool outside. Kensie hustled, careful not to slide in the snow as she yanked open the door to the tiny police station. Her stomach churned as reality set in. She was finally here.

This time will be different, she told herself, trying to bolster her courage.

The officer behind the counter looked up as she entered, but she wasn't sure if the scowl on his face was for her or the blast of cold air she brought inside. "Can I help you?"

Desparre probably didn't get a lot of outsiders, so she was going to stand out here. Kensie had gotten the same questioning looks each time she'd stopped to ask for directions on the outskirts of town.

If her sister Alanna really was here, maybe she'd be the one to find Kensie.

If only it could be that easy. But fourteen years of bright, painful hope drawn out for days or years and then dashed in yet another dead end, in yet another godforsaken town, told her that nothing about finding Alanna would be easy.

But if the note was real…

The hope that bloomed inside her now brought tears to her eyes.

The officer stood and rushed to her side. "Are you okay? Do you need help?"

She blinked the tears back and prayed her voice would be steady. "I need to talk to someone about the note you found from Alanna Morgan."

Frown lines dug deeper, creating grooves across the officer's forehead. He looked like he belonged in a rocking chair with a couple of grandkids on his knee, not wearing a police uniform. "Why?"

"I'm her sister."

The flash of emotions on his face was quick, so quick Kensie might have missed them if she hadn't seen them so many times in her life. Surprise, discomfort and pity first. Then something hard and distant—law enforcement probably learned to compartmentalize to keep themselves from going crazy case after case, victim after victim.

"You shouldn't have come all this way. Didn't you talk to the FBI?"

The FBI had spoken to her and her family, of course. They'd been the ones to call and inform Kensie about the note found in Desparre in the first place. But that didn't matter. "I needed to see for myself."

The frown was back, this time mixed with worry, but the officer nodded, patted her on the arm and then said, "I'll be right back."

He disappeared through a door marked Police Only and Kensie took a deep breath.

You can do this, she reminded herself. She was just out of practice. It had been years since the last lead on Alanna.

Standing in a police station now took her back to her childhood. All those years of waiting in hard plastic chairs, her mom's hand clutching hers way too tight, as they prayed for any shred of good news. Her dad standing stiffly beside them, his arm wrapped around her brother, holding him close as if that could keep him safe. Officers catching her gaze and then looking quickly away. Kensie's palms damp and her heart thudding way too fast.

Missing Alanna. Knowing it was all her fault her little sister was gone.

"Ma'am?"

Kensie looked up, realizing her eyes had glazed over as she'd stared at the floor, getting lost in her past. She stiffened her shoulders, tried to look like the professional woman she'd become instead of the terrified thirteen-year-old who always reappeared whenever she heard Alanna's name.

She held out a cold hand, shook hard and stared the new officer directly in the eye. Let her know she couldn't be sent off with a "sorry" and a pat on the back.

"I'm Chief Hernandez."

From the slight grin the chief gave, Kensie's surprise probably showed. She was young for a police chief, likely only a few years older than Kensie's twenty-seven.

But there was wisdom in her steady gaze and strength in her handshake.

"Kensie Morgan. I want to see the note that was left at the store."

Chief Hernandez held out her other hand and Kensie reached for the computer paper.

It was a photocopy, but her heart beat faster at the slanted cursive handwriting. She read it aloud. "My name is Alanna Morgan, from Chicago. I'm still alive. I'm not the only one."

"You recognize the writing?" the chief asked, skepticism in her voice.

"Alanna's? No." How could she? Her sister had been five years old when she'd been kidnapped out of their front yard. At five, everything had been big sloppy letters, forming words that were often misspelled. There was no way to know what Alanna's handwriting looked like now. If she was really still alive, she'd be nineteen.

Nineteen. The very idea made pain and longing mingle. What would a nineteen-year-old Alanna look like? What had happened in all the years between? Kensie had missed all of her sister's milestones.

Focus on now, Kensie reminded herself. *Focus on what you can change.* "What do you know?"

Chief Hernandez shrugged, then frowned, like she regretted the motion. "Not much, I'm afraid. We don't know who left it. We can't be sure it's even real. It says—"

"I know," Kensie cut her off, not wanting to hear a repeat of the FBI's depressing analysis. "But you must know something. What about the store owner who found it?"

"It was in a stack of bills. He couldn't even say who put it there or when."

Chief Hernandez tilted her head in what Kensie had long ago come to recognize as a pity gesture. "I'm sorry. You came a long way for nothing."

The tears surprised her. They rushed hard and fast to her eyes and Kensie ducked her head, trying to blink them back.

"Miss Morgan—"

"Thanks," she said, handing back the photocopy of the evidence—the photocopy of what might be her little sister's writing. Without another word, she rushed out the door.

This time, the cold was just what she needed. It slammed into her face, stinging her eyes and probably freezing the tears on her cheeks.

Get it together, she told herself. Ducking her head

against the wind, she hurried for her rental, parked across the street.

It didn't matter what the police thought. It didn't matter what the FBI thought. It only mattered what her heart was screaming.

Alanna was still alive. And Kensie might finally be able to bring her home.

The gunning of an engine ripped her from her hopeful thoughts. Her head jerked up and right, toward the source of the sound.

A station wagon the size of a small boat was plowing down the street, spraying snow and coming straight for her.

Colter Hayes didn't know what happened.

One second, his retired Military Working Dog, Rebel, was goofing off, chasing a stick as naturally as she'd once tracked dangerous bombers back to their hideouts. The next, she was racing away from him so fast he knew her injured leg would be acting up later.

He heard the engine a second after that, spotted the old station wagon careening around the corner, cutting through the slippery snow way too fast. And a woman frozen in the middle of the street.

"Move!" he screamed at the woman, cursing the injury in his own leg—sustained at the same time as Rebel's—as he raced for both of them.

He'd never make it in time.

The world around him seemed to move in slow motion as panic shot up his throat, mingling with the cold and making it hard to breathe. The car slip-sliding out of control. His five-year-old Malinois–German shepherd mix—the only friend he had left in the world—running straight in front of it.

Colter pushed his leg as hard as he could, trying to follow, trying to be of any use at all. But it was no good.

Rebel leapt up high, slamming into the woman's chest with her front legs, knocking both of them out of sight as the car raced past Colter. It slowed for a second, then sped off.

The panic dropped lower, making his chest hurt and his heart beat too fast. The memory of a year ago, of Rebel jumping on him as a bullet passed so close he felt its trajectory over his head, made it hard to breathe.

He tried to push it out of his mind, willed himself not to fall into that darkness as he raced across the street, sliding in the snow toward the two figures lying prone on the ground. He dropped to his knees, ignoring the *pop* in his knee and the pain that rushed up his thigh.

Another memory from a year ago, of surgery after surgery as he begged to know the condition of his unit. No one would tell him.

Colter blinked the present back into focus.

Rebel climbed off the woman, her movements a little stiff. She nudged her way under his arm, like she knew he was hurt.

Colter dug one hand into the soft fur on Rebel's back, reassuring himself she hadn't been hit.

Still lying flat, the woman groaned and reached a trembling hand up to the back of her head, poking around like she was searching for blood. But her hand came back clean and he helped her to a sitting position.

She stared at him with haunting brown eyes framed by dark lashes. Long, silky dark hair slid over her shoulders and across the back of his hand. The kind of woman he wouldn't have been able to resist once upon a time.

But she was as stupid as she was gorgeous.

"What were you thinking? Crossing the road without paying any attention?" His voice rose even as Rebel pushed her wet nose into his neck, something that usually made him laugh.

But nothing could make him laugh today. "You almost got yourself killed. You almost got my dog killed!"

"I'm so sorry," she whispered, sounding more shell-shocked than scared at her near miss. She reached a still-trembling hand out toward Rebel, gently stroking his dog's brown-and-black fur.

Rebel ate it up, the little traitor, giving the woman a solid push with her nose as if to ask for more.

The woman laughed, a deep, rich sound that seemed to curl around his body.

Colter scowled at both of them, but tried to keep his anger in check. Stupid or not, she had almost died a few minutes ago. And she wasn't a soldier in battle, but a civilian clearly out of place in Alaska.

To his surprise, his voice came out calm, almost soothing. "Let's get you out of the street before another car comes through. Everyone's going too fast today. Living here, they *should* know how to drive in the snow, but with the first snowfall of the season, it's like everyone forgets."

"Thanks," she whispered in that same soft, slightly husky voice.

It would have been a voice for his dreams, back when he had dreams. These days it was nothing but nightmares.

"Come on, girl," he told Rebel as he planted his hands in the snow and pushed himself clumsily to his feet.

"Are you okay?" the woman asked, her eyes even wider than they'd been a minute ago.

"Yeah, fine." It felt like his knee was on fire, but experience told him it didn't warrant a trip to the doctor. He'd just twisted it wrong and the rod and screws holding together his right thigh didn't appreciate it.

He had a few nights of ice and elevation in his future, but he'd been through worse. Much worse.

"I'm so sorry." Her voice wobbled, like she was on the verge of tears.

He prayed she'd keep them in check. "It's not your fault. It's a war injury." He held out a hand to help her up, but she frowned at it, climbing slowly to her feet on her own.

Colter felt his face redden. At six foot two and 180 pounds of mostly muscle—even after his injury—people had always looked to him for help physically. The snub now hurt more than the hit to his knee had.

Once they were safely on the sidewalk, she shuffled her feet. She shoved her hands into the pockets of her too-thin coat, another dead giveaway she wasn't from around here. It looked warm enough, but it wasn't cut out for Desparre's coming winter.

Her gaze darted from him to Rebel and then off into the distance, as if she was afraid he was going to yell at her again.

Colter held in a sigh. Beautiful or not, he didn't have the energy to coddle her. But she was starting to tremble, and he figured it was as much the realization of her near miss setting in as the cold. So he tried for a smile.

It felt unnatural, as if those muscles had forgotten how to work, but she seemed to relax a little. "I'm Colter Hayes. And this is Rebel."

She held out her hand. "Kensie Morgan."

He had her hand in a firm grip before the last name sank in. It had been all over the news a few weeks ago. "Morgan. As in—"

"Yes. I'm Alanna Morgan's sister. I came here to find her."

Although he could feel the tremble in her hand, her voice was strong, almost daring him to challenge her ability. Not that he'd dare. If there was one thing he understood, it was loyalty to a sibling, blood related or not.

And hope. He understood how hope could keep you going, when everything inside you screamed it was time to give up. "I hope you do find her."

"Thanks," she replied as he reluctantly let go of her hand. "Rebel is amazing. I froze and then she just— she saved my life."

"She was a military dog. A Gunnery Sergeant, in fact." One rank higher than his own, because the military taught soldiers to respect their K-9 partners.

"Really?" Kensie's gaze dipped to Rebel, whose tail wagged as they talked about her.

"Yeah." He didn't know why he'd shared that. Now that Kensie was looking less shaken up, he needed to get out of there. Away from the intensity in her eyes and the fullness of her lips. Away from the sudden physical attraction that took him by surprise.

"What did she do in the military?"

"Combat Tracker Dog," Colter said quickly, knowing that, like most people, she'd probably have no idea what that meant. "You should get out of the cold. You're not dressed for Desparre."

Even though her lips were taking on the slightest tinge of blue, she didn't seem to notice the cold—or his suggestion—as she stared at Rebel. "Tracker?"

There was too much hope in her voice. A dozen swear words lodged in Colter's brain. "Not that kind of tracker."

"But what—"

"She tracked back to perpetrators from explosion sites." Just saying the words filled his mind up with images of a military convoy, blown to bits. Bomb fragments lodged in everything. Limbs not attached to people. Friends, gone in an instant.

An L-shaped ambush that had come in two waves, one for the people he'd come to help and one for the responders. His chest started to compress again, the edges of his vision dulling.

"But couldn't she—"

"No," Colter snapped, more harshly than he'd intended.

Even if he and Rebel did the kind of tracking she wanted, she had no idea what she was asking. If he tried to help her, he knew what would happen. He'd have a mission again. A reason to reconnect with the world.

And connections meant pain.

"I'm sorry," he added over his shoulder as he spun away from her, whistling for Rebel to follow.

Chapter 2

Kensie Morgan was trouble.

Colter watched her image shrink in his rearview mirror and tried to tell himself he'd done the right thing. The truth was, he longed to turn around and promise to help her, even though he really *wasn't* that kind of tracker. And neither was Rebel.

From the back seat, she let out a short howl, as if she disagreed with his choice to leave.

"She's no good for us, girl."

His conversation with Kensie felt like the longest sustained chat he'd had with anyone in a year. He knew it wasn't, but maybe she was just the first person he'd felt connected to in all that time. The first person he'd actually wanted to stay and talk to longer. And that was dangerous territory.

Cowardly or not, he was finished with human connection. He had Rebel; he had the sheer, uncomplicated beauty of Alaska. That was enough for him.

Rebel didn't mind the nightmares. She probably had them too, poor girl. And now that they'd both been cut loose from the service, she wasn't going to go and die on him anytime soon. As long as she stopped saving people's lives.

She nudged her head between the front seats, resting her chin on his arm as he maneuvered up the winding, unpaved road toward his cabin. It was up high, which made the trek tricky during the worst of winter, but the view was worth it.

Staring out over miles of nothing but snow-topped trees and breathing in the crisp, cold air, so unlike the deserts where he'd served, brought him as close to peace as he figured he'd ever get. And once a military man, always a military man. There was just something about having the high ground that helped him relax.

His closest neighbor was miles away, down in the valley. He rarely saw other vehicles on his ride out of town, and never in the last few miles. A vehicle coming up the final hill meant someone was coming to see him. And no one came to see him.

His parents still called him regularly, certain he had to be lonely. But they'd been afraid of the trip to Desparre, of the wild animals they were certain roamed everywhere and the thick, heavy winters that sometimes prevented travel in or out until spring came around again. They couldn't understand why he'd come here. But then, they'd never really understood him. Not when he'd joined the military right out of high school and not a decade later when he'd been forced to leave it.

They loved him, but they didn't realize what he'd been looking for or what he'd lost. Brotherhood. A bond he shared with no one but Rebel these days, because she'd been in the thick of it with him.

As he slowed the truck to a stop in front of his cabin, his breathing evened out. All the open space did that for him. Beside him, Rebel seemed to relax, too.

He opened the driver's side door, telling Rebel to stay as he hobbled around to the back. Normally she hopped into the front and climbed out after him, but he knew her injury almost as well as he knew his own. She might not be showing it, but she was in pain, too.

"Come on, girl," he urged, watching as she stepped gingerly to the ground. She led the way up to the cabin, favoring her back left leg.

"We'll sit by the fire and take it easy tonight," he promised her, earning a half-hearted tail wag.

As soon as he opened the door, she walked straight over and claimed a spot in front of the fireplace.

"Greedy," he teased her, and she gave him a look as if to say, *Get a move on. It's cold in here.*

He'd had the heat set too low, not expecting the cold to come so soon, although he should have been used to it. By the time he'd moved out here last October, the snow had been so high the real estate agent had needed his help clearing it away so they could even open the door.

He cranked the heat up now, then got to work building a fire. He poured Rebel some dog food and dragged it over to her. He was hungry, too, now that dinnertime was approaching, but his leg was more demanding than his stomach. So, instead of cooking, he settled in his recliner, gingerly lifting his right leg and wishing he'd grabbed some ice for it first. But now that he was settled, he didn't plan to move for a few hours.

Between the heater kicking on and the fireplace warming the cabin even more, Colter's stiff muscles slowly started to relax. An hour later, his leg was still throbbing unhappily, but the pain was a lot more manageable.

With the fire roaring away on one side of him, the view of the valley covered in snow through a thick-paned window on the other and Rebel at his side, Colter felt complete. This was why he'd come to Alaska. Yes, his parents' claim was true—he was hiding here. But he was hiding from all the well-meaning but clueless people—them included—who wanted to *fix* him. Who had no idea what it meant to survive an ambush when all of his brothers had died.

Rebel whimpered and when Colter glanced at her, he could swear she knew what he was thinking. "It's okay, girl."

But instead of calming down, she stood, went to the window and started barking.

Someone was here. And since there was no one in Alaska he knew well enough to visit his house, it wasn't a guest.

He'd come to Alaska to hide from what was left of his life. Yeah, he could admit that. But there were plenty of other people who saw Alaska as the final frontier: a place to hide away from something they'd done, to run from the law.

Colter winced as he swung his injured leg to the ground, then hobbled over to the cabinet against the far wall and grabbed his pistol. He'd stopped carrying it into town, but right now he was happy he hadn't given it up altogether.

"Rebel, quiet," he commanded. In her three years as a Military Working Dog, never once had she disobeyed a command from him.

But today she just barked louder.

Colter released the safety on his pistol and eased toward the door, preparing himself for trouble.

Kensie gripped the steering wheel until her knuckles hurt, stomping her foot on the brake. But it didn't help. Her rental truck still slid backward, angling toward the edge of the road, toward the drop-off beside the steep hill she was trying to climb.

Why did Colter Hayes have to live in the middle of nowhere?

According to the few locals who would talk to her, he was an ex-Marine hiding from the world after being badly injured. No one seemed to know how he'd been injured or why exactly he wanted to hide. In fact, none of them seemed to know much more about him than the few details he'd shared with her on the street. And yet he'd lived in Desparre for almost a year.

"People come this far into the Alaskan wilderness for three reasons, honey," the grocery store owner had told her, then ticked off those reasons on gnarled fingers. "Either they love a good adventure, the kind that's as likely to get them killed as not. Or they want the entire world to leave them the heck alone. Or they've done something they don't want anyone to know about—probably something illegal—and they figure no one will ever track them down here."

Then she'd narrowed her eyes at Kensie. "We all assume Colter is the middle one. But you've got to be careful who you trust."

Her words echoed in Kensie's brain as her truck finally stopped its dangerous backward descent. She kept her foot wedged down hard on the brake, her hands locked tight on the wheel, afraid to move. Should she keep pushing forward or turn back?

She leaned forward, craning her head up at the hill in front of her. Snow was still falling on it, obscuring what was little more than a dirt trail. She had one more crest to go and she wasn't sure if her truck would make it. But she wasn't sure she could turn it around, either.

Now it was her brother Flynn's voice she heard in her head. "You're going to *Alaska*, Kens? Are you crazy? People venture out into the woods there and never come out again. You could die up there and we'd never even know where to start looking."

At the time, she'd thought he was overreacting. He always had when it came to her, even now that they were both adults. He'd already lost his little sister and she knew, somewhere deep down that he'd never admit, he was afraid of losing his big sister, too.

She realized now how ill-prepared she'd been for this trip. Desparre was insular. People here already distrusted each other, but they distrusted her double for being an outsider. Some of them had been nice but ultimately dismissive. Others had just eyed her suspiciously and refused to talk. Questioning as many people in town as she could had told her that either no one knew anything about Alanna other than what they'd read in the news, or they just weren't going to tell her.

But Colter understood this place. And regardless of what he'd said about his tracking skills, she knew one thing. Trackers found people. Whether it was someone who'd set a bomb or someone who'd been kidnapped, she had to believe he could help her.

And she might not be prepared, but she was determined. If Alanna was really here, Kensie wasn't leaving without her.

Assuming she could get up this mountain.

Gritting her teeth, Kensie switched her foot from the brake to the gas as fast as she could, not wanting to lose traction. The truck's wheels spun, spraying snow at a crazy angle, and then it shot forward, up the hill.

Kensie grappled to keep control of the wheel, her muscles aching. The truck veered left, then right, but it kept moving upward until she could see the top of the hill. She was going to make it.

As if thinking those words had been bad luck, the truck veered right again, straight off the side of the road. It sank down several feet, jolting her forward as the front end planted itself in a snowbank.

Kensie swore, tears of frustration pricking her eyes. For fourteen years, leads on Alanna had come and gone like rabbits in a magician's disappearing act. One minute promising and solid and right in front of them. The next minute *poof!* Like they'd never even existed.

This time might be no different. Her family didn't think it was. But they'd come to accept years ago what statistics said was a near certainty: Alanna was gone. She was never coming home.

Kensie had never been able to do that. And she didn't think it was guilt eating at her gut this time, telling her something was here. She had to believe that this time, if she looked hard enough, maybe the magic trick would become real.

Colter could help her. She knew he could. If she could find him. If she could convince him.

Was she even close to where he lived? She had no idea. She assumed she'd followed the directions properly, but what if there'd been a turnoff she'd missed? She could be miles from his cabin.

She peered through the windshield at the snowflakes, falling faster and thicker from the sky. It had been cold when she'd arrived, but temperatures had dropped to near zero in the hours since. And that was down in the main part of town, not up in the mountains where Colter lived.

Fear settled low in her belly as she zipped her coat up to her chin and slid her hood over her head, fastening it tightly. She didn't need to gun the engine to know there was no way she was getting her truck out of this snowbank.

She was walking from here. She just had to pray Colter's cabin was nearby and she wouldn't walk right by it in this snowstorm and then freeze to death.

Chapter 3

The moment she stepped out of the truck, Kensie wondered if she'd made a mistake. Her whole body seemed to ice over as her feet sank into a pile of snow, rising over the tops of her boots. The cold seeped through them, too, soaking her up to midcalf. She had to hold the tops of her boots to make sure they came with her as she climbed out of the snowbank and then her hands were soaked through her gloves.

Enormous snowflakes plopped on her head, sliding down the side of her hood, where some dropped off. The wind sent others flying into her face, where they left a watery trail down her neck and then slipped inside her coat.

She was going to die out here. She could already feel the icy cold in her lungs with every breath. What had she read about extreme cold bursting your lungs?

Calm down, she told herself. Colter's place had to be close. The grocery store owner had said the top of the final hill. There were no more hills to climb. And yet, no cabin.

There were a lot of trees, though, more than she'd expected this high up. She thought she could see a road marker ahead, leading a winding path through them. Colter's cabin could be behind the trees somewhere. But so could bears. Or she could get lost and not be able to find her way back to the truck. Every few steps, she glanced backward.

Soon she could no longer see the truck. Panic built inside her and she paused. Keep moving forward or turn back?

Then she heard it. Or maybe hypothermia had already started to set in and she was imagining the barking.

Kensie started to run. Her lungs protested every breath, painful from the cold, but as she rounded another copse of trees, there it was. A beautiful little cabin with a clear, perfect view of the valley below. She could even see a glacier from here. In other circumstances, she would have paused and soaked in the amazing vista.

Tears of relief spilled over and instantly froze on her cheeks and then Colter was there, his strong arm around her shoulders, leading her into his home.

She didn't even pause at the doorway, wondering if it was really a good idea to trust a man she'd just met. She simply let him help her inside.

As soon as she was through the doorway, Rebel pressed up against her side. The dog stayed with her until Colter pushed her into a big recliner near the fire.

Then Rebel sat primly next to her, soft brown eyes full of worry.

The heat from the fireplace made Kensie shiver. It didn't make any sense, but she couldn't seem to stop as Colter bent down with a pained grunt. He pulled the sopping wet boots from her feet and propped her legs up near the fireplace. Then he peeled the gloves from her hands, rubbing them between his own big, calloused palms until the warmth finally penetrated.

And so did his words. "What are you doing here? Wandering around in this weather is dangerous. Do you have some kind of death wish?"

Before she could bristle, he let out a heavy sigh and stopped rubbing her hands. "Hold them by the fire. I'll make you some cocoa."

"My truck hit a snowbank," she managed through chattering teeth.

"But why were you up here to begin with?" he asked, looking like he wasn't sure he wanted to know the answer as he walked into the connecting kitchen.

"I came to see you. I need your help. No one here will talk to me. But you know them. You know the area. You know how to track—"

"I told you, Kensie, Rebel and I don't do that anymore. And the kind of tracking you're talking about, we never did. It's not the same thing. Dogs are trained to do one thing. You can't just switch them over, make a drug-sniffing dog an explosives one. Doesn't work like that. And finding people without a direct trail? Even if we had a scent to work from, we wouldn't be able to do that."

Kensie felt her shoulders drop. She'd come all this way. This couldn't be the end of it.

Colter kept talking as he put a pot on the little stove and poured in milk and cocoa. She barely heard his words as she thought about the note that had been found. Thought about Alanna, somewhere in the Alaskan wilderness with her kidnapper.

"...Military Police don't do that. In a war zone—"

Kensie's head snapped up. "What did you say?"

"That kind of tracking work," Colter said, as the scent of cocoa filled Kensie's nostrils. "We don't—"

"No, not that. You said you were Military Police?"

"Yeah." The word was full of wariness.

"So, you know how to run an investigation."

"So do the civilian police. And they actually have authority here," Colter said as he handed her a steaming mug of cocoa.

The heat felt wonderful in her hands, the scent tempting her. But she just clutched it and stared up at him. "They don't want to help me."

He frowned as he lowered himself stiffly onto the chair on the other side of the fireplace. "Why not?"

Internally, she cursed her stupidity. If he knew the truth about what the FBI thought, he'd call her crazy, too. He'd probably join the chorus of people trying to get her to return home.

She postponed answering him by taking a gulp of the cocoa. It burned its way down her throat, making her eyes water, but it also seemed to warm her from the inside, so she took another sip and then another. When the mug was almost empty, she lowered it to her lap, realizing her teeth had finally stopped chattering.

Pins and needles danced along her feet and hands, but they'd gone numb when she'd been outside. The painful return of sensation was a good thing.

"Kensie," Colter prompted, staring at her with light blue eyes fringed with pale brown lashes.

He was more than just good-looking. The hard, battle-worn expression he seemed to constantly wear disguised it, but when he stared at her like he was now—with curiosity and sympathy—awareness settled low in her belly.

Suddenly, it wasn't just the scent of cocoa tempting her.

His dark blond hair was cropped close, military style, but she suspected it would be soft if she ran her hands through it. There was no hint of matching scruff on the hard planes of his jaw, but she wanted to slide her hands over the skin there, too, to pull him close and see how much control he'd have if she kissed him.

As she stared, his pupils dilated. Fire seemed to race over the icy surface of her cheeks and she ducked her head, trying to gain control of her emotions.

It had to be the fear of dying all alone of hypothermia. Or the stress of chasing after Alanna. Or maybe she'd just ignored her own needs for too long.

"It's old," Kensie blurted, hoping he hadn't noticed what she realized had been blatant ogling. But of course he had, or she wouldn't have seen the reciprocal attraction.

"What's old?"

She wanted to smile at the confusion in his voice, a little part of her hoping he was still as distracted as she was. The more sensible side of her brain reminded her that she was stranded in his cabin and she barely knew the man.

The voice of reason in her mind won. She straightened in her seat, meeting his gaze with an all-business stare. "The case is fourteen years cold." She shrugged, hoping he'd believe it, because it was the truth. It just wasn't the whole truth.

She rubbed Rebel's chin with her free hand, to distract herself from the lie by omission. She prayed he wouldn't read it on her face.

"So, they're not going to help you?" He sounded incredulous and a little outraged.

The combination just made her like him more. But she couldn't afford to be distracted by him. Not when Alanna might be out there somewhere. Not when everything inside of her was screaming that he could be the break she'd been waiting for most of her life.

And she had him. She could feel it. He sympathized with her pain and he had skills she'd never possess. With his help, they might really be able to bring Alanna home.

"It's a resources thing." She paraphrased what she'd been told hundreds of times over the years. Police always had to work on new cases, missing persons who hadn't been gone for years, who had a higher chance of rescue. The longer someone was missing, the less chance they had of ever being found.

Years ago, they'd first learned the realities about Alanna coming home as months went by with less and less interest from the police and the community. Her parents had made a promise. They'd do whatever it took to be sure that wasn't Alanna's fate.

But fourteen years of disappointment and two other children who needed them had taken its toll. Kensie knew it was her turn to take up the torch and keep that promise.

She stared expectantly at Colter, sensing his next words would be a wary agreement to try and help.

But he just shook his head sadly. "Believe me, I understand your pain, Kensie. Probably better than you realize. But I'm no good for you. I'm no good for anyone. I can't help you."

Maybe she *was* crazy.

It wasn't just her parents and Flynn who'd begged her not to fly out to Alaska on a questionable piece of evidence and a thin thread of hope. It was also her friends, the ones who'd been by her side since childhood, who'd watched how the constant surge of hope followed by inevitable, bitter disappointment had almost torn them all apart.

She'd overheard family friends talking about how Flynn's car accident had been a necessary wake-up call for her parents, reminding them they still had two children who needed them. And in some ways, it had. But it had also been the day they'd decided to accept something Kensie never would: that Alanna was gone for good.

But right now, hopelessness reared up.

After his announcement that he wouldn't help her, Colter had gone outside to dig out her truck over her objections. The whole time he'd been gone, she was worried he'd hurt his leg or freeze out there. But he'd bundled up in much better winter gear than she owned and forty-five minutes later, he'd reappeared.

She could tell he was trying to hide how badly his leg hurt, so she'd forced herself to keep quiet rather than asking. But guilt had followed her closely as Colter drove behind her rental all the way back into town. She'd parked by the police station where she'd first seen him playing fetch with Rebel, rolled down her window and debated what to say. She'd known him only a few hours and yet she'd been struggling to say goodbye.

Apparently, he had no such quandary. He'd given her a wave, a solemn "Good luck," and off he and Rebel had gone.

She'd probably never see them again.

The idea left a bad taste in her mouth.

But right now, she had to figure out how to move forward. She'd come here alone, with no expectation of help from an ex-Marine with investigative and tracking experience. Nothing had changed. She could still do this alone.

As many times as she told herself that, she still felt Colter's absence like a huge blow to her goal of finding Alanna. And maybe a little bit of a personal blow, too, although she didn't know him well enough to feel anything more than unsatisfied lust.

"Get over it," Kensie muttered. If Colter wouldn't help her, she'd do it herself.

After her experience slamming into that snowbank up near Colter's cabin, her first stop should have been to get better winter gear. But down in the main part of town, the snow was slowing and the accumulation was much less. Only an inch or two of slushy white coated the streets.

More than a pair of warm boots, Kensie needed a mental boost. Something had to go right, something to reassure her that she wasn't chasing a ghost. Maybe there would be a lead at the store where the note had been found. If she could locate the store itself.

Having an immediate goal made Kensie feel better. She steeled herself as she stepped out of her rental and back into the cold, but couldn't stop the shiver that raced up her spine. As quickly as possible, she stomped back into the grocery store where the woman had helped her before.

The instant Kensie walked inside, the woman—who was probably the owner as well as the cashier—looked up. Her steel-gray eyes, the same shade as her long braid, were sharp and knowing. "He was no help?"

Kensie shrugged in response, not wanting to bad-mouth Colter after he'd whipped her up a pot of cocoa, warmed her hands between his own and dug her truck out of the snow despite a badly injured leg. "It was a silly idea," she said instead.

The woman let out a grunt that sounded like she disagreed. "What else do you need?"

A small smile tugged at Kensie's lips. Living in a place like this must teach you to read people. As the bell dinged behind her, announcing another customer, Kensie said, "Colter Hayes has his own troubles. But I still need to find the store where the note was found. Do you think you could draw me a map? The roads are really confusing out here."

"That's because our roads are what you city folk

would call hiking trails. Honey, you might want to wait until the snow clears. It's out on the edge of town—so far out, most people don't even think of it as part of Desparre. Owned by a cranky old guy who's as likely to close for the day as not if the mood strikes."

Ignoring the little voice in her head reminding her what had happened when she insisted on driving to Colter's place in this weather, Kensie shook her head. "I want to try today. I need some good news right now."

"He might not have any."

"I know," Kensie said over the lump that had risen in her throat. She swallowed the discomfort back. She had to stay positive.

If she didn't keep searching for her sister, who would?

"All right," the woman agreed with a deep frown that told Kensie she didn't approve. But she drew a map and explained it three times.

Kensie thanked her, then headed back into the cold. She eyed the clothing store down the street, wondering if they'd have better winter gear, then looked up. The sun was hanging low, casting beautiful shades of red and orange across the sky. If she wanted to talk to the owner and get back to her hotel before it got dark, she needed to go now.

A tap on her shoulder made Kensie jump.

The man standing there backed up a step as she turned to face him. "Sorry, I didn't mean to startle you."

He was almost as tall and muscular as Colter. Almost as good-looking too, with jet-black hair and chocolate-brown eyes. Kensie lowered her arms.

"I heard you talking to Talise." She must have looked

perplexed, because he added, "In the grocery store. You're looking for Jasper's General Store?"

Kensie nodded, clutching the hand-drawn map she still wasn't completely certain she could follow.

"I can take you if you want. My truck's right over there." He pointed to a massive vehicle parked in front of hers.

It was probably much more solid in the snow than her rental, but what did she know about this guy? Back home, she'd never get into a truck with a stranger. Of course, back home, she never would have driven out to a stranger's cabin, either.

Because even though a little voice in her head kept insisting she and Colter had a connection, the reality was that she didn't know him.

As if reading her thoughts, the guy stuck out his hand. "I'm Danny Weston. Former military just like your friend Colter." He gave her a big, crooked, boyish-looking grin. "Although Colter was Marines. I was Air Force. Grunts versus high flyers. Just kidding," he added as she took his hand.

It closed loosely around her own, as if he was afraid to hurt her as he shook. Then he gave her a firm shake anyway. Must have been a military thing.

Kensie had an internal debate. She didn't know Danny, but she didn't know Colter, either. And that had turned out fine. Besides, this was about her sister. *If it wasn't for me, Alanna never would have been kidnapped.* Kensie nodded to Danny. "Yeah, that would be great. Thank you."

"Sure." He led her over to the massive vehicle and held open the passenger door. "We can talk to old Jasper and then I'll have you back here in an hour, before it gets dark."

The last of her doubts fled as she settled into the comfortable passenger seat. "That sounds perfect."

Danny smiled at her again, then slammed the door shut and ran around to the driver's side. He started up the engine and was just stretching his seatbelt across his lap when the driver's door was ripped open and he went flying out of the truck.

Surprise and panic shot through her as Kensie's gaze darted to the perpetrator. Colter.

"Get out of the truck now!" Colter yelled at her, his voice deep and commanding. Rebel stood beside and slightly behind him, teeth bared.

The panic intensified. She fumbled with her seatbelt as Danny climbed to his feet. She tried to open the door, but there was no door handle on the inside, just an empty space where it should have been.

Kensie shoved at the door, but nothing happened. She launched herself across the bench seat, straight toward Danny.

He was squaring off, facing Colter, as though he was about to take a swing. But across the street, people were starting to come out of businesses, maybe because they'd heard Colter's yell.

Danny paused, and while she still could, Kensie shoved herself out of the truck. Her body brushed past him and he started to turn toward her.

Her heart was pounding out of control, her limbs heavy and awkward in her fear. Then Colter's hand closed around hers, pulling her first to him and then shoving her behind him. The fear shifted, no longer for her own safety.

Two men who'd come out of the hardware store were slowly walking their way. Talise stood outside with a cell phone to her ear and her eyes on the police station down the road.

She knew Colter was strong from the way he'd practically lifted her off her feet just now, but with his bad leg, would Danny hurt him? Kensie's whole body began to shake as she glanced back toward the police station, willing officers to come outside.

"Drive away while you still can," Colter said in a low, menacing tone that sent shivers up her arms.

Rebel crouched low on her haunches and took a slow step forward, growling deep in her throat.

Danny took one last glance at the approaching townspeople, then gave Rebel a nervous look. He let out a string of nasty curses directed at Colter. Then he jumped in the truck and pulled away so fast she and Colter had to leap backward to avoid being hit.

As soon as Danny was gone, Colter spun toward her. The fury on his face was unlike anything she'd ever seen. His jaw was hard, his lips turned out in a near snarl. His eyes were narrowed into furious slits. But he took a deep breath and the tension disappeared, his face smoothing back into what seemed to be his default—not happy and mild, but serious and steady.

Next to him, Rebel straightened, then sat, as if nothing had happened.

"I'll help you," he told her.

"What?" She was almost more shocked than when he'd pulled Danny out of his truck.

"On one condition."

"Okay."

"It's just me, Kensie. You don't get into some random jerk's truck. That guy—" He broke off, blowing out a breath, then finished. "*I* help you and no one else."

The fear that had filled her a moment ago drained away, leaving her exhausted. But a smile built up inside. This was what she needed. This was *who* she needed. Colter was her best chance to change everything that hurt in her life.

He held out a hand. "We have a deal?"

Kensie placed her hand in his, liking the way his fingers closed solidly over hers, as if he knew she was strong enough not to be crushed. "Deal."

Chapter 4

Danny Weston had nearly kicked his ass.

Colter shoved down the embarrassment and tried to be thankful for the show of support from the townspeople. Despite the fact that he'd been here almost a year, the people of Desparre barely knew him. But they probably knew Danny. And what they knew, he was pretty sure they didn't like.

On a good day, Colter could take a guy like Danny down with ease. But it had been a long time since he'd had a good day. He knew his limitations and, right now, his leg was screaming at him.

It was a small price compared to the one his brothers had paid, but it stung to be so useless in a situation he should have been able to handle himself. Some badass Staff Sergeant he was.

Of course, he wasn't a military man at all anymore, except in his mind.

Turning around and heading back into town after he'd dropped Kensie off had been a fluke. A nagging sense that he'd regret it if he didn't help her look for her sister, even if he had no idea where to start.

He glanced at her now, absently petting Rebel from the seat beside him. Her lips were clenched in a tight line and her head was bowed slightly, as though Desparre was beating her. She'd barely said a word since she'd followed him back to his truck, but she'd done a poor job of hiding her shaking.

Anger at Danny for making her feel that way overtook his embarrassment, but even that was quickly eclipsed by fear. Fear over what could have happened if she'd ridden off in Danny's truck instead of his.

And nothing had been done about it. Police had shown up and taken his statement—and Kensie's, about the missing door handle inside Danny's truck. But the officers had shaken their heads, telling Colter he was lucky Danny wasn't pressing charges for assault. When Colter argued about the door handle—obviously meant to keep someone trapped—they'd said it wasn't a crime to have a broken truck.

As someone who'd run investigations himself, Colter understood their dilemma. But that same experience told him Danny was still a threat.

He shot another glance Kensie's way, unable to stop himself from drinking in a quick look at her. Reassuring himself she was safe.

Catching his look, she said softly, "Danny said he was Air Force. I thought I could trust him."

"I really am a Marine," Colter blurted.

Thankfully, she looked more perplexed than startled by his outburst.

"An MP. Military Police," he clarified. "I served for almost a decade, rose to the rank of Staff Sergeant. I doubt Danny Weston's gotten any closer to the service than walking past a recruiting booth."

"I shouldn't have believed him."

Her voice was so low he almost didn't catch it. His hands tightened on the wheel of his truck as he continued his slow, steady drive along one of Desparre's back roads out of town. "The guy's a creep, but he's smart. Good at getting people to trust him. Especially women."

"I think he was in the grocery store. He heard me talking about you. It seemed like he knew you."

"Yeah, he knows me. But we're not friends." Colter and Danny had crossed paths a few times since he'd moved to Desparre. Once had been in the bar where Danny was trying a little too hard to get a local woman to go home with him. Colter had walked her to her car, but he suspected if there hadn't been people watching, Danny would have come at him that night. A few times since, Colter had seen him around, and the guy had set his radar off.

He had no idea what had brought Danny to Desparre, but he suspected it wasn't good. And he didn't trust the guy within a mile of Kensie.

"Just steer clear of him, Kensie."

"Yeah, I got it."

There was an edge to her voice that he suspected came as much from fear as it did from anger.

He drew in a deep breath through his nose, trying

to calm his emotions. Yeah, it hadn't been smart of her to get into a stranger's truck, but how mad could he be when he'd essentially asked her to do the same thing with him?

She didn't know him. She was acting on blind faith and desperation. They were feelings he knew well. As much as he didn't want to get involved in anything remotely resembling a mission, he couldn't let that desperation lead her into danger again.

Because if Alanna had been grabbed by a guy like Danny, it was probably already too late to save her.

The errant thought left a bitter taste in his mouth and he shoved back the inevitable memories that followed, of the last moments he'd seen the brothers he'd loved. Brothers he would have traded his own life for if he could have.

He prayed Kensie wouldn't have to live with the same grief.

"So, the store," he said, trying to clear the fog that always threatened whenever he thought about that day, his last day in the military. "Tell me what you know."

She glanced his way, her beautiful eyes clearing, like this was the distraction she needed, too. "Not much. Apparently the owner found it in a stack of money. The chief of police told me Jasper didn't know who'd left it there, but I'm thinking we can ask him about everyone who came in that day. Or maybe he'll recognize me. My sister might still resemble me."

Her last words were full of hope and wistfulness, and he tried to remember how cold she'd told him the case was. "You said she disappeared fourteen years ago?"

"Yeah. She'd be nineteen now."

"How old were you when—"

"When she was kidnapped?" Kensie finished. "I was thirteen."

She didn't offer any more, so Colter let the silence remain, let Rebel take up the task of relaxing Kensie. His dog seemed more than up for it, leaning between the seats and practically hanging her head in Kensie's lap.

"I think she likes me," Kensie said, amusement in her tone.

"Yeah, she transitioned better into civilian life than I did. I think she'd be friends with everyone if she could."

It wasn't totally true. Like most dogs, she seemed to have an innate sense of who she could trust. But she definitely would like it if he'd let more people into his life, give her someone else to spoil her.

Kensie laughed as Rebel nuzzled even closer, her front feet practically in the seat with them now. "Well, thanks for making an exception and being my friend."

Was that what he'd done? He let the idea rattle around in his brain as they pulled up to the store out in a little strip of shops off the beaten path. Yeah, he guessed it was. He'd saved her life, she'd seen his home, and he cared about what happened to her. Plus, he sympathized over what happened to her sister. A year after leaving the military, he'd made his first new friend. As much as he liked Kensie, it left him unsettled.

"Let's go see what we can get out of Jasper." As he spoke the words, a familiar determination filled him, one he'd prayed wouldn't return. The feeling of a mission.

Instantly, his chest tightened and breathing seemed more difficult. The doctors at the VA hospital had told him the PTSD might always be with him. Sometimes it would be flashbacks, other times panic attacks or nightmares. They said he needed to learn to recognize the triggers and manage his response. But that was easier said than done.

Rebel's head swung toward him, her ears twitching. The first few months after he'd gotten out, there were times when something as simple as a branch snapping would send him right back onto that battlefield and the first crack of the sniper rifle. And he wasn't the only one; more than once, he'd found Rebel cowering in the bathtub during a thunderstorm. Or she'd leap on him, trying to protect him from a car backfiring, and re-aggravate both of their injuries.

Rebel knew exactly what was happening right now. But he didn't want Kensie to see his weakness, so he flung open the truck door and practically fell out of it.

The cold air shocked his system, filling his lungs and stopping the spasms in his chest. He clenched and unclenched his fists, a trick he'd learned at the hospital accidentally. It helped ground him, give him control over one small thing.

By the time Rebel leaped to the ground beside him and Kensie hurried around the truck, he felt back in control.

She squinted at him. "You okay?"

"Yeah. Let's do this." It was something he'd always say to Rebel when they were about to track a scent. It came out now without thought, but instead of provoking another attack, it straightened his shoulders and filled him with strength.

Beside him, Rebel seemed to strain forward, even

though she was always off leash. She sensed a new mission as much as he did. Unlike him, she seemed truly ready.

Thank goodness her injury hadn't fully healed.

The selfish thought hit unexpectedly. But if Rebel had healed while he hadn't, she would have been back at war, assigned to a new soldier. The only reason he'd gotten to keep her was that the huge piece of metal that had gone straight through his leg had also pierced her. Neither of them would ever be a hundred percent whole again. Which meant the military didn't want them anymore.

"Okay," Kensie said, obviously not realizing the dark place where his thoughts had traveled. She strode up the snowy walkway toward the store.

He followed, trying not to be distracted by the subtle sway of her hips under her parka. Rebel trotted along beside him, ready for the kind of action she'd been trained to handle.

As soon as they walked through the door, a bell dinged and Jasper Starn glared their way. With his chrome-silver hair slicked back on his head and his dark skin over-weathered by the Alaskan wind, he could have been anywhere between sixty and a hundred. He'd lived somewhere on the outskirts of Desparre and run this store for as long as anyone in town seemed to remember. And he was possibly the crankiest store owner Colter had ever met.

When they approached him instead of walking around the store, Jasper looked them up and down like he was cataloguing places they might be hiding weapons, then grunted.

Seemingly not put off by the less than cordial welcome, Kensie gave him a wide smile. It didn't seem to do much for Jasper's mood, but dang if it didn't make Colter feel a little lighter.

"I'm Kensie Morgan."

His lips pursed, but he made no other sign he'd heard her.

Kensie's smile faltered a little. "I'm Alanna Morgan's sister. I know you found the note—"

"I got nothing to say about that." Jasper cut her off, then angled his glare toward Colter. "No pets in the store. I've told you that before."

Colter nodded at Rebel, who promptly sat. At sixty-five pounds of pure, lean muscle, and always at attention, she could be intimidating. "We just have a few questions. The quicker you answer them, the quicker we're all out of here."

"I already talked to the FBI and the police. You want to know about it, ask them."

Kensie's smile dropped off. Probably she was used to people being accommodating—or at least polite—when she asked them about her missing sister.

Colter took an aggressive step forward, slamming his hand down on the counter. Sensing his mood, Rebel came up next to him, baring her teeth a little.

Then Kensie's hand landed on top of his. It was soft and slender and unexpected and it totally threw him off his game.

"I was there the day she went missing," Kensie said, her voice a pained whisper that made even Jasper freeze. "I was thirteen. I was supposed to be watching her, but

I was reading a book up by the house while she ran around the front yard."

A sudden, wistful smile broke across her face. "Alanna was five. She was wearing this blue flowered dress, covered in dirt because she liked to play with everything. She was so grubby—her hands, her face—but the cutest little kid. She had these dimples you wouldn't even know were there until she grinned, and then this sparkle in her eyes that told you she was about to be trouble."

Kensie took a deep breath and Colter felt the shaking through her hand. He flipped his over and closed it around her palm, trying to give her support even as his mind warned him he was treading in dangerous territory. Connection.

Kensie's fingers spasmed slightly in his, but that was the only sign she'd noticed. Her gaze was laser locked on Jasper. "I saw the car pull up. I saw the guy grab Alanna." Her voice broke. "I dropped my stupid book and ran after them, but they sped away. It was the last time I ever saw her."

Colter had been in Jasper's store more than a dozen times since he'd moved to Desparre. For the first time, he saw the man twitch and his glare soften.

"Look, I'm not playing games here," Jasper said, his tone conciliatory. "I found the note stuck in a stack of money in my cash drawer at the end of the day two weeks ago. I don't know how it got there."

"Okay," Kensie said, leaning forward. "Do you remember any of the people who came in the store that day? Maybe a young woman—about nineteen—who looked like me?"

Jasper's lips twisted as he stared at Kensie. "Maybe. Someone with dark hair like yours did come in that day, but she was with her family. I don't know who she was. Hadn't seen her before and haven't seen her since."

Jasper's was a regular stop for people who really lived off the beaten path. So if Jasper had only seen the girl once—if it was even Alanna—she might have just been passing through.

Kensie's shoulders dropped and her gaze sought his, as if she was looking for him to find a new path forward. But he wasn't sure there was one.

If Alanna had been in the store on her way to some even more remote part of Alaska, how would they ever trace her?

Colter knew what it was like to live with a desperate, burning hope, as painful as it was powerful. But he also knew that sometimes there was relief in release, too. He'd never return to the person he'd been before he lost his brothers. But when he'd woken in the hospital and no one would tell him if his brothers were okay, he'd been frozen. Sometimes he wished he could return to that state of hopeful ignorance, but it meant being stuck, unable to move forward at all.

Finding Alanna might be impossible. If it was, what if Kensie was frozen forever?

"We need to talk to the police."

Colter leveled his best Marine stare at Kensie across the table in the tiny restaurant off the main strip in Desparre. He'd pulled in on a whim because she'd looked so defeated after talking to Jasper that he hadn't just wanted to drop her at her truck all alone. And if he was being honest, he didn't want to say goodbye quite yet.

Because it was a place he came semiregularly and because Desparre was usually low-key, they let Rebel sit beside the booth as he and Kensie quietly sipped coffee. Her eyes were downcast, maybe to avoid his stare. But then, it hadn't worked on her the first four times he'd suggested this course of action.

"What's your hesitation? I know you talked to them once, but they're not going to spill everything they know just because Alanna is your sister. If we go in and ask pointed questions about the note, we might get somewhere."

"Yeah, maybe."

He frowned, trying to figure out if talking to Jasper had discouraged her as much as it had him or if something else was going on. "It's worth a shot, right?" he pressed, surprised with himself for playing cheerleader. He'd known this woman less than a day and already he'd spent more time with her than anyone else since his doctors at the VA hospital. Not only that, he was actually pushing her to press forward, when he'd been the one who'd wanted out in the first place.

Truth be told, he still wanted out. The last thing he needed was a mission. But Kensie had a pull about her he couldn't deny.

She took a heavy breath before meeting his gaze. "You're right."

"Okay, then," he said, forcing himself to sound more cheerful than he felt and praying he wasn't just giving her false hope. "Let's do this."

At his words, Rebel's head popped up and a grin

tugged his lips. This time, instead of leading him down memory lane toward a panic attack, the idea of having a mission just made him feel wistful. If only it happened like that more often. But although he'd gotten better at avoiding triggers, it wasn't the same thing that set him off every time.

"We're not working, girl," he told Rebel, who yawned and settled down on her tummy.

Kensie gave him an incredulous stare. "She understands you, doesn't she?"

His smile grew a little. "You've never had a pet, huh? Trust me, they understand way more than you'd think."

She shook her head. "Nah, we lived in the city until I was ten, then my parents finally decided three kids in a walk-up was too much and moved out to the suburbs. By then I'd kind of given up asking for a pet. I thought Alanna was going to be the one to wear them down about getting a dog. After she was gone, none of us had time for things like that."

Things like what? A childhood? He studied her, trying to imagine what her life had been like after her sister had gone missing. Trying to imagine the guilt she'd internalized at such a young age when it clearly hadn't been her fault.

He knew all about that. He understood how irrational survivor's guilt could be, just like he understood that knowing it didn't make it go away. But he'd been an adult, faced with an inevitable consequence of war. She'd been just a child. And yet, until she'd spoken those words to Jasper, he never would have suspected she blamed herself.

He barely knew her, but she came across as competent and positive. He supposed it showed that the front you put on for others didn't always match what was underneath.

He dropped some money on the table for their coffees and stood, trying not to cringe as his leg spasmed. They needed to do this before the police station closed.

Desparre wasn't big enough to warrant twenty-four-hour coverage. Officers here were on call after a certain hour, but the station would be closed. He checked his watch—8:00 p.m. They had one hour and then they'd be out of luck.

Kensie stood more slowly, taking one last, long gulp of coffee as if she was either preparing herself for something or delaying moving forward. Rebel followed Kensie's lead—probably her leg was hurting, too.

Twenty minutes later they were back in town. Desparre had a few old streetlamps casting dim light over the main road, but otherwise it had grown dark while they'd been inside the coffee shop. The place looked like a ghost town, except for the light and rock music spilling out of the bar.

Kensie got out of the truck first, moving quickly. Rebel trotted by her side, only a hint of her injury showing in the way she favored her back left leg.

Colter grasped the door hard and lowered himself out slowly. Sitting in the car and then the coffee shop had stiffened up his leg. Without giving it enough time elevated, the muscle above his knee felt knotted into an immobile mess.

He forced it to move, gritting his teeth as he tried not to limp, just in case Kensie looked back. The military had drilled into him that failure and weakness weren't options. He'd already failed, but he had no intention of looking weak in front of her. Not again.

Ahead of him, Kensie reached for the door to the police station, then jumped back as it opened from inside. Next to her, Rebel looked back to him, as if debating whether he needed her more than Kensie did.

She'd never taken to another human the way she had to Kensie. Not since he and Rebel had bonded on the battlefield had she so readily accepted anyone. Then again, he hadn't given her a lot of chances to spend time with civilians, outside his parents and the doctors at the various hospitals.

Apparently deciding he was fine, Rebel turned back to Kensie, who was now standing face-to-face with Chief Hernandez. She was bundled up, obviously heading out for the night, and she looked less than happy to see Kensie.

Colter picked up his pace, biting down against the pain. He'd be paying for this later, but he'd seen too many veterans get hooked on painkillers or booze after life-altering injuries. So he stayed away from all of it and just took the pain. Maybe it was his penance for living when everyone else had died.

"Miss Morgan, there's not much more we can tell you about your sister." Chief Hernandez nodded at him as he pushed his way up beside Kensie. "Colter."

"Chief. What about the girl who came into the store the day the note was found?"

"What girl?"

"The one who looked kind of like Kensie. She was there at the same time as a family."

The chief gave a tight smile. "You mean the one there

with her family? We don't know who that was, but we did talk to Jasper about what he remembered. And that was a family, not a scared girl trying to escape."

She looked at Kensie, who'd shrunk low into her oversized parka. "I'm sorry. I wish we could help."

When she started to walk away, Colter blocked her. "What's the problem? Is the case still open?" He heard the confrontational note in his voice, but couldn't stop it.

She frowned and shoved her hands in the pockets of her parka. "Technically, we let the FBI take over. We checked it out. There's nothing more we can do." She looked at Kensie. "I'm sorry. I understand this is hard to hear, but—"

"Hard to hear? What? That the police won't do their job?" Colter tried to keep the words inside. But either he'd lost his social skills during his self-imposed hideout this past year or he was just in military mode, assuming everyone was an enemy until proven otherwise.

He swore internally, but before he could figure out how to backtrack, Chief Hernandez stepped toward him, getting in his space.

Rebel bared her teeth and even Kensie sidled closer to him in a silent show of support, but the chief sounded more tired than mad when she finally spoke.

"We did our job. I think you're low on information, Colter. We worked closely with the FBI on this. It was their call in the end, but we agreed with them."

She looked briefly at Kensie, then focused her attention on him again. "Kensie already knows this because the FBI told her, but let me share what they determined after running down all the leads: The note was a hoax."

Chapter 5

He'd spent the entire day battling his re-injured leg and fighting the flashbacks of losing the people he'd loved most in the world. And the whole time, she'd been lying to him?

Colter bit back all the things he wanted to say to Kensie as Chief Hernandez walked away. *Get control of your emotions,* he ordered himself. But still, the anger and frustration bubbled up. He'd taken on a mission for her. All for a lead that had already been ruled a hoax.

"Colter, before you say anything…" Kensie put a hand on his bicep.

An hour ago, he would have leaned into her touch, however small. Now, his arm flexed instinctively, like a shove to push her away.

She must have felt it, because she withdrew her hand

and used it to stroke Rebel's fur instead. His dog tilted her head up, looking for more, and Colter couldn't help his frown.

"I know why you feel like I misled you—"

"Because you did?"

She huffed out a breath. "Yes, I did. But I wouldn't be here if I believed the FBI. I flew 3,500 miles for this. I know it's real this time."

His anger melted a little at the quiver in her voice. She was on a fool's mission. She probably knew it, too, but couldn't admit it to herself any more than she could to anyone else.

Maybe reason would help her get there. "Why does the FBI think it's a hoax?" He'd intended the question to be conversational, but it came out confrontational.

He really did need to work on his social skills. Before his accident, he'd had no problem relating to people. Apparently a year without practice was all it took to reduce him to a Neanderthal.

"The note said, *My name is Alanna Morgan, from Chicago. I'm still alive. I'm not the only one.*"

She said the words as if she'd more than memorized them. As if she'd internalized them. As if they were a direct link to the sister she hadn't seen in fourteen years.

"Okay," he said when she didn't continue.

"We didn't live in Chicago anymore. We lived in the suburbs. We'd moved there when Alanna was three, and Alanna knew her address. The FBI thinks someone just picked the details from a news story, because reporters usually simplified it to Chicago."

"What makes you think that's not what happened?"

"Who would do that, all these years later, so far

away?" Her voice was plaintive, desperation seeping through, and he understood.

It wasn't so much that she knew it wasn't a hoax. She just couldn't bear it.

"Kensie—"

"I know what you're thinking. You're right, okay? There have been so many false leads over the years. This can't be another one. It just can't. But there's more to it than that. I feel it deep down in a way I can't quite explain. There's something here. I know there is. And the FBI had their chance; I thought they'd come up with something. When they didn't, I knew I had to come myself."

"The FBI has a lot of experience—"

Her hand stroked Rebel's head more frantically. "The FBI didn't know my sister."

"So they can probably be more objective about this. Look." He cut her off as she started to speak again. "Why would your sister say she wasn't the only one? That sounds like someone looking for attention, not a real letter. If this were real, why wouldn't your sister provide some detail to prove it was her?"

"She was five when she went missing, Colter. How much does she even remember about us? What would she say?"

Kensie sounded defeated, but then she took a deep breath and pressed on. "For years, my parents spent all their time doing everything they could to try and find Alanna. She was the baby. We couldn't function properly as a family without her. And then my brother Flynn turned sixteen. I was twenty and Alanna had been gone for seven years, but my parents hadn't given up. I tried to watch out for Flynn better than I'd done for Alanna, but he got into a lot of trouble. He crashed the car, almost died. And it changed everything."

Colter sighed, knowing what Kensie was doing. The same thing she'd done with Jasper by telling the store owner personal details about the day her sister went missing. Playing on his sympathies to get him to continue helping her.

But as much as he sympathized with what she'd been through, dragging herself through a pointless search and him through the hell of a new mission wouldn't do either of them any good.

"I'm sorry for what you and your family have been through, Kensie, but—"

"We all worked so hard to stay close, to be good to each other, but sometimes I feel like we're just playing roles. That none of us has really been the same since Alanna went missing and we'll never be until we find her."

"Maybe you need to look for a new normal."

"Like you have?" Her hand lifted from Rebel's head and she crossed both arms over her chest.

"Yeah," he snapped back. "Maybe it's not perfect, but it works for me."

"It *works* for you? All alone up in that cabin, locking out the world?"

Rebel whimpered, nudging Kensie's thigh with her head, but Kensie ignored her this time.

"You don't know anything about my life, Kensie."

"And you don't know anything about mine! You don't know what it's like to lose your little sister, to watch her be taken right in front of you."

He clamped his jaw shut, trying to keep his words at

bay, but they poured out anyway. "I know more about loss and grief than you can possibly understand. You come here and insist I help you, but at the end of the day, you're selfish. You're hiding the truth from me, wasting my time as much as your own. Are you really thinking about your sister, or is this about you, about making up for a stupid mistake you made at thirteen years old?"

He regretted the words as soon as they were out of his mouth and he tried to backtrack. "It wasn't your fault. But this mission you're on is about *you*."

Her lips curled up. "Right, and everything you do is for someone else? I don't know what happened to your leg, Colter, and I'm sorry that you can't be a soldier anymore, but maybe you should get over it! All I'm asking is for you to do something you're already good at. All I need is a little help. The FBI is wrong. I *know* they are."

His leg twitched at her reminder. Rebel whined again and left Kensie's side, pressing against him as if to hold him up. He could tell her what had happened to his unit, about just how well he understood not wanting to let someone go when deep down you knew you had to. But he held the words in. They'd only make her feel bad and they wouldn't do him any good, either. He wasn't even sure he could talk about it.

Instead, he shook his head sadly. "I hope you're right, Kensie, but I don't think you are. And I can't follow you on a fool's mission. I'm sorry. I think you should go home."

Colter walked away.

Rebel followed more slowly. Every few steps, her head swung back toward Kensie, still standing outside the police station.

He was a jerk. He knew it. Yeah, some of his words had been true, probably even the part about her being selfish. She just assumed she understood him because she'd seen him limp. Instead of asking what he'd gone through, she'd been focused on her own pain.

Then again, hadn't he done the same thing? Walking away right now was only partly because her mission was likely to end in heartbreak for her and he didn't want to see it. The rest was because she was slowly pulling him back into the world.

He knew part of healing would require him to re-enter the world. And it wasn't because his therapists had told him so, back when the military had tried to force him to get some help. He wasn't blind to the fact that the way he was living wasn't the healthiest choice. But it was a choice that had brought him some measure of peace. Certainly more peace than he'd had in the hospital or even back with his family and friends.

Their platitudes and insistence they knew what he was going through hadn't made him feel loved. It had made him angry. Because no one who hadn't lived through a war and lost people could understand.

Maybe that had been part of the appeal of helping Kensie. She *didn't* know about his past. And he'd thrown that fact in her face.

He squeezed his eyes shut, slowing to a stop. He sensed Rebel pause beside him, always his loyal companion.

Holding in a curse, he glanced back. Just like he knew it would, guilt flooded him at seeing Kensie standing there.

She looked lost and alone. But she also looked unbeaten. Her head was still held high, her shoulders stiff. She wasn't going to give up on Alanna, no matter the odds.

He understood her loyalty. He admired it.

Semper Fi. It was the Marines' battle call, their motto. It was one of his own core beliefs.

Opening his eyes, he turned slowly. Rebel spun with more glee, her tail batting back and forth, slapping against his thigh.

With every step back toward Kensie, his heart pounded harder, warning him this was a mistake. Already, she was making him feel things that were dangerous. Connection to a mission, connection to another person.

He didn't want to care. He didn't want to re-enter the world, because eventually that would make him face the things he'd lost, face the grief over the *people* he'd lost.

He wanted to stay up in his cabin with Rebel. He wanted to let the peace of the mountains soothe his soul. He'd planned to stay there the rest of his life. He knew it would be lonely, especially after Rebel was gone. But that seemed like the safest choice, the happiest choice for him.

As he approached, Kensie watched him warily, probably with no idea what she was doing to his life.

"I'm sorry." His voice creaked with emotion and embarrassment heated his cheeks.

Rebel shoved her head under Kensie's hand, tail wagging enthusiastically.

A surprised laugh burst from Kensie at Rebel's antics and in that moment, Colter wanted to move forward. He wanted to laugh like that, unconstrained and free.

He wanted to spend time with a woman like Kensie. If this had been a year ago, not only would he have done everything in his power to help her, no matter the odds, but he would also have pursued her. Hard.

She still looked wary, as though she wasn't sure she wanted to accept his apology. As though she wasn't sure she wanted his help. "Colter..."

The idea of venturing back into the world, even this tiny bit with her, scared him. Terrified him might be more accurate. But he'd made the decision now, and he shouldn't have turned away just because she hadn't been totally up-front with him.

He'd accepted a mission. And whether or not it was one that could be accomplished, he owed it to her to try.

He owed it to himself, too. To see if he could really do it.

He cut off whatever response she had to his apology by stepping forward into her personal space. Close, so she wouldn't misunderstand.

She froze, her mouth still open.

He didn't hesitate. He wrapped an arm around her waist and yanked her to him before he could think better of it.

Kensie stumbled, but his bad leg didn't protest much as he caught her weight against his body. Then he captured her lips with his.

She tasted like coffee and peppermint. She tasted like every dream he'd ever had for himself, before his world was torn apart.

His other arm wrapped around her, pulling her even tighter against him, and then he lost himself. For a moment, everything else disappeared. The past, his broth-

ers, her sister, even the inevitable end of knowing her
when she returned to Chicago. For a moment, he was
living again. Truly living.

Every inch of his body seemed to come alive as her
hands slid slowly over his chest and hooked around his
neck. She was tall for a woman, but still a good five
inches shorter than he was, so when she went up on tip-
toes to give him better access, his knees almost buckled. And not because of his injury.

He might have thought it was the fact that he hadn't
kissed a woman in over a year. But it wasn't. It was Kensie. The smell of her, some faintly spicy perfume filling
his nostrils. The feel of her, little more than an outline
through her thick coat. The soft sounds she was making
in the back of her throat as she started to kiss him back.

It was less than twenty degrees out here, but he was
fast becoming as overheated as he'd been those first
days serving in the desert. The thought sent his heart
into overdrive, memories of his friends in happier times
mingling with Kensie, with the way she was clinging
to him.

It was all too much.

Colter let himself have one more taste of her and then
he pulled back, breathing hard. Staring down into her
dazed eyes, he tried to get hold of himself.

"I'm sorry," he breathed, barely able to speak.

Confusion knitted her forehead and then she tipped
her chin up. "I'm not."

She tapped the side of her leg like she'd probably
seen him do to get Rebel to follow, then headed toward his truck. When he didn't immediately move, she

glanced back, her hair flipping over her shoulder, full of sass. "You coming?"

Rebel was staring up at him, too, her expression plaintive, her tail sweeping slowly, clearing snow from the road.

After that kiss, she thought he might not follow? Still feeling as though his heart might pound its way right out of his chest, Colter hurried after her.

He barely even felt his leg.

Chapter 6

Kensie had hardly slept last night as thoughts of the kiss she'd shared with Colter played over and over in her mind. Instead, she'd tossed and turned in her surprisingly plush, comfortable hotel bed a few miles outside of Desparre. The outside looked like an enormous log cabin, but the inside was as opulent as anywhere she'd been in Chicago.

According to the manager, the hotel attracted mostly tourists from out of state during the summer months. They'd hoped to make Desparre a destination spot, a look at the "true" Alaska. Instead, they were slowly failing, the manager had whispered to her sadly. Kensie had the hotel practically to herself.

She should have felt pampered. But all she'd wanted to do was drive out to another log cabin, this one much smaller and filled with the overwhelming presence of a man who was no good for her.

She still couldn't believe he'd kissed her. Yes, she'd felt his reciprocated attraction from the start. But he was broken, possibly even more broken than she was.

He hadn't shared much about his time in the military besides his role and the fact that he'd been a soldier for almost a decade. Maybe he just didn't know how to do anything else. Or maybe the soldier in him couldn't live with a physical disability.

Kensie didn't care about his physical limitations. But she did know two things: he was too emotionally damaged to be relationship material, even if she was looking, and she couldn't let him distract her from this chance to find Alanna.

Right now, still yawning from her sleepless night, Kensie darted a furtive glance at Colter. He walked beside her, Rebel between them, near the store where Alanna's note had been found. The plan this morning was to canvass the nearby stores, see if they could find someone who knew anything.

Colter looked like he hadn't slept any better than she had. With his light skin, the circles under his eyes seemed even more prominent. Every twenty feet or so, his right leg dragged a little. For him to even let her see that much, she figured it was hurting him badly. That could have been the reason for both his lack of sleep and his grumpiness.

But she suspected the latter had more to do with the kiss they'd shared last night. When he'd picked her up downtown this morning, he'd handed her a disposable cup with the scent of coffee wafting from it and given her a gruff nod hello. Not exactly the slow, intimate smile she'd been expecting, but maybe it was a good thing.

Except right now, his continued brooding was beginning to annoy her. She didn't want to be ungrateful for his help, but she also didn't want to tiptoe around him.

"Maybe we should split up."

He frowned at her with the most direct eye contact he'd given her all morning. "Why?"

She pointed up ahead at the two businesses sharing a parking lot: a snowplow store and a diner that smelled like grease even from a distance. "We'll accomplish more, faster."

He grunted like he didn't believe her explanation, but she was actually grateful as he and Rebel headed off to the diner. The man may have been emotionally unavailable, but he was also six foot two of muscled temptation. Her willpower was pretty good, but even in his bad mood, walking beside him had made her unusually aware of his every move.

Time to focus on Alanna, Kensie reminded herself as she pushed open the door to the snowplow supply store. As the heavy door slammed closed behind her, she stared in awe. It was more like a warehouse than a store, filled with machines that dwarfed her. At the far end she saw a huge garage door and a checkout counter.

While most of the people she'd met in Desparre looked like they'd either been here forever or the extreme weather had aged them before their time, the guy manning the counter was young. Maybe twenty, with three piercings on his face and tattoos snaking out of both sleeves. He looked like part-time help.

She forced a friendly smile onto her face as she approached. Years of pleas on news stations and talk shows beside her parents, of trailing behind them as they questioned potential witnesses, had taught her that people responded to two things: a friendly approach and a sob story.

This was the part she hated most, selling out her memories of Alanna in the hopes of bringing her sister home. But if it worked, it was worth every sleazy guy who'd offered to "cheer her up," every ambitious reporter who'd salivated at the idea of broadcasting her grief to as many people as possible. It was worth every missed opportunity, every failed relationship. Even every possible relationship, cut off before it could begin.

"Hi," she started. "I'm Kensie Morgan. I'm looking for my sister and—"

The kid shook his head, already going back to the handheld game partially hidden under the counter. "No woman's been through here today."

"It wouldn't have been today. A few weeks ago, a note was left at Jasper's General Store down the road and—"

"You're looking for the kidnapped girl?" His head snapped back up, the game forgotten. "The news said she's been missing for fourteen years."

"That's right. She has dark hair like mine. And brown eyes, a little darker than mine." Were those things still true? Kensie assumed so, but had no way to really know. Maybe Alanna's hair had been dyed or she wore colored contacts. Or maybe, now that they were all grown up, they looked nothing alike anymore.

The kid shrugged. "I only started here this week.

I guess the last guy just walked out and didn't come back, so here I am. It's great, pretty quiet so I can do my homework."

Kensie's hopes sank. "So you don't know if the owner saw anyone like that over the past few weeks, maybe around the time the note was left?"

"Sorry. But can I ask you—"

"Thanks." She cut him off, not wanting to hear his questions about what had happened to her sister or what she worried had happened in all the years Alanna had been gone. Even the people who were sympathetic usually didn't know how to walk the line between support and morbid curiosity. That line was a lot thinner than most people realized.

As she headed back the way she'd come, the door opened and a man as tall as Colter, but who looked a decade and a half older, walked in. "Hey, where's Derrick?" he yelled across the store.

"Not working today," the kid called back.

"Excuse me," Alanna said, her hopes lifting again. "Do you live around here?"

"Yeah." The man turned deep brown eyes on her as he drew out the word, scowling.

That angry scowl. It was vaguely familiar. Kensie's heart rate picked up as she realized why. It reminded her of the man who'd taken Alanna.

Fourteen years ago, he'd climbed out of the passenger seat of a dark blue sedan, wearing all blue—jeans and a lightweight sweater. His long arms had stretched out and yanked her sister right off her feet. Alanna had let out a muffled squeak and then Kensie had screamed loudly enough that it should have brought the entire city running.

He'd met her gaze for mere seconds. She hadn't been able to tell his eye color from across the yard, but he'd been scowling. A deep, intense scowl she'd never forget. He'd been about the age this guy would have been back then, too. His hair had been more brown, whereas this guy had streaks of gray, but that might have just been time.

Kensie let out a small laugh, earning her a perplexed—and slightly concerned—look from the man. It was weird, but she'd done this repeatedly over the years. She'd see someone on the street and everything in her would go unnaturally still, even her breathing. Then adrenaline would kick in, sending her heart and mind into overdrive. A few minutes later, she'd come to her senses. The psychiatrist her parents had forced her to see for a few sessions as a kid had given it a name, but Kensie couldn't remember it.

She'd gotten such a brief look at Alanna's kidnapper. She probably wouldn't have been able to identify him fourteen years ago, let alone now.

The man started to walk away and Kensie grabbed his arm, surprised at the ropey strength beneath the thick jean jacket. His arm flexed and he jerked it free, almost knocking her down.

"You need something, lady?" He looked her up and down, studying her too intently. He might have been good-looking in some circumstances, but the anger curling his lips and raking harsh lines across his forehead ruined it.

She held her hands up. "Sorry. It's just—you've lived here awhile?"

"Yeah, why?"

She tried a smile, hoping it would soften him up. "You know the regulars, it sounds like, and I'm looking for someone."

He shifted, angling away from her. His gaze darted from the kid behind the counter to the big garage door at the other end of the space. Then he stared back at her suspiciously. "Who?"

"My sister. She was kidnapped a long time ago."

"Your sister, huh?" He scowled some more. "From where?"

"The Midwest." The words came out without conscious thought. Normally she said Chicago, but even telling herself she was being crazy, something about this guy was getting her radar up. He might just be unfriendly. Or maybe he actually knew something and she needed to tread carefully. Would getting too specific about Alanna—if he actually did know her, if by some crazy fluke he really was the person who'd grabbed her all those years ago—scare him away?

The guy's head swiveled back and forth between the doors again. "I don't know your sister, lady."

"But—"

He spun back the way he'd come, darting a glance over his shoulder as he threw the door open, then practically ran outside.

Kensie swore under her breath then ran after him, yanking her phone out of her pocket. She skidded to a stop in the snow outside as he leaped into a truck.

With shaky hands, she snapped a photo of him. For

one second, he froze, like he might jump out and rip the phone from her hands. Then the truck flew backward out of the lot, and slammed to a stop before changing direction and racing away.

He needed to get out more.

The thought surprised Colter. Usually, when he came to town and people wanted to ask him questions about his life or make small talk, he couldn't wait to get back to his cabin and shut the rest of the world out.

But today, carrying a homemade chocolate chip cookie that the grandfather of seven who owned the diner had given him, while Rebel drooled happily over a dog biscuit, Colter felt lighter than he had in a long time. His steps picked up as he headed toward the store where he'd left Kensie.

Once upon a time, she would have been everything he wanted. Back then, he'd been the kind of guy who'd had a map of his life drawn in his mind. He might have taken one look at her and sensed the possibility for marriage and kids. For a home waiting for him in between military tours.

That was the life he'd always imagined for himself. The kind of life his brothers in the Marines had: video calls with spouses, letters written in crayon arriving at bases around the world, pictures to carry inside their helmets. Something to fight for. Someone to go home to.

He'd never have any of that now. Without the military, the vision was a mess. He couldn't imagine a sedate life for himself, with a woman who didn't mind picking up the slack when his injury got to be too much, and kids who didn't mind that their dad couldn't run

after them like other dads. If he was being honest, he
didn't want that life at all now.

He'd come to Alaska not just to hide, but also to heal.
Somehow, over the past year, he'd lost sight of the *healing* part. But Kensie had forced him out of his comfort
zone, out of the solitude of his cabin, and it was reminding him of why he loved it here. Why he'd chosen it in
the first place.

Sure, there were guys like Danny Weston, people
who'd come here to take advantage of Alaska's wide-
open spaces and hide from whatever terrible thing
they'd done. But there were also people like the grandfather who'd owned this diner for the past thirty years.
Hardworking people who'd come here for the chance
to live a simpler life, to connect with nature and themselves. That's what he wanted.

Kissing Kensie last night had reignited in him all
the old dreams and this morning he'd woken with what
felt like a hangover. The inevitable disappointment he
felt whenever he dreamed of the past. Waking up and
remembering it was all gone had spiraled him into depression more than once. He wasn't going there again.

Kensie was never going to be anything more to him
than a memory. But maybe her entering his life was
exactly the kick in the butt he needed to make him re-
join the world.

No, life was never going to be the way he'd imagined when he was eighteen and just embarking on his
first military tour. But how many people's lives turned
out the way they planned when they were little more
than kids?

At his side, Rebel trotted along happily, with nothing left of her biscuit but a lone crumb on the top of her nose. A smile trembled on his lips. He could still be happy here. Just because his trajectory had changed didn't mean it was pointless. He could find meaning in his life, allow himself to enjoy the solitude of his cabin, the endless open views across the valley.

He drew in a deep, cold breath of Alaskan air. It was time to face his future.

Chapter 7

Kensie had barely spoken to him since he'd picked her up at the snowplow store.

Colter shot another glance at her across the truck cab. He hadn't known her long, but she wasn't usually this quiet. And while it could have been his own bad mood from when he'd met up with her a few hours ago causing her silence, he didn't think so.

It was probably the kiss they'd shared.

For the hundredth time since it had happened, he cursed himself. But this time it was half-hearted. How could he fully regret something that had reset his perspective on his life? Yeah, maybe kissing her had been a lapse in judgment, but hopefully it was the push he needed to get his life in order. To figure out how he was going to truly make this place his home, instead of just his hideout.

He gripped the wheel a little tighter, trying to find the right words. He'd never had to apologize for kissing someone before.

Eyes still on the icy road in front of him, Colter started, "The past year, I've been hiding out in my cabin. Not really on purpose. But I came here for the solitude and it was easy to turn that into a solitary life."

He glanced at her to see if she'd figured out where he was going with this meandering opening salvo, but she was just staring out the windshield, forehead furrowed. So he kept going. "Helping you wasn't easy for me. I know you don't get it, but trust me when I say that any kind of mission was the last thing I thought I needed."

She was silent, so he pushed forward, faster now, starting to feel foolish for not just blurting a simple apology and leaving it at that. "That's why I bailed on you when I found out you weren't telling me everything. And when I kissed you…"

Kensie stayed silent, lips pursed like she was waiting for a real apology. Or maybe she wasn't even listening to him. It was hard to tell.

"I'm sorry. I should have—"

"It was a mistake. I get it. I agree. We got carried away in the moment. It's not like it's going to happen again." Kensie cut him off suddenly, swiveling in her seat as far as the seatbelt would let her. She tucked one knee up underneath her, facing him even as Rebel tried to stick her nose in between to be petted.

It wasn't going to happen again? Even though that had been his plan, too, hearing her say the words made

him long to pull the truck over and see if she really
meant it.

Visions of her kissing him filled his head. The way
she'd fit inside the circle of his arms, soft and feminine but stronger than he'd expected. The way her lips
had melded instantly to his, like she'd been imagining
it since the moment he'd first helped her up off the icy
Desparre street.

Then the vision shifted, moved into territory he had
no business imagining. Of her back at his cabin, standing in front of the fire as she dropped her coat to the
floor. As his fingers found their way underneath the
hem of her sweater and his lips traced a path from her
mouth down to the pulse at her neck. As he lingered
there, pulling her body closer until there was barely any
space between them.

"I think I might have just met Alanna's kidnapper."

It took a minute for him to process Kensie's words,
for them to penetrate the increasingly erotic vision in
his head. Once they did, he slowed the truck to a stop,
pulling over as far as he could, and turned to face her.
"What?"

"I know it sounds crazy and at first I thought I was
just imagining things." Kensie spoke at warp speed,
reaching out to clutch his arm as if to keep his interest.

As if that was a problem. "Who is it? Why didn't
you come and get me?" And why was she just now
mentioning this?

"I don't know his name, but I got his picture." She
let go of his arm to fumble in her pocket and pull out
her phone.

When she turned it to show him, he squinted at it a

long minute, trying to place the guy. "I recognize him. He's lived here a long time." Colter tried to come up with a name, but couldn't. "I think he's got a place on the outskirts of Desparre somewhere. Comes in periodically for supplies. Usually to the spot we just visited, not the main part of town." He lifted his gaze from the phone. "Did you ask the store owner, Derrick? He could probably tell you this guy's name."

Kensie shook her head. "Derrick wasn't there. Just a kid who was working the counter."

"So, this guy who came into the store for supplies… why do you think he has Alanna?"

"He looked familiar."

Colter tried to keep the disbelief off his face. She'd been just a child when her sister had been kidnapped. "You got a good look at the guy back then? How close were you?"

How close had she come to being grabbed alongside Alanna? The idea made him nauseous.

"I was across the yard. I wasn't close enough to help her."

Kensie's voice was so mournful that Colter reached out without thinking and twined his fingers with hers. She clutched tight instantly, as if by instinct, and his heart pounded harder.

"You were thirteen years old, Kensie. What could you have done?" Besides get herself kidnapped—or worse?

"I should have done something. It was my responsibility to watch out for her that day!"

"That's not fair, Kensie. You can't carry that burden." He stared into her eyes, watching them darken with anger or frustration. Who was he to talk about the burden of survivor's guilt? But when it came to this, he knew he was right, so he pressed forward. "And look what kind of sister you've been. All these years later and you're here, searching for her, when even law enforcement won't."

It didn't seem possible, but she squeezed his hand even tighter. "Thank you for helping me," she whispered.

Kissing her yesterday had been a mistake. He knew it. But that didn't stop him from wanting to lean forward and do it again right now.

It took more willpower than he'd thought he had to resist that urge. Instead, he asked, "How sure are you about this guy you saw in the store?"

She let out a humorless laugh. "Not sure at all. But he *ran* when I asked him about my sister."

Colter frowned. He didn't even know the guy's name and yet he couldn't imagine the loner being a child kidnapper. But even though Desparre locals tended to be wary of strangers, running away from questions was suspicious. And, absolutely, something sounded off about the guy.

The question was, had Kensie spooked him? If so, would he run before they could figure out if he had Alanna?

"Either he's the one who kidnapped Alanna or he knows who did." Kensie spoke the words with certainty, tapping the picture she'd snapped before the guy had run away from her as fast as he could.

Colter frowned, like he was unconvinced.

But still, he'd brought her here, to a cozy restaurant-slash-food-store halfway between the snow supply warehouse and downtown. Apparently, the owner had lived in the area all his life and Colter claimed if anyone could tell them more about their suspect, it was him.

Their suspect. It sounded like something a detective would say, one of the overworked, tired-looking officers assigned to Alanna's case. *We have a suspect, but don't get your hopes up.* She'd heard those words a few times over the years, but they'd never led anywhere, even though she'd *always* gotten her hopes up.

This time had to be different. She refused to consider any other possibility. She wasn't sure she could handle another disappointment.

Just the idea of returning home without Alanna made pain lodge behind her breastbone, where it always did when she thought about how long her sister had been gone. Over the years, she'd had moments where she'd felt like maybe she could come to terms with the cold, hard statistics that said Alanna was long dead. But those moments were always fleeting, either because the idea was too much to bear or because she and her sister had always shared a special connection. Wouldn't she feel it in her heart if Alanna was gone?

The idea was foolish. Intellectually, she knew it. But she still believed.

"What are you thinking?"

Colter's words broke into her thoughts and Kensie looked up at him. Backlit by one of the restaurant's cozy lamps, which brought out the gold in his hair and softened the sharp lines of his face, he looked even sexier than usual. Her stomach flipped around for a different reason. Why couldn't she meet a man like this back in Chicago, with Colter's intensity and dedication, but without all of the baggage weighing on him so heavily she could practically see it?

"I'm thinking this has to be the break I need." Her words came out soft, almost sultry, and Kensie cleared her throat, ashamed of herself for lusting after Colter when all of her attention needed to be on Alanna.

To distract herself, she reached down and Rebel obligingly sat up, giving her easy access to stroke the dog's soft fur. Apparently, either Alaska was lenient about pet rules or everyone just knew and liked Rebel. She suspected the latter. Despite what people had told her about Colter not getting out much, the town seemed to be small enough that everyone knew of him and Rebel, if not the details of their lives.

"I hope so," Colter replied, but the lines between his eyebrows told her that her optimism worried him.

He probably figured she'd break if it turned out to be a dead end. If only he knew how many dead ends she'd survived over the years. Then again, she wasn't sure she had it in her to survive another.

Instead of replying, Kensie glanced around the lodge. She didn't have to look far.

The man approaching—with his long gray beard, weathered skin and seen-it-all gaze—had to be the owner. He shook Colter's hand, gave Rebel a slight frown, then glanced at Kensie. "New to Alaska?"

"Yes, I'm—"

"We're wondering if you could help us with something." Colter cut her off. He grabbed her phone and held it up. "You know this guy?"

The owner glanced from the phone to her and back again. "Seen him around over the years. Can't say I know his name. He's not really a talkative sort. Keeps to himself, seems to like it that way. You must understand the feeling."

Colter just lifted an eyebrow, but Kensie sighed, disappointed. "We should track down the owner of the snowplow shop. This guy was yelling his name when he came in. They know each other. Maybe the store owner knows where to find him."

"Why are you looking for him?" the owner prodded.

"I think—"

"We just need his help with something." Colter stood, dropping some money on the table for the cocoas they'd ordered but barely touched. Beside her, Rebel stood, watching Colter attentively. "Any chance you can tell us how to find Derrick Notte?"

"Guy who owns the snowplow place? Yeah, I can give you his address." He stared hard at Colter, ignoring Kensie and Rebel altogether. "But you piss him off and we're going to have problems."

Colter smiled, but it was hard and uncompromising. "He's not the one I'm planning to piss off."

The owner stared a minute longer, then let out a snort of laughter. "All right. Why don't you finish your drinks and I'll get the address."

Colter nodded and sat back down. Rebel followed suit, settling back on her hind legs.

Kensie lowered herself into her chair more slowly, waiting until the owner had walked away to whisper, "What was that about?"

"People like their privacy out here. He's giving me

Derrick's home address on faith. If Derrick gets mad about it, he'll start something."

"Seems a little dramatic," Kensie muttered.

"Yeah, it is. But I didn't want him to know what you were thinking. People out here don't like it when you assume the worst about us."

"I'm not," Kensie protested. "It's not a generalization. It's just this guy looks like—"

"I know," Colter cut her off. "But he didn't, and I didn't want to get into it. People here will help you if you need it, but they've got a live-and-let-live attitude. You probably hear about the ones running from the law, but we get the other side of it, too."

"What does that mean? People like you?"

Colter's lips twisted. "Yeah, I guess. I meant more like people running from someone who's hurt them. They rely on the residents here to respect their privacy. Domestic violence survivors, victims of stalkers, things like that."

"Oh." Kensie stared out the window of the restaurant at dense, snowy woods. The guy at the rental car place had told her Desparre had a higher population of bears than it did people. A smart place to hide from someone who wanted to do you harm. But too easy for a kidnapper to hide away with his victim, too.

"Kensie, can I ask you something?"

She refocused on the man across from her, and the serious expression on his face made her nervous. "Okay."

"There's something that's been bothering me since you first told me about your sister's note."

"What is it?" She almost didn't want to know the

answer. It felt like the trajectory of her entire life was riding on the outcome of this note.

Colter must have sensed her distress, because he set down his mug of cocoa, reached across the table and took her hand. His roughened fingers rubbed over her palm, sending shivers up her arm.

It was the kind of thing a boyfriend would do. Not a guy you'd just met who'd agreed to be your guide in the Alaskan wilderness. Kensie tried to ignore the emotions he was stirring up.

"If the note is really from your sister, why did she walk into a store and leave a message, but not run or ask for help? Surely if she was in distress or someone had her immobilized, she never would have been able to leave the note at all without the store owner noticing."

Kensie nodded, staring down at their joined hands. It had bothered her from the beginning, too, and for two entirely different reasons.

Taking a deep breath, she met his gaze. "It might be a sign that the note is fake." The possibility hurt, and she didn't want to even consider it, but she knew it was there.

Years of coordinating with law enforcement and private cold-case groups had also taught her the other possibility, which in some ways was even worse. "Or it could mean she's so afraid of her kidnapper or so conditioned to obey him that even given the chance to run, she won't take it."

In Colter's eyes, she saw understanding and sadness. As a soldier, he'd probably seen cases like that, captives who'd been tortured so badly that even when they saw a chance to escape, they were too terrified to try.

If that was what had happened with her sister—if the note was a final, desperate plea for someone to find her because she couldn't manage to run on her own—what shape would she be in if they located her?

Would the Alanna she'd known still be in there? Or would the woman Alanna had become be a hollow shell of the girl she'd once been?

If that was the case, Kensie wasn't sure either of them would ever recover from what happened in Desparre.

Chapter 8

Kensie was discouraged.

He never should have asked her about the note. If Colter had been thinking, he would have realized the implications without her having to tell him.

He didn't like that she knew what it meant. Not that he thought she was naive or clueless, but as much as he didn't want a connection, he couldn't deny that he cared about Kensie. Hopefully she wouldn't be in Desparre for long. He wanted a happy ending for her and her sister. He wished she'd had an uncomplicated life, without sorrow or tragedy.

Those things were for soldiers like him.

It was a ridiculous, unrealistic way to think, but there it was. He'd become a soldier for a lot of reasons, but one of them was because he wanted to make a differ-

ence. He liked to protect people. And that instinct was
kicking up harder than usual with Kensie.

Apparently Rebel felt the same way, because even
though she wasn't supposed to, she swiveled on her butt
and dropped her head into Kensie's lap. Kensie looked
surprised for a second, then laughed and started petting his dog again.

If he wasn't careful, Rebel was going to want to follow Kensie back to Chicago. If he wasn't careful, he
was going to want to do the same thing.

Colter pushed out the crazy thought and tried to
distract Kensie. After they'd talked to the restaurant
owner, she'd wanted to drive immediately out to Derrick's house. But his question had gotten her upset and
he didn't want her going to Derrick's that way. The guy
was prickly on his best day. He'd be a huge pain if Kensie was confrontational. Especially since Colter knew *he*
was likely to become confrontational if Derrick didn't
cooperate. If they were going to get answers out of the
guy, they needed Kensie's soft touch.

So, he'd ordered the restaurant's famous wild berry
cobbler and pushed the plate toward her as soon as it
arrived. She'd only picked at it initially, but the longer
they'd sat, the bigger her bites had gotten. The place
was famous for its cobbler for a reason.

"Tell me about your sister. What was she like?" Colter asked now, hoping to fill her mind with good memories she could draw on to win over Derrick if needed.

Kensie paused, a bite of cobbler halfway to her
mouth. A sad smile tugged her lips. "She was goofy
and fun. Even at five, we were already predicting she'd
be homecoming queen or class president when she got

older. Probably both. She was always the center of attention, always in the middle of the party. It was funny, because both me and Flynn—who's halfway between me and Alanna in age—were shy and serious. Bookish, my mom called us."

Colter smiled, because that wasn't how he saw Kensie at all. Maybe she'd outgrown her shyness or maybe she had an inaccurate perception of herself as a child, but she drew people to her with ease. He couldn't picture her ever being on the sidelines.

"Before Alanna went missing, I was teaching her to play violin." Kensie's smile turned wistful. "She'd seen me play and she wanted to be just like me."

"You were close?"

"Yeah. We were eight years apart, but we always had a special bond. Whenever I play now, I think of Alanna."

"You still play?"

"I'm a violinist in an orchestra back home. That's my job." Suddenly seeming to realize she'd been holding a forkful of cobbler, Kensie stuffed it into her mouth.

She played at such a high level that she did it for a living? He pictured her with a violin in her hand, bow flying across the strings, her eyes intense with concentration. "I'd love to hear you play."

Kensie's lips tipped upward, but there was still sadness in her eyes. She swallowed and told him, "I don't have my violin."

Of course not. It was back at home, with the rest of her family. A family who was probably waiting anxiously for Kensie to return—and hopefully bring with her the sister they hadn't seen in fourteen years.

It was a huge responsibility to carry alone.

He wanted to promise her they'd find Alanna. That he'd help her carry that load. But he knew it was an empty promise, so he didn't say it. Sure, he'd do what he could to give her access to the locals, to get her safely wherever she needed to go. But that was as much as he could do, and he knew it was nothing compared to what she needed. Compared to what she deserved.

"Why don't you have a boyfriend or a husband up here with you?"

The question was rude, and he regretted it the instant it came out of his mouth. Even Rebel lifted her head from Kensie's lap to eye him over the table, as if she disapproved.

"Sorry. None of my business," he said before she could answer.

"No boyfriend or husband. It's hard to…"

She trailed off, and it took him a minute to catch up and wonder what was hard about it, because he was too busy being pleased she wasn't attached. Which was selfish, because he had no claim on her and never would.

"What about you?"

"Why aren't I married?" The words popped out of his mouth full of surprise—both that she'd ask and that she didn't already know. He was broken.

"No," she said quickly, a flush rushing up her cheeks. "What do you do for a living?"

Half-relieved he didn't have to wade into that minefield and half-disappointed that she wasn't interested, Colter shrugged. "Since I left the military, I've been writing pieces for newspapers and magazines."

It was part-time work he sometimes loved and sometimes hated. He loved being able to share his perspective, to give civilians a more accurate look into how the military worked. But it reminded him that he wasn't where he belonged, in the middle of the action. It reminded him that he'd never be there again.

"The job is permanent?" she asked, probably picking up on his hesitation.

It was funny that he'd ended up writing, since his parents had always pushed him toward a career in communications. But it wasn't his passion, just a way to pay the bills. "Nah."

"So, what's next?"

He frowned, his instinct not to answer. But she'd been honest with him, so it was only fair he do the same. "I don't know."

Most of his life, he'd had a goal. He'd known from an early age he wanted to join the military, fascinated by stories from his grandfather, who'd lived in Poland during World War Two. He'd tried to help people escape, gotten caught and been thrown into the gulag in Siberia for his efforts.

His grandfather hadn't fought in the war. But he'd seen it firsthand and the injustices he'd described had made Colter long to change the world. It was a child's wish, but it had matured into a man's desire to make some kind of difference for people who couldn't do it for themselves.

When he'd enlisted right out of high school, his parents had been shocked. They'd been so sure he'd grow out of what they considered a childish dream. But to him, it was all he'd ever wanted. Being a man without a mission was an uncomfortable feeling.

But even more so was this new mission he found himself on, helping Kensie. Because the more she pulled him back into the world, the more he realized he was going to have to figure it out. He couldn't go back to the military. That part of his life was over, whether he wanted it to be or not.

He'd never again be Staff Sergeant Hayes. Now he was simply Colter. What exactly that meant, he wasn't sure. Once he'd helped her, he needed to move on and figure out what was next for him.

It was easier said than done. Desparre wasn't exactly teeming with opportunities for a guy who had no experience doing anything except being a soldier.

"Well, what about your family?" Kensie asked.

"What about them?"

"What do they think you should do next?"

"I have no idea. Move back home, probably." He hadn't asked and his parents hadn't suggested anything. He'd never thought about it before, but it was strange. They'd tried so hard to convince him not to join up. Once he'd come home damaged, they'd done their best to get him to return to the sleepy Idaho town where he was born. When he'd come here, instead, it was as if they'd finally given up trying.

Kensie was frowning, so he tried to explain. "I'm an only child. They had me late in life and in some ways I think they never quite knew what to do with me."

She frowned even harder, so he rushed on, "Don't get me wrong. They love me. They just never understood me. Never got why I wanted to join the military or what I was looking for there. The military gave me a mission, camaraderie and a brotherhood. I know it's different than your bond with your sister, because I didn't grow up with them, but it's a brotherhood all the same."

He trailed off, wondering how he'd gotten onto this subject. The faces of his lost brothers flashed in his mind and he gulped in a deep breath, praying he wasn't about to go into panic mode.

Rebel whimpered, scooting out from where she'd cozied up to Kensie to come around and nudge him. She was good at that, nudging him back to the present. Nudging him out of his panic.

Colter grounded himself by fisting his hand in her soft fur. He blew out the breath, focusing on evening out his heartbeat. It slowed and Kensie came back into focus, looking worried.

"I'm fine," he said before she could ask. "Hard subject."

"Why?" she asked slowly, like she was afraid she already knew the answer.

Colter pushed the words out fast, not wanting to linger on them. "They're all gone. Every one of my brothers, dead in an ambush. I'm the only one still here and it's not right. I should have gone with them that day."

Colter thought he should be dead?

Kensie had been shocked into silence at his admission, especially after Colter dropped that secret and then hadn't said another word about it. Even now, half an hour after he'd first told her, she was at a loss for words. She hadn't even known him for two days, but already she couldn't imagine the world without him.

And yet, how could she say that without sounding like she was infatuated with him or coddling him? Not to mention that now she felt horrible about the assumptions she'd made, thinking he was just hiding out in Alaska because he'd been injured.

She'd said terrible things to him when he'd gotten mad because she wasn't up-front about the FBI's assessment. Things about him not understanding loss, about how he should just *get over* his trauma. As if you could ever just get over losing your family, whether it was blood-related or chosen.

At least with Alanna there was still a chance. Still hope. Colter didn't even have that much.

"I'm so sorry," she said, and her voice came out a pitiful whisper as he pulled his truck up to Derrick's big log house. Her attempt at sympathy felt so insignificant next to what Colter had endured, and she knew she'd waited too long to say anything at all, trying to find the right words. As if there were any right words for that kind of loss.

He gave her a quick, sideways glance. "Not your fault," he answered briskly, flinging open his door. He stepped out and slammed it shut before she could say anything else.

Kensie glanced at Rebel, ashamed of herself, and the dog stared solemnly back at her until Colter opened the rear door and slapped his leg. Then she hopped out, leaving Kensie alone.

Focus, Kensie reminded herself. She had time to figure out how to give Colter a proper apology, since he was still helping her. Right now, she needed her attention to be on convincing Derrick to give them information.

Because the guy she'd seen at his store was connected to Alanna somehow. Kensie could feel it in her gut, as strong as the instinct screaming that Alanna was still here, that the note was real. That Alanna was still alive. Just waiting for Kensie to bring her home.

Kensie squeezed her eyes shut, praying she was right. Then she opened them and stepped out of the truck, hurrying up the unshoveled drive after Colter.

Derrick's house was nothing like Colter's, besides being a log cabin. It was at least twice as big, and the much smaller windows in front were all covered by shades. Still, Derrick must have heard them coming because the door opened before Colter could knock.

If ever she'd imagined a mountain man of Alaska, this is what she would have pictured. Derrick was huge—more wide than tall—with snow-white hair and an unkempt matching beard. He wore pants with a bulky vinyl appearance that looked like they were made for the outdoors and a thick flannel shirt that barely buttoned over his barrel chest. There was even an unlit cigar clamped in the corner of his mouth.

"What do you want?" he asked out of the side of his mouth not occupied by the cigar.

"We're looking for someone. We're hoping you can help us." Colter held out his hand to Kensie and she silently passed over her phone.

"Do you know this guy?" Colter held up the screen.

"He came to your store today looking for you," Kensie added.

Derrick blinked and then his gaze shifted to her. "Why do you want to know about Henry?"

"His name is Henry?" Kensie shuffled up closer, squishing Rebel between herself and Colter. The dog didn't seem to mind, just looked up at her and then back to Derrick, as if she was waiting for the answer, too. "Henry what?"

"How about you answer my question first, sweetheart," Derrick replied, the emphasis on *sweetheart* making it sound negative instead of an endearment.

Kensie heated with annoyance, but she gritted her teeth and gave him a smile instead. "I think—"

"She thinks Henry might be able to help her find her sister," Colter cut in.

"She can't talk for herself?"

"Let's not start something, Derrick," Colter answered, his voice low and hard.

Derrick smiled around his cigar. "You trying to scare me, soldier?"

"You don't want me trying," Colter shot back just as quickly.

Kensie stepped forward, slightly in front of Rebel, almost in Derrick's face. "Look, I get that you want to protect this guy's privacy, but—"

"Nah, I don't care about that," Derrick cut in. "Henry comes by the shop plenty, 'cause he knows I'll help him out. Advice. Best places to hunt, how to stay below the radar. I don't mind. But it's pretty clear the guy's hiding from something." He darted a sideways glance at Colter. "Then again, isn't everyone?"

"I'm not hiding from the law," Colter said, tipping his head meaningfully.

Derrick's eyes narrowed at Kensie. "He hurt your sister?"

"I don't know." Her voice broke and Kensie cleared her throat, embarrassed. She knew how to do this. She'd done this since she was thirteen years old. It was almost a role: dutiful older sister, willing to show whatever pain or desperation was needed in order to get information.

"Henry Rollings."

"You know where he lives?" Colter asked as Kensie breathed, "Thank you."

Derrick nodded at her, then looked back at Colter. "Up past the snowplow shop. He always comes in from the west. Off that old unmarked trail. Could be anywhere up that way."

Colter looked pensive, then held out his hand. "Thank you."

Derrick shook his hand and told him, "Look after this one."

Kensie stiffened a little at being talked about like she wasn't standing right there, but softened as Colter answered seriously, "It's my top priority."

"Good luck," Derrick told her, then closed the door on them.

Colter turned and headed back to the truck, Rebel trotting after him.

Kensie moved more slowly, staring at his back. This man working so hard to help her thought he shouldn't even be here. The idea filled her with a dangerous desire: to give him something to live for.

Chapter 9

Kensie was in his bedroom right now. Probably un-dressed.

The idea made Colter breathe faster and he couldn't keep his gaze from drifting over—yet again—to the closed door between them. No one besides Kensie had ever been inside his cabin. Now she'd been here twice. This time, it had been his idea.

Even though the reasons weren't personal, having her in his space *felt* personal. He imagined her right now, looking around his room. Taking in the simple spindle bed in the middle, Rebel's cushy dog bed in the corner. Maybe the pictures on his nightstand.

One of his parents from his graduation, younger and still convinced he'd change his mind about the military. Grinning with their arms around each other's waists, still madly in love after twenty-five years together. Back then, proud and excited about the future they imagined for him, so different than the path he'd seen for himself.

Another picture of Colter's brothers, taken not long before that final mission. Laughing and smiling, relaxed at the base. None of them knowing they had only a few hours left to live.

The memory sobered him, and images of Kensie changing out of her clothes into something more appropriate for the weather fled. But thoughts of Kensie herself stuck. Having her here didn't feel strange. It felt natural. And that made him nervous.

He had no room for anyone else in his life, especially not a woman whose time in Alaska had an expiration date. Because even though he missed his parents—and there were days he desperately wished he'd followed their dreams for him instead of his own, so he wouldn't know this pain now—he couldn't imagine ever returning to Idaho. Or going anywhere else, for that matter.

In the past year, Alaska had become his home. This cabin calmed him. The wide open spaces and cold, unforgiving weather relaxed him, helped reduce his panic. One day, maybe this place would even heal him, get him partway back to whole again.

The door to his bedroom opened and Kensie lumbered out.

Colter couldn't help the laugh that escaped. After talking to Derrick, she'd wanted to immediately try and track Henry Rollings. But he'd insisted on bringing her back to the main part of Desparre to get clothes more appropriate for Alaska's coming weather.

Instead of dropping her at her hotel, he'd brought

her here to change, because he'd wanted to stop off for a different kind of gear himself.

In early October, Desparre might hit twenty-five degrees midday if you were lucky. Lows regularly got down to two degrees. It wasn't really that bad, once you got used to it. But the problem was that Desparre wasn't a city like Chicago, filled with easy places to stop in and warm up if your car broke down or the wind chill got to be too much. October was also the snowiest month of the year and there was no guarantee when the snow would start—or stop. In a few weeks they could be so snowed in that no one was getting out until spring.

Keeping Kensie here until the flowers poked up in the valley below wasn't a half-bad idea. Even how she was dressed now, in boots appropriate for the mountains, snow pants and a jacket that would actually keep her warm if they got stuck out in the cold somewhere, he couldn't take his eyes off her.

She took big, exaggerated steps out of his room, as though she was weighed down by all the gear he'd made her get. But he shook his head, not buying it. Everything he'd picked for her was relatively lightweight.

"I feel like a snow monster," Kensie complained.

"You look cute." He hadn't meant to say it out loud, and her eyes widened. Hoping she wouldn't take that the wrong way, he added, "This is going to be much better if we get stranded somewhere."

"Why would we get stranded?"

"Well, hopefully we won't," Colter said, even though the idea of being stranded anywhere with Kensie didn't sound bad at all. "But weather here can be unpredictable. We get surprised by a blizzard or trapped on the hill by an avalanche and you're going to want real winter gear."

She looked nervous for a second, but then her expression shifted and her thoughts were broadcasted on her face. She'd definitely looked at the pictures in his room, and they'd made her think of his words earlier, about avoiding his rightful fate alongside his brothers. The look on her face now was one of uncertainty, as if she wanted to bring it up again but wasn't sure how. And mixed with that was pity. If there was anything he hated, it was pity.

"Stop staring at me like I'm damaged."

She looked startled. "I'm not."

Rebel lifted her head from the spot she'd claimed near the hearth, her head swiveling between them, ears perked.

He took a few steps toward Kensie. "Yeah, you are." He didn't know why he cared. They both knew it was true, so why did it matter if he could see it on her face? Was it better that she thought it, but kept it hidden?

Still, the idea of her thinking that he was *less* made tension build up inside him. Suddenly he couldn't think of anything he wanted more than to prove he was whole. Or, at least, whole enough.

He was still walking toward her. He hadn't intended to, but the closer he got, the better an idea it seemed. The closer he got, the more her eyes widened and her lips parted.

As he stared at the fullness of her lips, the rapidly increasing rise and fall of her chest, the past seemed to fall away. He reached out, letting his fingers drift over the puffiness of her coat, down to her bare hands. Some-

how, with Kensie so covered up, the act of sliding his
fingers between hers was intensified. The softness of
her skin, the delicate strength in her fingers, calloused
from playing violin. Pleasure shot up from the point
where their skin met, and he tugged her toward him.

Instead of pulling back like she probably should
have, she fell into him. He smiled at how huge her coat
suddenly seemed, putting unnatural distance between
them. But instead of unzipping it, he just wrapped his
arms around her, pulling her in tighter.

Her hands made a slow, jerky ascent up his chest, and
with her head tucked close to his shoulder, he wasn't
sure if it was desire or uncertainty putting the hitch
in her movements. But then she lifted up on tiptoe so
they were lined up perfectly, her beautiful eyes staring back at him.

Her lips were only inches away, her breath puffing
against his mouth, but he froze, captivated by the pure
toffee brown of her eyes, by the mix of emotions in
her gaze. Raw desire, yes. But also something softer,
more intimate.

If only that metal hadn't torn through his leg. If only
those bullets hadn't torn through his friends. He barely
knew her, and yet he could imagine if his life had gone
a different way. Kensie waiting for him through deploy-
ments, her letters putting a smile on his face when he
was away in some far-off country like he'd seen with
his brothers when they'd gotten messages from home.

As if she could read his mind, Kensie's expression
shifted, lines appearing between her eyebrows. Colter
didn't want her to think. He didn't want to think, either.
He only wanted to feel.

He leaned in, pressed his lips softly to hers, letting her decide. For a second, he thought she'd change her mind. Then her arms looped tight around his neck, her eyes closed and her mouth moved against his.

All the built-up pressure in his chest released and he sighed against her, loving the silky softness of her lips, the raspiness of her tongue seeking his.

It wasn't enough. He pulled her in even tighter, suddenly hating the sensible coat he'd had her buy. He kissed her harder, faster, desperate for more.

She met each stroke of his tongue, her fingers sliding through his short hair, not enough to grasp. She rose even higher on her toes, giving their kiss a new angle.

A different kind of pressure rose inside him. He could lose himself in this woman. Release all his pain and his past and try to forget himself with a few hours of pleasure.

He forced his hands away from her back, shifted them to her hips. Misunderstanding his intent, she tilted her hips toward him, almost changing his mind. But he couldn't do it. Couldn't use her to soothe the aches in his soul any more than he wanted her to do the same with him.

Because whether she thought so or not, this kiss wasn't really about him. It couldn't be. They barely knew each other. But, on some level, they understood each other.

He knew her pain, the way losing her sister must have followed her through her life, a silent, torturous ghost. He knew the razor-thin line between hope and desperation, between love and torment.

Using his grip on her hips to anchor her, he leaned

back, simultaneously peeling her off him. "We shouldn't do this."

His voice didn't even sound like his. It was deeper, gruffer than usual.

She blinked back at him, her cheeks flushed bright red and no comprehension in her gaze.

The fog of desire surrounding her made him want to pull her right back in. Instead, he told her, "Maybe I should be dead, but I'm not. So stop looking at me like I am."

Kensie's lips twisted up, lines raking her forehead. "What?"

Her voice wasn't right either. It was breathy, higher pitched. Way too sexy.

He steeled himself, trying not to lean back in. "You heard me."

Then he turned away so she wouldn't see how little this had to do with his proving something. He might have started walking toward her because of that, but it had quickly become something very different.

But not enough. And she deserved better.

Reaching on top of a cabinet, Colter pulled down his shotgun and dug out a box of shells from the drawer. When he felt like he had some control over his emotions, he turned back toward her.

She looked equal parts stunned and confused.

"Let's do this," he said, tapping his leg for Rebel to follow and heading for the door before he could change his mind.

How could a man who didn't think he belonged among the living make her feel so *alive?*

At twenty-seven, she'd had a handful of long-term relationships, even one that her parents had pushed her to make permanent. She'd had a handful of flings, too. But none of them had made her feel even close to what she'd felt with Colter for a few minutes up in his cabin. Minutes he regretted, if his abrupt stop was anything to go by.

He'd strode out of the cabin—with a shotgun, of all things—and Kensie had been left rooted to the floor. It had taken her an embarrassingly long time to get it together and follow.

Now here they were. Back on the edge of town where Derrick's store was located, except this time they were tackling a bigger stretch of stores. It was about the size of downtown Desparre, but the stores were more spread out, tucked away in a maze of side streets. That was Colter's excuse for them to split up and find out if anyone here could give them more precise information about Henry. That, and the fact that it was rapidly getting dark and he wanted her safely back at her hotel before the sun fully set. The reality, she suspected, had to do with that kiss.

It had started out slow, almost like a first kiss, even though they'd already shared one on the street. But then it had shifted. She wasn't sure which one of them had punched the gas, but suddenly, she hadn't been able to get enough of him. It had felt like a million degrees inside her winter gear as he'd heated her up, but she'd been certain she was about to shed all of it. About to fall into bed with a man she hardly knew.

The idea made her cheeks flush even now, and she'd barely been able to look at him during the drive over.

Embarrassment, yes, but also regret. Falling for Colter was a bad idea for so many reasons, and yet she'd take the heartache later for a night with him now.

That's how you feel right this minute, a little voice in her head whispered. *But what about when you're back in Chicago, all by yourself and missing him?*

The idea made her restless, antsy for a glimpse of Colter and Rebel, to reassure herself he was still close. Once he'd parked the truck, he glanced at her, his expression inscrutable, just staring for a long moment. Then he'd suggested she work her magic with some of the townspeople while he went into the rowdy bar and asked around.

As busy as the bar was, the rest of the town felt dead. It was beautiful, like a postcard, with snow blanketing the roofs and lantern-style streetlights lining the dirt roads, but also a little spooky. She turned down a side street, hoping to find someone to talk to. So far, she'd only run into a couple of shop owners and a father and daughter out for a stroll, none of whom knew Henry.

Back in Chicago, she'd be tripping over people. And yet, in some ways, she felt more connected to Colter here than she ever had to anyone in the city. Her apartment was great, a stone's throw from the lake, a brisk walk to work. Back home, she was always on the move. Going full speed from performances to working with cold-case groups to get attention for Alanna's kidnapping to a decently full social life. It was busy, but something was missing. And not just her sister.

She couldn't remember the last time she'd slowed down and really enjoyed life. Since she'd been in Desparre, she'd been moving at warp speed, too, searching for any possible leads before it was too late. And yet she'd had time to linger over cobbler and cocoa with Colter. Had time to relax with Rebel, pet her soft fur and enjoy the dog's contagious happiness. Had time to look out Colter's big window at the amazing scenery below and just *be*.

Two days in Alaska and here she was, rethinking the choices she'd made in her life. But she'd always done what seemed right, from trying to look after her brother during those years her parents were lost in the search for Alanna to trying to make them proud of her. Trying to make up for letting Alanna get taken in the first place and keep her sister's legacy alive through music.

Would Alanna even like the violin today? Kensie had no way of knowing, but every time she picked up the instrument, she felt her sister's spirit. It kept Kensie connected to Alanna in a way nothing else could. But had she traded her own path for the things she thought would make her parents proud, keep their love strong after what she'd done? Had she traded a chance to really live her life for the whirlwind that kept her from thinking too much about what she'd lost and what she really wanted?

The idea made anxiety rise in her chest until she clutched a hand there. It actually physically hurt. And she suspected it was only a fraction of the pain Colter felt whenever he suddenly seemed overcome by memories.

She couldn't dwell on it very long because, up the street, a man who looked like he topped six feet, with gray-streaked brown hair and a heavy jean jacket, stepped out of a store. Her heart rate took off and she walked faster, wanting to get close without his spotting her. Could it be Henry Rollings?

He headed away from her, walking with long strides,

but not seeming to realize she was behind him. *It was him.* Okay, she wasn't positive, but she was pretty sure. It was the same jacket she'd seen earlier, the same dark hair, shot through with gray.

Swallowing back her nerves, Kensie glanced behind her as Henry turned the corner up ahead. Where was he going? And where was Colter? If Henry really was connected to her sister's disappearance, she wasn't sure she wanted to face him alone. An ex-Marine with a shotgun at her side seemed like a good idea about now.

She dug in her pocket for her cell phone to text Colter just as Henry turned a corner. Scared of losing him, Kensie shifted from a fast walk to a jog. When she turned the corner after him, she slowed, stepping more carefully, softly. She didn't dare slip her phone out of her pocket now, afraid it would make too much noise. Even her breathing seemed too loud here.

There'd been a handful of people around on the last street, but this one was totally empty. The stores here were all dark, alleyways and parking lots dimly lit and quiet. Just the man she hoped was Henry Rollings striding along ahead of her. She had no idea where he was going. It didn't seem like there was anything here, unless his truck was down an alleyway or in one of the tiny lots peppering the small openings between some of the stores.

Had he spotted her reflection in a store window as she chased after him? Was he leading her into a trap?

Slowly, she slid her hand deeper into her pocket, bypassing her phone and groping instead for the key to her rental truck. It wasn't much of a weapon, but it was all she had. And there was no turning back now. Not if there was a chance he could lead her to Alanna.

She took another step and her right foot slid. Kensie pinwheeled her arms, trying to regain her balance as she realized there was slick ice underneath her.

Just as she caught traction again, the guy up ahead glanced back. His eyes widened at the sight of her. It *was* Rollings!

He whipped his head forward again and took off running.

Kensie raced after him, her new boots unfamiliar and sliding on random patches of ice. He turned another corner and tears pricked her eyes as she finally made it around the same spot.

He was gone.

She glanced both ways, desperately searching for a glimpse of him or any hint of where he could have gone. One way led to another alley and maybe back to the main part of town. The other led off into a group of freestanding storage units. And walking into those storage units, was that…?

Kensie craned her head forward, squinting into the darkness. A woman with dark, shoulder-length hair. Something familiar about the slope of her shoulders, the shape of her head. Was it even possible?

"Alanna!" Her sister's name erupted from her mouth in a desperate, high-pitched squeak, but the woman heard.

She glanced backward and Kensie almost fainted right there in the dark street.

After all these years, she'd actually done it. She'd found Alanna.

Chapter 10

She'd just seen her sister. The realization stunned Kensie so much she froze. And then Alanna was gone, disappearing into the maze of storage units.

Why would she walk away? Where was she going?

It *was* Alanna. It didn't matter that Kensie hadn't seen her sister in fourteen years, that she'd grown from a young child to a woman in that time. It didn't matter that Kensie had only gotten a brief, unexpected look at her face before she'd turned away.

It was *her*. Kensie knew it down deep in her soul, in the space that had been empty since her sister was taken. In the space that had burned with hope and determination, an unwillingness to let Alanna go, ever since.

Sucking in a deep breath as she realized she'd actually stopped breathing, Kensie stepped forward again and a glint of light in the store window she was passing caught her eye. A reflection from behind her. A person's reflection, moving stealthily toward her.

Kensie stared at it from the corner of her eye, not turning her head at all, not wanting to let whoever it was know she'd seen him. A jolt shot through her, leaving panic behind, as she figured out who it was. The guy who'd told her he was ex-military, who'd tried to lure her into his truck. Danny Weston.

Colter had called him dangerous, warned her to stay far away from him. Colter had been so certain Danny was a threat that he'd agreed to help her just to keep her away from the guy. Fear made her overheated inside her warm new winter clothes, but she tried to stay calm.

She could run from Danny, but could she actually *outrun* him? Her best bet would be to go down the alley, toward the main part of town. Toward help.

But if she went that way, she'd be going in the opposite direction from where her sister had disappeared. She'd lose Alanna again. And after fourteen desperate, painful years of searching, she couldn't risk it. So running wasn't an option.

Instead, she fumbled inside her coat pocket again, this time for her cell phone. Would Danny react if he saw her using it, come after her sooner instead of just tracking her? Assuming following her somewhere and then hurting her was his intent. Maybe he was just walking around.

But that was wishful thinking and she knew it. There was no one else here. All the stores were closed. And Danny had already tried to lure her off with him once. He'd failed. And she might not know Danny, but years of working with other families dealing with their own cold cases had taught her about people like him. Failure was a hit to his ego. He'd try again. It wasn't inevitable it would be with her, but she'd offered him an opportunity tonight. And she was pretty sure he'd try to take it.

Kensie pulled her cell phone out slowly, carefully, keeping it low in front of her body where he wouldn't see it. Thank goodness Colter had programmed his number in at his cabin.

She couldn't risk a phone call. So she typed out a frantic text, her hands shaking, praying she was giving him an accurate sense of where she was right now. Praying Colter could get to his truck, grab his shotgun and then get over here fast enough to help her.

She was a strong and capable woman, trained in basic self-defense, but Danny Weston was a lot bigger. In any other circumstances, she'd do the logical thing and run for help, screaming the entire way.

But logic didn't get a say when her sister was involved. Right now, Kensie could only think with her heart.

So, as she hit Send on her message to Colter, she kept moving. Toward those dark storage units. Toward Alanna.

As she did, a new reason to panic occurred to her. Could Danny and Henry be working together? Maybe they were luring her out here to grab her. Might she have found Alanna only to disappear with her?

Her parents might survive losing another child. Unlike a lot of families who'd gone through this experience, they'd banded together instead of being slowly ripped apart. The divorce rate was astronomical for parents who lost a child. But her parents had made it, in some ways seeming closer now than they had before Alanna went missing.

But what about her brother, Flynn? He'd already gotten so out of control at sixteen that he'd almost died while driving drunk one night, another dangerous stunt, probably crying for attention, for help. Yeah, he was much better now. But he relied on her regular check-ins, relied on a support group still. This might set him back so far it would destroy him.

Her chest hurt at the idea of choosing between Alanna and Flynn. She loved both of them. She was the oldest and although she'd failed Alanna, she'd always seen it as her job to look after them.

But did she really have a choice right now? She'd let Colter know where she was. Hopefully he'd see the text and come in time. If she turned or ran, Danny would know she'd seen him. And Henry had already spotted her following him, so would he stick around if she didn't catch up to him now? Or would he take Alanna and disappear somewhere else? Somewhere they'd never find her again?

Fear burned in Kensie's chest, the cold searing her lungs as she took too-fast breaths. She stepped off the sidewalk, crossed the snow-covered dirt road and stepped between storage units. Without store windows to show her Danny's reflection, she relied on her ears, listening carefully for footfalls. But the snow muffled most of them except for the occasional squish of a heavy boot in a slushy spot or the slight rustle of his clothing. Her phone was clutched tightly in her hand, but the screen stayed dark. Had Colter even seen her message?

The sun was sinking fast, casting beautiful reds and oranges across the sky, but the light didn't reach well between the storage units. It did a better job of casting shadows than providing light. Why would Henry even come back here?

She was an idiot. This had to be a trap. There was nothing here except plenty of places to hide between units and jump out at her when she was least expecting it.

Just as she was considering how to turn around without running into Danny, she realized where Henry and Alanna must have been going. Beyond the storage units was more parking. It looked empty, but she could only see a sliver of the lot, so she had to assume Henry had parked there. Maybe to keep Alanna out of sight while he shopped? Had she sneaked out of his truck, looking for help? But if she had, why had she kept walking when Kensie called her?

Kensie would figure that out when she found her. Glancing one last time at her cell phone, Kensie tucked it into her pocket and picked up her pace. She hadn't spotted Henry once since she'd started down this trail and for all she knew, he'd turned a different way.

But as she emerged from the storage units into a parking lot, she saw a black truck firing to life. And in the passenger seat was a woman with dark, shoulder-length hair.

No! The cry stuck in Kensie's throat. Without knowing what she was going to do, Kensie took off running, straight for the truck. Instead of trying to stand behind it—and probably getting run over for her trouble—she redirected toward the passenger side.

The truck was starting to back out, but slowly, like the driver hadn't spotted her. She could reach it! If the door was unlocked, Kensie could rip it open and pull Alanna out.

She was so close! A few more steps and her sister would be free. Then the driver's head tilted upward, like he was looking in his rearview, and the truck raced backward. It slammed to a stop—presumably as he shifted into Drive. But that was all the time Kensie would need.

She stretched her hand out toward the door handle, toward Alanna. Then an arm wrapped around her ribs from behind and a hand slapped over her mouth. Someone bigger and taller wrenched her off her feet, smothering her scream as the truck roared out of the lot, taking Alanna with it.

Where was Kensie?

Colter hadn't seen her in over an hour. He'd finished talking to the occupants of the bar twenty minutes ago, expecting to find her waiting by his truck. Although the stores were spread out, there wasn't a whole lot still open. Soon it would just be the bar.

He'd checked his cell phone, but nothing. So, then he'd started moving, peeking down most of the side streets, even popping into the few stores not yet closed. But no Kensie.

Nerves settled low in his belly, along with guilt that he'd let her wander around alone. Except she should have been perfectly safe here. Yes, it was quiet, but as far as he knew, the only trouble they'd ever had originated in the bar. Usually fights, which was why he'd suggested Kensie check the stores.

But there wasn't a lot to check, so why wasn't she back yet? And if she'd found anything, why hadn't she called? Yes, cell service could be spotty here, but it was usually okay as long as she stayed on the main streets.

Now, as the colorful streaks in the sky sank lower behind the trees, Colter glanced at Rebel. She'd sat patiently outside the bar waiting for him. He should have sent her with Kensie.

Rebel let out a low whine, as if she knew what he was thinking and agreed.

"Come on, girl, let's find Kensie," he said, picking up his pace even as his bad leg throbbed in protest.

Her tail wagged, but she watched him, as if he should know where she was. Which he should.

"Where are you, Kensie?" he asked out loud, making the woman closing up shop nearby glance at him sideways.

"Have you seen a woman with long brown hair and a purple coat come through here? She would have been looking for—"

"Her sister." The woman cut him off. "Yeah, I saw her about five minutes ago."

His heart picked up. Five minutes wasn't very long. And there wasn't much else down this street besides a few other shops, already closed up for the night, a couple of small parking lots and a group of storage units. Maybe she'd looped the long way around back to town and they'd just missed each other. "Do you know which way she headed?"

The woman silently pointed down the street—toward

the storage units—and then rounded the corner into the tiny parking lot next to her store.

Colter opened his mouth to ask if she was sure, but she'd seemed certain. He frowned, walking that way, but glancing down every alleyway he passed. A flash of movement caught his eye up ahead, and then a truck careened out from the side alongside the storage units. And in the passenger seat...was that Kensie?

"Kensie!" Her name ripped from his mouth as the truck did a dangerously sharp turn onto the street across from him. It would be gone long before he could get back to his truck and follow.

Panic and dread and loss filled him instantly, completely. They overwhelmed him, made his vision go dark like it had that day he'd learned about his brothers in the hospital. He slumped down into a crouch. His leg nearly gave out on him, but he managed to catch himself, resting his head on his knees, trying to get air into his suddenly uncooperative windpipe.

Beside him, Rebel let out a sharp bark and jabbed her head under his armpit. She nudged him with her nose over and over, grounding him, slowly settling the ringing in his ears.

And then he heard it. Kensie. A muffled shout of his name.

Was he hallucinating? He glanced at Rebel, who jerked to attention, straining forward without moving her feet.

It hadn't been Kensie in the truck. His hands shook so hard he could barely push himself back to a standing position, but he gritted his teeth and tried to get it together. Because from the sound of her voice, Kensie was in trouble.

He ran between the towering storage units, glancing back and forth, checking for threats far less effectively than he'd been trained. But Kensie's voice had come from the far side of the units; he was almost positive.

Rebel raced at his side, capable of outrunning him, but a loyal partner even now that they were both retired. She understood the Marines' code as well as he did; she'd never leave him.

"Good girl," he told her, pushing his leg even harder. Tiny knives danced up his thigh and he gritted his teeth, desperate to get to Kensie. Up ahead, he heard scuffling sounds, but nothing else.

Finally, the storage units ended and he shot out into a dark, dingy parking lot he hadn't even known was back here. At the far end of it was a dumpster. And Kensie, being dragged toward it by Danny Weston.

He had one arm manacled around her waist. The other hand was over her mouth, with his thumb jammed under her chin. Probably to keep her from screaming again. Or maybe she'd bitten him. He hoped she'd bitten him.

"Weston!" Colter barked, putting every ounce of command he could into it.

The man started, his gaze jolting upward as Colter ran straight at him, Rebel still at his side.

Right before they reached him, Danny swung Kensie violently sideways. She flew out of his grasp, slamming into the dumpster with a sickening, metallic thud.

"Kensie!" He stared at her, desperate to see movement, seeking out blood.

Before he could determine if she was okay, Danny was rushing him, ducking his head low and coming at him like a linebacker.

But Colter had been a Marine. He darted left, flicking his hand at Rebel in a silent command to go right.

She obeyed and Danny didn't adjust in time, flying between them. Colter spun, wincing at the trembling in his knee, but still ready to pound Danny into the ground.

But the jerk was faster than Colter had expected, already facing him, already realizing his weakness. Before Colter could react, Danny kicked out hard with a steel-toed boot, slamming into Colter's damaged leg, right above the knee.

Colter hit the pavement hard, face-first. Pain erupted in his head and thigh, and a million spots of light danced in front of his eyes until he thought he might throw up.

But Kensie was still in danger if he passed out, so Colter mustered up everything he had and flipped to his back.

Just in time to see that Danny had grabbed a pipe and was swinging it toward his head.

Chapter 11

The growl that emerged from Rebel's mouth in that moment was unlike anything Colter had ever heard.

Danny froze, pipe in midair, and then shifted, swinging that deadly metal at Rebel.

Colter knew he'd never get to his feet fast enough to stop it. There was only one option and it was going to hurt like crazy. He swung his bad leg as hard as he could into Danny's knees, knocking the man sideways.

Pain jolted up his leg to his head, then raced back down, until he couldn't tell what was damaged and what wasn't. But Danny toppled to his knees, dropping the pipe.

Then Rebel leaped on him, knocking him the rest of the way down. She wasn't an attack dog, but she was strong and Colter knew she'd do anything to protect him.

But he wasn't going to let her get hurt for him. Not again.

Colter wasn't sure he could stand, so he rolled sideways toward Danny, slamming a fist into the man's groin. He didn't like to fight dirty, but Rebel's life was at stake. So was Kensie's.

Danny yelped and curled inward, making Rebel jump off him. But it wasn't enough. And Colter wasn't going to win this battle from the ground. He needed to get up.

Danny was recovering faster than Colter, already rolling to his side and getting leverage to push to his feet. If Danny stood first, it was game over.

So Colter clamped his jaw against the pain and put his palms to pavement. With everything he had, he pushed upward, shoving himself to his feet.

It still wasn't going to be enough. Through eyes watering from pain, he could see Danny readying himself to deliver a knockout punch, fueled by rage and embarrassment and a dark soul.

His gaze jumped over to Kensie at the same time Colter's did. Somehow, while they'd been on the ground, she'd risen and crept up on them.

Time seemed to move in slow motion as Danny's eyes widened and he tried to swivel toward Kensie. But he was too slow.

Her punch was well aimed, despite the slight wobble as she pivoted toward him. It didn't take Danny down, but it knocked him back several steps and he shook his head, clearly seeing stars.

Colter didn't hesitate. He didn't know how long he could stand, but he had one last push in him. And it didn't matter if he collapsed as long as he took Danny down hard with him. He raced at Danny, ducking his head like Danny had done initially. But Colter made contact, slamming into him hard enough to make Danny buckle and send them both back to the pavement.

Danny landed beneath him, head smacking the concrete with an echoing bang. His eyes blinked open and closed and his arms drooped. Then his eyes popped open again and he shoved at Colter. But his strength was diminished enough that Colter had no trouble holding him down.

Then sirens were screaming toward him. Soon, someone was lifting him to his feet and rolling Danny over, slapping on handcuffs as Kensie talked a mile a minute to another officer.

Colter recognized both officers, and by how quickly they'd realized Danny was the aggressor, he figured they'd recognized him, too. He nodded his thanks as one of them explained, "We got a call from a store owner about a woman yelling for help."

The officer let go of his arm and Colter's whole right side seemed to collapse. He would have fallen if Kensie hadn't darted over to support him, slipping her smaller body beneath his shoulder. Still, the force of his knee giving out almost took them both down.

Colter fought it, shifting as much weight as he could onto his left leg. His right one screamed in agony and even without having to bear weight, it shook uncontrollably.

"You okay? You need an ambulance?" the officer asked as his partner dragged Danny away.

Danny screamed obscenities and threats the entire way to being shoved into the back of the police cruiser.

The officer who'd helped him up didn't even glance his partner's way, apparently assuming she had it under control as he continued to stare at Colter with concern.

"I'm all right," Colter said, as Rebel let out a dissenting whine.

"You need to go to the hospital," Kensie insisted.

"I know my injury. It just needs rest." Colter hoped he was right. "But what about you? You hit that dumpster hard. You were unconscious. I want a doctor to look at you."

"I'm fine." Kensie sighed, frowning down at his leg.

"Ambulance is right around the corner," the officer said. "We'll have them look at both of you and the paramedics can decide."

"But—" Kensie started.

"Let's go," the officer said, his tone brooking no argument.

Rebel barked her agreement.

Driving colter's truck made her nervous. It was a big, hulking beast, capable of handling the steep drive up to his cabin, but taking up more of the road than she was used to managing.

The man next to her made Kensie nervous, too. He looked like he belonged on a Marine recruitment poster, with his well-defined muscles and intense blue eyes. He'd gritted his teeth while the medic poked and examined his leg and suggested he get an X-ray to make sure all the metal holding his thigh together was still intact. Then he'd calmly shaken his head and limped to the truck.

But he'd been in no shape to drive and they both

knew it. So Kensie had gotten behind the wheel, after being cleared by the medic as having no obvious signs of concussion. Still, since she'd been briefly unconscious, they'd warned her to go to the hospital herself if she experienced any dizziness, vomiting or confusion.

Right now there was definite confusion, but it had nothing to do with Danny Weston throwing her against that disgusting dumpster. She risked another glance at Colter out of the corner of her eye. He looked terrible, his face so pale that she knew he was in a lot of pain. But he hadn't complained once. And she wasn't sure how to help him without hurting his pride.

Rebel looked just as worried as Kensie parked Colter's truck outside his cabin. She'd barely stepped out of the vehicle before the dog leaped over the front seat and climbed out after her. Rebel ran around to the passenger side faster than Kensie, but Colter had already gotten his door open and was trying to swivel himself out of the truck without bending his leg.

Kensie wedged herself in the door opening, sliding her arm behind his back and bracing herself for his weight. "Lean on me."

"I've got it," he said, sounding more frustrated than harsh.

"Yeah, I know, but this will be easier," she said, trying to sound cheerful. But she couldn't quite manage it. Residual fear still clung to her from her encounter with Danny. Fear about what could have happened to her. Fear about what had almost happened to Rebel and Colter.

His eyes narrowed on her, as if he could read her thoughts, and then he did lean on her just a little as he hauled himself out of the truck. The step down to the ground was shaky and Kensie did her best to absorb the impact, but she could still tell he was hurting.

It took them several minutes to make the short trek to the cabin door, with Rebel running circles around them most of the way.

"Rebel, chill," Colter finally said, a smile cracking through as she plopped down on her butt.

"She loves you," Kensie said as he fumbled with the key and got the door open.

"Yeah, well, I love her, too," Colter replied, bracing himself on the doorjamb to take some of his weight off her. "We saw three years of combat together. We train as partners and that's what she is. I'd take a bullet for her and she almost took one for me."

Kensie glanced back at Rebel, who was waiting patiently for Colter to make it through the doorway before she followed. "You saved her today."

"She saved me in Afghanistan," he answered simply, pulling away from her a little to peel his coat off and drop it on the floor.

"You saved me today, too." Her text had never gone through, but he'd come for her anyway, taking on Danny despite his own injuries.

Colter glanced at her briefly before continuing a slow walk toward his recliner. "We saved each other."

His words were filled with so many emotions. Honesty and admiration, yes, but also embarrassment. Probably because he hadn't been able to take Danny down on his own. But it wasn't a fair fight when Colter had a damaged leg.

She knew saying that would only fuel Colter's resentment and frustration at his situation. Instead, she stayed silent, helping him lower himself into his recliner.

Once seated, he sighed and rested his head back against the chair, closing his eyes. It gave her the chance to stare at him, at the very faint lines on his forehead, the thick blond-tinged eyebrows, down over a strong nose to strong, full lips. Lips she'd tasted more than once. Lips she wanted to taste again right now.

His eyes flicked open. There was heat in his gaze, but amusement in the tilt of his lips. "You mind shutting the door, Kensie? It's cold in here."

She hurried toward the door, feeling a flush shoot up her face. Although what reason did she have to be embarrassed? They'd already kissed twice. He knew she was attracted to him. She faltered as she pushed the heavy cabin door shut. But did he know that what he'd done had drawn her to him even more?

He deserved to know that. He deserved to know that while he was sitting there, obviously feeling like a failure for not taking down Danny Weston all alone, in her mind, doing it despite his injury made Colter more heroic.

"What are you thinking?" Colter asked softly, making her realize she'd been standing there too long without turning back. "If you think you're up for it, you can head back to your hotel. I don't mind if you take my truck."

"That's not…" She turned to face him, clutching her hands together. To make sure he knew she had no intention of leaving, she tossed her coat and yanked off her boots. "I know, being a Marine, you're used to being able to take on any threat all by yourself."

"Not really." He cut her off, looking uncomfortable. "Marines work in units. I mean, yeah, I was an MP and a K-9 handler, which is a little different. But I still had a partner." He glanced at Rebel, whose tail swung back and forth as she glanced between them.

"I don't know what you're thinking right now," she continued, even though she was pretty sure she *did* know. It was in the slump of his shoulders, the down-turn of his lips, the way he'd hung his head as he'd told the officers what happened. He felt like less of a man.

Well, screw that. She walked slowly toward him, forcing herself to keep eye contact even though the strength of his gaze made her too warm inside. Made it hard to concentrate on her words.

But she tried, because she owed him that much after what he'd done for her. And not just in that parking lot, but every moment since she'd met him. "Having an in-jury doesn't make you less."

He blew out a loud breath through his nose, like he disagreed, but she didn't give him time to cut her off.

"You could have used that as an excuse. Not just today, but for everything I've asked you to do. But you haven't." She kept approaching, her tone gaining con-viction with every word, because it was all true. "You acted anyway. You put yourself in harm's way to help me and Rebel." Her voice broke as she reached the side of his chair and took his hand. "You're the most incred-ible man I've ever met."

She hadn't realized she thought it until the words came out, but they were true. No one had ever put so much on the line for her, and she barely knew him. What must he be like when it was someone he loved?

He stared back at her, the expression on his face shifting from disbelief and self-disgust to contemplation to something soft and raw that made her legs feel weak. Then his fingers were sliding through hers, his touch making nerves all over her body fire to life.

On Colter's other side, Rebel let out a short bark, startling her and breaking the spell. But as soon as she turned her smiling gaze back to Colter, the feeling returned. Because he was still staring up at her with an intensity that said her words had penetrated. Maybe she'd even made him believe them.

She slid her palm over the scruff coming in on Colter's cheek, then leaned in. It was an awkward angle, but when his lips grazed hers, it didn't matter. Happiness filled her, instant and so powerful that it overwhelmed everything else. She pushed forward, pressing her mouth more tightly to his, and almost fell into his lap.

She caught herself on the recliner arm just in time. "Sorry," she breathed.

"Come here," he whispered back, tugging her toward him.

Carefully, she pivoted her body over the chair, so she was straddling him without putting any weight on him. Her knees were on either side of him, her butt arched awkwardly in the air, but it didn't matter, because now her hands could slip around his neck.

He stared at her a long moment, all of that intensity directed solely at her making her squirm. Then he cupped her face with his big palm, drawing her closer until her lips settled on his again. He kissed her softly at first, the merest grazing of his lips and tongue against hers that left her whole body aching for more. When she couldn't take another moment of the slow torture, she fisted a hand in the front of his shirt and picked up the tempo until her head started spinning.

Colter's kisses grew deeper, more demanding, until everything else in the world ceased to exist. Slowly, she became aware of his hands slipping underneath the back of her shirt, his long fingers caressing their way up her back. She'd been content with just kissing him; knowing the way his leg was, he wasn't up for more. But suddenly she craved the feel of his skin against hers.

Her hands shook as they felt their way down impressive pecs and a muscled torso. Then she grabbed a fistful of his T-shirt and pulled upward. He leaned forward and helped her pull it over his head.

She'd planned to peel off her own shirt next, but got distracted by the expanse of bare skin in front of her. Drinking the sight in, her gaze stalled on his left biceps. Script circled his arm and as she traced the words, the muscles there leapt under her fingertips. "Semper Fi," she read aloud, her voice husky.

"Latin," he told her, his beautiful blue eyes fixed on hers even as his hands returned to their trek over her rib cage. "The Marines' motto. It means always faithful."

Loyalty. A smile trembled on Kensie's lips as her body responded to his touch, arching forward. Of course. A man like Colter lived by those words. He was loyal to Rebel, loyal to the memory of his lost brothers, even loyal to the promise he'd made her.

And right now, she wanted to show him how much she appreciated it. She leaned back in.

"I'm so glad you're not hurt," he whispered against her lips.

She jerked back, a jolt of realization and horror slicing through her. She'd been so distracted by Colter—by his reinjuring his leg, by her feelings for him—that she'd forgotten to tell him what she'd discovered.

With tears pricking her eyes, she scrambled off him. "Colter, I found her."

"What?"

"I think I found Alanna."

Chapter 12

Kensie's words filtered slowly through Colter's haze of desire. "You *what*?"

"I think I found her, Colter." She crossed her arms over her chest, pacing in front of him.

Rebel stood near the bottom of his recliner, her ears perked, head swiveling to follow Kensie's frantic movements.

"Okay." Colter leaned forward, then grimaced as pain jolted up his thigh. It had faded into the background with Kensie's soft lips on his, her skin beneath his fingers. Now it was back, full force. Swallowing nausea, he studied her.

A minute ago, she'd been fire and energy in his lap. Now, she was all nervous agitation and desperate hope. "Tell me what happened."

"It's that guy. The one I saw in the snowplow store."

"Henry Rollings?"

"Yeah. I followed him toward the end of the shops and then he turned a corner and I lost him. I was trying to decide which way he'd gone when I saw Alanna heading into the area with the storage units."

Colter absorbed her words more slowly than he would have liked, still a little distracted by the swollen pinkness of her lips, the rapid rise and fall of her chest. By the memory imprinted on his mind of her climbing on top of him, of the touch of her fingertips still searing his skin. "Why would she go back there? Was he dragging her?"

"No." Kensie stopped moving, her shoulders slumping, lines knitting her forehead. "She just walked in. It was after I'd lost him. I was trying to decide his most likely route when I spotted her."

Rebel moved as soon as Kensie stopped, hurrying over and shoving her nose under Kensie's hand. Without seeming to realize it, Kensie started petting Rebel, who sat and made herself comfortable.

"So, you followed this woman you think is Alanna?" Colter clarified. "Not Henry?"

Her head jerked back slightly. "Well, yeah, I guess so. I just assumed he went that way, too, once I saw her."

"And what about Danny? Was he with her?"

"No, Danny was following me."

Colter held back the slew of questions that bubbled up. When had she spotted Danny following her? Why had she gone into a deserted location if she'd known Danny was on her trail?

Colter didn't ask because he knew the answer. Her sister.

Kensie's lips folded upward, contrition in her gaze as her hand went still on Rebel's head. "I had to try and get to her, Colter."

"I understand." And he did. He didn't blame her for it, either, no matter the state of his leg. "But what would you have done if you'd caught up to her? If she was really walking that way without being forced…"

The thought trailed off as he realized that the truck that had flown past him moments before he'd heard Kensie's scream—the one he'd thought carried Kensie away from him—must have held Alanna. He'd been devastated, thinking it was Kensie being ripped out of his life. So how must Kensie feel, knowing it was the sister she'd been searching for since she was thirteen?

"Are you sure it was her?" He had to ask, even though he couldn't deny the resemblance. But then, he'd only gotten a brief glimpse of the woman in the truck's passenger seat. Dark hair, similar profile. He'd just assumed, because he knew Kensie had gone in that direction.

Maybe Kensie was just assuming, too, because she wanted so desperately for it to be Alanna.

The woman he'd seen hadn't been tied down in the back, out of sight. She'd been sitting up in the passenger seat as if she was there of her own free will. None of that sounded like a woman who'd been kidnapped.

"I-it had to be her," Kensie said. He must have looked unconvinced, because she started petting Rebel again, faster, as she rushed on. "I yelled her name. She turned toward me when she heard it, Colter. It was her. It was Alanna."

"Are you sure? Then why did she keep going? Maybe she just turned because you startled her, Kensie." He didn't want to destroy her hope, but he had to ask.

"Long-term kidnapping victims bond to their captors," Kensie told him haltingly, like she didn't want to know about such things, let alone talk about them. "They do it just to survive. Someone like Alanna, grabbed when she was only five…" She broke off on a sob that she quickly stifled. "It's possible she doesn't even know she was kidnapped, that she doesn't remember her family. That she doesn't remember me."

"I'm sorry." He cursed himself for not thinking it through. It made sense. Long-term prisoners of war sometimes did the same thing.

Not wanting Kensie to dwell on what her sister might have endured over all those years, he turned the conversation in another direction. "Are you sure she was with Henry? Did you ever see them together?"

Kensie squinted up at the ceiling, like she was trying to recall, then finally shook her head. "No, I can't be positive. I assume it was him driving the truck I saw her in, but I couldn't actually see the driver. But what are the chances he led me that way and then Alanna just happened to be there? Especially after he ran from me at the snowplow store when I started asking questions?"

Unless he was trying to lead Kensie to her sister. Trying to lure her into a trap she couldn't resist and then grab her, too. But Danny Weston had almost beaten him to it. Colter kept the dark thoughts to himself.

He also didn't voice a more immediate concern. If

Henry thought Kensie was following him around, if he knew she'd seen Alanna, would he disappear now?

He should suggest the possibility to Kensie, but he didn't want her running off trying to find Henry alone. Especially if Henry *had* hoped to take both sisters. Because, right now, Henry had a big advantage. He knew Kensie would do whatever it took to save Alanna. And they still had no real idea where to look for him.

Besides, no matter how much he wanted to be, Colter was in no shape to go anywhere right now. Not even to help Kensie. No matter how badly he wished he could.

"It had to be Henry, right?" Kensie pressed when he stayed quiet too long.

"Probably," Colter agreed, but his mind was only half on Henry now. Because maybe they were both letting their hopes run wild.

Alanna had been missing for a long time. What was the likelihood Kensie had just spotted her walking around town, no matter how deserted it was? Especially after that note had shown up and drawn the FBI, making the townspeople more alert for a possible sighting of the missing woman? Would a kidnapper really let her out into public with that added scrutiny?

Kensie told him she was pretty sure she'd seen Alanna, but maybe that was just because she wanted it so badly. The FBI thought the note was a hoax. Maybe this wasn't real, either, just a woman who looked like Alanna might have after fourteen years of growing up.

Maybe the best thing he could do for Kensie wasn't to help her chase these potentially dangerous men, but to help her move on with her own life. Help her accept that Alanna was gone. Help her realize that her own life was still worth living, that she deserved to have her own future.

Except how could he do that when he didn't believe the same was true for himself?

The way a person changed between the ages of five and nineteen was enormous. Colter had been right to ask if she could be sure the woman she'd seen was Alanna. The very idea that it might not be made Kensie's chest constrict and her brain want to shut down. She'd spent so long searching. She wasn't sure she could bear another dead end.

But this time really did feel different. She couldn't explain it, except that it had been years since she'd felt this surge of hope, this restrained happiness waiting to burst free. In the beginning, she'd experienced it often. But over the years, that had faded, leaving behind a hope that was much more jaded, much more cautious.

Since she'd first heard about the note in Desparre, though, something had taken hold of her, something deeper than desperation. She wanted to believe it was the bond she and Alanna had always shared, rearing up and screaming at her not to miss her chance to bring Alanna home.

"Kensie."

Colter's voice broke through her thoughts and she realized he was stretching his hand toward her. She stepped closer, threading her fingers through his and hanging on tight.

Rebel scooted forward, too, nudging up to Kensie's side the way she'd seen the dog do with Colter.

With the two of them beside her, Kensie's tension

eased a little. Knowing she truly wasn't in this alone cleared the panic from her mind enough to strategize. "I think we should go to the police. They must be able to get an address for Henry Rollings."

"Not necessarily," Colter replied. "And they don't really have a reason to give it to us even if they have it. But I have to be honest, Kensie. From what I've heard about this guy, I think he lives off the grid. No one in the bar could tell me quite where, even the longtime locals, which says he doesn't want anyone to know."

"Well, the police should at least be able to help us—"

"We don't have any evidence that he's done anything wrong," Colter reminded her. "We can't even be sure this woman was with him or that she's actually Alanna."

"But—"

"We can try the police if you want. I just don't want you to get your hopes up for their help. Look, a military investigation is different, so maybe I'm wrong or we'll get lucky. I'm just telling you what I know about the process. You've probably encountered it, too."

"Yeah." Evidence was king. Police generally weren't interested in the theories of civilians. It was fair, but frustrating.

She stared at Colter, and she couldn't stop her gaze from drifting to his bare chest. For a man who'd sustained a serious injury a year ago, he was in amazing shape. Running her hands over all of those muscles had made her giddy with lust. Her fingers twitched in his now, wanting a return visit.

Forcing her gaze back up, Kensie said, "I don't need the police. I know you can help me track Rollings."

Colter's lips pressed together into a hard line. "I'm

going to do my best, Kensie, but tonight…" He sighed heavily.

"I know. It's okay. We should wait for the light anyway, and honestly, I'm still a little shaken up from earlier."

It was true. If she let herself think too long about how close she'd come to being Danny Weston's prey—for whatever terrible thing he had planned for her—she'd lose it. Only Colter's kisses and his soft touch had swept away the lingering feel of Danny's aggressive, sweaty hands.

Still, the words were hard to say, because the truth was that she wanted to rush back out now. She was terrified that since Henry had spotted her following him, he'd skip town for good and take Alanna with him. But Kensie also had fourteen years of practice watching how investigations worked. Right now, she had no clue where to find Henry. And she'd learned her lesson about going after him alone.

She needed Colter. And she needed him uninjured. "Are you sure you don't want to go to the hospital?"

"I know my injury, Kensie. It probably seems like I'm being a typical boneheaded man, but I've lived with this for the past year. It hurts pretty bad right now, but it's nothing compared to what it was like even six months ago. It'll heal. It'll suck in the meantime, but it'll heal. I need elevation, ice and rest."

She peeled her hand free and hurried into the attached kitchen to get him some ice. "How much rest?" It was insensitive, but as much as she wanted Colter's help, time mattered right now. If he was going to be out of commission for a week, she'd have to find someone else to assist her.

The idea of having anyone else by her side while she searched for Alanna made anxiety gnaw away at her. Somehow, in two days, Colter and Rebel had managed to become much more than just local help. Much more than tools in the search for her sister. They'd become her friends, her support system.

She faltered, a bag full of ice in her hands. Colter had done so much for her, and when he'd said he should be dead alongside his brothers, words had failed her. Just like she'd failed him in that moment.

"Kensie?" Colter called. "What's wrong?"

How could he read her so well already? She'd never been someone who wore her feelings all over her face. Slamming the freezer door shut, she strode over to him and carefully placed the ice on his thigh.

Colter flinched at the contact, but didn't make a sound, except to say, "Thanks."

There was another chair on the opposite side of the room, but Kensie didn't want to be that far away when she broached the topic of his lost friends. So she perched on the edge of the hearth, her heart pounding frantically.

Since she'd gotten involved with groups chasing cold cases, she'd met a lot of families of victims. Some had gotten the worst possible news during the time she'd known them. When she could, she'd tried to support them, all the while praying she'd never be one of them. But she'd learned quickly that what helped one person hurt another. And she didn't want to hurt Colter. He'd faced too much pain already.

"Colter…"

He turned toward her, his beautiful blue eyes narrowing like he knew what was coming. Rebel rose from her spot on the other side of his recliner and ran around, plopping down between them. Ears perked, chin up, she stared at Colter like she was waiting for him to say something.

Kensie spoke first. "I like the picture in your room. The one where you have Rebel on your shoulders."

At her name, the dog's head swiveled toward Kensie, her tail wagging.

A short burst of laughter, half amusement at Rebel and half nervousness about the conversation, broke free. "Those were your brothers with you, right? Your Marine brothers?"

The picture had been perched sideways on his nightstand, as though sometimes he wanted to see it and others he turned it away from him. The photo showed everyone covered in dust, looking exhausted, and she'd wondered if they'd just returned from a mission, wondered what they'd been doing. Colter was in the middle, Rebel's front legs dangling over one shoulder and her back legs dangling over the other, with Colter holding both. Her tongue had been lolling out, her eyes a little droopy, like she was just as tired as the soldiers. But they'd all been smiling. Even Rebel's mouth was stretched outward, like she was happy, too.

"Kensie, you've seen what happens when I even think about that day." His voice grew quiet, like he hated admitting it. "I break down. I can't function. I don't want to talk about—"

"You don't have to tell me how they died, Colter. I want to know how they lived. You loved them, right?"

"Yeah."

"And they loved you."

It wasn't a question, but he nodded anyway.

"Don't you think they'd want—"

"Me to live?" Colter interrupted with a humorless laugh. "You think psychiatrists haven't played this game with me, Kensie?"

"It's not a ga—"

"It's not about that. Of course they'd want me to live. We all lived and breathed by the same code. Loyalty. We did everything together. And maybe that's half the point. They all had families at home waiting for them. Every single one of them. Except me." He leaned forward, pain all over his face—but from his wound or his memories, she wasn't sure. "How is that fair?"

"It's not fair," she answered softly. "But you deserve a chance at happiness, too. You deserve a family."

As she spoke the words, she could actually imagine a family for him. A little boy with Colter's sky-blue eyes. Twin girls with Colter's slow grin and her own dark hair. Rebel chasing after all of them in a yard behind a cheerful yellow house. She and Colter watching, holding hands and laughing.

Kensie swayed backward at the intensity of her fantasy, at how *real* it felt, how possible. But it wasn't. Not even close. Her time with Colter was temporary.

Colter said something, but the words didn't process over the roaring crescendo of her heartbeat in her ears. Somehow, over the course of two days, she'd done more than just develop a silly crush on Colter.

She'd gone and fallen halfway in love with him.

Chapter 13

She was falling in love with Colter Hayes. A man she barely knew.

It was ridiculous. It shouldn't even be possible. And yet, her heart thumping madly and her face flushing with the fear he might read her feelings in her eyes told her it was true.

"Kensie."

The way Colter said her name suggested he'd been repeating it. She jerked her gaze up to his, seeing the mix of confusion and concern.

His hands were braced on the recliner, all the distracting muscles in his arms outlined. "You swayed backward like you lost your balance. I think it might be from hitting your head. Maybe we need to get *you* to the hospital, get you an MRI."

How did she explain what had just happened without admitting her newly realized feelings? A burst of nervous laughter escaped.

Colter shoved himself forward, sliding down the recliner. At the motion, his jaw clamped so tightly that his lips turned inward and moisture filled the corners of his eyes. "What's going on? You need a doctor to check you out."

Jumping to her feet, Kensie held up a hand. "Stop! Don't move. I'm fine. I promise. I was just thinking about something and it surprised me. I feel normal, no headache, nothing. I don't have a concussion." She stood on one foot and pivoted in a circle. "See? My balance is fine."

He froze halfway down the recliner, eyes narrowed. "What were you thinking about?"

What could she tell him that was believable but wouldn't scare him into suggesting she find someone else to help her? Someone she wouldn't fall for after just a few days?

"Um…"

"Kensie." This time her name was filled with warning, like he already didn't believe her.

"I think I've spent most of my adult life trying to make up for letting Alanna get kidnapped." The words that burst from her mouth surprised her. Not the fact that she thought it; she'd realized it while she'd been wandering around town, searching for information on Henry. But it surprised her that she'd shared it.

Colter looked equally surprised. He stayed suspended halfway down the chair, his mouth open in a silent O.

Not wanting him to feel sorry for her—or think she didn't have a life—she backtracked. "I know it's not my fault. It's just survivor's guilt rearing up."

Great. Now she sounded like one of the psychiatrists her parents had insisted she see as a teenager.

"Of course it's not your fault."

Colter sounded almost offended by the idea, but he must have believed her, because his biceps bulged out again and then he hauled himself back up the chair. Leaning against the headrest, he closed his eyes, exhaustion in the slump of his shoulders and the way his chest heaved from the effort.

She hoped he'd drop the topic, but when his eyes opened again, they were soft, understanding.

"Why isn't your family here with you, Kensie? Helping you search for Alanna?"

It wasn't the question she'd expected him to ask and she felt herself flush for a new reason now. She didn't want him to think her family was mean or uncaring. "Because of what the FBI told us," she explained. "We've all been through this so many times over the years. There's been a lot of false leads. Once, two years after she was taken, we even drove down to Indiana to see a girl who'd been rescued. She wasn't talking and police thought it could be Alanna. It wasn't, but—"

That experience had scarred her. The girl had been a broken shell. Gaunt and terrified, and the same age as Alanna would have been then. Police had eventually found her family, but Kensie had kept track of her over the years. At thirteen she'd committed suicide.

"Anyway," Kensie rushed on, realizing she'd stopped talking long enough for concern to put lines across Colter's forehead. "My parents handled that one better than Flynn and I did."

"Of course they did. How old were you?"

"Fifteen."

Colter swore, and Kensie continued. "My parents did try hard to keep me and Flynn away from the search. But we wanted to know. We missed Alanna, too. We still do. And the longer Alanna was gone, the harder it was to get interest from the press, help from the public for tips. But they were a lot more interested if they could talk to me or Flynn."

"Oh, Kensie—"

"Flynn was younger than me, so I tried to do most of the press interviews. I thought I was protecting him, but it wasn't enough. It was never enough. My parents did their best for us, but they were trying to do their best for Alanna, too. And over the years, Flynn just got more and more out of control. Hanging out with a bad crowd, doing dangerous things just to cheat death or get some kind of rush—he's explained it to me, but I still don't totally understand."

Rebel let out a low whine and scooted closer, resting her head against Kensie's leg.

Kensie smiled at the dog, who seemed to have a finely tuned sense for when someone was hurting. Running her hand over Rebel's soft fur released a bit of the tension knotting Kensie's shoulders.

"When he was sixteen, he drove his car off a bridge. Not intentionally," she added, thinking of the girl in Indiana. "He was drunk. Thank goodness no one else was hurt. Flynn spent a month in the hospital. And that changed everything."

"What do you mean?" Colter asked softly.

"We have close family friends who say it woke my parents up to the fact that they had two other kids who needed them." When Colter frowned, she told him, "I don't think they ever forgot. But it was hard growing up with Alanna's disappearance always overshadowing everything. My parents missed birthdays chasing possible sightings. Flynn and I probably spent too much of our childhood talking to police and being interviewed by reporters and talk-show hosts. I wanted to do it, but Flynn..." She shook her head.

"So, if Flynn was sixteen when this happened, how old were you?"

"Twenty."

"So there was no do-over on your childhood at that point."

Kensie shrugged, uncomfortable with the implication. "I love my parents. They love me. They tried to do what was best for all three of their kids. I understand that. Heck, I pushed them hard not to stop. And when they did—"

"You took over," Colter said, his intense gaze never leaving her face.

She shrugged. "Yeah. My parents needed to focus on Flynn. But we couldn't just give up on Alanna. She's my baby sister."

"So, now you chase after these leads all by yourself, with no one to lean on?"

"It's not like that. My family is only a phone call away. And I can't expect them to drop everything every time I think there might be a chance."

"They dropped everything for your sister when you were a kid."

"That's not fair," Kensie said, but it lacked heat because she knew Colter was just trying to take her side. The problem was, there were no sides. There was just sadness. Her parents' way meant accepting Alanna was long dead, lost to them forever. Her way meant the possibility of an endless cycle of hope and heartbreak.

"You're right," Colter said. "I'm sorry. But you shouldn't have to do this alone."

"I'm not doing it alone," Kensie said softly, her hand still absently stroking Rebel's head. "I've got you."

And that had changed everything. She stared at him, the soft understanding in his gaze, the ice hanging sideways off his leg, dripping unnoticed onto the chair.

She'd never met anyone like Colter Hayes. She'd probably never meet anyone like him again.

If this was what being halfway in love with him was like, she was in trouble. Because it would be far too easy to fall the rest of the way.

And she had a feeling if that happened, she'd never recover from the hard landing.

"I've got you."

Kensie's words echoed in his head, the soft, shy certainty in her voice tugging at his heart. She deserved someone to stand next to her, to help shoulder her burden for more than just a few days or a week or however long she was going to be in Desparre.

That was something he could never give her. But he could support her while she was there.

And he could open up to her, the way she'd opened up to him.

The very idea made his lungs constrict too hard with each breath, made his skin burn with clammy heat despite the ice melting all over his leg. But he pushed the words out anyway, praying he wouldn't have a full-blown panic attack in front of her.

"When I woke up in the hospital, the doctors told me they weren't sure they could save my leg."

Kensie's back straightened at his change in conversation, her hand slowing on Rebel's head.

As if sensing he needed her now, his dog came to the recliner and dangled her head over the chair arm. She nudged at his elbow, encouraging him to pet her, and he laughed at her antics.

But his laughter faded fast. "Pretty quickly, though, it didn't even matter what happened with my leg, because they told me none of my brothers had made it out of that ambush. Rebel got out, but they weren't sure she was going to pull through."

He smothered the sob that lurched forward at the memory. He could almost smell the hospital's nauseating mix of bleach and sickness. Saying the words was a softer blow now than it had been then, but it still felt like someone had punched him right in the chest.

Kensie lurched forward. She gripped his shoulder, not impeding the quickening motion of his hand petting Rebel. "You don't need to talk about this, Colter."

"I do. I want to tell you." As he spoke, he realized it was true.

He hadn't talked about that day since it happened, refusing to get into any detail with the shrinks the military kept offering him. Refusing to go into detail with his parents, who wanted to help him, but just couldn't move past their own mix of fear and joy that *he* was alive to understand his depression.

"You know that picture in my room you liked?"

"Yeah." Her voice was soft, barely above a whisper. He could actually hear her swallow, waiting for him to continue.

"It's the last one I have of them. We weren't technically a team. I was Military Police, K-9 Unit. Rebel's role was pretty new to the military then. She'd been serving for three years as a Combat Tracker Dog. It meant the two of us were partners. Sometimes we'd go with a unit, other times we'd get dropped into a site by ourselves."

"Dropped?" Kensie asked, her hand absently rubbing his shoulder.

He wondered if she even knew she was doing it. "Yeah. Helicopter would take us in and we'd rope out together. Rebel would be attached to me and we'd be set down somewhere, usually out in front of a unit to check out a location. Rebel's job was to start at the site of an explosion or an ambush and then follow the trail back to the person who set it. She was good at it, too."

At the praise, Rebel's tail darted back and forth a few times. But it settled fast, either because she knew what he was talking about or she recognized the serious tone of his voice.

"Anyway, for almost a year, Rebel and I had been attached to a Marine Special Operations Team. The guys you saw in the picture in my room were that unit. We all bonded fast. That day—the day the picture was taken—we'd just come back from a mission. We thought we were finished for the day. We should have been finished for the day."

He blew out a breath, remembering the moment the call had come that they were going back out. There'd been nothing out of the ordinary about it. They'd all had just enough time to get cleaned up, get comfortable. But that was the way of missions sometimes. You might not see any real action for weeks and then, all of a sudden, you'd barely get any rest.

That day they'd heard about a bomb going off, listened to the initial reports. One of his brothers had said he hoped they'd be the ones to check it out. They all knew Rebel's success rate. They believed she could find the bomber who'd taken the lives of what he'd later learned were twenty-six soldiers.

That moment in the command tent was the last time they'd all been together before heading out. He could picture the whole group, in a combination of fatigues and fresh T-shirts, looking exhausted, but with a seriousness that said they were ready to go.

He blinked the image of his brothers away and Kensie refocused in front of him. She waited patiently, quietly, her hand still on his shoulder.

"It was an IED—improvised explosive device. A strong one. Blew up a couple of transports. A lot of our people were killed. The area was dangerous and reports said there were no expected survivors, so the Special Operations Team I was assigned to was sent out. Their job was to clear it for a Medevac unit to come in—with the hope that reports were wrong and there'd be people left to save. Rebel and I were supposed to get a scent on the guy who'd set the bomb."

When they'd arrived, the scene had been terrible. The trucks had been caught in a remote pass, an area known to be dangerous because of the terrain. The trucks could go between the rocky hills or all the way around. Around meant losing a lot of time. Between meant making a tempting target for the snipers who were known to hide up in the hills if they got word of a transport coming through. But this had been the first time someone had tried an IED there.

"I admit, I was nervous about the call once we got details. I had a feeling we'd be tracking this bomber up into territory well controlled by insurgents. But Rebel and I were going to wait for the rest of our team to finish their work and come with us if we needed to. But we never got the chance."

The wreckage had still been smoldering when they'd trekked in, alert for snipers looking to finish off anyone trapped in what remained of the transport vehicles. But there'd been no one left to hurt, no one left to save.

The smell of smoke and fuel had been overwhelming, the craters much bigger than anyone had expected. He'd known from a single look that it was too late for anyone who'd been in those trucks.

His vision blurred over at the memory. He'd known most of those people, and just like that, they were gone. It hadn't been the first time. But in that moment he'd tried not to linger on the pain. He'd tried to hold on to the anger. That's what would push him forward into the rocky hills with Rebel, looking for the bomber.

"Rebel got a scent," he told Kensie, realizing that it

was tears blurring his vision. He felt her soft finger-tips swiping them away for him as he pressed on. "It's probably why we made it. We were out in front of the rest of the team. They'd already cleared the immediate area, but the hills above? All we could do was watch those. So, Rebel and I were the first targets."

"Targets?" Kensie's voice wobbled and her hand clamped harder on his shoulder.

"It was an ambush. Once the bomber took the trucks, the others waited up in the hills until we'd searched the place, called it in as clear. Then they fired. An L-shaped ambush. Seems like all the fire is coming from one spot, so you move, and then you realize it's there, too. Probably the plan had been to get soldiers and then the first responders. Which isn't exactly what we were, but a Special Operations Team is a pretty tempting target."

Colter couldn't believe it had been a year now. The official after-action reports estimated that it had taken less than three minutes for everyone else on his team to be killed. And he'd missed all of it, hadn't been able to take a stand alongside them, because he'd already been out of the fight. It was one of the biggest regrets of his life.

The cabin was so silent he could hear Rebel's soft breathing, Kensie's more uneven breaths.

"How did you survive?" Kensie finally asked. Her voice was shaky and something wet dropped onto his arm that he realized was her tears.

"Rebel. That first shot was fired and she leaped on me. Kind of like she did with you the day we met you." He'd actually felt the next bullet slice right over his head, but by then he'd already been falling.

Rebel whined at the sound of her name, pressing her

head against him, maybe recognizing he was moving into dangerous territory.

"It's okay, girl," he told her. Because it was. He'd already gotten through most of the story and he hadn't broken down.

Colter stared up at Kensie. Her lips trembled despite how hard she'd pressed them together. She was blinking rapidly, trying to contain the moisture covering her beautiful toffee-colored eyes.

She cared about him. The thought filled him with joy and pride and fear. He didn't want to hurt her.

Dropping his gaze from hers, he continued. "We fell into one of the bomb craters. Down through rubble. A piece of metal went all the way through my right leg."

Kensie gasped as he finished. "Rebel landed mostly on top of me, so the metal that went through me also sliced her back leg open pretty badly. I passed out. I woke up later in a helicopter airlifting me and Rebel out of there. Apparently the insurgents had come down from the other side and finished off the rest of my team."

"I'm so sorry," Kensie whispered, her hand like a vise on his shoulder.

"I guess they thought we were already dead. I was out cold, but Rebel wasn't. She must have kept totally still while they were searching. The team who came to help us said they wouldn't have even known we were down there except Rebel alerted them. We were flying out of the site and I was trying to stay conscious long enough to ask about my team, but no one wanted to answer me."

When they'd avoided the question, he'd known it was bad. But as hard as he'd tried, he hadn't been able to hold onto consciousness long enough to force the issue.

It had been days later, in the hospital, when a representative from the military he'd never met before had finally broken the news.

"I had two surgeries, the first one to get the piece of metal out of me and then later to screw the leg back together to try and save it. Rebel had three, poor girl, though her leg has healed better than mine. Then there was PT for both of us, for a good six months. We both made it back home, but our career together was over."

His physical therapy had been driven by an equal mix of unrealistic determination to get himself back into fighting shape and the desire to just be mobile enough to go and see his brothers' families in person. Apologize.

He'd never done it. By the time he'd healed enough to be released, he'd broken down every time he'd picked up the phone to book the travel. Since then, one of his brothers' wives had given birth to their first child. Another's oldest had graduated from high school. So much they should have been around to see.

Instead, it had just been Colter. And no one had been waiting for him because he'd never made that commitment to anyone or anything outside the service.

It wasn't fair. But staring at Kensie now, as she sniffled and swiped a hand over her face, where tears ran freely, he realized how much had changed for him. For the first time since that day, he was actually glad he'd lived through it.

For this moment. Her hand clutching him so tightly as she tried to get control over her emotions. It wasn't pity in her eyes, but deep sadness and understanding.

He knew she understood why he'd never felt like he

should have gotten another chance when none of his brothers had. Because somewhere deep down, she probably felt the same way about her sister.

But the bond he felt with her was more than one of loss. Because she made him want to live again, to reach for things he had no business wanting.

He couldn't do it.

She had a shot at finding Alanna, at moving on with her life and finding happiness. But how could he smile and go on with life like everything was fine when eight other families had buried their happiness?

The answer was simple. His living that day had been a fluke, an act of love from his partner. But it wasn't what was supposed to have happened. He should have gone with his brothers. And he wasn't going to betray them by leaving them behind a second time.

Chapter 14

His leg was killing him.

Colter bit the inside of his lip until he tasted blood. He leaned heavily on the cane he'd reluctantly pulled out this morning when he'd discovered even getting out of his recliner was a challenge. He hadn't used the thing in more than six months, when he'd vowed never to rely on it again. Thank goodness he'd stashed it in a closet instead of tossing it.

He hated that he needed it now, but it was better than not being able to keep up with Kensie. Because as much as he could have used another day or two to recover, he knew she wasn't going to wait. And he didn't trust anyone else to help her.

She'd slept twenty feet away from him last night, tucked into his bed. Every time she'd rolled over, he'd heard the rustle of his sheets and every nerve in his body had fired to life. Especially since, before she'd headed to his room to sleep, she'd leaned over and pressed the softest, briefest kiss on his lips.

The feel of that kiss had lingered through the night, tingling every time he heard her move. Even before his accident, he'd never connected with anyone the way he had with Kensie.

He still couldn't believe he'd shared his story with her. Even more, he couldn't believe he'd done it without having a bad flashback or a panic attack. But her touch on his shoulder and Rebel's head under his hand had kept him grounded in the present.

Today, he felt wrung out from the inside. But in a strange way, it felt good, like some of the tension and anger he'd been carrying around for the past year had been swept away, too.

Maybe it was looking at the way she lived her life. She'd said she spent too long trying to do everything at two hundred percent to make up for what happened to her sister. But when he looked at Kensie, he didn't see a woman doing everything at warp speed to avoid having to really live. He saw someone capable and strong, someone who would never give up on the people she loved.

Right now she was walking beside him. He could practically feel her restrained energy as she took short strides, her hand resting on Rebel's head.

They'd agreed last night that, since her truck was in town and he was in no shape to drive, she'd stay with him. Then, today, they'd go back to the part of town where she'd spotted Henry. With all the stores open, they'd be able to talk to more people and hopefully get some better answers about the man and where he lived.

The plan had been to set off in the morning, but his leg had refused to hold his weight for very long. The concern on Kensie's face had mixed with an anxiousness to get going and he'd promised he'd be ready by midafternoon. She'd seemed doubtful, but here they were. He would be paying for this later, but he wasn't taking any chances. His pistol was holstered under his shirt on the left.

Danny Weston was still in a holding cell, so he wasn't an immediate concern. But Colter didn't know enough about Henry to have any clue what to expect if they found him. If Kensie was right and he'd had her sister for the past fourteen years, Colter wasn't messing around. Whatever it took to free Alanna, he was willing to do.

"How can no one know this guy?" Kensie asked now, sounding as frustrated as she looked.

They'd spoken to half the store owners so far, plus a handful of locals braving the cold. The temperatures weren't abnormal for this time of year—hovering around twenty degrees—but the windchill had been brutal all afternoon. He'd tugged up the collar of Kensie's coat for her, but her cheeks were already windburned.

"Someone will know," Colter promised.

It was clear Henry was trying to stay off people's radar, and while locals embraced the idea of "live and let live," they were also a wary bunch. You had to be, with people like Danny Weston trying to take advantage of that attitude.

So the locals might try to stay out of other people's business, but a guy like Henry would have raised flags for someone. They just had to find the right person—the one who'd not only gotten suspicious but was also in a position to notice details about where he might be hiding out.

And Colter had an idea who that right person might be. He held open the door to a check-cashing place that looked like it had been built fifty years ago and never cleaned in all that time. It was crammed into a corner of the town, mostly hidden behind a grocery/hardware store, but that's how the locals liked it—out of sight. And so did the people who frequented it. People who wanted as short a paper trail as possible, who didn't believe in keeping their money in banks.

"Let's try here," he suggested.

Kensie gave him a doubtful look but preceded him into the store, Rebel on her heels.

"That dog better be a service dog," the owner snapped. He was perpetually scowling, a guy who looked as unkempt and old as his store. But his eyes were sharp, zooming in on Colter's side immediately as if he could tell Colter was carrying.

"One of the best," Colter replied, purposely misunderstanding what the guy meant by "service."

The owner—Yura something—screwed his lips up in a semiscowl, but his gaze drifted from Colter's side to his cane and his dragging leg. "Yeah, okay. You looking to cash a check?"

"No, I'm looking for some information on someone who might have been in here."

"Don't give out information on my customers," Yura

said, turning his attention to the TV mounted in the corner, playing a soap opera on mute.

"We think he kidnapped my friend's sister," Colter said, nodding toward Kensie.

Yura narrowed his gaze on Kensie, then frowned harder at Colter. "What's his name?"

"Henry Rollings."

"Henry, huh?"

"You know him?" Kensie's voice was full of hope as she leaned closer to Yura.

"Yeah," Yura said slowly.

"What can you tell us about him?"

Yura stared so long at Colter that Colter thought he was going to have to ask again. Finally, Yura asked, "Why do you think he kidnapped this woman?"

"I saw her," Kensie blurted. "I tried to follow them and then someone else got in my way and Henry drove off with her."

Yura's gaze shifted briefly to Kensie, then returned to Colter. "You were a Marine, huh?"

Colter wasn't sure how Yura knew that, but he supposed it was a sign his instincts were correct—Yura noticed things about people. "That's right."

He nodded at Rebel. "Her, too?"

"Yes."

"So was I. Long time ago." Yura sighed heavily. "Henry's a strange guy. Lot of the people who come in here are hiding from something. Not really my business what it is. But kidnapping a woman? You sure about that?"

"No," Colter answered, sensing Yura would respond better to honesty. "But there's a really good chance. And if he did take her, he knows that we know. So we don't have long to find him."

"Please," Kensie said, her voice barely above a whisper. "If you can help us…"

Yura nodded. "Henry cashes checks in here sometimes. I think usually he gets paid in cash, but every once in a while he does odd jobs for a couple up north. Untrusting sort, the Altiers. They like to stay off the radar, too. They pay well but keep a couple of guns on hand and only pay by check. Say it's a safety thing and I don't blame them, the way they hire drifters. Plus, they've got a bunch of kids to think about."

"Up north?" Colter asked. "Is that where Henry lives? Near this couple?"

Yura dug around under the counter and then dropped a piece of torn notebook paper on it. He sketched out a rough map, then turned it around for Colter to see. "You know where this is?"

Colter held in a curse. "Yeah, I think so."

"I can't be sure he lives up that way, but if I had to guess, this is what I'd pick. The couple he works for is here." Yura tapped the hand-drawn map, marking a spot in the middle of nowhere. "No one lives within two miles of them. They're seriously paranoid. But Henry's come in here a half dozen times over the past few years with checks from them. My bet is he lives somewhere in this area, close enough that they feel comfortable hiring him repeatedly."

"It's out of the way," Colter agreed. "Perfect for someone who wants to hide. And in the direction that the warehouse owner said he sometimes sees Henry go."

"It's not going to be an easy area to get into unnoticed." Yura pushed the map toward him. "Semper Fi, brother."

Hearing the words sent a jolt through Colter, part shock, part energizing. It had been a year since anyone had spoken them to him. "Semper Fi."

"Thank you," Kensie added as she trailed Colter out the door. "How long will it take us to get there?"

"We're not going tonight."

"What?" She slapped her hands on her hips, over the warm coat he'd forced her to buy the other day. "Why not?"

Even though he knew it was windburn, he liked the pink in her cheeks. It matched the fire in her eyes right now. But he wouldn't let himself be swayed. He'd agreed to help her find her sister, not get her killed in the process.

"For one, it's going to be dark in a couple of hours and we don't even know if he lives here. This is Yura's guess. Two, the terrain is seriously treacherous. We don't want to be stuck out there at night."

"Colter—"

"I know time is crucial, Kensie. Believe me, I get it. But we're not doing your sister any good if we get ourselves killed. And I'm not kidding about the area. There's no easy way to access it other than one trail, and even that's blocked half the time. We've already had enough of a snowfall that it's possible snow has dumped off the side of the hills and made it inaccessible."

"But we saw Henry in town just yesterday. He got here somehow."

"Yeah, and that probably tells us the road is fine, but some of the locals who live way out in the wilderness use snow mobiles and keep a vehicle somewhere else. Besides, if Henry is anticipating us, he'll know to watch that road. Not to mention that Yura's map just gives us a general area. It'll take us hours to investigate it all."

"So, maybe night is better," Kensie argued. "If Henry is watching the road—"

"We get people stuck up in that area who freeze to death every year, Kensie. There are no cell towers for miles, so no cell service at all. And the houses are miles apart, too, so you'd be lucky to reach help."

"But you know the area—"

"Not that area. Not well enough. I'm not taking you up there tonight."

Frustration and disappointment mingled on her face, but they couldn't hide what was underneath: fear. Fear that even as they stood there speaking, Henry was already rushing her sister out of town. That they were already too late.

"Tomorrow morning," Colter promised. "We'll go with supplies and a plan. Okay?"

"Okay," she agreed reluctantly.

He nodded. "I'll drop you at your hotel so you can get fresh clothes and I'll pick you up tomorrow at eight. Sound good?"

"Oh. Sure."

The surprise in her voice told him she'd half-expected to go back to his cabin with him tonight. The idea made desire curl in his belly, but he ignored it.

He couldn't take her with him tonight because he wasn't going home.

After he dropped her off, he planned to scout the area himself.

* * *

She should be with Colter now, not tossing and turning in her ridiculously soft hotel bed, unable to sleep.
It was mostly worry about Alanna keeping her up, but
part of it was the man helping her find her sister.

If they did locate Alanna tomorrow, Kensie would
be going home. She'd never see Colter again. Just the
thought of it made her chest tighten with dread.

Why hadn't she spoken up when he'd told her he'd
drop her off at her hotel? Based on the way he'd returned her kiss last night before she'd headed off to his
room, if she'd asked to go with him, he would have said
yes. Instead of sitting here, heart beating too fast and
a million different scenarios about what could happen
tomorrow running through her mind, she could be with
Colter right now.

In his bed with him. Or on his lap on his recliner.
She'd even take a spot curled up on the floor by Rebel
if it meant she could be close to Colter.

Who was she kidding? Even if she started out on
the floor—which she knew Colter would never let happen—she wouldn't stay there long. She'd end up beside
him, underneath him, on top of him, arms and legs en-
twined, lips pressed against his until she could hardly
breathe.

Normally, she backed away from relationships that
had too much potential to hurt her heart. Her mom said
it was her way of protecting herself from losing anyone
again. So she left them first. It was probably true, but
then, she'd never met anyone she couldn't stay away
from. Until Colter.

His loss had been different than hers, but he understood the mingling of grief and guilt in a way most people couldn't. And maybe that was part of why she felt connected to him. But it was only a small part.

The rest of it was about the man. The way he'd risked his own safety for hers and Rebel's. The way he smiled at Rebel when she sat by him. The way he looked at her sometimes with those soft blue eyes, focused so intently on her as if he never wanted her to leave his side.

She knew exactly where it would lead to sleep with someone she cared too much about and then walk away. She'd never been remotely tempted to try it. But right now, she was pretty sure *not* staying with Colter tonight was going to be one of the biggest regrets of her life.

So do something about it. The thought hit like a sledgehammer and Kensie shoved off her covers, heart pounding. What would Colter do if she just showed up at his cabin tonight?

Only one way to find out. Kensie felt a goofy smile lifting her lips as she flipped on the light next to her bed.

As the light went on, there was a soft thump from the other side of her door.

Kensie froze, listening. Had Colter gotten the same idea and come to her hotel tonight? No. He'd never stand out there skulking if he'd made up his mind to be with her. He'd knock forcefully and then wait patiently for her to decide.

Maybe someone else had checked into the hotel. Except the sound had come from *right* outside her door. Too close to be someone going into another room.

Maybe she was imagining things. She sat perfectly still, straining to listen. Another sound reached her ears, this time a drawn-out metallic scrape, as if someone was working the lock.

She jerked in response, banging her head against the headboard as panic took hold.

At the sound, whoever was outside stopped being quiet. There was a loud *thud*, like a big body ramming against the door. The door actually curved inward near the ceiling, but the lock held.

Why had she chosen the big, luxurious failing hotel with hardly anyone staying in it instead of the beat-up motel closer to downtown? The only other person staying on this floor had checked out yesterday. The manager was four floors below her, probably asleep at his desk like he had been last night. Screaming was useless.

Fighting back panic, Kensie practically fell out of bed, groping for her cell phone. *Colter.* His number popped up first, the last person she'd texted.

Need help right now, she typed frantically, even as she wondered if she should call 911. But Colter knew exactly where she was, knew who was a threat to her in this town. Had Danny Weston been let out of jail already? Why wouldn't the police give her a heads-up?

She'd call the police as soon as she finished texting Colter. *Please hur—*

There was another thunderous *bang,* and this time the door burst inward, splintering away all around the lock.

Even knowing it was useless, Kensie screamed. Dropping the phone, she grappled blindly for anything she could use as a weapon, her gaze locked on the man backlit in her doorway.

Not Danny. Henry Rollings.

He rushed into the room, igniting a million fragments of memory in her mind. Alanna glancing back and smiling at her as she danced. The tire swing her dad had hung in the front yard. A big dark sedan rolling slowly down the street toward them. A quick hand reaching out and yanking Alanna away.

Everything suddenly sped up, in her memory and right in front of her, as Henry darted around the foot of the bed.

He was older than he'd been fourteen years ago, more gray in his hair, more lines on his face. But he still outweighed her by a lot, still had ropey muscle in his forearms and a dangerous gleam in his eyes.

"You never should have come here," he said, his voice low and deadly.

Kensie stopped groping for a weapon. Instead, she leaped on top of the bed. Running instead of fighting suddenly seemed like her best option.

He changed direction, reaching for her, but she jumped over his arm, landing awkwardly on the floor on the other side of the bed.

Something pierced her bare foot and pain exploded in her arch, but Kensie ignored it, her focus solely on the door. She could hear him behind her, catching up, and she ran faster, tears pricking her eyes at what she realized was a splinter from the broken door in her foot.

She was so close. If she could just get through the door, the emergency exit for the stairs was a straight shot down the hallway. There was a fire alarm right next to it she could pull on her way, maybe attracting attention from the hotel staff who knew she was up here.

She'd almost cleared the door when a big hand closed

like a vise around her elbow and yanked her back into
the room, hard enough to send her to the ground. Her
head smacked the floor and even the thick carpeting
wasn't enough of a cushion to stop the shock. The air
whooshed out of her lungs and her vision wavered
briefly.

Then he was kneeling over her, one knee on either
side of her hips, and a new kind of panic exploded in
her chest. What was he going to do to her? What had
he done to her sister?

Tears filled her eyes, but rage almost instantly overtook the fear as she thought of Alanna. Where was her
sister right now? Was Henry planning to get rid of Kensie so he could continue hiding here with her sister?

But it was too late for that. Colter knew about him.
Even if she was gone, Colter would search for Alanna.

It wouldn't come to that, Kensie vowed. Yanking her
arms upward before he could pin them down, Kensie
used her nails and went straight for his eyes.

He jerked out of the way just in time, but before she
could use his shifted position to her advantage, he was
back, leaning closer. Blowing rancid breath in her face,
he snarled, "I don't know how you found me, but you're
not taking me down."

With his face so close to hers, Kensie instinctively
tried to shift her head away. Then she realized her mistake and went after him again, this time getting her nails
deep in the skin of his cheek as he jerked backward.

But it wasn't enough. Calling her all kinds of names,
Henry pressed his big hands around her neck. They
closed around it with ease and then he was pushing
down, stealing all her air.

"I didn't even know she had a sister," Henry growled. "You should have let her go. Let *me* go."

Kensie gagged, grabbing his hands with hers, trying to peel them off. But he was even stronger than he looked. Spots formed in front of her eyes, even as she kicked up, trying to knee him in the groin.

He moved his knees inward, pressing her legs together, keeping them pinned to the ground. His hands closed tighter around her neck, his lips moving into a satisfied smile before his face started to blur.

Kensie flailed, a last desperate attempt to break his chokehold, but it was no use. She couldn't breathe; she could barely see.

She was going to die.

She would never know what happened to her sister. She was going to put her family through the trauma of losing another member. She was going to put Colter through the grief of losing someone else who mattered to him. Because, as gruff as he acted, she knew he cared for her.

He'd never know how much she cared about him.

Kensie's hands shook as she tried to peel Henry's fingers away from her neck, tried to gasp in another breath. But none came.

Her hands stopped working. She felt them hit the carpet beside her, useless, as everything went dark.

Chapter 15

Kensie wasn't answering. Not her cell phone and not the phone in her room.

Warning Rebel, "Hang on, girl," Colter jammed his foot down on the gas.

Rebel lurched forward anyway, letting out a brief whine.

"Sorry, girl," he said, both hands clenched tightly on the wheel as he took the unpaved road way too fast. His truck bounced and rattled, sliding on sudden patches of ice, but always gaining traction again.

Why wasn't Kensie answering? Her text had cut off midsentence and that had been several minutes ago, with nothing since.

Colter gritted his teeth as he took another curve at speeds that made his truck teeter right. It set back down again, earning another warning whine from Rebel. But he was all the way out by where Henry Rollings might live, using the map Yura had given them earlier. Despite the dangerous roads, he needed speed to get to Kensie.

"Call 911," he told his phone, glancing down to be sure it picked up his voice properly. If the police thought he was overreacting, so be it.

"Nine-one-one. What's your emergency?"

"This is Colter Hayes." He didn't know the voice on the other end of the line, but it was a small town, so hopefully whoever it was recognized his name and knew he wasn't prone to false alarms or overreactions. "My…" he stumbled over "friend," the word not feeling right on his tongue, then he hurried on "…is in trouble. She just texted me that she needed help. She's staying at that big luxury hotel outside of town."

"I need you to stay calm, sir," the woman replied, her own voice way too even and slow, making him realize he'd been talking at warp speed. "What kind of trouble is she in?"

"I don't know. She didn't give me any details. Her text cut off midsentence and she's not picking up her phone. I need police to get there now."

"Okay, sir, we'll send someone out to see what's happening," she said in that same exasperatingly slow voice, telling him she definitely didn't know who he was. "But do you think it's possible she just needed help with something simple? That it's not an emergency?"

"No, I don't think that's possible! She'd never text me to hurry if it weren't an emergency." His voice gained volume with every word and he took a deep breath, trying to stay calm. "Are officers on their way?"

As he asked, he left the treacherous unpaved trail he hadn't wanted Kensie on tonight for a smoother road. At the transition, his truck bounced high enough that his head almost smacked the cab ceiling. In the rear-view, he saw Rebel hunkered down, trying not to get thrown around.

At least Kensie was staying at the overpriced luxury hotel outside of Desparre instead of the cheap motel downtown. He was much closer to the hotel. Of course, the police were closer to town. But then, it was late enough that probably no one was left at the station anyway.

"Who lives out by the luxury hotel? I want the closest officer sent out."

"Don't worry, sir. We'll get someone over there to check it out. Now, I want you to remain calm and—"

"She's on the fourth floor, room 409." He cut her off, then hung up. He didn't want to waste time with her focused on his panic. Not when he needed every bit of his attention on the dangerous roads ahead.

"It's going to be okay, girl," he told Rebel, partly because he knew he was making the ride hard for her and partly to reassure himself about Kensie.

She had to be okay. He didn't think he could handle losing someone else.

The very thought of something happening to Kensie made his breath stutter and his lungs lock up as his heartbeat thundered painfully against his chest.

Not this. Not now.

A hundred curses screamed in his mind, but he couldn't get enough air to voice them. He clenched the wheel harder and eased his foot up off the gas, fighting the panic and impending dizziness. He couldn't afford to lose control, especially not here, not at speeds his truck could barely handle with him on full alert.

Suddenly, Rebel's nose pressed against his arm and he realized she'd stood and pushed her head between the seats. He breathed deeply, slowly, focusing on the feel of her head leaning into his biceps.

"Thanks, girl," he said when the panic eased and his heart rate started to slow.

He could do this. He wasn't going to let his mind wander to all the possible reasons Kensie had sent that text, all the possible dangers she could be facing. He was going to put all of his energy into getting to her as fast as he could.

"I've got this, girl," he told Rebel, pleased when his voice came out strong and determined. "Lay back down," he told her, not wanting her to get thrown around as he punched the gas again.

She listened, obviously sensing he'd conquered his panic.

"Call Kensie," he ordered his phone, but once again, it went to voice mail. Instead of hanging up immediately, he said, "Hang on, Kensie. I'm coming."

Then he jammed the gas pedal into the floorboards. The turns came too fast as he put the truck's suspension to a serious test. It still seemed to take forever to get to the hotel, but he knew it was less than ten minutes since Kensie had texted.

Squealing to a stop, Colter yanked the truck into Park and then grabbed his cane before jumping out of the cab. Rebel was right behind him, so fast that he suspected she knew Kensie needed them.

But where were the police cruisers, sirens wailing? Instead, the parking lot was dark and silent, only a few vehicles scattered up near the entrance.

Colter swore as he pushed his leg as hard as he could, doing a ridiculous hobble-run to the front of the hotel, not even bothering to shut the truck door behind him. Rebel kept pace beside him, tension in the lines of her back that told him she was ready for battle.

When they burst through the doors into the hotel lobby, the older man behind the desk jerked his head up in surprise. "Can I help—"

"Have you seen Kensie Morgan? She's staying—"

"Fourth floor," the man interrupted. "From Chicago. Nice lady. She—"

"Have you seen her in the past ten minutes?" Colter demanded.

"No."

"She's in trouble. Call the police." Colter didn't care that he'd already done it. The fact that they weren't here yet—regardless of how far the drive was for the closest officer—pissed him off.

"What?" The man pressed a shaky hand to his chest. "What's going on?"

Colter didn't answer. He just bolted for the elevator and jammed his hand against the Up button. If he'd been in fighting shape, stairs would be quicker, even at four stories. But these days, elevators were a faster option.

Thankfully, the elevator must have been at the ground floor, because it opened up fast and then he and Rebel were inside it, heading up. "Please be okay," he chanted, watching the numbers beep by as they rose too slowly.

Finally the elevator arrived with a loud *ding* and Colter slid through before the doors finished opening. Rebel charged out after him.

He'd never been up here, but over the blood racing in his ears, he heard…something. Almost like a gurgling. And way down the hall, something lying in the hallway. Small, like a piece of wood. But it didn't belong.

Colter headed that way, almost stumbling as he pushed his leg as hard as he could. Rebel ran beside him, following his silent command.

Before he reached the room, the noise stopped. When he finally peered inside, Henry Rollings glanced back from where he knelt on the floor.

And beneath him was Kensie, her head lolled to one side and her eyes closed.

With a roar that didn't even sound like him, Colter dropped his cane and rushed Rollings.

Panic shot across Henry's face as he tried to scramble to his feet. But he wasn't fast enough.

Leaning on his stronger left leg, Colter grabbed the man by a fistful of shirt and yanked him off Kensie and onto his back. Not letting him regroup, Colter let go of his shirt and grabbed him by the forearm, twisting up and back as he dragged Henry farther away from Kensie.

"Check Kensie, girl," he told Rebel, who leaped right over Henry and landed beside Kensie.

Colter said a silent prayer that she was okay, but right now he had to focus on neutralizing Henry before the guy realized Colter's weakness and went for his bad leg like Danny had.

From the corner of his eye, Colter watched as Rebel nudged Kensie, then did it again, harder. Kensie didn't move and Colter felt panic rising inside of him.

Then Henry yelped and twisted, yanking his arm free while Colter was distracted. Pushing against the floor for leverage, Henry shoved himself upward.

Colter's panic shifted into rage. His focus narrowed onto just Henry, all of his fury and fear directed at the man. He could feel his lips twisting back into a snarl as he raised his fist.

He'd been to war, survived multiple tours where he'd seen others die. He'd faced an enemy with the desire to eliminate a threat, but he'd never felt this kind of primal hatred before. His fist connected with Henry's face, fueled by all of that rage, too hard and fast for the man to block it.

Henry hit the ground hard, lights out.

For a split second, Colter wanted to keep pounding on him. But his worry for Kensie quickly overcame his hatred for Henry.

Colter twisted toward her. His knee popped as he dropped down beside her. His eyes watered at the pain, but he brushed the moisture away and pressed his fingers to her bruised neck. Rebel let out a long, low whine as Colter prayed.

Then he felt it. A pulse. Slow, too weak, but it was there.

Dropping even lower, he placed his hand in front of her mouth and nose, waiting for the soft brush of her breath. It, too, was faint but there.

Suddenly, he couldn't see as he stroked his hand

down her cheek. "Kensie, Kensie, wake up." A drop splattered on her face and he realized he was crying.

Her eyes blinked open, confusion and pain in her gaze. "Wha—" she croaked.

"Don't try to talk." He sucked in a long breath of relief, swiped away tears so he could see her better, then folded her hand in his. It felt so fragile, so delicate. "You're okay. You're okay."

Beside him, Rebel's tail thumped the ground and she dropped to her belly, resting her head on Kensie's arm.

Down the hall, he heard the *ding* of the elevator and footsteps running toward them. "We're in here," he called. "We need an ambulance."

"Colter Hayes?" a voice called back.

Chief Hernandez had come herself. It had taken way longer than Colter would have liked, but he knew the chief didn't live nearby. If she was the closest, then she'd still made good time.

"Yes. We're in here. Kensie needs an ambulance."

Kensie started to lift her head, but Colter put a hand on her shoulder. "Don't move."

He glanced back as Chief Hernandez poked her head around the door, then entered, holstering her weapon and lifting her radio. "Get me an ambulance."

She strode into the room and cuffed Henry's hands behind his back as he groaned and started moving.

"Where's Alanna?" Kensie croaked, her words barely intelligible.

It hurt Colter just to hear her speak. Neither his hand on her shoulder nor the chief's admonishment not to move until an EMT had looked at her prevented her from struggling to a sitting position.

Colter braced his hand behind her back and Rebel jumped up, rotating her body until she was sitting half behind Kensie for support.

"Good girl," he told Rebel, but she didn't even wag her tail in acknowledgment, just kept her serious gaze on Kensie.

"Where is she?" Kensie demanded, her voice raw but gaining volume.

Chief Hernandez yanked Henry to his feet and he groaned some more, shaking his head.

Trusting Rebel to have Kensie's back—literally—Colter stood, ignoring the new stiffness in his knee. He got in Henry's face even as the chief gave him a warning look and angled the hip where her weapon was holstered away from him.

"Where's Alanna Morgan?" he demanded, so close he could feel Henry's disgusting breath on his neck. "If I have to repeat my question, it won't matter that there's a cop here."

"Colter…" Chief Hernandez's voice was full of warning, but also worry.

She'd known him since he moved here. He'd even helped her break up a bar fight once when her backup was slow and his leg was in a cooperative mood. For the most part, they got along. But she'd never heard this tone from him. And he knew if he had to make good on his threat, she'd have to do her duty and protect the guy in cuffs.

But he wasn't going to let Henry hide behind an arrest now. "Tell me," he growled.

Henry's face went pale as his gaze darted to Kensie. "I don't know what you're talking about."

"Colter," the chief snapped before he could respond. She yanked Henry back a few steps and he went willingly with her. Then her backup was in the room, a couple of cops Colter probably could have taken down in better days, but not now.

"Colter." Kensie's softer voice came from behind him.

He turned and realized she'd gotten to her feet. She sounded and looked terrible, with blue and purple streaks all the way across the front of her throat. But her balance was steady and her eyes were clear.

"Let me do this," she croaked.

"Everyone just calm down," the chief said as the other officers stood in front of Kensie, blocking Henry. "Jennings, give me your fingerprint kit."

"Hey, *he* attacked *me*," Henry shouted, starting to struggle.

"And you broke into this hotel room and attacked the occupant," the chief replied calmly as she yanked her arm upward, pulling his cuffed hands up, too.

Henry yelped and then Jennings was pressing his finger into a machine the size of a cell phone as the other officer kept his gaze locked on Colter and his hand locked over his pistol.

"This is pretty cool, huh?" Jennings asked, excitement in his flushed cheeks and too-high tone. "Pretty much only the FBI has these, but we got a grant after this serial case a few years ago and…oh."

"What?" the chief asked as Jennings stared at the machine.

He turned it toward her and she shook her head.

"Guess we know why you didn't want us to take your prints, now, don't we, Manny Henderson?"

Henry/Manny let out a string of curses, then insisted, "I didn't kill her."

At his words, Kensie whimpered and Colter spun, grabbing her as she swayed.

But she pushed him off, tears streaming down her cheeks as she rushed forward. She leaned around the officer who stood in her way, croaking, "You killed my sister?"

"Look, I didn't even know Shoshana had a sister," Henry said. "But I didn't kill her. Someone framed me, okay? I ran because someone framed me."

"What?" Kensie and Colter asked together.

Chief Hernandez sighed loudly. "Manny Henderson here skipped town in Kansas a decade ago after murdering Shoshana Lewis."

"I didn't kill her!" Manny shouted.

Ignoring him, the chief continued, "Apparently he's been hiding out here ever since."

Kensie dropped to the floor so fast Colter didn't have time to move. He realized belatedly that it was a semi-controlled fall as she sat and buried her head in her hands.

"He didn't come after me because of Alanna," she whispered.

"Who the heck is Alanna?" Henry snapped.

From the floor, Kensie looked up at Colter and he knelt closer, ignoring the way his knee protested. "He thought I knew about the murder in Kansas. When I said I was from the Midwest…" A sob burst out, then she turned her gaze on Henry. "I was wrong. He looked so much like the guy I remember, but he had nothing to do with Alanna's kidnapping."

"I didn't kidnap anyone!" Henry yelled. "And I didn't kill anyone, either. I was—"

"Get him out of here," Chief Hernandez demanded, pushing Henry toward Jennings, then stepping closer to Kensie.

"I'm so sorry," she told Kensie. "But I think you're right. You stumbled onto a fugitive. And I know I could have been more patient with you before, but the FBI really did work hard when they came up here. I don't think the note was real."

"I've been chasing a ghost," Kensie whispered, staring into the space where Henry had been.

"I think it's time you go home," the chief said.

A jolt of dismay shot through Colter as Kensie's defeated voice agreed. "I think you're right."

Chapter 16

It was time to go home.

The very idea made Kensie want to curl up in a ball and weep. But she just gritted her teeth harder, until her jaw and her head hurt.

"Are you in pain?"

Blinking moisture away, Kensie looked up at the nurse checking her vitals. "No," she croaked, even though speaking made her throat feel like she'd shoved sandpaper down there and was scrubbing as hard as possible. Then again, not speaking didn't feel much better.

Apparently, her throat was so swollen the doctors had considered putting a tube in to help her breathe. But she'd fought them on it until they'd agreed to keep her under observation and on some kind of intravenous medicine for a while.

For the past few hours, she'd been here alone. Colter and Rebel had come with her in the ambulance, but they wouldn't let the dog in the hospital no matter how much Colter argued. So finally he'd agreed to go to the police station and give his statement while doctors checked her out.

"You're doing good, hon," the nurse said, patting her arm and leaving the room.

Once she was gone, Kensie stared blankly into the empty room, still feeling blindsided. Henry Rollings's claims that he hadn't killed the woman in Kansas had been forced and full of denial. His confusion about her sister had sounded so real.

Even though he was a killer, Kensie believed him when he said he didn't know Alanna. He'd come after her because he thought she was onto his real identity and the murder he'd committed in Kansas. She'd played right into his fears when she'd told him she was from the Midwest instead of being specific and saying Chicago.

So whoever she'd seen that day with Henry wasn't Alanna. It couldn't have been. It was another woman, someone who just resembled what Alanna might have looked like if she'd had the chance to grow up.

Because the truth was, Alanna had probably never gotten that chance.

Kensie knew the statistics about stranger child abductions. Her family had come to accept the truth long ago. And Kensie had been running from it ever since her parents had given in and decided to move on with their lives.

Instead of following their example, she'd chased a ghost, seeing leads where there were none because she was so desperate to undo a mistake she'd made when she was thirteen. Maybe it was time to forgive herself. Maybe it was time to let Alanna go.

The sob that burst forward made Kensie choke and gag. Her throat felt like it was closing up and her chest felt like it was on fire. A nurse ran into the room as Kensie got control of her breathing. She swiped the tears off her face and managed, "I'm okay."

She wasn't. But hopefully she would be.

Her parents' wake-up call had been Flynn's accident. Apparently she'd needed a fugitive to try and kill her to find her own wake-up call.

"Kensie?" Colter's voice reached her from the hallway.

She stared at the open doorway and then he appeared, moving as fast as he could with his cane. Kensie closed her eyes and held out her arms.

Then his arms were around her and her head was on his chest. She squeezed her eyes more tightly closed, breathing in Colter's scent—clean and slightly musky—and tried to relax. Because as badly as she needed a good cry, doing it would hurt too much. And she didn't want a sedative or a tube in her throat.

Finally, he leaned back and stared down at her face, brushing hair out of her eyes. "Are you okay?"

She nodded, not wanting to speak, not even sure she *could* speak without losing it.

He didn't move his arms from around her and she kept hers looped around his back. It felt right, like something she'd do with a boyfriend instead of a man she'd only known for a few days.

"I gave the police my statement, Kensie, and the reason it took me so long to get back here—besides dropping Rebel off somewhere safe—is that I talked to them about Henry."

From the way his lips twisted up, she knew bad news was coming. She held on tighter, waiting.

"They've contacted police in Kansas and I asked the chief to beg for a little professional courtesy and get the station there to look into his whereabouts when your sister went missing."

Kensie's heart thumped madly, a brief hope, but he shook his head.

"The day Alanna disappeared, Henry Rollings was serving a one-month jail sentence for a DUI. He's not the guy, Kensie. I'm so sorry."

She ducked her head, pressing her face against his chest and letting the relief and disappointment roll over her in waves. Relief because Henry was a killer, but he hadn't killed Alanna. Disappointment because, yet again, she had no real answers.

And it was time to accept that maybe she never would.

She wasn't sure how long she stayed there, not moving, but she didn't want to let go. Her time in Alaska was about to end and that meant leaving Colter behind.

She was falling for him more with every day. There was no question about it. But that wasn't enough.

Not when he was too broken to move on with his life, even if he cared for her, too.

Besides, her family was waiting for her. A family who'd been scared for her to come here, who hadn't been whole for too long but had always tried. They'd stood by each other instead of letting Alanna's loss tear them apart. And even though she blamed herself, they'd never blamed her. Not once, even in anger, had anyone suggested it was her fault. Except for Kensie herself.

Leaving Desparre—leaving Colter—was the right thing to do. So why did it feel so wrong?

He didn't want to let her go.

Colter glanced at Kensie, sitting silently in the passenger seat of his truck, staring out the window. In the past four days, he'd come to think of it as her seat. And now she was leaving.

In the back, Rebel sat quietly beside Kensie's suitcase. His dog had let out a low whine when Colter loaded it and he'd petted her softly. "I know, girl," he'd whispered. "I know."

The doctors had cleared Kensie to leave this afternoon and she'd booked a flight home tonight. In the brief time between, they'd held hands and walked the streets of Desparre without speaking. Then he'd left her at her hotel to pack while he picked up Rebel so they could both say goodbye.

He couldn't believe he was about to drop her off at the airport and never see her again.

Stealing a glance at her, he tried to memorize her profile. The thick, glossy hair framing her face. The full lips, always tilted slightly up at the corners like she was on the verge of a smile. She was staring out the window, so he couldn't see her eyes well, but he didn't need to. He could picture the exact shade of light brown, like a delicious toffee. He could see the serious intensity there.

Redirecting his attention to the road ahead, Colter blew out a heavy breath. He never used to be the guy who didn't know what to say, but since Kensie had told him she was leaving, he'd been at a complete loss for words.

He'd known it was coming eventually, of course. He even knew it was the right thing for her. But knowing it was different from watching her walk out of his life for good.

Don't go wanted so badly to erupt from his mouth, but he squeezed his lips closed. She had a family to return to, a life to rebuild—and maybe to rethink. In the hospital, he'd seen it on her face that she was reevaluating the choices she'd made in her life. He hoped she'd keep playing the violin. Even though he knew she'd chosen the career path because of Alanna, he could see it on her face when she talked about playing: she loved it.

He'd never get to see her play. Never meet her family or walk hand in hand with her down the street in comfortable silence again.

And for the first time in a long time, he knew exactly what he wanted: her. He could picture a life with her. A home. Babies.

It was an impossible dream. But it felt good to dream again. He actually felt *alive* in a way he hadn't since the moment that first shot had rung out in the desert and Rebel had slammed into him.

"Kensie—"

She turned toward him, her face full of expectation and hope.

Words about staying in touch, about making plans to see each other down the road—someday, somehow—died on his lips. She deserved more than empty promises.

What could he really offer her from 3,500 miles away? A relationship of phone calls? The burden on her to fly out to see him since he'd vowed to remain in Desparre, since the very idea of going anywhere else made his chest hurt?

She was falling for him. He'd felt it in the lingering touch of her fingers on his face as she kissed him the other night. He saw it in the way she stared at him now, with the kind of unrealistic hope she'd once shown for finding her sister.

He might not be worthy of her, but he cared enough about her to try and do what was best for her. And that was giving her a clean break. As much as it hurt, what she needed most from him now was for him to let her go.

He slowed his truck to a stop in front of the airport, unable to believe how fast the time had come. "I'm going to miss you, Kensie."

Her mouth opened into a silent O, the hope in her gaze fading. Then she gave him a forced, trembling smile. "Thank you for helping me, Colter."

She unbuckled her seat belt and twisted to pet Rebel, pressing her cheek briefly to his dog's head. "I'm going to miss you, Rebel."

Rebel whined, looking at Colter as if trying to tell him, "Make her stay, stupid."

Everything in him ached to comply, to beg Kensie not to go, or at least to stay in touch. Instead, he gave her his own forced smile. "We're going to miss you, Kensie."

She threw her arms around his neck, pressed a brief kiss to his lips and then stepped out of his truck. She grabbed her luggage from the back seat and strode into the airport before he could recover.

And then she was gone.

Chapter 17

How could her heart feel this full and this empty at the same time?

Kensie stared out the window at the plane pulling up to her gate. It had only been four days ago that she'd left Chicago, terrified and full of hope for what she might find in Desparre. She'd never expected to find someone like Colter. She'd never expected to lose someone like Colter.

And she'd never thought she'd be returning home without Alanna and with a total loss of hope of ever finding her. The idea of giving up on her sister made guilt gnaw at her, but it was time to move on. Colter had taught her that. If only she could have taught him the same.

She didn't like picturing him and Rebel alone in their cabin, cloistered away from the world with only pictures of their dead brothers to sustain them. It wasn't a way to live. She wanted so much more for him.

But she couldn't force him to change. And she'd spent too much of her life living for someone else. It was time she started living for herself.

As much as it hurt, she had to go. For the briefest moment, she'd thought he was going to suggest they stay in touch, maybe even pursue something long-distance. If he had, if he'd felt as strongly as she did, she would have ignored her head telling her it would never work. She would have followed her heart.

But he'd simply said goodbye, so she'd tried to do the same. A clean break. It was the right thing for both of them.

She'd practically run from his truck when he stopped outside the airport. If she'd dawdled, she knew she would have broken down, or worse yet, admitted how she felt about him. And telling a guy you were falling in love with him after knowing him for four days wasn't the best idea. Especially when you were about to leave and never talk to him again.

That wasn't how she wanted him to remember her, as needy and heartsick. She wanted him to remember her as strong and determined. She wanted him to think of her and recall the feel of her kiss, the warmth of her smile. Not an awkward goodbye.

"Are you okay, honey?"

Kensie looked up at the elderly woman holding out a tissue to her. She took it, nodding her head and swiping at tears she hadn't even realized she was shedding.

The woman frowned but walked away, and Kensie stiffened her shoulders. It was time to stop looking backward. Even if he didn't know it, Colter had done so much for her. She'd always cherish him for that.

Being with him had made her look at herself differently. She'd seen herself through his eyes and it had made her want things she never even knew she was missing.

Colter had looked at her, not knowing the accomplished violinist, the steadfast volunteer for cold-case searches. He'd seen *her*. He'd looked at her and seen her determination and her optimism and even her stubborn side and he'd liked her for those things alone. Staring back at him, she'd realized she'd spent her whole life measuring herself by the wrong things. And suddenly, she wanted more for herself.

More than a life lived in the spaces between searching for a sister she hadn't seen since she was a child. It wasn't her fault Alanna was gone. The person who'd kidnapped Alanna was to blame. And maybe by not living her own life to the fullest, Kensie was doing her sister's memory a disservice.

Alanna had only been five when she'd disappeared, but Kensie wasn't putting a shiny fantasy on her memory. Alanna had loved Kensie for playing games with her, reading to her before sleep and for the silly humor they shared. Those were the memories Kensie needed to keep alive, not a single moment she couldn't change.

"Now boarding for Flight 1850 to Seattle with continuing service to Chicago. Boarding all rows, all seats."

The announcement startled her and Kensie glanced up, realizing the plane had already off-boarded and been cleaned while she sat thinking about Colter and her life. She watched a short line of people file up to the entrance.

It felt like a lifetime since she'd been in Chicago. Closing her eyes, Kensie whispered, "Goodbye, Alanna."

Saying the words out loud seemed to lift a weight off of her. Her breathing actually came easier, even with the lingering pain in her throat and chest.

Her trip had been a failure, but she would be forever grateful she'd come. Colter had opened up a new world for her. If only she could have done the same for him.

Standing, Kensie shouldered her travel purse and joined the last of the passengers. She'd just handed her ticket to the gate agent when a familiar voice startled her.

"Kensie! Wait!"

Her heart seemed to give an extra-hard thump as she spun toward Colter.

He was running toward her as fast as his cane would allow, and dread and hope mingled. A long-distance relationship with a man who still couldn't move past his own grief was the wrong decision when she was finally trying to move forward. And yet, if he asked, there was no way she'd refuse.

"Colter," she breathed, envisioning trips to Alaska, warm nights in his bed, love letters to hold them over between visits.

He slid to a stop and her heart took off, unable to believe he'd come back for her. Heck, he'd probably bought a ticket just to get in here. To ask her in person instead of over the phone.

"Yes," she agreed before he could say anything.

The challenges of long distance didn't matter. The fact that he wasn't in the right place in his own life to enter into a relationship didn't matter either. They'd make it work. If he cared about her a fraction as much as she'd started to care for him, they'd figure it out.

"Kensie," he said, "Don't go."

Her heart pounded even faster. She had to leave now. Her family was waiting. She had so many decisions about her life to make back home. But she could come back. Soon.

Before she could voice any of that, he rushed on, "I think we were wrong. There's still a chance your sister is here. I think we can find her."

She was going to stay.

Thank goodness he'd pushed his leg so hard and gotten to the gate in time. If he'd been a minute or two later, Kensie would have already been gone. And even though he'd convinced himself he could let her go, the relief he felt right now was overwhelming.

"Final boarding for Flight 1850 to Seattle, with continuing service to Chicago," boomed over the speakers. "Passenger Kensie Morgan, please proceed to Gate 17. Aircraft doors close in two minutes."

Kensie blinked at him, then glanced over her shoulder at the aircraft entrance.

Colter dropped his cane and gripped her upper arms, wanting to shake off the incomprehension on her face. "Kensie. Did you hear me? I think we were wrong. We still have a shot at finding Alanna."

She turned back to face him, creases forming between her eyebrows. Her lips turned up in what he'd come to recognize as her apologetic look. "Colter, I…"

"Kensie." This time, he actually did shake her a little. "I talked to Jasper," he said quickly as Kensie glanced again at the airplane, as if she was actually still considering leaving on it.

Colter talked even faster, wondering what had happened since he'd dropped her off. Yesterday, if he'd suggested the remote possibility of a lead, she would have jumped up immediately. She would have ignored all the dangers, optimistically insisting this time could be it.

Then again, someone had just tried to kill her. And while being in the military meant he'd gotten used to being a target, he'd never had violence get so up close and personal, either. People trying to shoot you in a war zone was one thing; breaking into your hotel in a quaint Alaskan town and trying to choke you to death was another.

Sliding his hands down her arms, he twined his fingers with hers, and she finally gave him some real eye contact. "I know there have been a lot of dead ends. And some scary threats, between Henry and Danny. But this is different. I can feel it."

He wasn't just saying it to get her to stay. Jasper had repeatedly said he couldn't be sure of anything. But underneath his words, there'd been a restrained excitement, as if even he thought he was onto something.

"Jasper said a guy just came through his store asking about all the hubbub with the FBI and wanting to know if they'd given up already." He squeezed her hands a little tighter. "Kensie, Jasper remembers this guy from the day the note was found. This guy could have been with the girl he saw, the one he thought looked like you. Jasper said seeing this guy brought it all back. He says that day he assumed it was the guy's daughter with him."

Kensie's gaze darted to the gate and then back to him as they called her name once more over the speaker. "Did he say what this guy looked like?"

"No. But we can go and talk to him. He's waiting for us right now. I told him I was coming to get you and we'd be over as fast as we could."

She stared down at their locked hands a long moment, then shook her head. "Colter, I can't spend my life chasing long shot leads." She raised her head and there was something new in her eyes, something strong and bright. "I deserve to find my own life, to figure out what I want for *me*. You taught me that," she added softly.

He had? Her words made him sway backward slightly. He wanted that for her, but... "There's a time to move on, Kensie. But right now is the time for blind hope and optimism."

She started to shake her head, to pull her hands free, and he held on tighter.

"*You* taught me that," he told her. "You don't give up on the people you love."

Saying the words made him flinch a little, thinking about the day his brothers had died. Thinking about whether he was inadvertently leading her in the wrong direction, trying to force her attention back into her past when she had a real shot at a good future. But his gut was screaming at him that this was a true lead, and he wasn't sure he could follow it on his own.

Her shoulders dropped and hurt passed across her

face, but just as quickly, she lifted her chin. "How do you know this isn't another dead end?"

"I don't," he said as the attendant at the gate announced, "Doors are closing for Flight 1850."

His leg was starting to throb from putting weight on it for so long, but he ignored it and pulled her a little closer. "Kensie, please come with me. This isn't over."

She stared up into his face for a long moment, then pulled her hands free. "It's not over," she repeated softly.

Then, she launched herself into his arms.

Chapter 18

Kensie sneaked another glance at Colter, heart pounding madly. She was in the passenger seat of his truck, flying away from the airport at speeds that couldn't be legal. All of his attention was on the road ahead, his knuckles white against the steering wheel like he was on a mission.

She still couldn't believe she'd walked away from her flight. There wasn't another one to Chicago for three days.

Three more days with Colter. He was a dangerous temptation she needed to resist. Because whether it was three days from now on the very next flight, or three days after that, she'd eventually be leaving. And when it came to Colter, nothing had changed.

Falling halfway in love with him already meant

heartache was waiting for her. Falling right into his arms would only make it worse.

"I'm glad you're staying, Kensie," Colter said, shooting her a sideways glance, as if he could feel her eyes on him.

When she'd thrown her arms around him at the airport, he'd actually lifted her off her feet and pressed his lips to hers for a long, tantalizing moment. People around them had cheered, clearly misunderstanding what was happening.

Now that they were back in his truck, she could read his nerves in the tense lines of his arms, the flexing of his jaw. He was worried he'd talked her into staying for just one more false lead.

Fear and hope blended, making her heart race even faster and her fingers tap a nervous beat against the armrest until Rebel pushed her nose between the seats and stilled her hand.

Kensie smiled at the dog, realizing how much she was going to miss Rebel, too, once she actually did leave. The thought added anxiety to the mix and Kensie took a deep breath.

This is just like every other lead on Alanna, she reminded herself. *Approach it like you always try to, with low expectations but high hopes*. It was a hard balance, but one she'd gotten fairly good at over the years.

But this time felt different. Maybe because she'd finally decided to let Alanna go and then gotten yanked right back into the search. It really felt like her last chance.

"I'm sorry."

It took her a minute to comprehend Colter's words and then she frowned over at him. Had she spoken out loud?

"I should have followed this lead on my own, instead of dragging you back into it. I was being selfish. I'm sorry."

Selfish? He'd spent the past four days running down leads on someone law enforcement had already given up on. He'd rushed to her side whenever she needed him, twice saving her from dangerous men.

Kensie let out a snort of disbelief. "Nothing you've done since I've known you has been selfish."

He was silent for a long time as they navigated the long drive back toward Desparre. Finally, as the roads beneath them changed from pavement to dirt, he spoke slowly, deliberately. "I didn't want you to go."

His words stunned her briefly into silence, but while her mouth refused to work, her mind and body shot into overdrive. Her skin tingled with sudden awareness of how close he sat to her, her lips aching for another kiss. Her brain started cataloguing how far they were from his cabin and how soon they could get there.

She'd stayed for Alanna. Mostly. But part of the reason she hadn't gotten on that plane was the man sitting next to her. Intellectually, she knew it was better to keep her distance, to focus on her sister for her remaining few days here. But her heart had other ideas. And the fact that she was still chasing after Alanna all these years later instead of moving on with her life proved that her heart almost always won.

Before she could figure out how to respond to his surprising admission, Colter spoke again. This time, his voice was all business. "Jasper says he tried to play it cool with this guy, act like all he knew was the FBI had decided it was a hoax. But he's not sure the guy bought it. So whatever he tells us today, we need to act cautiously. I don't want another situation like Henry."

Kensie's fingers instinctively grazed her still-bruised throat. It seemed to tighten at the touch. "Neither do I."

He shot a pensive glance at her, then hit the gas even harder. Before she knew it, they were pulling into the lot in front of Jasper's General Store.

Rebel ran circles around her and Colter as they made their way up to the door until finally Colter laughed and said, "Relax, girl." He looked at Kensie. "She's happy you're back."

"So am I." The words came out without thought, but they were true. Even if this turned out to be one more in a series of disappointments, she couldn't regret anything that gave her a little more time with Colter.

He held open the door for her and his gaze seemed to caress her face, as if he felt the same way.

It put a light, giddy feeling in her chest. But as she preceded him into the store and Jasper ran around the counter as soon as he spotted her, the feeling shifted into a different kind of nervous hope.

"Kensie." Jasper reached for her hands, folding them between his lean, weathered palms.

The first time she'd met him, he'd been gruff to the point of rudeness. But now he was staring at her like they were long-lost friends, and she realized her story about the day she'd watched Alanna get ripped away had touched him.

Jasper glanced up as Colter and Rebel came in be-hind her, nodding at them and not saying a word about

Rebel being in the store. "A guy came into the store today. I recognized him from that day. And I think he might have been with the girl." His gaze went back to Kensie, his eyes wide as his words tumbled out. "I didn't recognize the girl that day, so it didn't stick, but I recognized the man."

"What?" Colter stepped closer. "You didn't mention that on the phone."

"I know. I called you as soon as he walked out and I've been trying to place him ever since. He's not a regular. Not even a semiregular. But that day wasn't the first time he's come in the store. I've seen him before. I think he could even live around here."

Kensie's heart picked up speed. If he lived around here, they had a real chance at finding him. At finding Alanna.

"I have to be honest, I probably wouldn't have connected him to that day except he was asking questions. And they were just too casual. It all felt forced, like he was desperate for the answers but didn't want me think he cared. And then I realized he'd been there. I think he walked out at the same time as the girl." He gave Kensie an apologetic look. "I can't be positive they left together that day, or even that it's your sister, but it all seems suspicious, doesn't it?"

She slid her fingers from between his palms, patting the top of one of his hands. "Yes, it does." She glanced at Colter, wondering where they went from here.

"What can you tell us about how to find him?" Colter asked.

"I walked out after him today. Tried to act all casual, but honestly, I'm not sure he bought it any more than I bought his questions just being simple curiosity. So I waved at him and grabbed the shovel I'd left out there, like that was why I'd gone out. Anyway, I saw him get into a truck, but the way he peeled away, it was like he was trying to avoid me getting a plate number."

"Which way did he go?" Colter asked.

"Now *that* I can tell you. As soon as he peeled out, I booked it upstairs. Most people don't know it, but this store has roof access. Gave me a good view of him for a while."

Jasper walked behind the counter and pulled out a map, drawing a line away from his store and out toward what looked like nothing but forest to Kensie.

But as soon as he drew it, Colter's gaze darted up to hers, tension in the line of his jaw. "That's the same area where Henry lived. There's not much out there. It was true for Henry and it's true for whoever this guy is. It's a great place to hide."

Kensie nodded, her nerves shifting to determination. "Let's go do a little tracking."

Rebel barked her agreement.

This might be hopeless.

Colter didn't speak the words out loud, but Kensie glanced at him as if she'd heard him anyway and shook her head.

"We need to keep going," she told him, voice tight as she leaned toward the windshield like she could lead them there by pure force of will.

It had started to snow. Big, fluffy flakes that plopped onto the windshield and slowly slid down. They were sticking, making the forest surrounding them look picturesque.

Right now, it wasn't accumulating much. But Colter knew how fast that could change out here. Although his truck was in good condition, with a nearly full tank of gas, he didn't want to take any chances. Even locals could misjudge Alaska's weather, which could turn brutal fast.

"Ten more minutes," he told Kensie, "and if the snow hasn't stopped, we'd better turn back. We can make another trek out here tomorrow."

"But—"

"Kensie, we're three hours deep into this forest. We don't want to get trapped out here if the weather turns."

"I'll check the radar."

He glanced at her briefly, most of his attention on navigating the dirt road winding between huge fir trees. "You're probably not going to get any service. No towers out this way."

She held her phone up, testing it in different directions, then sighed. "You're right. No service."

They drove in silence for a few more minutes, but Colter could feel Kensie's tension ratcheting up. The snow remained steady, not letting up, but not getting worse, either. And still no sign of any homes.

"Do you think we missed it?" Kensie asked.

"It's possible. Usually people who live out this way don't want to be too far off of a main trail, because even these can get buried when the snow gets deep. But the road did split ten miles back. If we'd taken the other way, we would have ended up near where Henry lives. I went this route because I figured if Henry had seen your sister—if she really looks like you, the way Jasper said—Henry might have spoken up."

"Why would he? He seemed too busy trying to kill me."

He reached for her hand, squeezed it briefly. "I mean afterward. When the police were there and we were talking about your sister. If he lived near someone who looked like you, he might have put it together and said something, tried to get a little leverage."

She leaned back against her seat, twisting to face him. "Maybe we should pay him a visit and ask."

"Maybe," Colter replied, less enthusiastic about that idea. If they asked, Henry was likely to lie if he thought he could get anywhere—or just to torture Kensie, because he was a sick SOB. If he knew anything, he probably would have already volunteered it.

"Hey, what's that?" Colter slowed the truck until it was barely creeping forward as he peered through the thick trees.

"Where?"

Colter pointed. "Up ahead, at the one o'clock position, about a hundred feet ahead of us."

Kensie leaned forward again, squinting through the snow, which was beginning to fall a little faster. "I don't see anything."

He gave the truck a little more gas until Kensie exclaimed, "Oh!"

"It *is* a cabin," Colter muttered. And it was about as well hidden as you could get. If they hadn't been looking, they might have driven right past it. Positioned close enough to the road to get in and out, but far enough back to remain unseen unless you were looking. And on the other side was a mountain, so no one would notice it from that direction.

The wood cabin looked like it might have been hand constructed, but as they continued to drive forward, he realized it was a lot bigger than he'd originally thought. "You could fit a whole family in there."

His shoulders slumped as he said it. How likely was it that the person who'd grabbed Alanna lived in a cabin this big, just the two of them?

He swore as he spotted a sign at the entrance of the long unpaved drive leading up to the cabin. Two slabs of wood, one underneath the other, were staked into the ground at the entryway. The bottom one read *Trespassers will be shot*. The top one read *The Altier Family*.

"Isn't that the name of the couple Yura mentioned when we stopped by his check-cashing place?"

"What?" Kensie was still staring intently at the cabin.

"The Altiers. I'm pretty sure that's the couple who paid Henry with checks sometimes for odd jobs. It's not the guy, Kensie. Yura said this is a couple, with a bunch of kids."

Her disappointment was all over her face as she turned toward him. "Well, maybe they know who else lives around here. Let's go talk to them."

"I'm not sure that's a good idea." He pointed at the *Trespassers will be shot* sign.

As he did, he spotted a station wagon in the distance, up beside the cabin, and his heart rate doubled. Most people who lived around here drove huge trucks. The last time he'd seen a station wagon was the one that had nearly run Kensie down on the main road in Desparre.

He'd assumed it had been an accident, an idiot driving an even more idiotic car for Alaska weather. But maybe it hadn't been an accident at all. Maybe, right from the start, Kensie had been a target.

"Kensie, what did you do when you got to town? Before Rebel saved you from that car?"

She frowned at his change of topic, but answered anyway. "Not much. My plane landed and I rented a truck, then drove into town. I had to stop for directions a couple of times."

"Did you tell people about why you were here?"

"Sure. I figured I might as well, in case someone knew something. Why?"

Colter pointed through the trees again, at the station wagon. "I think that's the car that nearly ran you down. I think word got around that you were here, looking for Alanna, and someone didn't want you to find her."

Instead of fear, excitement shot across Kensie's face. "This could be it," she breathed.

"We need to go back and get the police," Colter told her, his gaze returning to the sign warning off trespassers.

"But—"

"If we've really found her, Kensie, it's not going to do her any good to get ourselves killed."

She glanced over her shoulder, back behind where Rebel sat, to where Colter had his shotgun. Her gaze lingered on it a long moment before she nodded. "You're right."

Not wanting to turn around in the Altiers' driveway and draw attention, Colter shifted into reverse, hoping there was a wide enough gap in the trees somewhere nearby for him to change direction. The truck was just starting to move backward when Kensie blurted, "Wait!"

Jamming his foot on the brake, Colter glanced back at the cabin. A group of kids had stepped outside and he scanned through them, looking for anyone who resembled Kensie.

In a way, they all did, at least from a distance. Dark hair, slight olive tone to the skin. But as he scanned them, he realized none were the right age. The youngest girl looked to be about six, then there was a boy who was probably twelve, another girl who might have been sixteen and an older boy who had to be in his early twenties. They looked like siblings.

Colter swore. "Kensie, Jasper might have seen that girl there, the oldest one. She looks a little bit like you. He might have mistaken her for Alanna."

But she was too young. It wasn't her.

From how pale she'd gone, Kensie must have realized the same thing. He reached for her hand again, all his focus on apologizing for bringing her out here for nothing.

"Colter," she breathed, pulling her hand free and pointing toward the cabin.

When he glanced back, he saw that the oldest boy was no longer there. In his place was a girl, about nineteen, with dark hair, cut to shoulder length. She had strong, thick eyebrows and lush, full lips like Kensie.

And Colter recognized her. It was the girl he'd seen in the passenger seat of the truck that had flown past him in town, when Danny had cornered Kensie. At first glance, he'd even mistaken her for Kensie.

"It's her." Kensie's voice was barely above a whisper, and he could hear the tears and joy in it at once. "It's Alanna."

She reached for the door handle and he grabbed her arm, stopping her. "Kensie, we still need the pol—"

Before he could finish his sentence, a loud *boom*, like a firecracker that had gone off way too close, split the air. Colter recognized the sound immediately: a rifle.

Chapter 19

Kensie had found her. After fourteen years of searching, she'd finally found Alanna.

She was still reeling as she stared at Alanna through the forest. Her body felt frozen with disbelief, but her mind had figured it out and was screaming at her to move. To run, grab Alanna and get out of there fast.

Except Colter was yanking the truck into reverse. Then it was speeding backward fast enough to wrench Kensie hard against her belt and send Rebel sliding into her seat with a yelp.

And it still wasn't fast enough. Another *boom* blasted the air, making Kensie flinch as the front of their vehicle erupted with smoke.

"We're hit," Colter said, his voice way too calm.

Kensie stared through the smoke, realizing the blast had come from a rifle. The truck had been hit.

Panic started to break through her daze. Fear for herself, Colter and Rebel, and desperation not to lose Alanna now that she'd finally found her.

Up near the front of the cabin, the oldest boy who'd gone inside was back, pointing at their truck and yelling something. The woman next to him—in her early forties, who looked like his mother—lifted that rifle again.

"Colter—" she started to warn him.

"Get down!"

Before he'd finished speaking, Rebel's teeth were gripping the arm of her coat, tugging down until Kensie was scrunched awkwardly with her head between the seats.

But what about Colter? He was still sitting straight, jaw clenched tight as he steered the truck. A visible target.

The smoke pouring out of the engine was getting thicker and darker, and her fear intensified. "Is the engine going to blow?"

"No," Colter answered tightly, his knuckles white against the wheel as the truck sputtered, barely moving even though Kensie could see his foot jammed down on the gas.

Then, the rifle blasted again and the whole right side of the truck sank.

Kensie let out a shriek as Colter swore, struggling with the wheel as he turned the truck directly toward the trees. "She got the tire. Climb into the back seat."

"What?"

"Do it now. Hurry!"

Hands shaking, she fumbled with her seatbelt as he fought with the wheel, until finally she realized what he was doing. Angling the truck the other way, so his side was facing the rifle and giving her more protection.

"Colter—"

"I'm right behind you. Go!"

Kensie launched herself into the back, squashed up next to Rebel, who'd been smart enough to get down on the floor behind her seat.

Colter twisted, jamming himself between the front seats. His shoulders were too broad and he seemed to get stuck, but he stretched his arm out and grabbed his shotgun.

Kensie tried to press even closer to Rebel, making room, and Rebel squeezed tighter into the door without complaint. "Get back here," she demanded.

But Colter was going the other way. He stayed low, but he shimmied back into the front.

She yanked on the sleeve of his coat, even as he popped open the glove compartment, grabbing a box of shells. He jammed several into the shotgun, stuffed the rest into his pocket and told her, "When I tell you to, open that door and make a run for the trees."

"Colter—"

"Get ready," he barked, lifting the shotgun.

There was another ear-splitting blast and the windshield shattered, spraying glass into the truck. It pricked her arms and Kensie shrieked. Then she gagged as heavy, dark smoke rushed into the cabin.

Colter. Had he been hit?

Kensie twisted, lifting her head, trying to get a better look at him. Almost instantly his hand was there, shoving her head back down. But not before she saw two things. Colter wasn't hit. And the woman who'd been shooting at them was now running toward the truck, rifle still raised.

"Colter," she warned, choking on the smoke, her words coming out gravelly, in a voice that didn't sound like it belonged to her. "She's coming!"

"Plan hasn't changed," he said gruffly, calmly. "Grab the handle. You're about to go."

"But—"

"On the count of three! One, two, three, go!"

Heart thundering, pounding hard enough to hurt her chest—or maybe that was the smoke she was inhaling—Kensie shoved open the door.

"Go, Rebel! Trees!" Colter yelled.

Rebel shot out the door, and Kensie scrambled after her even as her mind screamed for Colter.

She heard the blast of a shotgun, once, twice, as she choked on the fresh air, as she took huge, desperate strides. She ran in the path Rebel made, the dog easily outpacing her.

"Colter!" She thought she screamed for him, but maybe it was only in her mind as another *boom* seemed to make the ground shake.

Then pain raced up her leg, intense as fire, and Kensie crashed to the ground.

Kensie was down.

Colter's whole world narrowed to just her form, falling into the snow. The edges of his vision darkened as he gasped for breath, and the blast of a sniper rifle went off somewhere above him. Then there was a crushing weight on his chest, Rebel's paws slamming into him.

He barely had time to register any of it before he was falling, falling…

Colter's hands darted out, reaching for something, anything to break his fall. The shotgun he was holding smacked the truck seat and smashed his fingers. But it made no sense. There was no truck here, only debris. Only the blasted-apart remains of a transport vehicle, the unexpected grave of too many soldiers.

"Colter!"

Kensie's panicked voice broke through his confusion, pulled him out of that nightmare overseas where he'd lost all his brothers. Brought him back to her.

Only he wasn't with her. She was shot and he was inside a truck that was rapidly filling with smoke. And although he'd fired at the woman with the rifle, it was too hard to see through the black smoke. He had no idea if he'd hit her.

Move, his brain screamed. Colter gasped for breath, trying to subdue the panic as he choked on smoke. From a distance, Rebel's bark reached him, as if she was urging him to hurry.

It was a tight fit between the seats, but even with the smoke obscuring everything, he didn't want to make too big a target. He was no good to Kensie if he was dead.

Colter shoved and twisted, finally managing to get his shoulders between the seats. He dragged the shotgun behind him, the only weapon he had. At the open back door, he paused, getting a better view of the cabin.

The woman was still standing, but she was no longer shooting at them. Instead, she was taking cover behind the door, pulling the youngest two kids with her. Still standing in the yard was the oldest boy, who was holding a pistol, taking aim at Kensie.

"No!" His voice mingled with someone else's and before Colter could launch free of the vehicle, the girl they thought was Alanna tackled the boy.

Colter didn't wait. Leaving his cane behind and gripping the shotgun carefully, he darted out of the truck, dropping to his haunches beside Kensie. Her calf was bleeding, but it wasn't the kind of wound made by a rifle. It could have been ricochet, but most likely, it was a bullet from the pistol.

Relief gave him his first full breath. The cold air hurt, but seemed to clear some of the smoke from his lungs. Keeping hold of the shotgun while lifting her wasn't easy, but he knew they were probably going to need a weapon. His right leg trembled, pain burning his thigh, and he prayed it wouldn't give out on him.

Thankfully it held as he draped Kensie over his left shoulder and started to run. "Go, girl!" he told Rebel, who was ahead of them, in the cover of the trees.

His dog took off, darting from one tree to the next, a blur of brown and black fur. She left an obvious trail of paw prints in the snow and Colter knew he would be doing the same. They'd be easy to track.

There was only one main road in and out of the area, the one they'd come in on. They'd be easy targets there, but he wasn't sure this was much better. He hadn't given Rebel instructions other than to run, which was all they could do right now. There was no time to strategize with a family carrying weapons potentially right behind them. But they were heading deeper into the wilderness, toward the edge of a mountain, farther away from help or shelter.

His leg throbbed, shaking each time he put weight on it, especially at the pace he was going. Every twenty feet, Rebel stopped, glancing back at them, waiting for him to catch up.

Kensie was light. He'd once run with a fellow soldier, someone double her weight, over his shoulder for two miles. But that was before his leg had been irreparably damaged. Now it was all he could manage to keep his grip on her and the shotgun, keep his feet from sliding out from under him. It got even worse once the ground started to slope downward.

He wanted to glance behind him, see if the woman with the rifle or the boy with the pistol were following. But he knew if he did, he'd lose his balance. With each step, the slope was getting steeper. He wanted to double back, go the other way. Seek higher ground, the way he'd been trained. But there was no chance of that. It was too steep now, and it would take them right back toward the Altiers.

He needed a plan, because they'd managed to head right down the side of a mountain, when he'd hoped there'd be a straight route alongside the edge. Anyone standing at the top of the mountain would have a good view of them, no matter the trees. Then again, the trees were getting thicker the farther down they went. And a moving target wasn't easy to hit. He needed to move faster.

"I can run!"

Kensie's voice penetrated his thoughts and he realized she'd been repeating it, her words muffled against his back. But he also knew it was wishful thinking on her part. She'd taken a bullet to the calf. She might be able to push herself for a while, but he didn't want to test that theory now. Not while they were still so close to the cabin.

He didn't respond. He couldn't. With every step, the mountain was getting steeper, until he found himself leaning backward for leverage, slowing his steps so they wouldn't both go tumbling down. Up ahead even Rebel had slowed, and he realized she, too, had started to limp. Her back leg was acting up because she'd pushed it too hard.

Colter wanted to use the trees for support, grab them to slow his descent. But he couldn't, not with Kensie slung over his left shoulder and the shotgun barely grasped in his right hand.

The cold burned his throat and lungs and made his eyes water. The tears seemed to freeze on his cheeks, the wind brutal as the slope continued to get steeper. It was too steep. He slowed even more, taking slightly sideways steps, back and forth, to help him navigate down.

Rebel was handling the terrain better, but she'd looped back for him, sticking by his side. He wanted to tell her to go ahead, but he couldn't manage to get the command out. And he wasn't sure she'd obey it even if he did, especially when his bad leg buckled slightly, and his foot slid dangerously forward. He managed to catch himself by angling his free shoulder right into the trunk of a tree. The branches whipped against his face, against Kensie's legs hanging over his chest. It ripped the shotgun out of his hand, sent it tumbling down the mountain, bouncing off trees as it crashed downward. The path he and Kensie would take if he slipped again.

Keeping his shoulder pressed into the tree, Colter regained his footing. Lungs screaming, heart thundering, he stopped, finally glancing back. Scanning the ridge of the mountain, he saw nothing. No woman with a rifle, no boy with a pistol.

He strained to hear over the racing of his heart, but he couldn't make out the sound of an engine, either. Not a truck or even a snowmobile, which would be much more agile to come after them and which the Altiers surely had, living so far from resources.

"Rebel," he wheezed, tapping his thigh.

His dog scooted under the tree with them and Colter eased down, lowering Kensie off his shoulders. Setting her down made his legs tremble violently. When he had her on the ground, he allowed himself to slide down, too, praying he'd be able to get back up.

"Are you okay?" she asked, her eyes huge, before he could ask her the same thing.

"Let me see your leg," he said instead of answering.

She scooted around, grimacing as she lifted her left calf onto his lap so he could get a look at it.

Her jeans were saturated with blood below the knee. The bullet had ripped a hole through her pants that he didn't want to open further in this weather. But he could see the swollen, damaged skin that was exposed, and the injury was still pumping out blood.

Colter probed it as gently as he could. There was no exit wound. Probably because of the distance, maybe the angle. He couldn't tell where the bullet was, if it had lodged right below the entrance or if it had ricocheted around inside of her, redirected by bone until it made a mess.

He had basic medic training, but he didn't have the supplies to deal with a bullet wound. All he could do was stop the bleeding and get her to a hospital as soon as possible.

The second he peeled off his winter coat, his body tensed up as the cold penetrated deeper. Ignoring it, he peeled off his shirt, then the undershirt he wore beneath. Swearing, he quickly pulled his shirt back on, zipping his coat over it. Then he wrapped the undershirt around Kensie's leg, knotting it tightly enough to make her yelp.

"Sorry. I've got to stop the bleeding."

Thankfully, it did stop. Not instantly, but his shirt went from white to a pale pink and then didn't change. He prayed it would stay that way if she had to run on it. Because he wasn't sure he could carry her out of here.

He wanted to stay under this tree, rest a while. But as Kensie traced a finger over the welts on his face from the branches, he peeked out from underneath the tree. Still no sign of the family on the top of the mountain. But the longer they stayed in one spot without moving, the more the cold would seep into them. The more likely they were to slowly die from exposure.

"Do you see them?" Kensie whispered, reminding him of the problem of running: the possibility that one or both of them would get shot.

"No."

"They're not coming after us." Kensie's shoulders slumped and moisture filled her eyes. "They're running. They know we found Alanna, and now they have time to disappear."

Chapter 20

It was starting to get dark.

Kensie peered up at the sky for a split second and lost her balance. Her arms darted out, seeking something to grip, and found a tree branch on the left. It slowed her, but then the branch snapped and her feet slid again, her boots not getting enough traction in the snow.

It had been falling faster since they'd taken shelter briefly under the fir tree where Colter had wrapped her leg. She'd suggested waiting to see if it slowed, but Colter had insisted they keep moving.

He'd looked worried then. He looked even more worried now as his arm shot out in front of her, giving her something to hold.

She grabbed on with both hands. He grunted as he stiffened his arm, stopping her downward slide.

"Sorry," she wheezed. It hurt to talk. Colter had pulled her hood over her head earlier, knotting it tight, reducing her peripheral vision but helping her retain heat. Supposedly.

But since they'd left the shelter of the fir tree, the cold had seemed to invade her from the inside out, settling in her lungs and even her bones. Her left leg throbbed and the shirt Colter had wrapped around it was now bright red. She was unbearably tired and scared that the exhaustion was less from the trek and more from loss of blood.

She had no idea how long it had been since they'd run from the cabin, just that it was long enough for the sun to settle low in the sky. The three of them were still picking their way down the mountain. She and Colter were using the trees for support. Rebel was better at keeping her balance, but even she was sliding periodically and she'd started favoring her injured back leg.

She and Colter were both limping badly. She knew Colter hated himself for not being able to carry her, so she was doing her best not to show how much her leg hurt. But the truth was, the pain was more excruciating than anything she'd ever experienced.

With every step, no matter how gentle, a jolt went up her leg, all the way to her hip. More and more, she felt like she might throw up from it, so she clamped her jaw tight and tried to focus on each new goal. First the big fir tree fifty feet ahead of them, then the boulder twenty-five feet away. Now it was just getting from one tree to the next, simply taking each step without slipping and tumbling down the mountainside.

The warmer coat Colter had made her buy was back

in her luggage, in his ruined truck. She was wearing the one she'd arrived in, which could handle Chicago's tough wind chill, but not this. Not being stranded on the side of a mountain, only the trees blocking the sudden gusts of ice-cold wind. Not the dampness seeping into her bones as the snowflakes soaked through her jeans, slid into her gloves whenever she grabbed a tree branch for support.

"Hang on," Colter said.

Kensie grabbed the nearest tree, sagging against it as Rebel pressed close to her side. Kensie suspected it was to lend her warmth, but even the dog was starting to look cold. Kensie's eyes slid shut and she tipped her head, resting it, too, against the tree. It felt iced over and it soaked her hood even more, but right now, she didn't care. More than anything, she craved sleep.

When she heard Colter swear, it was harder than it should have been to open her eyes again. "What 'sit?" she slurred. Her mind felt foggy, but not so foggy she didn't realize that was a bad sign.

Hypothermia did that. Kensie focused on her fingers and toes, trying to decide if she could feel them. It was strange that she couldn't tell. She tried to wiggle her toes and almost lost her balance. "What is it?" she asked again, enunciating carefully.

Lines raked Colter's forehead and she wanted to smooth them away, wanted to make the worry in his sky-blue eyes disappear. But it was all she could do to stay on her feet.

"I thought we might have gone far enough to get service."

For a long moment, his words made no sense. Then

she glanced at his hands, which were stuffing his cell phone into his pocket. Despite having warm gloves, his hands were bright red, the fingertips an alarming white. As soon as he'd returned the cell phone to his pocket, he shoved his hands back into his gloves, rubbing them together.

"We walked that far?" she asked, happy she wasn't slurring anymore. At least she didn't think so.

"No. We're headed sort of perpendicular to the path we took to the cabin, down the mountain. We're not going toward Desparre, but there's another town out this way. It looked like I might have a signal, but the call kept dropping. I tried texting 911 anyway."

"How will they find us?" Her words ran together, barely comprehensible, and Kensie tried to focus, tried to get her sluggish mind to connect properly with her mouth. She tried it again, and this time he understood.

"We've got to keep moving."

She whimpered, the idea of continuing on any farther seeming impossible.

In response, Colter slid closer, wrapped an arm around her waist, taking some of her weight even as his jaw clenched.

The sight gave her strength and she stiffened, took a deep, cold breath. If she gave up, she knew he'd carry her as far as he could. But what if her extra weight was the difference between his making it or dying on this mountain? "I'm okay," she told him, surprised when her voice came out determined and clear.

She had to make it. For Colter and Rebel, who'd put their lives on hold to help her. And for Alanna, who might already be packed up in the Altiers's car, on her way to some other out-of-the-way town, where she might stay hidden for another fourteen years. If Kensie died here, no one would know the truth about who had taken her sister.

That wasn't going to happen.

She stiffened her shoulders and took a step forward. Her injured leg gave out on her and she hit the ground hard, her head smacking the dirt and snow. The world rotated in a dizzying swirl and then she was sliding, picking up speed as she went.

Reaching out, Kensie grappled for anything. Her hand snagged a low-lying branch and she held tight. Her back arched up off the ground, then came back down, but somehow she held on, the image of Colter's worried face giving her strength. She couldn't die like this. She couldn't give him one more loss to grieve, one more reason to blame himself when it wasn't his fault.

It took her a minute to realize she'd stopped moving, but she didn't let go of the branch, because it was still steep. Then Colter came sliding down next to her, half out of control, Rebel right behind him.

"You okay?" Colter's voice was panicked.

She tipped her head back toward him and tried to smile. Tried to reassure him without words that she was all right, that she wasn't giving up. That they'd make it.

But the truth was, she wasn't sure. Because when she tried to push herself to her feet, no matter how much she gritted her teeth, her leg kept giving out on her.

"It's okay," Colter said, bending next to her.

Then she was up, dangling over his shoulder again. Tears spilled over, even as she tried to stop them, knowing the moisture was just going to freeze on her skin.

Colter grunted, using tree branches for leverage, his right leg dragging slightly behind him. Keeping pace beside him, Rebel pressed close against him and Kensie saw the dog's back left leg was barely taking weight.

She didn't need to be able to see down the mountain to know they were far from the bottom. Far from civilization or help.

Dread filled her, bone-deep and exhausting. They weren't going to make it. And it didn't matter if she begged. Colter would never leave her behind to save himself.

But if they were going to die out here, she wanted him to know how much his help meant to her. How much meeting him had changed her life. Had changed the way she thought about herself, the way she thought about what she wanted.

Meeting him had changed everything.

She'd been lying to herself, thinking she was halfway in love with him. When it came to Colter, there was no halfway. She was straight-up in love with the man. And after everything he'd been through—all the loss and guilt—she wanted him to know he was still worthy of love.

Yes, he was damaged, but so was she. And damaged was far different from broken.

Sucking in a breath full of frigid air, Kensie projected, wanting to be sure her words weren't lost on the wind. "I love you, Colter."

Was he starting to hallucinate?

Colter had wanted to give his coat—better suited for the freezing climate—to Kensie hours ago, but he'd known he wouldn't survive without it. And with her injured leg, he wasn't sure she'd be able to make it out on her own. Her makeshift bandage had been saturated with blood more than an hour ago, the wound bleeding freely again. He'd tightened it repeatedly, stemming the flow more than once. But it always started up again.

Even with his better gear, he knew they were both in serious danger of frostbite and hypothermia. Every breath hurt his lungs and his fingers had felt clumsy and uncoordinated on the too-tiny numbers of his phone. Maybe his mind was going, too. It was the only explanation for the auditory hallucination he'd just experienced, Kensie saying she loved him.

He snorted. Maybe in his wildest dreams.

But then he heard it again, and there was no denying it was her beautiful voice speaking the words, even though her voice was rough from the chill. Joy filled his heart so fast it actually hurt, but worry followed immediately.

She thought they were going to die. It was the only reason she'd admit something like that.

He wanted to say it right back to her. The thought shocked him, made him set his right leg down crooked, twisting it sideways. He slipped, but righted himself quickly, even as it registered that he hadn't felt pain like he should have. His body was shutting down.

Or maybe the joy of her words was just overriding any pain.

He glanced at Rebel, sticking to his painfully slow pace beside him. She was struggling, too, whimpering every once in a while when she put weight on that back leg. "I'm sorry, girl," he whispered.

Louder, to Kensie, he said, "You're just scared. We're going to be fine. Save your strength."

But his mind was screaming at him to say it back. He loved her.

The very idea was shocking. He hadn't thought he was capable of loving anyone new. Hadn't thought his heart had any room left in it after the loss of his brothers.

He loved his family, loved Rebel. But that was all he could handle. A woman like Kensie deserved so much more than he could give her.

And yet…he wanted to give her the world. He wanted to stand beside her, not just when they made it off this mountain, but years beyond. Wanted to experience a life with her, have children with her.

The thought was a betrayal of the promise he'd made that day when he'd woken up in the hospital and the doctors had finally admitted to him what he already knew in his heart. They were gone, all of them. He was the only survivor.

He'd looked up at the ceiling and promised never to forget them, swore he'd bide his time until he joined them. He'd never felt suicidal and yet, for the past year, he hadn't really wanted to live. Probably the only reason he'd come this far—pushed through the agony of his surgeries and the long recovery—was Rebel. His partner. His family.

But somehow, in the past four days, Kensie had become his family, too. He loved her.

He loved her.

It didn't even seem possible in such a short time, but he couldn't deny the emotion rising up in him. The protectiveness, the desperation to save her, no matter what it cost him.

"I love you."

For a second, he thought he'd spoken his thoughts aloud. Then, he realized she was repeating herself.

"Kensie, we're going to make it," he told her. "I know you're scared, but you have to believe." When she tried to speak again, he cut her off, lungs burning as he kept pressing forward, one slow step at a time. "Tell you what. When we make it out of here safely, if you still want to, you can tell me. Okay?"

Getting so many words out made his lungs scream, but he had to do it. If she really did love him, maybe it would help her hold on. Even if his leg gave out, maybe he could get her far enough. He'd tell Rebel to lead her out. His dog wouldn't want to leave him, but he knew she'd come to love Kensie as much as he had. And Rebel was tough, just like Kensie. With a break, with Rebel by her side, Kensie could push through. The two of them could make it. He just had to get them as far as he could.

But his leg was slowing him down more with every step. The pain was back now, the numbness from before gone, and he wasn't sure if that was a good sign or a bad one. Because he could barely feel the rest of his body. He had no idea how he was keeping hold of Kensie, but he knew if he adjusted his grip at all, it would break.

He'd never felt this much agony in his life, not even when he'd woken on that airplane, with a piece of metal slicing straight through his thigh. His face burned, like he'd scalded it. His lungs felt frozen, as if they had to chip free of his ribs with every breath. And his leg was the worst. It shook so much he knew it was only a matter of time before it gave out entirely. And each step sent pain from his knee up to his hip and then back down, as if that metal was still impaled there.

He wasn't going to make it. He was going to fail her, like he'd failed his brothers. They were going to die out here.

"You've made me believe I'm worthy of a life that's truly mine." Kensie's voice cut through his thoughts, a strange raspy croak that sounded nothing like her normal voice. "I want you to believe what I already know. That you're worthy of a good life, too. Even if it's not with me."

She thought he didn't want a life with her? He didn't have the energy to correct her, but keeping her talking wasn't a bad idea. It would keep her awake. Falling asleep was a quicker trip to hypothermia.

But she was wrong. He wasn't worthy. His right leg was failing him. He couldn't even lift it anymore, just slide it forward and pray he didn't lose traction and send them both tumbling down the mountain.

He glanced at Rebel and her soft brown eyes stared back at him, weary but determined. Rebel was still going on force of will and love for him and Kensie. She'd never give up, his dog, his partner.

In that instant, a new kind of strength filled him. A strength that wasn't his own.

He glanced at the sky and he could almost feel his Marine brothers, watching over him, helping him. "Thank you," he rasped.

Then he heard the most beautiful sound he'd ever heard in his life. The familiar *whomp whomp whomp* of a helicopter.

He lifted his gaze skyward once more and there it was, circling overhead. A spotlight shot past them, then darted back. They'd been found.

Colter's leg gave out and he collapsed.

Chapter 21

Colter woke with a start in an unfamiliar hospital bed. The beeping of the heart monitor next to him accelerated as the past few hours came back to him. "Kensie!"

"She's okay," a nurse reassured him.

Colter took a few deep breaths, getting his heart rate under control. This had happened several times already.

The helicopter he'd spotted from the mountain was a police chopper, sent out after his text to 911 had gone through. It hadn't been able to set down for them on the wooded mountainside, so Colter had forced himself up. Beside him, Kensie had managed to do the same with Rebel pressed against her side. Together, the three of them had limped as far as they could, until finally a rescue team met them.

Now they were here, getting checked out. As hard as he'd tried to stay awake, Colter kept drifting off to sleep.

Beside him, Rebel pushed wearily to her feet and the nurse gave his dog a stern look.

"She shouldn't be here." The nurse repeated the same thing she said every time he woke.

"She's my service dog."

The nurse grunted, clearly not believing him. But hospital administration had—or, at least, that's what he'd assumed, until a doctor had winked at him then bent down and checked Rebel's leg, too. The doc had said his wife was military and he knew a soldier dog when he saw one.

Rebel seemed to like that and let the doctor examine her. He'd put ointment and gauze over each of her paws and then gently wrapped her leg. Thankfully, she hadn't torn anything, just aggravated the old injury. It just needed time, the doctor told him. Much like Colter's own leg.

They'd stripped off his wet clothes and soaked his hands, feet and nose—which all had minor frostbite—in warm water. Now his hands and feet were bare, wrapped in gauze, and he was in a hospital gown.

He knew Kensie had also suffered from frostbite, that she'd been experiencing hypothermia. But they'd assured him she would survive, then rushed her off to surgery to remove the bullet from her leg. That was the last he'd seen her.

Colter glanced at the clock on the wall, trying to remember what time they'd arrived. "What's taking so long?" he asked the nurse.

"We're making sure we address everything," she replied, a little more patiently than she'd responded to

Rebel's presence. "She'll be okay." Then she glanced over at the door. "You've got visitors."

His gaze shot up. Rebel's did, too, surely expecting the same thing he did. To see Kensie standing there, smiling tiredly. Instead, he discovered a pair of police officers.

He didn't know either of them. They were wearing uniforms from a town northeast of Desparre, closer to where the helicopter had found him, Kensie and Rebel.

The pair stepped into his room, both serious cops who looked like they'd been on the force a long time. The nurse left, closing the door behind her, and Colter's heart pounded. "Did you find them?"

When the rescue team had arrived, Kensie's first words had been about her sister. She'd been frantic and desperate, barely making sense, so Colter had filled in as best he could with aching lungs and a body that wanted to just lie down and sleep.

He'd been asking for updates every time he woke, but no one seemed to know anything.

"We sent a tactical team out to the cabin," one of the officers replied. "It was partially cleared out. We're tracking the Altiers now. We've talked to the nearest neighbors—a couple of miles away—and learned it's a family of seven. The parents and five children. The neighbor confirmed the oldest girl is named Alanna."

The news sent a shock through Colter, even though Kensie's reaction when she'd seen the girl had already told him it was her.

"Our team is still searching. We'll let you know as soon as we find them."

The officer spoke with confidence, as if locating the Altier family was a foregone conclusion, but Colter's shoulders slumped. They'd managed to keep Alanna hidden for so long. What if they got away again? How would Kensie survive coming so close, only to lose her sister once more?

Colter's heart ached for her. He'd do anything he could to help her, assuming she wanted his help. But in all the time since they'd arrived, while he was worrying about how she was faring, he hadn't been able to stop thinking about one other thing.

When they'd gotten to safety, she hadn't repeated her words from the mountain. She hadn't repeated that she loved him.

He wanted to say the words back to her anyway. But should he? Or should he give her a clean break, let her focus on her family, on trying to make it whole again?

A shriek outside his door jolted him out of his thoughts and he realized the officers had left. Rebel jumped up at the sound, recognizing the voice, even though it didn't sound quite normal. Kensie.

Together, they moved as quickly as they could to the door and Colter flung it open, ready to handle whatever threat faced her. Instead, he saw a different pair of officers walking down the hall, Alanna between them.

Kensie was in the hallway, too, in a hospital gown, her leg wrapped up. She limped awkwardly toward the trio, not even noticing him as she breathed, "Alanna?"

"Kensie!" the girl replied, racing toward her sister and wrapping her in a hug.

After fourteen long years, Kensie was finally hugging her sister again.

It didn't feel real. The last time she'd wrapped her

arms around Alanna, she'd had to bend down to reach the five-year-old. She'd buried her head in her sister's unruly curls, breathed in that little-kid scent of sugar and dirt that she still smelled whenever she thought of Alanna.

Now her sister was nineteen and only two inches shorter than Kensie. Her hair was thick and straight, cut in a blunt line at her shoulders, highlighting the elegant lines of her face.

Kensie pulled back, holding Alanna at arm's length to get a good look at her.

"We still look like sisters," Alanna whispered.

Her voice was different, too, and yet a hint of the five-year-old was still there. Tears filled Kensie's eyes and she swiped them away, not wanting to miss a single detail of her sister's face, all grown up.

They *did* look like sisters. Kensie's hair was longer, but if they twined strands together, Kensie doubted they'd be able to tell whose was whose. Alanna's eyes were a darker brown, closer to Flynn's than Kensie's, but she and her sister had the same long eyelashes, the same strong eyebrows. People would have known they were family at a single glance.

What would it have been like to grow up with Alanna? With eight years between them, they never would have been in school together, but Kensie would have wanted to be her protector. Just like she had when she was thirteen.

"I'm so sorry," Kensie whispered back, remembering that moment in their front yard, the defining moment in her life. When she'd read a book while Alanna had run around the yard, too close to the street. When a car had sped up to their curb, slammed to a stop, and the man inside it yanked Alanna away from them.

Alanna took her hands. "It's not your fault."

Kensie burst into tears. It hurt her lungs and her face, which she'd only started to feel again in the past hour. Wiping her tears away with her arm so she could keep hold of her sister's hands, Kensie gave a shaking smile. "I've missed you so much."

From the corner of her eye, she spotted Colter and Rebel, standing in the doorway of a hospital room. They were sliding quietly backward, obviously trying to let her and Alanna have a private reunion.

But there'd have been no reunion at all if it weren't for the two of them. Keeping her right hand gripped in Alanna's, she turned her head and held out her left for Colter.

He seemed a little unsure, but Rebel limped over immediately, pushing her way in between Kensie and Alanna and making Alanna laugh.

Kensie's heart felt so full at the sound. As her sister petted Rebel, Kensie stretched her hand out farther, silently imploring Colter.

When he stepped carefully toward her on bandaged feet and placed his hand in hers, she squeezed tight. She never wanted to let go of any of them, ever again.

She wasn't sure how long they stood there, in the hospital hallway, huddled together and smiling at each other, until Alanna suggested, "Let's sit."

The pain in her leg had actually been forgotten, seeing Alanna safe, but now it returned in a wave of agony. She wasn't supposed to be standing on it yet, let alone walking.

They must have been quite a sight, limping into her hospital room. Once she was seated, Colter beside her, Alanna on the empty bed across from them and Rebel on the ground between them, Kensie asked, "What happened all these years, Alanna?"

As soon as the words were out, she wanted to call them back. What if her sister had been terribly abused? What if it hurt her too much to talk about it? Was Kensie prepared to hear what Alanna had endured?

Colter's fingers slid through hers, squeezing gently, lending her strength, and Kensie tried to stay strong for Alanna.

But her sister shook her head. "It's not what you're thinking. They were…good to me."

"*Good* to you? They *kidnapped* you, Alanna! They stole you from us for fourteen years!"

"I know. And all that time, I tried so hard not to forget you and Flynn, and Mom and Dad. I tried so hard to protect my memories. It wasn't easy. I was five. But I still have good memories. I was one of the lucky ones."

"What do you mean?"

"You saw them, right? At the cabin?"

The other kids. Kensie had assumed they were the Altiers's own children, that only Alanna had been abducted. Realization made the blood seem to drain from her body. "They were all kidnapped?"

"Yeah. The younger two don't remember their birth families at all. Sydney—she's twelve—remembers best. She was the oldest when they took her and I guess they learned from that, because they started picking younger kids. Johnny—my older brother—he was five, like me. He barely remembers his birth family. It's why they've been able to mold him so much. It's why he shot at you. To protect the family."

Kensie swallowed back her instant response. Johnny wasn't her older brother. *Flynn* was her older brother. And she and Flynn and their parents weren't Alanna's *birth* family. They were simply her family.

Colter pulled her hand into his lap, stroking her palm gently, like he could read her mind. Across from them, Alanna sighed.

"I guess it's hard to understand," she said. "But I lived with the Altiers for fourteen years, most of my life. They picked kids who looked like them. They wanted a family and couldn't have one, so they kidnapped kids. They treated us well, never hurt any of us. They wanted us to be happy, but the way we lived—it was like kids probably did a long time ago. We worked hard, all of us. We lived off the land. We were all homeschooled. And we moved around. A lot. Especially at the beginning. Until eventually we came here. I guess they felt Alaska was safe, because we built the cabin. We finally stayed in one place."

"You were happy?" The question was hard to get out, because she hoped her sister would say yes, but some part of her felt like it was wrong for Alanna to have been happy with her kidnappers.

Alanna's gaze dropped to her lap and she fiddled with a worn gold and garnet ring on her right hand. It looked like an antique, something that would get passed down in families. But it hadn't come from the Morgans.

"Mostly." She met Kensie's gaze again, her eyes imploring Kensie to understand. "I never forgot you, Kensie. I never forgot any of you. I wanted to come home.

I tried not to let them know, but I always wanted to come home."

"And at that store, you finally had a chance to write a note without being seen?" Kensie asked, trying to contain her emotions. There were so many. Happiness at having Alanna back, regret at missing most of her childhood, anger that the people who'd stolen her had pretended *they* were her family, relief that Alanna hadn't been hurt or abused.

Alanna bit her lip. "Sort of. I—"

When Alanna looked like she might cry, Kensie assured her, "It's okay. Whatever it is, you can tell me. We're sisters."

Alanna smiled. It trembled on her lips, her eyes still watery, but it was fueled by happiness. Kensie knew because it looked just like her own smile.

Happiness burst inside of her at sharing that with her sister. In that moment, she knew whatever Alanna had been through, whatever Alanna needed to help her move forward, they could do it together. They could rebuild their family. Finally.

"I had chances before. I was allowed to go places. I mean, they watched me, but they trusted me, too, once I'd been with them for a while. It's just that…"

"What?" Kensie whispered.

"I love them."

The words made Kensie's chest hurt, made her whole body tense up. But she tried not to show it.

"I'm sorry," Alanna said. "I know that has to be hard to hear. But they raised me. I knew they'd kidnapped me, but they treated me well. They took care of me and over the years, I just—"

"It's okay," Kensie assured her. It *was* hard to hear, but she understood. And although she didn't want to owe the Altiers anything, she was grateful they'd given Alanna a good childhood.

"But last month, Johnny started talking about wanting to get married. He'd met this girl and he was so excited about adding to our family and I just… I realized if I didn't try, I'd never get any milestones like that with you, Flynn, Mom or Dad."

"Were they mad when they learned what you'd done?" Kensie asked, not wanting to think about what the rest of her life might have been like if Alanna hadn't taken that risk.

"Yeah. They thought we'd lucked out when the FBI called it a hoax, but then they said you'd come to town. They were talking about leaving. I convinced them to let me go into town, to just see it one more time. It was the only place I'd lived for more than a year—except back in Illinois with you. Da—Mr. Altier took me into town late at night, figuring not many people would be around."

The day she'd followed Henry. He must have gone the other way, down the alley and back toward town, instead of into the storage units, like she'd thought. But without knowing it, he'd led her right to Alanna.

Alanna burst into tears. "When that man attacked you in the parking lot, I thought I'd gotten you killed."

Kensie shoved to her feet, her leg screaming as she put weight on it, and folded her sister into a hug. Hopefully just one of many, many hugs to come. "No. You saved me. You and Colter and Rebel. You saved me."

"Alanna Altier?"

Kensie's head swiveled at the question and she saw a doctor waiting in the doorway. She wanted to correct him about her sister's name, but kept quiet. There would be time for that. Right now was a time to reunite.

"I need you to come with me so we can make sure you're okay."

"I'm fine," Alanna said, her arms still looped loosely around Kensie.

"I'm sure you are, but this won't take long," the doctor insisted.

Alanna looked at Kensie and she nodded. "I'll be waiting for you," Kensie promised.

As the doctor led her sister into another room, Kensie sank onto the bed Alanna had just vacated, staring at Colter as disbelief and joy mingled. "I can't believe any of this is real. I can't believe we found her."

Colter smiled back at her, the sight of it already so familiar and comforting. "Believe it," he told her. "This is your new normal."

"I've got to call my family," Kensie said, even as her mind screamed that she wanted *him* to be part of her new normal, too.

"I can go," Colter said, standing. "Let you call them."

"No." Kensie reached out for him and he let her pull him closer. Her heart beat a frantic, frightened tempo as she stared into his eyes, wanting him to see the truth of her words as she spoke them.

Obviously sensing something important was happening, Rebel scooted closer, pressing against Colter's side.

"I meant what I said on the mountain," Kensie blurted before she could lose her nerve. "I know it's fast and I know it's not what you were looking for, but I can't help it. I love you."

She had to tell him. He'd done so much for her. He'd lost so much in the past year. Even if he couldn't love her back, she wanted him to know that he was worthy of someone giving him everything they had.

She expected his face to twist with regret and discomfort, but instead he smiled. It started out slow and sexy, putting crinkles beside his eyes. Then it burst wide and Kensie's heart seemed to do the same.

"I love you, too, Kensie."

Epilogue

His journey was coming to an end. He hoped.

Colter stared up at the apartment complex across from the lake, frozen in place. The wind coming off the water was cold, but nothing compared to the brutal weather Desparre was getting right now. Beside him, Rebel nudged his leg with her head, as if to say *get moving*.

Colter laughed. "Be patient, girl."

It had been a month since he'd seen Kensie. He'd dropped her and Alanna at the airport, watched as Alanna stared nervously up at the sky. She'd never been on a plane. The people who'd raised her since she was five were in custody and she hadn't wanted to leave behind the siblings she'd grown up with. But they all had families, too, people who'd been waiting for them, praying for this day to come.

Kensie had stared back at him, a smile trembling on her lips and tears in her eyes. She needed to go, needed to help Alanna transition back into a life she barely remembered. Needed to be with her family as they all reunited.

And his place was in Alaska. Over the past year, it had truly become his home. The noise of a city brought on unexpected panic, while the quiet solitude of his cabin soothed his soul. Gave him a little peace.

He hadn't wanted to let her go, but he couldn't go with her.

The truth was, they hardly knew each other. A long-distance relationship from Alaska to Chicago seemed a little crazy, but they'd vowed to give it a shot.

But over the past month, he'd realized it wasn't right. He couldn't move on like this. There was still too much baggage from his past weighing him down.

So for the past three weeks he'd been lying to Kensie. He'd pretended he was still in Alaska whenever they talked. But the slightly guarded tone her voice had taken on lately told him she suspected something wasn't right. Or maybe she was starting to have second thoughts about their arrangement, too.

Swallowing his nerves, Colter tapped his leg for Rebel, but she was already up and moving. He had to follow her into the complex. He almost forgot to use the cane he'd brought along for show as they hurried through the doors. He'd done his research beforehand— this apartment complex didn't allow pets.

The guy sitting behind the security desk frowned and Colter leaned heavily on the cane. "Sorry. I forgot her service vest."

The guy looked like he was going to argue, so Colter rushed to the elevator, ignoring the man's calls to sign in. The doors slid closed behind him and Rebel before anyone could stop them.

As the elevator rose, so did Colter's stress level. He hated enclosed spaces, especially ones made of metal. Closing his eyes, he breathed slowly in and out through his nose as Rebel pressed hard against his side.

"Thanks, girl," he said as the elevator dinged and the doors opened, letting them off on the fourth floor. Kensie's floor.

Swinging the cane back and forth as he walked, Colter followed Rebel down the hall. Although they'd never been here, his dog seemed to know right where to go. She ran up to Kensie's unit and sat on the welcome mat, then thumped her tail frantically.

Before he caught up to her, the door swung open and Kensie was standing there. She wore workout gear and carried a yoga mat under her arm, which fell to the ground as soon as she saw Rebel. Her gaze darted up, eyes comically wide as they met his.

He smiled, but it was shaky. "Hi, Kensie."

Rebel lifted her front paws off the ground, almost knocking Kensie over as she rested them on Kensie's forearms.

"Rebel," Colter admonished, but it lacked heat. He wanted to jump on Kensie himself.

Kensie laughed and dropped to her knees, wrapping her arms around Rebel's neck as his dog's tail swung back and forth. "Hi, Rebel." She looked up at Colter. "Her leg healed well."

"It's as good as it will ever be," Colter agreed. The

same as his. Neither of them were quite whole, but then again, if they were good enough for a woman like Kensie, maybe they didn't need perfect.

Finally Kensie stood, wariness in her gaze. "What are you doing here, Colter? I thought—"

"You thought I'd never leave Alaska?"

She laughed, but it sounded more like nervous energy than amusement. "Sort of. I figured the next time I saw you would be when Desparre thawed out and I could get back up there."

"It's not enough," he told her. "Phone calls for six months."

She bit her lip and the hand petting Rebel sped up.

"Can I come in?" he asked, not wanting to have this conversation in the hallway.

"Sure. Of course." She snagged her yoga mat off the ground as she spun, her hand shaking as she held the door for them.

Her apartment was just like he'd expected it to be, with bright, happy colors and—if you angled your head just right—a view of the water. But he didn't give it much of a look, because he couldn't take his eyes off Kensie, staring back at him like she was afraid of what he'd come all this way to tell her.

He set his cane against the wall. He hadn't needed it for weeks. "How's your sister?"

She looked thrown by the question, probably expecting him to dive right into the question of their relationship. "It hasn't been easy. She's still adjusting. But my family feels whole again, Colter." She clutched her hands together, betraying her nerves as she added, "No matter what, I'll always be grateful to you for helping bring her home."

Not wanting to draw out why he'd come and make them both anxious, Colter started at the beginning. "Rebel and I have been traveling across the country for the past few weeks."

"What?" She sank onto the couch, shaking her head. "I don't understand. We've been talking. You were in Alaska."

"No. I just didn't want to tell you about it until I was finished." He sat on the chair next to her, taking her hands in his as Rebel scooted her way between the couch and the coffee table to lie on Kensie's feet.

"Rebel and I made a journey to see the families of each of my brothers."

"Oh, Colter," Kensie breathed, squeezing his hands tighter.

"It's something I've been meaning to do since that day. Something I haven't been able to bring myself to do. First, it was the injury and then it was guilt. Guilt over being alive when they were all gone." His voice cracked, but he forced himself to continue. "I always felt like it wasn't fair for me to move on when none of them would ever have a chance to do it. But you know what every single one of those families told me?"

"What?" she asked softly, lifting one hand to swipe away the tears he felt on his cheeks.

"I was dishonoring their memories by refusing to live my life." He took a deep breath, trying to get control of his emotions. "And my life is you, Kensie."

Her eyes widened even more, the nervousness that had filled them before replaced with hope.

"And then Rebel and I went to see my family."

Her eyes filled with tears at his words. She knew he hadn't seen them since he moved to Alaska.

"It was tough. They still don't understand me, but they love me. And they're happy about what I'm doing now."

"What's that?" Kensie whispered, her eyes still huge.

"I found a nonprofit organization that wants my experience. I'm going to be helping others like me, coming out of the military. Or families who need support after facing loss. It's downtown."

She blinked a few times, looking confused. "Desparre has a nonprofit downtown?"

He grinned. "Not in Desparre, Kensie." He squeezed her hands tighter, hoping he wasn't moving too fast, springing this on her instead of talking it over first. "Downtown Chicago."

Her mouth moved a little, like she wanted to speak, but didn't know what to say, so he rushed on.

"I'm looking at an apartment across town this afternoon." He'd wanted to be as close to her as possible, but he couldn't afford anything near the waterfront. Not yet.

"That's…" She shook her head. "You don't need to look for one. You can stay with me."

His heart picked up speed, not from nervousness now, but excitement. "Your place doesn't allow pets. I pretended Rebel was a service dog to get her up here, but I'm not sure how long that will—"

"No," Kensie interrupted. "I'll move. Wherever you want. I mean, I can't go to Alaska. I would, if things were different. But my sister—"

"I know." He cut her off, hardly able to believe she

was saying *yes*. That she was going along with his crazy plan—even upping the ante—after knowing him barely more than a month.

"I'm going to keep my cabin in Alaska. I'm hoping we'll visit. And the city isn't easy for me. I didn't just pick Desparre because of the solitude, but also because it helps with my anxiety. I'll probably need some help adjusting. But I want to," he added when it looked like she was going to say something. "I want to deserve you."

She scooted closer to him and Rebel lifted her head off Kensie's feet, staring up at her as if she knew something important was happening.

"Are you kidding? How could you not deserve me? You brought me back my sister. You saw me for *me*. You're *here*."

He smiled, so much joy inside him it was hard to breathe. He couldn't remember the last time he'd felt this way, but he knew it was before that fateful day he thought he'd lost everything.

But she was wrong. He didn't deserve her. Not yet. He needed to reclaim his life to be the man she deserved in hers. And he wasn't there yet. But with her help—and her love—he knew he could do it.

Kensie shifted closer still, until she was almost hanging off the edge of the couch. In response, Rebel scooted backward, out from between the couch and table. She ran around the edge of the room, so she could force her way between Colter's chair and where Kensie sat.

Colter laughed as Rebel rested her head on his arm, her gaze going back and forth between him and Kensie, tail wagging faster and faster.

"I guess we should start apartment hunting," Kensie said. Her voice was full of wonder and surprise, but it was also filled with love.

In that moment, he knew without a doubt he'd made the right choice.

"It doesn't matter where we end up," he told her. "You're the only home I'll ever need."

At his words, she launched herself off the couch and onto his lap, throwing her arms around his neck. "I love you, Colter," she breathed.

He barely had time to respond before she was kissing him.

Beside them, Rebel barked her approval.

* * * * *

Brooklyn K-9 Unit Officer Jackson Davison caught movement out of the corner of his eye: a face in the trees fading out of view. His heart beat a little faster. Was someone watching him? The hairs on the back of Jackson's neck stood at attention as a light breeze brushed his face. Even as he studied the foliage, he felt the weight of a gaze on him. The sound of Smokey's barking brought his mission back into focus.

When he caught up with his partner, the dog was sitting. The signal that he'd found something. "Good boy." Jackson tossed out the toy he carried on his belt for Smokey to play with, his reward for doing his job. The dog whipped the toy back and forth in his mouth.

"Drop," Jackson said. He picked up the toy and patted Smokey on the head. "Sit. Stay."

The body, partially covered by branches, was clothed in neutral colors and would not be easy to spot unless you were looking for it.

He keyed his radio. "Officer Davison here. I've got a body in Prospect Park. Male Caucasian under the age of forty, about two hundred yards in, just southwest of the Brooklyn Botanic Garden."

Dispatch responded, "Ten-four. Help is on the way."

He studied the trees just in time to catch the face again, barely visible, like a fading mist. He was being watched. "Did you see something?" Jackson shouted. "Did you call this in?"

The person turned and ran, disappearing into the thick brush.

Jackson took off in the direction the runner had gone. As his feet pounded the hard earth, another thought occurred to him. Was this the person who had shot the man in the chest? Sometimes criminals hung around to witness the police response to their handiwork.

His attention was drawn to a garbage can just as an object hit the back of his head with intense force. Pain radiated from the base of his skull. He crumpled to the ground and his world went black.

Don't miss
Scene of the Crime *by Sharon Dunn,*
available wherever Love Inspired Suspense books
and ebooks are sold.

LoveInspired.com